WINTERSFALL
GEN-HEIRS: THE GUARDIANS OF SZIVERIA
BOOK I

SARAH WESTILL

OTHER TITLES BY SARAH WESTILL

GEN-HEIRS: The Guardians of Sziveria

(in reading order)

Levkaseon – A Prequel

Wintersfall

Raiventon

Kynhaven

Asherwick

Ericksen - A Wintervail Special

Survaine

Wolvenguard

Voklane

Bella and the Beast Master

Gen-Heirs world novella series

Frozen Flowers Fallen

Perfect Melody Silenced

Dreams Never Seen

Fiery Nights Tempted

Broken Heart Questioned

Winter Wishes Scattered (2025)

The Ralston Brothers

A Gen-Heirs world series

Captivated by Dominik (2026)

For world maps be sure to visit www.sarahwestill.com

To get the latest updates, follow Sarah on Instagram

@authorsarahwestill

CONTENT WARNING:

THIS BOOK CONTAINS MATURE
CONTENT, INCLUDING BUT NOT
LIMITED TO –

Consensual sex (non-graphic)
Action violence
Abduction
Death of a parent and sibling

Reader discretion is advised.

WELCOME TO THE GEN-HEIRS WORLD

In the distant future, a major cataclysmic event not only reshaped the world as humanity knew it, but left entire lands uninhabitable. As generations of survivors struggled to endure a fight for territory and resources, humanity regressed into what became known as The Primal Years. A dark and dangerous time that lasted for centuries.

Slowly, civilizations formed in the new nations. Limited means of transportation and communication began to develop in a resource-poor world. Powerful countries arose known as Sziveria, Ruthenia, Italyssa, Westica, and Cairo. New cultures, with their own standards of honor, became global powerhouses.

By 830 Post-Cataclysmic Event (PCE), strong talents are now inherited traits, passed down through genetics. The recipients of an unavoidable hereditary legacy are known as Gen-Heirs. Trains, ships, carriages and if one can afford them, small magnetically powered vehicles move people. Radios are the only means of quick communication besides handwritten messages. Heated water is a luxury. Extreme drops in temperature and harsh arctic winds have forced most food growth indoors, in greenhouses. A dangerously lethal virus known as Human Rabies Syndrome (HRS) plagues the globe. The inhabited world is growing at a slow rate, each unique country striving to exist in harsher, cold climates, and those who survive have become ruthless in their quest to thrive in this new, forsaken world...

THE RANKING SYSTEM

Guardians of Sziveria
Queen/King Elect
Prince/Princess Elect
Arch Guardian
Prince/Princess
Shield Guardian
Master Guardian
Primary Guardian
Key Guardian
Guardian (anyone who serves the realm)

Enforcement Services
First Prefect (FP)
Master Prefect (MP)
Prefect
First Tribunii (FT)
Master Tribunii (MT)
Tribunii
First Guardsman (FG)
Master Guardsman (MG)

Guardsman

Other Key Terms –
  First Intelligence Office (FIO)
  Sziverian National Investigative Division (SNID)
  Haven City Enforcement Services (HCES)
  Medical Science Officer (MSO)
  Medical Science Investigator (MSI)
  Uninhabited Zones (UZ)
  Human Rabies Syndrome (HRS)

❧ I ❧

S ziveria, June 7th, 832 P.C.E. (Post-Cataclysm Event)
Old Helston locality

CHAOS ERUPTED IN THE WAKE OF A BULLET PIERCING A target secured to a giant oak tree. Birds squawked, taking flight in a mass exodus of feathers and trembling leaves. The satisfaction of another perfect shot failed to ease the fiery pain in Katria Nachemir's side from the rifle's recoil. A side effect of not being healed enough to practice.

The exercise provided a much-needed distraction, but the ache served as a reminder of the devastation she had attempted to escape. Tears burned her eyes, and with a quick breath, she pushed on, loading two more bullets into the bolt-action chamber.

Shooting at a target wouldn't change anything. Her mother and sister were still dead, buried in what would now become a family cemetery. A bullet wound would forever mar her body. Escaping was nothing more than a mental game now. Anytime she looked down at herself, she made the nightmare real again.

The gunman who stole their lives remained elusive, the reason for the fatal attack unknown. Focusing her pain on something productive was all Katria could think to do. Sitting in the too-quiet house with her despairing father wasn't an option anymore. At some point, perhaps hours after the massacre, he'd forgotten he had one daughter left alive. Katria refused to endure the pain of being ignored any longer.

The target became the manifestation of her pain, and the bullet a means to an end. Taking a long, slow inhale, she wrapped her hands around the gun. Her fingertips formed a connection with the rifle. All the working mechanisms became a map in her mind, while the wind blowing across her skin became an adversary. Without effort on her part, the calculations flowed through her.

Before she could pull the trigger again, a twig snapped behind her. She swung around and aimed at the stranger before he moved another step. His hands flew into the air. Strong morning light cast his face in sharp relief, drawing attention to a firm jaw, high cheekbones, a patrician nose, and a mouth that didn't look to smile often.

"I'm just here to talk," he stated in a deep, soothing voice, his foot lifted midstride. "My name is Ryan Voklane, I work with the First Intelligence Office."

Katria didn't lower the weapon or allow her surprise to show. The FIO guardian was a long way from home. "Are you here about my mother and sister?"

He slowly removed a tan ivy cap he'd been wearing, revealing neatly combed pale blond hair. He lowered his foot and sank into a non-threatening, relaxed stance. "No, local enforcement is handling that, I believe."

Anger flared. Somehow, Katria managed to keep her

temper in check. "And getting nowhere. It wasn't a local murder."

"I'm sure you're aware of your father's past. They may never find who killed them," he said gently.

Fresh tears burned, and she looked away from the pity in his silvery blue eyes. "Then what do you want to talk about?"

"You."

That brought her attention back. "Me?"

"Yes. Do you mind lowering your gun?"

Katria looked him over. Though broad-shouldered and fit, his neatly pressed black pants and jacket, along with his well-tailored gray vest and red knit cotton scarf, spoke of days spent in an office. There were no telltale bulges of a hidden gun or knife, at least from his front. If he opted to pull something from his back, she'd be quicker. She decided he likely wasn't much of a threat and lowered her gun. "You're from Haven City?"

"Correct."

"Am I in trouble?"

"No, I'm here to offer you a job. A position on one of our elite guardian teams."

Katria kept her surprise internal. "A position? As what?"

"Sharpshooter."

She glanced down at the worn rifle in her hands. "There's nothing special about my shot."

"On the contrary, Miss Nachemir. You may be the best shooter in Sziveria. Perhaps even the world. You're a Gen-Heir."

Katria kept her expression carefully neutral. Inside, she panicked. She couldn't have been more stunned if he'd slapped her. Yes, she was her father's genetic heir, or Gen-Heir as society preferred to call those who inherited more than looks and health. Her unique capability to connect on a cellular level with a gun, and her ability to know, by touch alone, how all its variables—distance, wind, humidity, air temperature, and air density—affected a shot. With only a rifle, scope, and target, her mind calculated and adjusted in a split second. Despite Aleksandrov Nachemir's best efforts, someone had learned the assassin's daughter shared his talent.

"How could you possibly know that?" she asked. "I've never competed, never done anything outside this property with my father."

"We have our ways."

She frowned. "Of course you do."

"I know this is a delicate time for you, but if you work with us, I promise I'll put the full resources of the Sziverian National Investigative Division into the death of your mother and sister. We'll find who killed them and bring the murderer to justice." He took a tentative step forward, his cap clutched in his hands. "Your country needs the skills you have to offer, and you'll be working with the best."

A tightness formed in her chest. *Justice*. A month ago, the word hadn't had much meaning. Now it meant everything. But at what cost? She looked down the length of the field to the target on the thick tree trunk. "I'll be doing what someone did to us... won't I?"

"No, no, you'll never take an innocent life. Our queen elect has no desire for personal vendettas. She's only interested in national security. When they call you to work, you can be sure the person will be bad. Someone like the person who came after your family. Justice *for* another family, for your country."

The words were careful in their assurance, pretty in their seduction to compel her agreement. Katria looked him over again. The handsome planes of his face remained unthreatening, open, almost warm. She *wanted* to say yes. "My father will never agree."

"You're eighteen, and if I'm correct, uncontracted for marriage?"

"Yes, correct."

The guardian took another brazen step closer. "You wouldn't have to tell him."

Lie to her father? The idea made her stomach curl with acid, and yet the suggestion had merit. If he didn't know, he couldn't stop her, and the greatest investigative force in the country would examine the murders of their family. "Will I get any sort of training?"

"Training, along with so much more."

"And if I don't like the idea in the end?"

"You can walk away. However," he added, frowning, "you must understand I can't promise the investigation if you don't keep up your end."

She nodded. "I understand."

"Good."

In the course of their conversation, he'd managed to inch forward enough to reach out and touch her bare wrist. Katria froze. His hand disappeared into his jacket pocket. Now he stood too close for her to use her rifle without falling back onto the ground if he posed a danger after all. A flash of white caught on his emerging fingers. He handed her a card.

"Be at this address in one week."

September 3rd, 832
First Intelligence Office
Haven City

Sean Blackbain's booted feet echoed down the long,

empty corridor. The dancing flames in the glass lamps, every few feet, barely penetrated the heavy darkness of the third floor, below ground level. The musk of dank walls and the absence of sunlight thickened the air. A dense folder weighed down his left hand. He studied the name hastily scrawled across the edge.

Katerina Nachesa.

No one had ever told him about the woman reputed to be the best shot in the world. No reputation or experience backed up the claim made by the FIO. Yet he was supposed to take her under his wing, turn her into a valuable team member. He glanced at the markings on the doors he walked past. A few feet farther, he arrived.

The door opened with ease. Three people sat inside. A lamp on the table and a low-burning fire cast the room in heavy shadow.

Ryan Voklane straddled a chair in his usual unprofessional style, his arms braced across the back. The woman's back was to him, her long black hair reflecting the meager golden light. An old man slid sheets of paper to her across the table faster than she could gather them. Shadows danced off the deep wrinkles of his face and over his gnarled hands.

Ryan glanced up and caught Sean's eye. The faint movement caused the woman to turn around, aware of his presence.

Impressive.

No emotion shone in her vivid blue eyes, not even curiosity as her gaze met his. As he stood and opened himself to read the emotions floating through the room, he couldn't make out any feelings from her. Like the tranquil, undisturbed surface of water, she was a void. Sean remained calm despite the phenomenon that made him want to ask a million questions. Would she still be an emotional abyss if he touched her?

He flexed the fingers on his free hand with the thought of her skin under his, and the need to encounter any emotion now. His Gen-Heir sympathetic empath senses, known as a Sympath, helped him pick up the bored annoyance of the old records keeper, and... *well, how interesting*, Ryan's carefully concealed anxiety. What did the liaison to the arch guardian of Sean's intel team have to be nervous about?

The soft, warm light danced across the woman's ivory skin. Softly rounded cheeks, high-arched black brows, a full mouth, and a straight nose, he could spend hours staring at her and learning all the beautiful curves of her face. She was also young. Too young. Sean quickly looked away from her and back to Ryan.

"Can I speak with you for a moment?" he asked, motioning to the hall.

The chair's feet scraped across the floor as Ryan stood. They stepped into the corridor, and Sean waited until the door closed completely before speaking.

"She's a child." Sean tried to control his frustration.

"She's of age, a legal adult for almost a year now. She'll be nineteen in a month."

"Voklane, what are you doing? She's not old enough, and you know it. She has zero experience and limited field training."

"She's perfect. She's completely moldable and eager to learn. Did you read her training record?"

Sean glanced down at the file in his hand. "I looked it over."

"And?"

"And I admit she has potential. Bring her to me in a year or two."

The normally calm demeanor Ryan portrayed shifted into hard angles and stiffened muscles. A preternatural silver glow shone across his pale blue gaze. Sean resisted the urge to step back. "We don't have a year or two. We need her now. No one else has the capabilities she has. Your team will be the greatest asset this country has, and the greatest threat to our enemies. Your intel guardian team was created to be the best, not to come second to anyone. You'll take the woman, or I'll find someone else to lead your team."

Sean clenched his jaw. They both knew he needed to leave not only Haven City, but the whole of Sziveria. The team assignment was his long-trip ticket. He couldn't afford to mess this up. Still, there were too many concerns to ignore. Especially one. "A woman, specifically one so young, can't travel alone with three men. No story in the world we give will work."

"We already figured out how to handle that. You won't travel as a cohesive team. At least it won't appear that way. That's for the best as well. She'll travel mainly with you since you're her superior and team leader. At other times, she may be with Merrick as a niece or Dandridge as a sister. Their coloring is close enough to pull that one off."

Sean was almost afraid to ask, but he had to. "And with me?"

He gave a little smile Sean didn't trust. "Probably your ward, or whatever we need her to be." Ryan clapped him on the shoulder in a reassuring manner that irritated Sean. "I'll be sure to make a note of her cover story role in each assignment."

"I'm sure you will."

"Oh, come on, Blackbain. She's a beautiful woman. Things could be worse, really."

Sean slapped the folder against his thigh. "I'll take your word for it."

"Let's sign paperwork, shall we?" Ryan held the door open for him.

With a sinking sensation in his stomach, Sean reentered the room. The woman's gaze followed him to the table. The warm light from the fire and candle accentuated the delicate planes of her face. With her sleek midnight hair and startling blue eyes, he wasn't sure how they were supposed to travel unnoticed anywhere. He suddenly found himself thankful she wasn't standing. He didn't want to know if an equally attractive body was attached to her pretty face. Besides, he preferred women closer to his own age of twenty-six years.

Sean flipped the chair around and took the seat closest to her, then threw the folder onto the table. "Sean Blackbain. I'm your—"

"Team leader. They told me," she said softly, accepting yet another paper.

Sean barely caught the stack that the old man slid to him. He shot an impatient glance in the man's direction. "And this is?"

"Your contract," the old man rasped.

"I already signed my contract years ago."

"New team, new contracts, and promised obligations."

Sean looked at the stack and drummed his fingers in thought. "I see."

Ryan came to stand behind Sean. "You know how it is. Merrick and Dandridge signed theirs yesterday."

"Right." Sean flipped through the pages, trying to make sense of the lines of text.

"I hate to make this quick, but the MagnaRail leaving for Port Scarborough departs in thirty minutes, and you both need to be on it. Henry, the pens please, and show them where to sign."

Sean's gaze snapped up to the old man, who offered him a pen. The process was happening too fast. He was supposed to have time to explain the job to this woman. To review her contract, outline what expectations would be placed on her and what would happen if she failed. He needed to ensure she had the proper gear, the latest rifle model, and that she understood how communication worked on his team.

She'd pushed the edges of the initial few pages away, revealing the lines for her first signature, which she was poised to sign. Sean placed his hand over hers. Like threads pulling between them, the first inclination of emotion filtered through the skin-on-skin contact. Nervousness. Uncertainty. A hint of... fear. Though buried, his Gen-Heir Sympath senses drew the feelings forward. Her full lips parted, and she met his stare.

He leaned in close enough to smell the soft, floral notes of her soap and see the pure, glacial blue color of her irises. He whispered so only she could hear, "Are you *sure* you want to do this?"

Katria's heart pounded so loudly in her ears that she *knew* the man sitting next to her had to be able to hear. And then he touched her. His large hand covered hers, and he somehow expected her to form some sort of coherent thought as awareness settled where their skin met. His amber eyes searched hers. She'd never seen eyes like his before. They seemed to glow with an inner fire.

"You have your entire life ahead of you," he said softly.

He was so close, his mouth, with a too-sensual, bow-shaped upper lip and full bottom lip, inches from her face. Katria's throat went dry. The uneven light accented the stubble covering his strong jaw and brought out the lighter streaks in the dark blond hair hanging around his face. Not a fashionable cut like Ryan's, but more rugged, his long hair falling past his shirt collar in the back. A thick piece shifted across his brow, half covering his eye, and she had the sudden urge to brush it from his forehead. She quickly looked away. This man was essentially her boss. She couldn't be thinking about anything more than the orders he would give her.

Orders.

The thought brought her back to reality.

"I'm sure I want to do this," she whispered. Then with more conviction, "I'm sure, yes."

His hand slid away from hers, and she was startled by the sudden cold left behind. "Very well. Continue, please."

The old man leaned forward and, with a quickness only decades in the job could provide, flipped directly to the pages they needed to sign. Katria took a deep breath with each applied signature, knowing without a doubt she signed her life away. But if joining an intel team meant finding who'd destroyed her family, it'd be worth it. She'd do anything she had to now.

Ryan had assured her that operatives from both the First Intelligence Office and the Sziverian National Investigative Division were working on the case. She just had to keep her part of the deal, and the investigation would continue. If she helped them, they'd help her.

She chanced a glance back at Sean. Before he'd walked in the door, attraction had been something other people experienced. No other man had ever been able to make her notice much. This man proved different. Over six feet tall, built like he knew how to use his body as a weapon, and with an appearance any sane woman wouldn't reject, he had Katria noticing more than she cared to. More than she should.

He was her boss. Nothing more.

They signed the last document. A sense of finality swept over Katria. She stared at the stack of pages and swallowed against the panic. A heavy hand landed on her shoulder, and she looked up.

His eyes, filled with a compassion she didn't understand, stared down at her. When had he stood? "Come on, time to go."

Closing her eyes, she filled her lungs with a soothing inward breath and then released it. This was the last time she would allow herself to feel distressed at her decision. She had made her choice. Whatever happened from this day forward was the life she'd chosen. She opened her eyes and stood to follow him.

"Well, Katerina, let's see what they're having us do first."

"Katria," she corrected.

"What?"

"My name is Katria."

He cast her a quiet, searching look. "I see. How about I just call you Kat?"

A little ache formed in her heart, along with guilt she couldn't afford. "My dad calls me that... called me that, I mean. So yes, okay."

"Kat, it is."

Ryan clapped in exuberance. "All right, Intel Guardian Team Blackbain, let's get this production on the rails, shall we?"

❧ 2 ❧

A*pril 23ʳᵈ, 835*
Wilhelm, Gaula

Katria carefully set the black barrel of her bolt-action combat rifle, model eighteen, referred to as a BACR-18, into its padded case, laying it open on her hotel bed. Next, she placed the shoulder rest and then the scope into their designated spaces. She checked her rounds for the third time, ensuring she'd have enough for the night's mission, and then locked the case.

Heavy booted steps fell outside the room she occupied in the shared suite, and by their determined, methodical pace, she knew it was Sean and not one of the other guys. For three years, she'd been a sister, niece, ward, wife, cousin, and in one instance that none of them could still figure out, an aunt. Usually, she was a sister or niece to Mason Dandridge, a ward or cousin to Kevin Merrick, and a ward or wife to Sean. Thankfully, the *wife* role had happened only twice in their three years.

Katria did not need the reminder that she couldn't have him.

A soft knock sounded at her open door, and she glanced up to find him standing at the threshold. "I'm almost ready."

Sean crossed his arms over his broad chest. The rolled sleeves of his dark gray cotton shirt pulled tight, revealing the defined muscles beneath. Katria fiddled with the latches on the rifle case. Anything to keep from staring.

"Mason found the house where our suspected infectious diplomat is staying," he said.

"Good, we were cutting it a little close this time."

"Can't fault ourselves, we just received the assignment last night."

She gave a small smile. "Well, emergencies work that way, I guess."

He pushed off the doorframe and motioned with his head toward the other room. "Come on, I'm about to go over the plan."

Katria smoothed her hand down the front of her soft black dress and followed Sean to the large living area in their two-bedroom hotel suite. Kevin looked over a map laid out on the table, motioning to the area Mason had tapped his finger against. Over a head taller than the other two men, with a deceptively lean build, Kevin radiated coiled strength. Katria barely came to his chest. His gold wedding ring glinted in the fading light filtering through the dingy third-story windows. Kevin refused to take the ring off *or* even pretend he and Katria were anything but relatives. Needless to say, Kevin and Mason had become the brothers she never had.

Mason glanced up when she entered the room, his silvery gray eyes showing warmth at the sight of her. He tossed his long black hair over his shoulder as he straightened. "Hey, Kat."

She smiled as she rounded the table and accepted his bear hug. "Nice map, as usual."

"Thanks, didn't have much time for this one."

Sean braced his knuckles on the table and leaned forward, looking over Mason's meticulous handiwork. "All right, this morning I was given orders for the team to evacuate a Cairoen diplomat suspected of having human rabies syndrome. Since there's no way to confirm if he's infected with the deadly virus or just a common cold, we can't do anything more than get him contained and away from the population. Cairo wants him handled with care. They will assume responsibility once he's on a ship back home. Mason did the recon we needed for a successful extraction."

He nodded towards Mason, who returned the gesture in acknowledgement before Sean continued. "The Cairoen is here for a trade meeting and has been sick with cold-like symptoms for a week now. His lover in Cairo died of the infection eleven days ago. He's in denial. His country is in a panic. We're the only ones who can get him out, and hopefully home, without causing an international incident. Cairo will owe Sziveria, so we're under strict orders to get this handled."

Katria took a nervous breath. "An entire week. He has to be close to turning."

"Too close," Kevin chimed in. "That's why I'll be doing the extraction. If he goes, I can take care of him before he infects anyone else. If he's feeling as bad as the report claims, he should be holed up in his room. At least until the meeting."

"Which is tomorrow morning," Mason pointed out grimly.

"Correct. That's why we have to move this evening." Sean tapped a building across from a large house. "Kat, you'll set up here. I don't foresee any opposition. On the other hand, if we're too late, or Kevin can't contain our diplomat friend, you'll be in a good position to make sure things stay confined." He slid his hand a couple of blocks away on the map. "Mason, you'll make sure transportation is secure, along with a direct means of getting him onto the ship without any delays. Kat and Kevin, you'll meet us at the ship. Kat, I won't have time to wait for you to get down to the street once we have him, so you and Kevin will walk the five blocks. The Cairoen's a ticking viral bomb as it is."

"Understood," Katria said.

"I'll be waiting in the carriage line with the tranquilizer ready," Sean said.

"It won't work if he turns," Katria softly pointed out.

Sean sighed. "I know, but we can't forcibly detain a diplomat. If he's not infected, he won't remember much of the night with sedatives, and he can't implicate Sziveria in his abduction."

"Maybe at least cuff him after he's out. It'll slow him down if the virus goes active while he's in the carriage," Kevin suggested.

"Okay." Sean nodded. "We can do that, but only after he's completely unconscious."

"The ship is supposed to have isolated quarters for us. First Intelligence is paying a large sum for it, and so far, no questions asked," Mason stated.

Katria leaned over the map and touched the building Mason had drawn on the sheet, directly across from their target location. "How many stories?"

"Seven, I think," Mason answered. "The bottom floor is a shop, the upper floors didn't look to be in use, so you'll have your choice." He leaned forward and tapped a narrow alley to the left of the building. "There's an access door here, and if the lock is stubborn, a small window just down from it."

Katria nodded. "Perfect."

"We'll do a secondary communications check on location," Sean stated, glancing around. "But everyone's magnacoms worked fine when we checked yesterday?"

They all confirmed.

"Good, just make sure to charge them fully before we begin. For this mission, we need to be in step-by-step contact," Sean ordered.

Mason and Kevin left for their rooms to prepare. Sean rolled up the map and tossed it on the low-burning fire behind him.

Katria tsked. "I always hate that you have to burn those."

Sean looked at her. "You'd rather someone know what we're up to?"

"No, it's just Mason works for hours on those maps for us, and they're always so... real. Like you're staring at the streets from the sky. I don't know how he does it."

"Because he's a Gen-Heir," Sean replied, as if she should know as much.

Not all genetic talents were as cut and dry as hers, or even Sean's. Being touch-based, their capabilities were never in doubt. Some, like Mason, were logic-based and required testing for proper placement in a guardian position. Along with his high-value strategy talent, Mason's artistic abilities made him a vital member of the intel guardian team.

She flexed her jaw in annoyance. "Yeah, I'm aware of Mason's ability. I guess I'm still impressed by it."

He gave a small smile. "Well, we're still pretty impressed with yours."

Katria was *not* impressed with her birthed ability. So often she wished she hadn't inherited what had raised her father to rather dangerous fame. But if she dwelled on her *gift*, she'd spiral into a bad place, so she simply offered Sean a rather shallow smile. "Thanks."

Sean seemed to sense her angst. He leaned across the table and met her stare. "You aren't one of them, Kat. You aren't bad, unlike the people we're assigned to go against."

A twinge of pain constricted her heart. She had to look away from his fierce amber gaze. Over the years, they'd had variations of the same conversation. She'd always assured him she was fine, that whatever he *felt* about her was incorrect. She had always put on the mantle of the emotionless assassin they'd recruited and expected. But lately, doubt grew. The kills were becoming too easy. The last handful, she hadn't even bothered to learn about her targets.

"I don't know anymore," she found herself whispering.

"I do, and I know you've read most of the files on those individuals, and you know it too."

At one time, that had been true, and the information on her targets had been enough. She couldn't stop herself from wondering, though, at what point the lack of morality in taking a life begins to take its toll? What would happen when she truly stopped caring? "Do you still care? I mean, do you care about the choices you have to make, the orders you have to give?"

He furrowed his brow. "Like tonight? No. Others, sometimes. But that's not our job to mind."

"How much longer do you think they'll keep us away from Sziveria?"

Annoyance flickered in his gaze; he lifted his chin towards her. "Why are you asking all this?"

She shrugged. "I don't know. Finally getting homesick, I guess."

He sighed and turned his attention back to the fire, poking the unburnt pieces of paper into the flames. "I'm not."

His answer took her by surprise. "Really? There's no one you miss?"

"I left nothing behind in Sziveria."

Katria recognized from his tone that the topic was closed. Spending three years in the man's company had given her unique insights, and this was one of them. When Sean finished talking, he was done. Since he rarely spoke about his life, she'd get nowhere with more questions.

Neither of them had given up much personal information in their three years together. Since nothing could grow beyond what was written on a piece of paper for them to accomplish, they worked hard at keeping their relationship professional.

As she walked past his brooding form, watching the hint of muscles play under his shirt, she reminded herself that the less she knew about Sean Blackbain, the better.

"Coms check one – Kat reply. Over," Sean's deep voice came into Katria's ear. She gritted her teeth against the little thrill that rolled in her belly. An unwelcome reaction she wasn't allowed to have.

"This is Kat, coms check one. Over," she replied, and then released the mic button. The bulky black radio box attached to the belt at her hip utilized magnetic power through friction. She'd shaken it the entire trip to make sure the unit was fully charged.

The rest of the team checked in as Katria sprinted up

flights of stairs, rifle case slung across her back. Small windows let in dying golden light, barely illuminating the narrow passage up. By the fifth floor, her muscles protested, but she pushed through the burn in her thighs and the ache in her chest. On the seventh floor, she conducted a thorough sweep, ensuring she was alone. Only a rat scurried into a dark corner in the last room she checked.

She pressed her mic button. "Seventh floor secure, setting up in the center window. Over."

"Acknowledged."

Katria knelt and pulled the case off her back. She set the bulky container on the dusty wooden floor in front of her. Long shadows blanketed the floor. Dying light provided enough illumination for the task at hand. Years of practice allowed her to assemble the rifle in seconds. She eased a window open enough to slide her barrel into position and then looked through the scope.

"Making entry onto the second floor," Kevin's voice said into her earpiece. *"Ballroom is full of guests, I wasn't noticed. Over."*

A faint creak sounded behind her. Katria snapped her head around and stared at the door to the room where she sat. Her free ear strained to hear another sound while she watched for telltale shadows that she wasn't alone.

Nothing.

Stupid rats.

She let out a breath and went back to looking through the scope at the party in the house below, watching for any signs that someone suspected Kevin's intrusion.

From her vantage point, she had a clear view of the entire street, the front of the house, the gardens, and the walkway. A house staff meandered up a path, lighting lamps as the last of the sun's rays disappeared over the horizon. The party seemed to be going smoothly enough for her to relax some. She crossed her legs and rested her rifle on the floor in front of the window. When Kevin gave the word, he was on the way out, she'd reengage.

A board creaked, sharper, closer. Katria sucked in air. That was definitely not a rodent. She lifted her rifle and swung around as a groaning man, eyes rimmed red, drool flowing from his slack mouth, shuffled into the room. At one time, he appeared to have been a builder, if the simple canvas pants, suspenders, and long-sleeve shirt were any indication. Fingers twitching at his sides, his feet lumbered in heavy boots unevenly, his sole purpose now to find a victim. Gone was the man he'd once been.

Katria suppressed the urge to scream and reached for her mic button. The movement made the infected man notice her. He charged, fast. His weight slammed her into the rotting wall between the windows. The thin plaster caved beneath the force, splintering into the air around her. Brick and pieces of broken wood bit into her back.

All her strength focused on keeping him at arm's length. His power was no longer his own, driven by the virus's impulses. She'd seen how this story played out far too many times. It took all her mental fortitude not to panic. If his gnashing mouth bit any part of her flesh, or the spittle foaming at his mouth made its way into hers, she'd suffer the same fate within two weeks.

The diseased man pressed closer until her biceps burned and trembled with the effort to keep him away. Terror ate at her, and she cried out. Sweat dotted her forehead and slid between her breasts. The only choice she had was to somehow kick him far enough away to reach one of her pistols under the window, which would send her to the ground, more vulnerable than she was now.

"Something's not right," Kevin's voice said across the

coms. *"He's not in his room, and I'm looking at his itinerary. The meeting is happening now. Over."*

"Say again, over," Sean replied.

"We were given the wrong information. The trade meeting was scheduled for tonight, started almost a half hour ago, not tomorrow. Over."

Shouts and screams drifted up through the open window. Katria tried to twist and get her legs between her torso and the infected mans.

"People are running from the building in chaos," Sean's voice said over the com, the faint clomp of horse hooves on brick echoing across. *"Kevin, get out of there. Mason, meet us at the dock we were supposed to go to after we delivered the diplomat. Kat and Kevin, meet me at the carriage in two blocks."* When she didn't respond, Sean said again, *"Kat, do you copy?"*

Katria gave another cry of distress as her body strained to keep the infected at bay. Teeth gnashed too close to her face. Twitching fingers attempted to grab at her, their movements uncoordinated. The stench of sickness and rot made breathing difficult. Stuck, without much hope, she couldn't stop a tear from sliding down her cheek. How was she going to escape?

The silence on the other end of the radio made Sean's heart thump too hard. He didn't waste another second. Jumping off the carriage, he bolted across the street. The side door into the building Kat occupied hung open, and he slipped in on a soundless stride. Adrenaline flowing through his veins, he took the stairs two at a time, sliding across the dusty landings. He wanted to call out. To hear her voice. To know she was okay. But if she wasn't, he didn't want to alert anyone waiting.

Just a communication failure, he assured himself, to keep calm.

When he reached the seventh floor, he unsheathed his knife and entered the quiet hall on light feet. He did a quick visual search and saw no one else on the floor, at least not in the hallway. A strained shout from a central room told him where to go, and that she wasn't alone. He pressed his back to the wall beside the door and glanced in. Cornered into the wall, Kat attempted to keep her assailant at bay. Sean let out a curse as he took in the man's thin frame, disheveled clothes, and his sharp snapping of teeth.

Sean vaulted into the room. The second he reached the attacker, he grabbed a handful of greasy hair and yanked. "Move! Now!"

The infected man jolted back. Sean dropped the knife and broke the man's neck with a rapid twist. Kat landed on the floor with a heavy thump. She quickly scooted away, the body slumping near her legs in a loose pile of flesh and bone, the teeth still snapping, the reanimated brain not knowing the body was now useless. Sean grabbed the back of the infected man's clothes and dragged him to the farthest corner, careful to keep from coming in contact with any fluids. In a few minutes, or a few hours, the virus animating the corpse would die, too, and only a dead body would remain. The eerie gnashing of his teeth was something they'd have to tolerate.

"Are you okay?" He knelt beside Kat and examined her, looking her over, turning her wrists. He took her chin in his hand and lifted her jaw, checking her throat. He searched her clothes for any damp spots.

"I'm fine," she said, breathless. "He didn't get to me."

Before he could stop himself or even realize what he was doing, Sean gathered her into his arms and held her tight to his chest. Trembling, she wrapped her arms around him. His hand smoothed down the long length of her braided hair as relief flowed through him. Little chunks of grainy plaster fell through his fingers to the floor.

"You're okay," he assured himself more than her.

"I checked... I don't understand. I searched, Sean. This floor was empty. And... the infected don't have the cognitive skills to climb stairs. H-how did he get in?"

Sean pulled back, his hand still resting in her hair. "I don't know. You didn't hear anything?"

"Just a board creak. I thought it was a rat, and then I heard another, and that's when he..." She closed her eyes and took a deep breath. "That's when he came in."

"Maybe he was in a closet. They can still open doors."

She shook her head. "No, I searched everywhere."

"Okay," he spoke in a calm tone to subdue her rising panic. He rested his chin on top of her head. "What does that leave?"

Her fingers tightened on his back. Every muscle in her frame went rigid. "That someone is as skilled in covert missions as we are, and dropped an infected man onto my floor to kill me?"

Sean sat back on his heels and resisted the urge to take her face in his palms. He wouldn't take the chance touching anyone's skin, especially hers, until after he washed his hands. "They failed. You are fine. And if they sent in a zombie for a man, it's because they knew they couldn't best you. They would fail."

She nodded, her lips parting, and Sean made the mistake of focusing on them. For three years, he'd avoided becoming too personal with her unless necessary, such as needing an accurate gauge of her mood or treating her for an injury as the team's medical science officer. Now he found himself inches from her mouth. He moved closer, the slightest shift of his weight. She didn't shy away. Her anticipation was strong enough to saturate the air, settling in his blood, urging him to act on the compelling need to kiss her.

"What's going on? Sean? Kat? I'm at the carriage. Where are you two? Everything all right?"

Kevin's interruption pulled them both back to reality, and Kat's arms fell away as Sean stood. She cleared her throat and blinked. Sean did the same, turning his back to her. What had he been thinking? He hadn't been. A mistake he couldn't make again.

Katria stared at the corpse and the puddle of infectious saliva pooling from its gaping mouth. The body twitched and shivered, but the snapping of his jaws had stopped. She shuddered in revulsion tinged with fear and quickly looked away, gathering her case and rifle. Slinging the closed carry case over her back, she kept the gun free. Positioning it under her arm, she followed Sean out, not bothering to glance behind. She kept close, as per her training. Of course, if she were sincere, she'd also admit she felt safer near him.

Rescues were part of their job description. Each of them had needed one at some point. This one had been different. After it was over, Sean had held her. Actually held her close to his strong chest, near enough for the warm, smoky scent of him to envelop her and make her forget rational thought. For the first time in the three years since she left home, she'd felt safe, secure in a moment. She *knew* nothing would happen to her. Sean wouldn't allow it.

There was also the matter of the near kiss, but she quickly pushed that away. Under no circumstances could a repeat happen.

They arrived at the alley. Cool air brushed her face. She ignored tendrils of loose hair floating around her and kept her focus on getting to the safety of the carriage. Whoever had attempted to unleash a rabies-syndrome-infected man on her might decide to go double with the three of them, or worse.

Kevin held the carriage door open for Kat, and she threw her case in before climbing inside.

"What happened?" Kevin inquired, helping her since she refused to release her rifle.

Sean jumped into the driver's seat. "Someone managed to get an infected man onto the seventh floor *after* she'd cleared it."

"What?" Kevin asked, shocked.

Sean shrugged and shook his head. "I have nothing. Well, nothing I want to consider."

"I do... and I don't like it," Kevin stated as he closed the door.

The carriage jostled as he joined Sean, and Katria rested inside against the seat. She wanted to know their theory, but the adrenaline from the attack was wearing off, and she suddenly found herself exhausted.

Slowly, her fingers slid along the cool metal of the gun's barrel, lying on her lap, to the slightly warmer wood, her mind lost in thought. The trusted weapon had been ineffective to her this time. Even her pistols had been of no use. She'd had no way to get to them. Before the next directive, she'd find a way to remedy that. There had to be another means to make her method of safety more accessible.

They came to a stop, and Katria sat up, glancing out the window. A small cutter ship sat bobbing in a soft current, the rising full moon casting long silvery shadows along the single sail.

Sean opened the door and motioned for her to exit. They walked at a clipped pace to the boarding ramp. Mason was waiting on deck. The deep frown on his handsome face made Katria's stomach drop.

He held up a slip of paper. "Summons to return to Haven City."

Sean took the note from him and unfolded it. His scowl matched Mason's. "Well, it appears someone set us up to fail. They knew we wouldn't accomplish the mission. No way we could have with the information we were given. The diplomat was infected and I bet he went active, like the man Katria had to deal with."

Kevin cursed. "Who would have done that?"

"Either we'll find that out in Haven City, or we're in some deep trouble because someone purposefully made sure this night was a fiasco."

❄ 4 ❄

T hree days later
        First Intelligence Office
Haven City, Sziveria

DESPITE A STRONG URGE TO REACH FOR KAT'S HAND,
Sean resisted. Anxiety flowed from her in waves, crashing
into him and setting him further on edge. She kept fisting
and unfisting her hands at her sides, exhibiting the nerves
the rest of them were too proud to show. The moment
they'd set foot onto Sziverian soil, a member of the FIO
had been waiting for them.

While Mason and Kevin had returned to their home-
land in the past three years, Sean and Kat had not. The
homecoming wasn't the one he had been expecting. Then
again, he wasn't sure what he'd ever anticipated of a city
that held nothing except bad memories.

One more certainly wouldn't matter.

Ryan Voklane's office door was partially open. After a
quick knock of warning, the team stepped inside. Two

chairs sat before his desk, and he motioned towards them. Sean gave a nod for Kat to sit, and he took the chair beside her. Mason and Kevin lingered closer to the door.

Perhaps it was just a show of power, but Ryan ignored their presence, continuing to work on a document in silence. When he finished, he folded his hands over the paper and looked at each of them before speaking. "I'm sure I don't need to say why you're here."

"One failed mission and suddenly we're at the bottom?" Sean couldn't help but ask.

"You don't fail."

"We aren't given misinformation, either."

Voklane tilted his head. "Misinformation?"

"Our instructions were to given to us on the day of the assignment. We barely had time to prepare a plan, let alone enact one."

"Those orders had been delivered three days before."

Sean furrowed his brow. "We didn't get them."

Ryan sighed and shuffled through a stack of papers on the corner of his desk. He removed a pale green folder and opened it. "Sent on the seventeenth of April to Wilhelm, Gaula. Delivered on the twentieth of April for execution. I have all the signatures here."

Sean accepted the folder and looked it over. "Who is Kenneth Linray?"

Ryan shrugged. "A courier we hired."

Handing it back, Sean said, "Well, he didn't do his job. He lied."

"I'll look into it," Ryan said as he accepted the closed folder. "In the meantime, you're home until further notice. I'm sure you already know, but the diplomat did indeed have HRS. He killed every person in the meeting and managed to get into a party taking place down the hall, where he infected several attendees. They aren't dead yet, but they might as well be. Cairo is understandably upset. We'd promised to take care of it."

"And we would have."

"Yes, well, *would have* doesn't work for them," Ryan sighed. "I'll look into this failure of assignment notification and try to talk to Arch Guardian Synintel. As you said, one failed mission in three years is more than acceptable. You all set an impossibly high standard for yourselves."

"So just go home?" Mason asked from the doorway.

Ryan nodded. "Yes, go home. Sean and Kat, you need to maintain your cover nation-side, so I'm sure you'll understand if you keep your marriage up for appearances' sake."

Sean's heart skipped a beat. *Their what?* "Excuse me?"

"Your marriage," Ryan said slowly, looking at Sean as if he should have understood the words the first time.

Sean glanced at Kat, who'd gone ashen. "So... we're expected to be on an assignment in Haven City as husband and wife?"

"No, you *are* husband and wife, just as you have been for three years. Come on, you two, nothing has changed just because you are home. Your government contract work isn't over yet, so neither is the marriage."

Kat raised a shaky hand. "Um, we never married, Mr. Voklane."

Ryan rolled his eyes. The legs of his chair scraped against the floor as he stood. He went to a cabinet and, after thumbing through it, pulled out a file. He placed it on top of the cabinet and sifted through pages until he found the one he needed. Back at his desk, he handed it across to them. "Three years ago, signed and dated, done deal."

Kat reached for the page, but Sean was faster. He

scanned the contract, focusing on his name and the concise, binding document that legally united them in marriage. Behind him, Kevin let out a bark of laughter.

"Well, I think we have completed our part here," Kevin said. "Mason?"

"But," Mason protested.

"Let's go," Kevin said, dragging the sputtering logistical expert from the office.

Sean suppressed the rising anger filling him and held up the paper. "Is this our copy? The copy you didn't bother to give us?"

"Yes, you can keep that one. We have several more, including the one filed with the Records Department."

The urge to crush the paper in his fist was almost too strong to ignore. Instead, he handed it to Kat and stood. "I suppose you'll be in touch when you have information about the communications failure for our assignment."

Ryan turned his attention back to the documents he'd been working on when they walked in, effectively dismissing them. "Of course."

Sean left without another word. Behind him, Kat's quick footsteps fell. He knew he should stop, say something, anything, but words escaped him. While neither of them deserved what had just happened, she *really* didn't deserve it. Husband material, he was not. Sean wasn't looking forward to the moment she realized who the government had forced her to marry.

Black wooden cabs for hire, their horses waiting in trained patience, formed a long line in front of the imposing drab, gray building. Sean bounded down the wide stairs to the sidewalk, weaving his way through the moderate traffic. He motioned to the first cabby, who looked his way. When he reached the vehicle at the start of the line, he opened the door and waited for Kat.

She hesitated before climbing in. Sean gave the address to his Haven City house and then joined her.

Once they were moving, he chose to look at Kat. The view outside wasn't one he relished. He knew he'd see clean, red brick buildings of varying heights lining neat, brown brick streets. Carriages of different classes, from wealthy, ornately painted boxes to small open buggies, mixed with ariots, vehicles run by magnetic engines harnessing the power of positive and negative attraction, on the wide roads. Since only the extremely wealthy and the government could afford the small vehicles, they found themselves outnumbered. Any part of town they'd travel through would yield the same sights, plus a few trees or ornately decorated front yards, and towering greenhouses in the back.

Kat stared down at the document that had sealed their fate so many years ago without their knowledge. The clop of hooves on brick kept uncomfortable silence away.

"Anything we should know specifically?" he asked.

She gave a slight start, her eyes meeting his for the briefest second before returning to the paper. "Like, how to get out of it? Only if one of us dies."

"Great," he replied sarcastically.

"Are we going to your house?"

"Yes."

Her jaw tightened, and her fingers gripped the paper tightly enough for it to crinkle. "What sort of announce-ment do you think they made?"

"I don't know. I'm positive, though, that Voklane was kind enough to make sure a copy is waiting for me."

"I never thought I'd *want* to shoot someone before today," she remarked softly.

"Yeah, he has a way of doing that to people," Sean

agreed. With a sigh, he sat forward and braced his elbows on his knees. "Listen…"

Kat shook her head quickly and pressed her back into the seat. "I'm not ready to discuss specifics. Not yet."

"Fair enough. However, there's one thing we need to discuss, and I don't want to wait."

"All right."

"We've been married for three years," he began, a tightness forming in his chest. "And I…" He ran his fingers through his hair, suddenly unable to meet her gaze. "I wasn't exactly…"

"You didn't know," she whispered, seeming to understand where he was going with his inept confession.

"Well, I know now, okay?"

She simply nodded.

The carriage came to a stop in front of his three-story brick house. Kat gasped as she looked out the window. "This is where you live?"

"It's fairly small by society's standards for a ranked guardian."

She raised a brow. "You're a ranked guardian?"

Sean stared at her. Was it possible she didn't know him beyond the first and last name he'd given her all those years ago? The urge to punch something finally got the better of him, and he slammed his fist into the wooden frame of the carriage. "I'm going to kill him!"

Katria couldn't remember a time when she'd seen Sean angry enough to have a physical reaction. He leapt out of the carriage and stormed to the house as if an enemy needed to be conquered within. She wasn't sure why her question had unraveled his final string, and she didn't know if she wanted to.

The front door stood open in his wake. Katria took a

deep breath. For the second time, she'd be stepping into a new life, a new identity. Only this time, she had a strange feeling this one would somehow be much harder. Options were limited, or rather, nonexistent.

Three years ago, in a stack of papers they had forced her to sign in a rush, she'd managed to marry Sean Blackbain. No ceremony making promises to their future, no romance, no love. No family. Tears burned her eyes, and she had to breathe them away quickly. What family would have been there anyway?

The negative thoughts would lead nowhere. Time to see her new home. She walked up the brick stairs to the door. On any other occasion, she would have admired the beautiful flowers blooming in pots leading up to the entrance, but today their colors seemed muted. Inside, a small commotion bustled as men and women dressed in neat gray and white attire filed into the spacious foyer. Sean was wealthy enough to have a staff. Just who had she married?

A tall, regal man with perfectly styled hair stepped forward from the small crowd and gave a rigid bow. "Primary Guardianess, I'm Davis, at your service. Sean is in the library. It's right this way."

The lost expression she likely wore must have tipped him off. She smiled and went to thank him, and then his words fully registered. "I'm sorry, who?"

"Sean, he's in the library."

She cleared her throat and touched her hand to her chest, an odd sensation building. "No, before that, y-you called me *Primary Guardianess?*"

"Yes, of course. Are you not his wife?"

Play the part, woman! she scolded herself. Straightening her back, she nodded. "Yes, sorry, I'm only used to what he calls me." Which was not a lie.

Davis gave a polite smile. "Of course."

He guided her to the library, off a narrow side hall from the wide staircase leading to the second floor. She gave a polite nod in thanks and waited until he'd closed the doors to provide them with privacy. Sean stood hunched over a small table, a newspaper open before him. He gripped a glass filled with amber liquid.

Katria pointed at the closed door, even though he wasn't looking at her, and stated, "Davis called me Primary Guardianess." Afraid to ask, but knowing she had to, she continued, "What exactly should I know?"

In one swift motion, Sean drained the entire glass. Fantastic. Her husband would be incoherent before dinner. He didn't say a word, simply held out the newspaper to her. Katria crossed the distance to him. She furrowed her brows as she took the paper, folded to an article in her hand.

Have we got a juicy exclusive for our beloved readers of The Haven City Chronicle. *Whisper about the rumors no more, it's official! The ever-dashing Primary Guardian Wintersfall has tied the knot, and not just with anyone. His mysterious bride? None other than the stunning Katerina Nachesa of Ruthenia, the daughter of a distinguished diplomat with ties in all the right places.*

But wait, of course, we have more to share with you! The star-crossed pair didn't just sign on the line. Oh no, that would be too dull for the Blackbain family, don't you agree? So of course you will be delighted to learn, they eloped! That's right, three whole years ago! And where have they been since? Off on a globe-trotting escapade that would make even the most seasoned adventurer blush.

Now, the glamorous duo has returned at last, simply glowing with the thrill of their whirlwind love story. And you heard it here first.

Katria stopped reading. Confused, she glanced at the name they'd given. "Katerina Nachesa?"

"That'd be you. Did they spell something wrong?"

Katria thought quickly. If they'd lied about her name in the paper, maybe... She unfolded the marriage license. Her shoulders fell. Her real name was listed on the marriage contract, making it a completely legal document. And yet, could it be that Sean didn't *know* who she really was? How? He'd held the same legal paper she did. She wasn't going to worry about that for now, just count herself lucky. Slowly, she refolded the marriage license.

"Yes, of course, it's fine. My father wasn't a diplomat, though," she replied to cover her slip. "They built us a backstory? Do we have it? Or is this newspaper *it*?"

Sean straightened. "I think the newspaper is all we've been given." He leaned against the small table and crossed his arms. "Who was your father, then?"

"He just did government work, but not anything diplomatic." *Unless one considered contract killing a means of diplomacy.* Her attention returned to the paper. "What about you? It says here, Primary Guardian Wintersfall."

"Oh, I'm sorry, where are my manners?" He straightened and then executed a perfect deep bow. "Sean Blackbain, Primary Guardian Wintersfall."

Katria's mouth went dry. "So I'm..."

He gave a sarcastic smile. "The Primary Guardianess Wintersfall. Of course, you were already a guardian, but now you're married to a ranked one."

Confused, Katria raised her hand. "Wait. I was a guardian already?"

Sean nodded, returning to his relaxed stance against the table. "Yes. Anyone who serves Sziveria, either in a city role such as enforcement services, or a national role, like in the Investigative Division or First Intelligence, is a guardian. Voklane is a guardian, but he doesn't hold a ranked position."

"And how exactly do the rankings work? How did you become a primary guardian?" she asked.

"Old roles that hold voting seats in the Hall of Laws are ranked according to the community they used to, or continue to serve. Later, as specific talents were needed to fill other official roles, Endowment and Revocation assigned ranks to help recruit the necessary gifts. Only specific Gen-Heir talents can fill certain ranked guardian positions. My family holds an old Primary rank, first assigned to the family Wintersfall as a voting seat for the Wintersfall Lake community. My rank will always carry that name as a means of tradition, regardless of what family is endowed with it, though I'm the first Wintersfall to not serve in a voting seat. The names are the way the founders of our nation chose to preserve our early history. Didn't you learn about guardians and ranking in academia?"

Katria absorbed this information, ignoring his question. Not only had she always been a guardian, carrying the responsibility of her nation, it seemed, but now she had a husband to support, who was ranked. A duty beyond simply taking an order. In fact, in the eyes of society, they were seen as having an equal partnership. If Sean had an issue, he'd come to her to help solve it.

"Voklane is a dead man," she breathed out.

"Twice over."

$ 5 $

S ean had waited for any indication that Kat recognized his name. The only distress she'd shown was at her sudden position within society. Most women would be thrilled. This woman seemed honestly troubled, and not because of who he was.

For almost an hour they'd sat in silence. She sitting on the floor, scouring over a law book she'd found, and he sitting in a chair not far from the fire, silently watching her.

His wife.

The realization both thrilled and terrified him.

"Where did you grow up?" he asked softly, suddenly wanting to know the little things he'd avoided for so long.

"Outside of Old Helston, on a cliff overlooking the Sovereign Channel. My father liked his privacy."

"And your mother?"

She froze, and for a moment, he didn't think she was going to answer. Then she relaxed and continued running her finger down the page of the book. "She was an botanist. What about you? Did you grow up here?"

"Mostly here, yes. My mother was very involved in the social scene. She didn't like being away from all the parties, dinners, and theater shows. My father didn't care so much. Where I lived at any given time depended on whether my mother insisted that he keep me. Then I was at the lake property."

"Hmm," was her only reply. "I'm not seeing anything here in this contract book."

Sean sighed and leaned his head back against the chair. "Wouldn't matter anyway, we're government service agents. Civilian laws don't apply to our contracts."

With a growl of frustration, she snapped the book closed. "Then what's the end game?"

He straightened and stared down at her. "What do you mean?"

"I mean, they keep our marriage secret until we're forced back after a failed mission, and then they make us stay and act as a married couple. Someone is playing at something."

Leaning forward, he clasped his hands between his knees. "I don't see who would have anything to gain by forcing us to play out a marriage."

She tapped her index finger to her lips. "It has to be something."

Sean considered her words, along with all the people he worked under. None of them rang any alarms for possible enemies. "I don't know."

"Voklane had to know when he handed you the contract that you'd be upset. Could he be the reason?"

"Doubt it, three years ago, he was nothing but an order giver. He handed down information, but little else. I'd only known him for a year by that point. Not long enough to piss him off to this extent."

"Okay then," she sighed thoughtfully. "So, something else."

"Maybe they just figured we'd make that great of a team," he threw out more sarcastically than he intended, slumping back into the chair. "Then again, I think you would have done fine with *any* team they placed you on, or with any leader."

"But they didn't marry me to another leader... or another man," she remarked quietly.

No, but they should have, Sean stopped himself from saying. "No, and they had no way of knowing we'd manage to keep things entirely professional."

She fidgeted some, drawing her knees into her side, and avoided his stare. "Do you think they figured we wouldn't keep things professional?"

Only someone naïve about the ways of men and women would ask that question. Kat wasn't exactly what he'd consider innocent. Then again, they'd taken great care to treat her as nothing more than a colleague, at least in his case. While she may have become seasoned in many things, intimate relationships were not one of them. They couldn't pull off being married in front of people if she didn't even know the intricacies of a liaison.

His troubles seemed destined to continue to mount.

Sean ran his hand down his face. All the things about her he'd forced himself not to see were no longer forbidden. Her long, silky black hair, the full pout of her lips, and the soft curves of her body, small by the societal standards she was about to face, but perfect for what daily life demanded of her. Fit and firm, yet clearly defined enough to be still feminine. A sudden quickness rose in his pulse.

Kat wasn't like any of the other women in his life. She held a trust in him no one else had, one he didn't want to break. Despite their relationship changing on paper, he had to tread carefully with her. She deserved so much more than he'd ever be able to offer. The more often he reminded himself of that fact, the better.

Ignoring her question, he stood and made his way over to an aluminum tray sitting on a small, ornate table beside the door, which was overflowing with an array of colorful envelopes in various sizes. "Let's see who's interested in having us in their house."

Sean's disregard for her question didn't go unnoticed. Katria bit her bottom lip and tried to make sense of it. At no point during their three years of serving together had he made any advances towards her, nor had he given any indication that he wanted to. Except for their last mission. And she'd done her best to make sure he never knew the storm of emotions she felt whenever he walked into the room.

Even now, as he tossed envelope after envelope back onto the tray, she couldn't help but notice the way his shoulders moved, the hair that fell ruggedly around his face, or how the stubble covering his strong jaw made him seem even more dangerous than usual.

And he was her husband.

Little tremors danced in her stomach, and she quickly looked away. While the sensation wasn't unfamiliar when it came to Sean, she still buried the unsafe emotions. Now her infatuation could cost her something.

He gave a soft grunt that brought her attention back to him. Only a handful of envelopes remained in his grasp, and he flipped one open, releasing the seal. "Interesting."

"What?" she asked, rising.

"Three years ago, this family..." His words died off, and he shook his head as if dismissing a bad memory. "They didn't care for mine much. Now it seems they wish to have us over for a dinner party." He flipped the card over and snorted. "They want to be sure they can toast the happy couple."

"A dinner?" Katria fidgeted with the soft fabric of her skirt. "Aren't those rather expensive?"

"To host, immensely."

"And to attend?"

Sean tapped the stiff card against his chin. "I suppose we'll have to get clothes for it. We didn't exactly need to be fashion-conscious on most assignments."

"I've never owned a formal gown. I think the last time I needed one, Mason or Kevin rented it for me."

"Ah, yes, I remember that. Mason did, and it was a fiasco."

She laughed and nodded, recalling the fluffy olive-green monstrosity Mason had proudly procured for her. "Yes, it was hideous, and equally as uncomfortable."

"I think he was trying to make sure he looked every bit the part of a protective big brother."

"He succeeded. No one came within five feet of me that night."

"It was lucky for them," he said in a tone that had her gaze meeting his. For a second, the intensity in his tawny eyes forced her heart into her throat. Then, as if she'd imagined it, he flipped the card. His expression shifted just as quickly to neutral. "We'll need new clothes, and I suppose you'll need to accept the invitation to keep up appearances. After all, the supportive spouse usually decides what functions the couple attends."

"They do?"

"Yes, but since you have no idea who any of these people are, we'll do it together until you learn. Or until we figure out what's going on, and if getting into certain homes will aid us."

Three years ago, she'd been overwhelmed with the sudden change in her life. Alone, with three brawny men, being given orders to protect them from a distance, or execute a death warrant on a complete stranger, she'd been in over her head.

In retrospect, it was nothing compared to what she faced now.

Forced to function in a society she'd only heard rumors of, married to a man whose reputation she could break within it. And somewhere out there could be an unknown enemy who'd watch their every move, and every mistake she was about to make.

"How many days?" she asked softly.

"A week."

"How am I supposed to learn a lifetime of etiquette in a week?"

Katria accepted the narrowed-down invitations he handed her. "The same way you learned how to be a sister to a primary guardian and cousin or ward to a master guardian." He gently grasped her chin in his hand and met her gaze. "You've played the part of ranked society so many times, and you didn't even know. Now you're just playing the wife to one."

"But I'm not playing," she whispered. "I really am one."

His hand dropped, and he sighed. "I know."

Then his words caught up to her, and her eyes widened. "Mason and Kevin are ranked, too?"

Sean gave a low, deep laugh. He threw his arms up as he walked past her to the tumbler of rum he'd left sitting by his chair. "Yes, because those of us who don't want to sit in and dictate law or rewrite tax code are still required to do our part to the elected crown." He took a heavy drink. "So we take the orders and make sure the *good guys* win where they need us to."

"What are Mason and Kevin's rankings?"

"Mason is Primary Guardian Kynhaven, and Kevin is the Master Guardian Raiventon, and his wife is the daughter of an arch guardian."

"Kevin's father-in-law is an arch guardian, and he's running around the world as an interceptor?"

"Yes, because he's the best, you know that."

"And his wife is okay with it?"

Sean took a deep breath. "I don't think she knows."

"Oh," Katria breathed. Good, at least she wasn't the only one keeping a secret.

"So if you happen to meet her..." he began.

"No speaking of our work together."

"Correct. Which is really for the best anyway."

"I imagine so. I'm not sure how to introduce myself, anyway. Hello, I'm Kat. I kill people when the government asks me to. I don't think it'd go over well."

He cracked a smile as he raised the glass to his lips. "Probably not. Keep that in mind as you're introducing yourself to people in a couple days."

"What about you?"

Sean raised a brow. "What about me?"

"Do they know who you are, what you do?"

His eyes met hers in questioning. "My name has never changed."

Katria's pulse quickened a bit, but she reminded herself that her false name was a lie only she seemed to know. "And how about the work you do for the intel team?"

He shook his head. "No, no one knows what I do, just that I work for the First Intelligence Office in place of my seat. As for in what capacity, only very few have that knowledge."

"And me? Am I just your wife, or will they know that I'm an operative too?"

Sean gave a smile that didn't reach his eyes. "Just my wife. The daughter of a diplomat, I met while doing my job."

"How am I supposed to live a lie for days, possibly weeks?" she couldn't help but ask, trying to subdue the sudden panic. "I was raised in a tiny, obscure village. My only knowledge of life outside of this country is everything I've done with you. It hasn't exactly been high society. I've done things, seen things..." She wrapped her arms around herself. "They can't even begin to imagine."

Sean crooked his finger, motioning for her to come near. Against her better judgment, she rose and slowly moved one foot in front of the other until she stood inches from him. Her heart pounded, a mixture of anxiety and anticipation. Though what she possibly had to antici-pate, she wasn't sure.

"That's where you're getting it all wrong," he said gently, sitting down so they were near eye level. Even though he didn't touch her, the distance between them was small enough for his smoky, warm scent to surround her. "They don't know you at all. They know what's in the paper. You're the daughter of a diplomat, and we've been on this grand romantic adventure for three entire years. No society, no reputations to build or to keep. Just us, gallivanting to every exciting destination, testing our luck outside the Uninhabited Zones. Whatever you want. You're Katerina Blackbain, Primary Guardianess Wintersfall."

She desperately wanted to correct him. She was *Katria* Blackbain. But to do so would mean revealing what someone didn't seem to want him to know, and until she could figure out why, she decided she'd keep her identity a secret for now. She also didn't want to discuss the dark details of her past. Three years still wasn't long enough.

"We'd be incredibly comfortable with each other," she found herself pointing out.

"Yes," he agreed, his frame stiffening in the chair.

She resisted the urge to take a step back from him. "We can't fake that."

"I don't think we'll have to."

Katria frowned. "What do you mean?"

"We have traveled the world together, and we have taken our chances outside of many Uninhabited Zones. They just weren't..."

"Romantic," she finished when he didn't.

"Correct, and again, something they will never know. You'll see for yourself that we'll be all right the first time we have to interact in a public setting. Treat it as any other assignment and you'll do fine."

But this wasn't an assignment. It was her new life, and his, and the decisions she made had lifelong consequences. Unlike their unsuccessful mission, a failure in some folder to be filed, what happened now mattered for months, if not years. Every aspect of their life would be affected. From what would be written about them for all to read, to where they'd be allowed to shop. How did people live with that sort of pressure?

Then there was another matter they were both ignoring altogether. Intimacy. If she stood next to her husband like the subordinate she'd been for years, everyone would know something was wrong. But what did she know of being a wife? Or of anything romantic, for that matter? She'd never even experienced a kiss.

"Are husbands and wives affectionate in a social setting?" she asked as casually as she could muster.

Sean shrugged and set his glass down on the small side table. The smooth roll of his shoulders, close enough to touch from where she stood in front of him, had Katria balling her hands to resist temptation. "Some are, some aren't. I suppose it depends on their relationship. Society doesn't frown upon spouses who display affection, but they don't necessarily expect it either."

"Depending on the circumstances," she reiterated.

"Yes, and they've never met us together, so they have no idea how we should or shouldn't act."

Comforted by his response, she nodded. "Okay, that's good."

"However," he began, scooting forward until he rested on the edge of the chair, "I suggest you read the article in its entirety."

Katria glanced at the floor where she'd left the paper sitting next to the useless book on contract law. "Why?"

His fingers suddenly touched hers, and Katria jumped at the contact. "Because you won't be able to react like that."

She let out a steadying breath. "I'm sorry, I didn't—"

"Nothing to be sorry about, not right now. In a week, though, that response could mean disaster."

Of course, acting as if her husband repelled her wouldn't do. He moved his fingers to her wrist and along her forearm, his soft touch creating an unfamiliar tremble deep in her belly. Katria's breath grew shallow. With a bit of pressure on the inside of her arm, he urged her to move dangerously closer to him. She more leaned than took a step, though her feet betrayed her, sliding along the soft carpet. His hand slipped from her arm to her waist, pulling her near enough that if she took a deep breath, her breasts would press into his shoulders.

"They *will* expect me to touch you." He straightened his back until he was almost level with her, his mouth so close to her neck she could feel his warmth. Katria's heart raced, and she closed her eyes, a pleasant sensation building where his breath fell along her skin. "They will expect me to..."

"Miss, miss, please!" Davis's voice pleaded from the other side of the door.

The library door burst open. Katria leapt away from Sean. He, however, didn't seem the least bit fazed as a stunning woman swept into the room. The rush of air from the door swirled long black hair around her face and ruffled the silky, pale blue length of her gown. A playful gleam danced in her silvery gray eyes and on her red lips.

"So it's true," she remarked, coming to a stop, a hand on her hip. Her gaze moved from Katria and came to rest on Sean.

Katria suddenly found herself conscious of her lack of fuller curves. Compared to this woman, she was a stick. Sean sat back in his chair, a frown darkening his eyes.

"That depends on what you've heard," he replied.

The woman sauntered over to him. "Well, that is true. Besides, I should know better than anyone that you can't trust what you read in the *Haven City Chronicle*."

"You write for them," Sean said, deadpan.

A wicked smile toyed at her lips and she curled a finger into the hair at his shirt collar. "Exactly. And I don't see a wedding ring." She glanced Katria's way and looked her over in a manner that left Katria bristling. "On either of you."

"We have to pick them up from the jeweler."

"Ah." The woman smirked, sliding between Katria and

Sean, forcing Katria to take a step back. She wrapped her arms around Sean's neck and sat on his knee, smiling at him. *Who was this woman?* "Which jeweler?"

"Cora!" Mason's deep voice called out from the foyer. Breathless, he appeared in the doorway. "Cora, get off Sean's lap." He held his hand up as he bent over, gasping for air. "I am so sorry, I tried to stop her, I don't know how she moves faster than me."

"She was just getting up." Sean helped Cora rise, though much slower than Katria cared for.

Mason stopped before Katria, his breathing heavy. "Again, really sorry. She's so stubborn."

"Oh, and you're not?" Cora chirped with a raised brow.

"It's fine," Katria said tersely.

"No, it's not. Sean is your husband, and she knows better," Mason chided, more to Cora than as a conversation.

"She knows better," Cora mimicked.

Katria rose on tiptoes and whispered to Mason, "He's been my husband for three hours."

Mason met her gaze, his lips in a tense line. "No, Kat, he's been your husband for three years, and you need to make sure every other woman knows it." He turned his attention back to Cora. "And that goes double for my wicked twin here."

"Your... *twin?*" And here she thought she knew these men she'd served with for the past three years. *Arrive home to learn they're entirely different people.* The unexpected urge to slink off into a corner to process all she'd discovered today rode her hard. Katria took a steadying breath and remained fixed at Mason's side. "Sean said you're ranked as well. What else do I need to know about all of you?"

Mason arched a dark brow and crossed his arms over

his massive chest. "I figured you knew about our ranks. We're guardians, after all."

"Yes, but Sean said not all guardians are ranked. He said I was one. I know I'm not—or rather I wasn't —ranked."

"Technically, you have always been in a ranked position as his wife," Mason said.

With her hands on her hips, Cora came to stand before Katria. "And my brother here could have filled the same seat our mother filled in the Hall of Laws, or as an enforceman, but he felt it wasn't exciting enough."

"That's not true, I just didn't want to chance on my work following me home as an enforceman. And the Hall of Laws?" He shuddered and frowned. "No, thank you." Frown still in place, he looked at his twin sister. "Happy now? You've seen her. Can we go home?"

"So you're the woman who replaces me when he's running around the world." Once again, she looked Katria over, from the floor up to her gaze. "I guess I can see how that would work. Is that all they needed you for? To play little roles for the big boys?"

Maybe it was the condescending tone or the smirk on her far too pretty face that made Katria give a little smile of her own. "No, I was the one who made sure your brother came home alive. Every time." Then she leaned forward and said softly, "I'm a perfect shot from five hundred yards. Don't make me prove it to you."

Cora's response started as a gentle chuckle and grew into a barking laugh. "So perfect!" She turned her attention back to Sean. "She'll fit right in with the family name, won't she?"

That seemed to be the final straw for Sean. He stood and grabbed Cora's elbow, propelling her towards the door. "Say goodbye, Cora."

"Goodbye, Cora!" the infernal woman sang into the air as Sean escorted her out of the library.

"I can't believe she's your sister, let alone your twin," Katria told Mason.

"Yeah, I get that a lot. She wasn't always this... vibrant." Mason sighed. "Life has a way of doing things to us."

Wasn't that the truth. "I seem to be in one of those moments myself."

He gave a small smile and patted her back gently. "You'll do fine. You will. And if you get harassed by someone, just remember, you can always find out where they live."

Cora yanked her elbow from Sean's grasp once they were free of the library, but Sean made sure she kept moving, placing a hand on the small of her back.

"What game are you playing at?" he asked, once he was positive they were far enough away for Kat not to hear.

"No game," Cora replied, coming to a stop. "What about you? From the little bit I gathered in there, she doesn't know much about anyone on your team. Did the woman come from a cave?"

Sean flexed his jaw and sighed. "Close enough."

"She knows nothing?"

He simply stared at her.

"I see. You won't be able to hide the truth for long, Sean."

"I'm aware of that."

"You know, she may not care." Cora reached up and fiddled with the collar of his shirt. "I didn't. I still don't."

He took her hands and squeezed them until her gaze met his. "I *am* married to her, Cora."

Slowly, she pulled her hands free and looked down. "I

know... I may have gone to the Records Department to confirm when my editor handed me the piece to write."

"*You* wrote that article about us?"

She shrugged, a coy smile tugging at her lips. "Now and again, they have me write something that won't put me on a hit list somewhere. Besides, they know I know you personally and could add something no one else could. I guess it's your luck I know what *not* to say."

Curious, Sean crossed his arms over his chest. "Who gave your editor the information?"

"I don't know, it arrived on his desk in an envelope with a memo to have it printed within twenty-four hours. They didn't care who was bumped from the gossip column. I don't think I've ever seen anyone get an entire page. Someone wanted to make sure all of Haven City knows you two are in town." She pushed a long strand of black hair over her shoulder. "I can't be too upset about it, though–I did get an entire page in the most-read section. The invitations haven't stopped rolling in. I'll know anything I want about anyone before the month's over."

"Be careful," Sean warned. "Drug brokers and shady merchants aren't the only ones who like to keep their secrets secret."

She pushed a hand into his shoulder playfully. "Worried about me?"

"No, I'm worried about what your brother will do if someone comes after his sister while he's home to do something about it."

She exhaled heavily. "Point taken, I'll be careful."

When she turned to leave, he asked, "Do you think you could get the envelope and memo for me?"

"Of course," she said as if he should have known already. "And I also know an investigator with Haven City Enforcement Services. He's a good man, trustworthy. If you need an inside look at what's going on in the underground, I can see if he'll meet with you."

"Maybe. I have a feeling if anything is going on, it'll be very much above ground."

She shrugged. "He knows them, too. He's a key guardian."

"I'll let you know."

Nodding, she turned to leave again, but not before calling over her shoulder, "And Sean? You don't live up to your family name, so don't worry, she'll think that's who you are."

Sean took a deep breath as Cora slipped out the front door. How he wished she'd be right. But he figured Kat had been through enough in one day. Finding out exactly *who* she'd married could wait a little longer. Hopefully a lot longer.

"Where did she go?" Mason asked as he walked past Sean to the closed front door. "She's as bad as Kevin, just disappearing."

"She caused the trouble she wanted, so she left," Sean remarked with a slight smile. "She mentioned someone left the information about me and Kat on her editor's desk. She's going to get it to me and speak to an investigator with the HCES about meeting."

"How do you think the HCES can help?"

"I don't know, probably with nothing, but right now I'll take anyone who may be on our side."

"I agree something isn't right, but do you really think we need to be *that* worried about it?"

"I'm not sure yet. Do you know who the investigator might be?"

Mason flexed his jaw in thought. He groaned and dropped his head back. "He will *not* be on your side."

"Who is it?"

"Key Guardian Asherwick."

"Jonathon Hunter?" Sean cursed. The day kept getting worse. Jonathon Hunter was the last person who'd help him, even if Sean lay on the street dying. "Yeah, that meeting will never happen. What was she thinking?"

"I don't think she was. I'll talk to her."

"She is a disaster," Sean bit out.

"Yep. Now you know why I had to leave Sziveria."

Sean accepted Mason's handshake. "I'll let you know if I discover anything."

"Same here. And sorry again for the intrusion."

"It proved insightful."

Mason grinned. "Among other things."

Once the door closed behind Mason, Sean headed back to the library. He stopped at the door. Kat turned from staring into the fire, exhaustion clear on her beautiful face. Unlike Cora, everything about Kat was genuine. A flicker of emotion danced in the back of his mind, and he forced it away.

"Come on," he told her, "I'll show you to your room."

She bit her bottom lip. "Is it your room, too?"

Sean simply motioned for her to follow. They headed to the second floor, Kat trailing behind at least three steps. The upstairs of his house was much simpler than the downstairs. Only a solid runner adorned the long hall branching to the left and right. No paintings hung on the walls beside the sconces, and only a small table, placed beside every other door, held a small crystal oil lamp.

"We have eight rooms on the second floor and three on the third, accessible via a stairway at the end of the hall to the right here." He stopped at the second door to the left and pushed it open. "And this is your room. It's not mine, but it does adjoin, which you're fairly accustomed to."

She nodded, stepping past him and into the room. She

went to the chest left in the center. "Everything I own is in this. Funny, the lack of things I possessed never mattered before now."

"You weren't home before now." He glanced around the room he'd ordered decorated but had never bothered to inspect after the house became his years ago. Now, he took in the elegant yet simple oak dresser and the full bed adorned in cream and navy accents, matching the walls and curtains.

"Home." She said the word slowly, as if the meaning itself were foreign to her.

Sean took a chance and stepped into the room, closing the door behind him. Propriety was no longer something they needed to worry about, except perhaps with each other. As far as his staff was concerned, he could be alone in his wife's room. To do otherwise might raise red flags they couldn't risk.

"I know this isn't what you're used to, but I hope you can make this home, at least for the time we're..."

"Stuck together?" she finished when he failed to find the words.

"I was going to say 'in this contract.'"

"According to the contract, we're in it until they no longer have us assigned together, or—" Her words suddenly died, and she looked away. She slowly lowered herself to sit on the chest.

Sean raised a brow and came to a stop in front of her. "Or what?"

"I don't think it'll be anything we have to worry about," she replied briskly.

When she still wouldn't look up at him, picking at a green destination label beside her leg, he crouched down before her. "If you don't want to say, hand me the contract and I'll try to focus on more than just my name this time."

"I left it downstairs, with the newspaper and book," she said softly.

He frowned. "Not exactly something you want to leave lying around."

"You don't trust your staff?"

"The only person I trust is Davis, and that's because he's been working for my family since I was a boy. The others? No. They're likely already writing what they're going to sell to the *Chronicle* or *The Havener* in the morning."

"Do I need to go get it?"

Sean shook his head. "No, Davis will make sure it's placed safely in my desk, either in my room or my office. However, do I *need* to go get it, or are you going to share?"

A flush crept into her cheeks and along the exposed skin of her chest. "We're bound permanently if we..." She took a deep breath and in a whisper he almost didn't catch, said, "conceive a child."

"Conceive?" Sean asked, making sure he heard correctly.

She nodded.

"Well, there are ways around that," he said before he could catch himself.

Her wide-eyed stare would have been comical at any other time. "What?"

"I mean... I'm not saying that we will...you know," He gestured between them. "I'm just saying... never mind." He cleared his throat. "We're married until we're unassigned, then?"

"Yes."

A board creaked in the hall. Sean turned his head slightly and listened. The doorknob began to turn slowly. He leaned forward and braced his hands on the trunk beside her hips. Her vivid blue eyes met his in alarm.

"Do not pull away from me," he whispered, leaning his body in close enough to hers that each heavy breath she took pressed her breasts into his chest. He fell to his knees and pushed himself between hers before she could object. A gasp escaped her lips, which turned into a forceful breath as he wrapped his arm around her waist and pulled her completely against his torso. She braced a hand on the trunk behind her, the other grabbing his shoulder.

The faint groan of the door hinges sounded behind Sean, giving away whoever entered. He didn't release Kat, keeping her close, his forehead practically touching hers. Her fingers dug into his shoulder, either for balance or because of the anxiety rolling from her.

Her breath fanned over his mouth in soft puffs. Sean found himself wondering if she'd breathe the same way if he kissed her. Every curve of her form fit against his, making him very aware of the planes of smooth muscle under the fabric of her gown.

"Your guardianship?" a woman asked behind him.

"What?" he growled, real annoyance rising in him. He unexpectedly found himself *wanting* to kiss his wife. And now nothing stood in his way, a dangerous thing to be aware of.

"A message c-came for you."

"Leave it on the dresser." Fabric rustled, followed by quick footsteps. "And close the door behind you."

He waited until the click of the door signaled they were once again alone before reluctantly moving. Taking a calming breath, he stood.

"There, now they'll have something worth selling tomorrow," he commented as he made his way to the dresser.

"You did that for gossip?"

Tearing open the envelope, he replied, "No, I did it because we have a very real role to play. As I told you earlier, you can't shy away from me. If I take your hand, you accept. If I move in to kiss your cheek, you offer it. If I put my hand around your waist, you move closer. Every time we step foot outside our bedroom, people will be watching. We can't give them the wrong things to talk about."

"And what Mason's sister did?" she asked, defiance clear in her voice.

Sean paused in pulling the message free. "I've known Cora a long time. That she misbehaved in her usual manner will come as no shock to anyone. Plus, her brother was with her."

"Was that always the case?"

Sighing heavily, Sean didn't pretend not to understand what she asked— had Mason always accompanied Cora when she visited? He gave an honest answer. "No."

"Is she..." Kat took a steady breath. "Is she still—"

"I thought I made myself clear on the ride home," he said low, a sliver of indignation welling up in his chest. "There's no one except you now."

The words hit Katria like a derailed train. The dangerous glow his eyes took on when he was angry hitched her breath in her chest. How she desperately wanted to be the only woman in his life. But a piece of paper didn't change their circumstances.

Despite her better judgment, she couldn't stop herself from asking, "How can that be when we aren't truly married?"

He returned his attention to the note in hand. "Careful, I might take that as a challenge."

Katria knew she wouldn't be much of a challenge if he

opted to test her resolve when it came to him. Her heart still pounded from their close encounter. Once again, she wouldn't have shown any resistance *if* he'd chosen to kiss her. Something she really needed to work on. She couldn't afford to fall for... her husband.

Her husband.

Why did the knowledge seem more real now? A temptation she wanted to admit and test the boundaries of?

If she'd been alone, she'd have dropped her head in her hands in defeat. To focus on anything but her impossible situation, she asked, "What is the message?"

"A personal invitation to a small gathering held in our honor from Key Guardian Wystone," he answered, somewhat distracted as he turned the small notecard over.

"What makes the event so special that we needed the invitation right away?"

"I'm not sure." He glanced over his shoulder at the closed door.

"Should we go, then?"

He tapped the card against his palm. "Maybe."

Katria was used to his cryptic thought patterns, and she knew she'd get little more out of him now that a plan was formulating in his mind. "When is it?"

"Two nights from now. We're attending a dinner in five days, which was the earliest one anyone invited us to."

"The key guardian wants to make sure we attend his party."

His gaze met hers. "Yes, and someone wants to make sure we're in Sziveria, and that everyone knows about it."

❧ 7 ❧

Sean handed the invitation card over to Kevin once they were inside Kevin's foyer. "I'm glad I decided to check your little apartment here for you first before going to the manor."

Kevin glanced at him before turning his attention to the invitation. "Me too. I'm too suspicious to bring the potential danger we might be in home to Raina. If anything happened to her..." He sighed. "How is Kat handling everything?"

"I don't know yet, it's still day one."

Kevin chuckled softly. "All right, how are *you* handling it?"

Sean raked his fingers through his hair. "I can't bring myself to tell her... anything."

"She's not the judging type," Kevin told him, leading the way to his study. He held up the card as they walked into the small room. "Do you expect a kind welcome at this event?"

"I didn't anticipate an invitation to any event, let alone

one in our honor," Sean admitted. "I don't even know what to expect."

"Well," Kevin began, sitting behind his desk, "then I think we can assume, at least for the first social event, it'll be a bunch of fawning and nothing more. That'll give you some time. But I think we both know it won't be much. We don't live in a kind society."

Sean knew all too well how cruel ranked society, and those who ran in the same circles, could truly be. "Agreed. And it's not that she'll judge me," he stated in honesty. "It's that she had no choice. She doesn't deserve what I bring to the table."

Kevin met his stare. "Let her decide that."

"We both know it's true."

Kevin shrugged. "Perhaps. But neither I nor Mason allowed it to affect our friendship with you. You aren't your family's mistakes."

Sean managed a slight smile as he sank into a leather chair before Kevin's desk. "Cora said the same thing."

"Cora might always be two seconds from setting herself on fire, but she's still a smart woman."

Sean filled Kevin in on the rest of his conversation with Cora. "Between the order to print my marriage to Kat on the most-read page, to this invitation, I'm positive something isn't as it seems."

Kevin held up the small cream-colored card. "My question is, why try to deceive the top covert minds in the country?"

Shrugging, Sean clasped his hands in his lap. "I don't know, maybe they think they're better and we won't figure out their plan, if there is one to find."

"Or maybe they think they have someone better organizing whatever may be going on."

"Who knows you're home?"

Kevin flipped the little card between his fingers. "Just Voklane."

Sean rubbed his index finger along his temple in thought. "Mason went riding across half of Haven City chasing after his sister, so he was likely seen. But if you're not known to be home, it may be something we can use to our advantage."

"If someone is after us, they'll be watching, and I don't want to give them a reason to go inside Raina's house. If I'm noticed, I want to make sure they can find me here, at *this* apartment."

"Hopefully it won't come to that." Sean accepted the invitation when Kevin handed it across the desk. "We do, however, need information."

Kevin gave a sinister smile. "Yes, we do, and I know just whose office to start in."

Fighting against the tangle of sheets around his legs, Sean bolted upright, heart pounding in his ears. His fist held tight to a pillow while his other hand searched for a weapon he didn't need. Breathing heavily, he sagged against the thick wooden headboard, dropped his head back, and closed his eyes. Sweat beaded on his naked chest and trickled along his temples.

For three years, he'd evaded the nightly nightmares his childhood induced. He'd hoped the passage of time would be enough to silence the past once he returned home.

Apparently not.

With slow, even breaths, he brought down his heart rate. Tossing the sheets back, he threw his legs clad in cotton pajama pants over the edge of the bed. For a quiet moment, he simply sat. He hated this house and all the memories held within its walls. If it hadn't been part of his ranked property, he'd have sold the house once it became legally his.

Heaving a sigh, he stood and made his way to a small table with a water pitcher and glasses. After pouring himself a full glass, he downed the cold liquid, allowing the cool sensation to ground him in the now. He set down the cup and braced his weight against the table. A faint glow along the floor caught his attention, and he followed the soft stream to the bottom of the adjoining door. Evidently, he wasn't the only one battling demons tonight.

"Bad idea," he whispered to himself as he walked to her door. Taking a deep breath, he chided himself again, "Very, very bad idea."

Yet he still tested the knob, and found it unlocked. Slowly, he pushed her door open. His heart clenched in his chest. The soft, dying light of the fire cast her in warm, deep shadows. With her knees drawn into her chest, her arms wrapped tightly around them, she sat pressed against the headboard.

A thin peach satin slip barely concealed her form. The soft fabric shimmered in a pool around her exposed thighs. Sean didn't think he'd ever seen her look so small. He'd certainly never seen her so alluring. His bad idea shifted into a truly poor decision.

She stared off into nowhere, not even acknowledging him.

Against his better judgment, Sean crossed the short distance to the bed. When she still didn't seem to register his presence, he sat on the edge of the mattress.

In a second most wouldn't have discerned, she reacted, pulling a hidden pistol free.

Sean wasn't most. He dodged the weapon, grabbing her wrist in the process. Giving a swift yank, he brought her tumbling across the distance between them and caught her before she could fall off the bed. Her silky black hair slid across his arm in a long cascade. He squeezed her inner wrist, forcing the gun to the floor with a heavy *thunk*. She twisted under his arm and pushed against his chest as her knees drew up in a coil to fight further.

"It's me!" he barked, pulling her close.

Immediately, all the resistance left her. Breathing hard, she dropped her forehead to his shoulder. The silken length of her hair caressed his bare chest, teased his damp flesh. Sean closed his eyes and loosened his hold on her wrist until she pulled it free.

"I'm sorry," she whispered.

"I guess I can be thankful that the last three years of Kevin's training worked."

She sat up, her blue eyes glistening in the faint light. "I could have shot you."

Tenderly, he pushed the wayward strands of hair from her face. "I should have known better than to startle an assassin. I doubt I would have reacted much differently if our roles were reversed."

"Normal people don't live like this." She dropped her head back to his shoulder.

He stroked her smooth tresses. "We gave up normal a long time ago."

"Why did you come in here?"

Why indeed. Sean leaned back, putting a slight distance between them until she met his stare. "I saw the light under my door. I had a nightmare, and I wanted to make sure you were okay."

"*You* had a nightmare?" she asked in disbelief.

"Yes. Haven City doesn't exactly hold the best memories for me. They all seemed to want to return on the same night," he confessed, frowning.

She bit her bottom lip. "Mine too."

Sean searched her face. So she had a few secrets in her past, too. Interesting. When she didn't elaborate, he didn't push. Since he wasn't ready to divulge his own, he wasn't going to ask for hers.

In the silence, he became keenly aware of her soft curves accentuated by the delicate fabric falling over them. The smooth mounds of her breasts showed over the low swoop of the neckline. A strong desire to feel her, to test her reaction, coursed through him. The urge overtook him. Without breaking her gaze, his hands slid slowly up her bare arms to pull her forward again, all rational thought escaping. Her lips parted as his mouth found hers.

He kept the kiss soft and even, toying at first, his lips brushing and teasing across hers. She made a delicate, yet desperate whimper deep in her throat, and he eased the tip of his tongue along the seam of her lips. She opened immediately, accepting the unhurried glide of his tongue along hers, allowing him to explore, leisurely. Sean had never kissed anyone for the simple joy of the moment. He kissed to seduce. For the first time, he wanted something more. Wanted to discover if a slow burn could be as enticing as fast and frantic.

Against his chest, her breathing quickened. Her arms wrapped around his shoulders, closing any remaining distance between them. Sean knew taking the kiss deeper would be easy, that she wouldn't resist. The thorough, seductive assault was having a dizzying effect on him. Under his fingertips, the rise of desire swelled within her, flowing into him, mingling with his own response. Every inch of her molded deliciously to his body. The warm satin of her nightgown teased his senses, and he found temptation winning.

No! She doesn't know the truth about you, or what she'll be stuck with forever.

Sean pulled his mouth from hers. Breathing hard, he stared at her. In equal shock, she stared back, as if taken entirely by surprise. Her fingers shook as she brought them to her mouth. Slowly, he moved away from her, and she braced herself on the mattress but made no move to cover her exposed skin. Her nipples stood out in harsh relief against the thin layer of satin. His tongue pressed against his teeth as he imagined how she'd respond if he leaned just a little closer and closed his mouth around one.

"I don't know if this is good or bad," she admitted softly.

"Oh, it was *very* good," he said, and she flushed, looking away from him. "However, we're going to go with bad... for now."

She nodded. "Agreed."

Good. Now that they'd officially set a boundary, he needed to make sure he stuck with it. As she watched him rise, a subtle hunger still clear in her impossibly blue eyes, Sean knew the task would be easier said than accomplished.

Katria fell back against her bed once Sean closed the door between their rooms. *What in the inhabited world had that been?*

A mistake, that's what. Though as far as first kisses went, she couldn't have asked for better. Her body hummed in a confusing, yet delicious way. An unfamiliar, yet not unwelcome ache throbbed at her core. She pressed her legs together and grabbed a pillow, hugging it tight, trying to ignore the strange condition she found herself in.

She had one purpose for agreeing to take on the role of a government operative: to find out who'd killed her mother and sister. Not to fall in love with her team leader or build some life she knew for certain she could never have. Her hand fell to the long-healed wound on her side. A reminder of just how dangerous the choice had been. At one time, her father thought he could escape the carnage he'd wrought and live a normal, happy life. All his hopes and dreams had shattered around him with the crack of a rifle. She wouldn't make the same lapse in judgment.

After turning down the lamp, she crawled back under the covers, knowing sleep would allude her. Somewhere out there, someone waited to finish a job they hadn't accomplished three years ago. Maybe they had already killed her father, leaving her as the last member of her little family. Tears welled in her eyes. He never knew what had become of her. She wondered if he'd ever noticed she'd left at all. Hugging her pillow close, she breathed the sadness away. She hadn't cried for her family since she'd buried them, and she wasn't about to start now.

The light of dawn arrived much earlier than she expected. Sighing, she reluctantly left the warmth of the blankets. Being home didn't mean she could neglect what had kept her alive for years: her training. She'd need the skills more now than she had abroad.

She found her training clothes neatly folded at the bottom of the chest. After carefully hiding her rifle, she changed into them. A quick rap sounded on her door before it opened a crack.

"Are you decent?" came Kevin's voice.

Katria raised a brow. "Kevin? What are you doing here?"

"It's five. So, are you?"

"I'm aware of the time, and yes."

He pushed the door open the rest of the way. "Come on, we need to be finished before the staff arrives."

"Where are we going?" she asked, joining him in the hall. She glanced around. "Where are Sean and Mason?"

"They had things to do."

"And you don't?"

"I can't be seen, so no. Not until after dark."

"But you're here," she felt the need to point out.

He just smiled cryptically.

"Where are we going?" she asked again.

"Underground."

"There's an underground floor to this place, too?"

They went to the far end of the hall, where Sean had said the stairs led to a third floor. Kevin went to the last room on the right. He motioned for her to go in first. She walked into an empty room with nothing more than a small rug in the center. Kevin searched for a panel. When he gave it a gentle push, the wall opened into another set of stairs leading down.

Katria sighed. "Of course, he has a secret level."

"I think his mother had it put in. Don't ask. He just repurposed it."

"I see." She tried not to think too hard about why Sean's mother would have needed a secret room.

The stairs led to a expansive space covered in thick mats, workout equipment, and in the far back, what looked like....

"No way," she whispered as excitement bubbled up in her. She rushed across the room. Her hands pressed to cool, thick glass as she peered into the dark, narrow chamber. "An indoor range?"

"Yes, but you can practice that on your own."

His lack of enthusiasm dampened her spirits somewhat, and she reluctantly left the area behind. Kevin pointed to the mat in the center of the room where he stood waiting.

"Let's begin."

Two hours later, sweat soaked Katria's clothes. Long

strands of hair had come loose from her braid and stuck to her face and neck. Bending over in exhaustion, she managed to get out, "Enough!" before her lungs, already struggling for air, erupted into a fit of deep coughs. "No more."

She collapsed on the floor as Kevin bounced away from her and to a heavy sandbag hanging from the ceiling. He leapt around the bag, jabbing at it with cloth-wrapped fists. Katria drew her brows together, never having seen him so agitated.

"What's wrong with you?" she asked when she could draw in enough breath to speak again.

"I do not want to be in this country," he stated between punches.

"Seems to be a recurring consensus. What about your wife?"

Springing up into a powerful front kick, he sent the bag flying back and up. "What about my wife," he repeated softly, more to himself, it seemed, than to her. "I can't bring this home to her."

"You managed to get into this house. Are you telling me you can't manage to get into yours unseen?" Katria wrapped her arms around her knee.

Kevin reached out and stopped the bag from swinging wildly around. "She'll tell people. She doesn't understand the need for secrecy."

Understanding dawned on her. "And right now, no one knows you're home except us."

"Good thing I'm used to your charming company."

Katria stuck out her tongue at his sarcasm. "How can she be married to you and not know how to keep things private?"

"Because she doesn't know exactly what I do. She can't. For her safety as well as ours."

"I'm sorry." Katria frowned. "It can't be easy to compartmentalize like that."

Holding the bag in his arms, he let his stormy gray eyes meet hers. "Don't you?"

The words hit a little too close, and she found herself looking away. "For some things, I suppose."

He unwrapped the tape from his fists, leaving a long trail of white cloth behind him as he slowly walked back towards her. "We all do. I think people would go insane if they couldn't compartmentalize the tasks we have to accomplish."

Katria glanced at the stairs leading back to the central part of the house. She could just imagine the gasps of shock at seeing them emerge from a room, sweaty and winded. The staff would fight over themselves to be the first to grab the newspapers. "We can't be seen together, not looking like this."

"Don't worry, no one will ever know I was here." He went to a bench next to the stairs, pooling the fabric on the wood. "I'll see you again tomorrow morning."

An unladylike, and rather un-adultlike, whine escaped her. "Really?"

"Really. It won't be my fault you can't run five flights of stairs with an enemy chasing after you. You know where to be now. Five a.m."

Drained, Katria sluggishly headed up the steps. Back in her room, she took the time to explore the space, delighted to find the small bathroom came complete with hot running water for a small tub, a luxury only the rich possessed. The means to heat water required resources in short supply, making them as rare and expensive as an ariot. She wouldn't complain. The indulgence had only been hers to enjoy on a handful of occasions over her life. On a small shelf beside the tub, various ornate colored bottles sat in a neat row. Pulling one down, she removed the stopper and inhaled a sweet, floral fragrance.

An argument in her head didn't last long, and hot water won. She ran the bath. While she waited for it to fill, she went into her room and found something decent to wear, laying it out on the bed. She knew the dress wasn't likely ranked guardianship-worthy, but until she could obtain something that was, it would have to work.

She swirled the water around, mixing the cooler flow with the hot, and poured in a subtle, clean scent that reminded her of the ocean. The water changed from clear to a soft milky white. After discarding her clothes in a pile on the gray stone floor, she climbed in. Sinking into the water, she let the tension of the past few days melt away.

The warmth enveloped her, drowning out all sound. Katria stayed under until her lungs begged for air. Despite the tub being small, she managed to remain submerged, the water lapping at her shoulders, and lay her head back. Closing her eyes, she relaxed.

What seemed like only seconds passed before she heard Sean call her name. But as she tried to move, pain erupted from her knees and hips, and she realized the water had grown cold. Not only had she fallen asleep, but her legs had fallen asleep as well.

Wincing, she used the strength in her arms to pull herself into a sitting position in the water. A terrible crick had formed in her neck, and she rubbed the tense muscles. "I'm in here," she yelled when she heard her name again.

He peered around the doorframe and then immediately disappeared. "I'll come back in a few."

"No!" she cried out, mortified. Needles penetrated every inch of her lower body, and she squeezed her eyes shut in pain. "I can't move, I fell asleep, and my legs..."

She swore she heard a long string of curses come from

him, but when he appeared holding a huge, fluffy gray towel, he was calm.

"Can you stand at all?" he asked, holding out the towel.

Katria held tight to the edge of the tub and attempted to rise. Water sloshed over the edge as she failed, sliding down with a pained cry.

"All right, stop." He grabbed her hand. "Just... just hold onto my shoulders, okay?"

He crouched down, and she wrapped her arms around his neck. Water dripped from her skin, darkening the white fabric of his shirt. In a swift, smooth motion, he lifted her and wrapped the towel around her. Once she was completely free of the water, he picked her up and carried her into her bedroom.

She held the towel tightly with one hand. Sean sat on the bed, positioning her on his lap so her feet dangled over his legs. Carefully, he began to massage the blood back into her traitorous limbs.

"Any better?"

She grimaced and shook her head. "Not yet."

"How long were you in there?"

"I'm not sure. Long enough for the water to get cold." She licked her lips and pulled the towel up a little higher, as though it would somehow preserve any modesty she had left. "Thank you. I don't know what I would have done if you hadn't come in."

Sean didn't look at her as he grumbled, "You're welcome."

Nervous, Katria found herself fiddling with the lengths of hair around his collar. A sudden need to fill the silence between them seized her. "Kevin said you had somewhere to be this morning. Where did you go?"

He stopped rubbing her calf, but kept his eyes averted, his frame growing stiff. "Kat, I don't think I need to point out that you are sitting naked on my lap. My self-control is paper thin where it comes to you right now, so can we *please* not have a conversation?"

Taken aback by his admission, she stared at him. "It is?"

The intense, fiery color of his eyes made her heart lurch in her chest. "Yes, *wife*, it is. And unless you want this marriage to become very real right this moment, I suggest you sit perfectly still and keep your mouth shut."

She pressed her lips together, biting them to keep from saying another word, and dropped her arm from his shoulders. The same enticing tingle low in her belly that she'd experienced with his kiss made her want to squirm, but the rigidity of Sean's body told her it would probably be a bad idea. Gradually, the painful prickle in her legs gave way to a dull throb, and she was able to move her toes.

"I'm okay now," she said as soon as she could move her ankle. "Thank you."

He released her and eased out from under her legs, leaving her sitting alone on the bed. With rapid strides, he crossed the room. "Once you're dressed, I'll be in the library."

Katria stared at the door after he let the force of his exit close it. She heaved a sigh, her heart pounding in her ears, her cheeks hot. How was she supposed to face him again?

For three years, Sean had forced himself to see Kat as a valuable member of his team. Nothing more. A colleague under his leadership. Sure, he did basic care for her, like ensuring she ate, because her focus often went sideways on days they engaged in their assignments. Or making sure something she dealt with or witnessed didn't keep her awake at night. While her well-being had been in his hands, it'd been as her superior, not her partner. In less than twenty-four hours, a single sheet of paper had turned his entire world upside down.

What in the arctic, man?

First a kiss, then a confession of desire. At the rate he was going, the next twenty-four hours didn't bode well. Usually, he prided himself on his restraint, but Kat was proving to be a challenge he hadn't anticipated or encountered before.

The lines of print on the papers before him blurred together. Sighing in defeat, he ran his hands down his face and sat back in his desk chair. He needed to focus on their situation and solve the puzzle they seemed to be caught in.

But Kat's soft skin under his hands, her passionate response to his kiss, the way her body flared to life under his touch—to the point where if he'd moved his hands higher under her towel, she'd have given zero resistance—kept invading his thoughts.

Shoving the chair back, he stood. With his hands clasped behind him, he made his way to the tall window overlooking the greenhouse gardens. Now that he was home, he had to undo years of neglect. A small army of workers on ladders and knee pads scrubbed at the algae-covered panes of glass. Very little of the once majestic garden remained. Taking a deep breath, he returned his thoughts to where they needed to be.

The door opened, and the object of his turmoil walked in. Dressed in one of her simple black gowns, Kat looked every bit the woman he always remembered. And yet she was completely different to his eyes now. She paused when she saw him, and a delightful flush spread across her pale skin. Sean went back to looking out the window.

Deciding conversation was quite important now, he said, "I think we need to go to the party tomorrow night."

The soft click of the door closing them in alone together sent his nerves on edge.

"Why?" she asked.

Sean returned to his desk. He pushed papers around until he found the one he wanted and pulled it free. "Vernon Payce, Key Guardian Wystone. Recently released from the First Intelligence Office."

Kat took the sheet from him. "And he'll be there tomorrow?"

"He's the one who sent the invitation."

She glanced up at him, eyes wide. "What was he released for?"

"I'm not sure yet."

Her attention went back to the paper. "How did you get this?"

"I didn't. Kevin did."

"They just handed it to him when he asked?"

Sean rubbed his knuckles along his stubbled jaw. "Not exactly."

"So it says here that Key Guardian Wystone worked in partnership with Import and Immigration about foreign ships coming into port, both passenger and trade. He seems to be some sort of cultural expert? He helps determine if a ship, or her passengers, may be a threat to Sziveria."

"And he's been relieved of his duty," Sean stated quietly.

Kat set the paper down slowly, her face drawn and somber. "I see. Another FIO guardian who seems to be on someone's bad side, like us."

"This could all be a coincidence."

"Yes, but you need to be sure our situation and his aren't related."

"I need something more than I have, which is nothing right now."

She glanced down at her simple dress, pulling at the fabric. "And I need something different to wear."

"I have that handled. Davis and your stylist elite I had him hire today are going to take you. The carriage is ready when you are."

The color drained from her face. "You aren't going?"

"No, you'll be fine, it's just Extilis Square. Get what you need and return."

"What do I need?"

He searched through the mess of papers again and retrieved a narrow slip. "I wrote them down."

"Of course you did." She sighed, taking the list from him. A gasp escaped, and she stared at him. "This is a lot."

"Society requires a lot."

"Sean, I don't shop."

"Today you are."

She ground her teeth together, the paper crumpling in her hands. "And my budget?"

"You don't have one."

She batted her lashes, then spun and gave a wave over her shoulder, singing out, "The words every wife longs to hear. Diamond-crusted bodice, I can't wait to own you."

"Funny!" he shouted after her as she flounced out the door, but couldn't stop the smile that crept onto his lips.

In a flurry of silvery blue silk, Katria collapsed onto her bed. The fashionable gown she wore was one her stylist elite insisted she purchase *before* being seen by anyone shopping, and it was fuller than she was used to wearing. Her single-layer black gowns flowed with her movements and didn't get caught between her legs or rise in a burst of sheer waves on a breeze. A translucent, intricately beaded silver top layer covered her from neck to wrist to ankles, gathered at the waist with a thick-tied, rich blue ribbon, and accented the same vivid blue fitted bodice gown beneath. The style would take some getting used to. And she would wear twice as much fabric for a formal event.

Thankfully, the stylist elite, Rebeka, had explained her job to Katria, so at each boutique, Katria simply chose a gown style and fabric. Everything else, Rebeka handled for her. The woman even chose color palettes for Katria's face and decorative clips in various styles for her hair.

A quick knock sounded at her door before it opened. Katria reluctantly rose from the bed. Rebeka entered, arms filled with a mountain of colorful, opulent fabric. The curly brown ringlets piled high atop her head barely showed over her armload.

"Your purchases have arrived. The custom orders will be here in a few weeks, but these few will suffice until then," Rebeka said.

Katria stared as the woman swept into a massive closet she hadn't even noticed. "But you're holding enough clothes for all I'll need. I mean, when will I ever need more?"

"Oh, don't be silly," Rebeka chided. "You'll need a different gown for each dinner party, luncheon or brunch, theater show or dance you attend. What we purchased today will last you the week, no longer."

"I can't wear the same gown twice?"

"You can next season, or when you travel. It doesn't do to make it look as though your husband can't afford to clothe you properly, does it?"

"But I won't need all those after spring is over," Katria argued, frustrated. "What a waste of money and clothes."

"Of course, you will. Summer and early fall are very busy social months. And then, of course, there are the Wintervail parties, which are a flurry of dances and greenhouse gatherings before the first heavy snowfall traps everyone inside. Or, you may even decide to take advantage of one of the many winter-over invitations you'll receive to spend all the snow-bound months in a more social setting at someone's estate." Rebeka hung the last gown, brushing the folds out of the fabric. "I know you both have been traveling for years, but I'm sure with your father, you attended many functions. You'll get used to it again."

Right, because she was supposed to have come from a similar background of socializing and glamor. Katria knew all the questions she asked exposed her inexperience, but with so much at stake, she couldn't risk seeking answers from the wrong person. She needed to understand how this new world she found herself in functioned. "And after the year?"

Rebeka smiled as she closed the closet door. "I study the newest fashion trends and plan accordingly."

Katria gasped in horror. "A completely new wardrobe?"

"Not always, but many things do change, yes."

"I see. Thank you, Rebeka."

The woman gave a quick nod in acknowledgement and then left. Katria ventured into her closet, opening the door into a room half the size of her bedroom. Shelves, made especially for shoes, lined an entire wall. A padded bench sat in the middle, with a mirror on either side of it. Four oil lamps, when lit, would completely illuminate the cream-painted space. The handful of gowns she now owned barely filled the rack they hung from, a bright burst of color in the neutral room.

Overwhelmed, Katria sank onto the bench, her fingers toying with the beads on the silver silk of her skirt. A life of luxury was never something she'd wanted or expected to have. A row of long, slender drawers between two gown racks caught her attention. She went to them and slowly pulled one open. A rainbow of jewels glistened in the faint light coming through the open door. Necklaces, bracelets, rings, and earrings were neatly arranged in rows along white velvet padding.

Katria gasped and leapt away from the fortune. The bench caught the backs of her calves. She tumbled backward over the piece of furniture. Landing heavily, she groaned as her shoulders slammed into the edges of the shelving.

"Good grief, woman," Sean said from the doorway.

Katria fought with the onslaught of fabric she found herself stuck in. She couldn't even see him through the haze of silk and tulle.

"When did you become so ungraceful?" he asked.

Letting out a heavy breath, she emerged from the layers, not even caring that her legs were on the bench while the rest of her was on the floor. Her husband had already seen her in a worse position today. "Since becoming a ranked guardianess."

Sean helped her rise, a smile tugging at the corners of his lips. "That's supposed to inspire grace, not lessen it."

"Are those real?"

He glanced at the open drawer of jewelry. "Yes. Did you look at them all?"

"There's more?" she asked in disbelief.

"Yes." He stepped over the bench and motioned to the rest of the row. "All of these contain generations of my family's collection. Jewelry doesn't go out of style. One of my ancestors, my great-great-great grandfather I think, was a collector of pre-Cataclysm pieces. There are several in the collection that are priceless and garner much envy."

"I've never even worn a necklace," Katria confessed.

"Not even a simple chain?"

She shook her head. "My mother didn't like jewelry. She said it'd just collect dirt when she worked or get lost when she took it off, so my father never purchased any."

Sean slowly closed the drawer. He opened two more before stopping. "Then wear this for your first piece. It's light and will go with any dress your stylist puts you in."

A woven silver chain glittered as he lifted it, a single teardrop opal dangling from the end. Katria cupped her hand as he dropped the dense stone into her palm, the cool silver chain pooling around it. "Whose was it?"

He glanced up in thought. "I think my great-grand-mother. According to my mother, she didn't like flashy, heavy jewelry. Most everything simple was hers."

Katria ran her thumb over the smooth surface and smiled. "I think I'll like her collection best."

Sean lifted a velvet lined panel free of the drawer, angling it for her to see the glittering simplicity. "You're in luck. Her collection is so modest in design, the entire thing fits into this drawer in multiple layers like this one. My great-grandfather could afford to spoil her, and he did."

Katria gently replaced the necklace back onto the panel and Sean settled it back into place. "Rebeka said what she bought today will be enough for a week. How do you afford so many clothes?"

Sean clasped his hands behind his back as he exited the closet. "Men don't care if they wear the same pants all day. A woman, however, *is* expensive to keep in society's standards."

"I don't want to own a store's worth of clothes," she argued, following him out. "It's ridiculous."

"I agree it's absurd, *but* if you break with tradition, it'll reflect badly."

"Rebeka said as much," Katria replied with a sigh.

He gave her a teasing wink. "Don't worry. As you saw, it's not as though I'm hard-pressed for much. If you get too expensive, I'll just sell a necklace or two."

Katria's stomach fluttered at his playful nature. A side of him she wasn't used to seeing. "You joke."

"Of course, I do. My family is like Mason's, we've been in a ranked guardian role for generations, and when I took over, I started investing well. Also, you have to remember, we haven't paid for so much as a meal in three years. Where do you think the money we've made has been going?" He crossed the room to his bedroom door.

She hadn't considered that. "Mine too?"

"We're married, so they've been sending our income to the same place. Don't worry, I set up an account for you this afternoon and transferred all your earnings to it. I have the papers for you to sign when you're ready. It still has to be attached to mine for now, but we can remedy that another time."

Astonishment and a little nervousness filled her. She had money, a means of starting an independent life when all this was over. Assuming, they'd let her just walk away from her government service. She was a little sketchy on the details of life after intelligence work.

"Thank you. I guess you took everything I had to spend today out of the balance?"

Sean shook his head, his hand settling on the doorknob to his room. "Right now, you're my wife, and any of your expenses are mine to handle."

"I'm only your wife because *they* say I am. You aren't responsible for me like that," she said softly.

"I am completely responsible for you. And not because *they* say so, but because *I* do."

The flutter returned, and all she could do was nod, knowing it was useless to argue. She wouldn't win. Taking a deep breath, she watched as he slipped from her room. When it came to Sean, she was beginning to believe she wouldn't win against anything.

❧ 9 ❧

A cloud of powder enveloped Katria's face. Rebeka gently patted a large cotton applicator along her jaw and up towards her ears. Katria coughed and waved the fine particulate away.

"Is this necessary?" Katria asked, annoyed.

Rebeka inspected her work and then patted a few more places. "You don't want to be all shiny a half hour after you arrive. These parties can get hot."

The butterflies that had begun dancing in her stomach the moment Rebeka arrived in her room intensified. When her stylist finished setting her makeup, she pulled out over a dozen glittery flower clips and laid them out in a neat row on the dressing table.

"What are those for?" Katria asked, looking over the golden baubles.

"Your hair."

Katria raised a brow. "All of them?"

"Yes."

"No... I don't think so."

Rebeka's hazel eyes widened. "What do you mean?"

"You can use two."

"But, fashion—"

Katria met Rebeka's gaze in the mirror. "I said two."

The young girl frowned and took a step back. She tapped her chin and then raised her index finger. "Very well, I know what I can do."

Katria flexed her shoulders. "Good."

As the girl went to work, she kept glancing at Katria's reflection, worrying her bottom lip. Finally, she spoke. "I wanted to thank you for giving me a chance."

"I didn't have anything to do with your hiring, you can thank Davis for that," Katria admitted, rolling an eyeshadow brush along the table.

"Yes, but you could have denied my application."

"I never saw your application. But why would I have denied it? You've been competent so far."

Rebeka flushed and smiled faintly. "Thank you. I've had a hard time finding someone to hire me since I graduated."

"Why?"

Katria didn't think the young lady was going to answer as she silently brushed and folded the long lengths of Katria's hair. Then she softly said, "I didn't test as a Gen-Heir."

"In your chosen field?"

Rebeka shook her head. "At all. I'm... common in my genetics. It turns out ranked, or wealthy, society only wants to hire a Gen-Heir when it comes to stylist elites. I wasn't aware of that when I chose my profession."

Being a genetic heir, or Gen-Heir, herself, having inherited her father's genetic ability to sharp shoot, Katria never really gave much thought to what it would be like to have only common genetics. Of course, she'd not have her current position on her team, or be married, or... she sighed. Life would be simpler. "Being a Gen-Heir is not everything they say it is."

"I guess for some talents that might be true, I bet they don't get much say in what they can do. But, for others, like me, it's the difference between an arch guardianess or a banker's wife."

Katria smiled. "But not this time. Though I'm not an arch guardianess."

A huge grin broke out over Rebeka's face. "No, not this time, and I think I prefer a primary to an arch anyway."

I know I do. Katria couldn't imagine what she would have done if Sean had been any more powerful.

"There," Rebeka remarked with pride, taking a step back.

Hesitantly, Katria lifted her gaze to meet her reflection in the mirror. Her lips parted in surprise. She couldn't believe the regal woman who stared back. Rebeka had gently clipped her sides back and worked soft, flowing curls into the ends of the cascading hair. Subtle smoky gray color on her eyelids brought out the vivid blue of her eyes, and a sheer dusting of pink drew attention to her full cheeks. The fine layer of powder smoothed out her pale complexion, making her skin appear flawless. Katria turned her face one way, then the other, noting how the warm glow from her table lamp accented the curves of her face.

"I didn't know I could look like this," Katria said.

"You're beautiful," came a deep, masculine voice from behind.

Both the ladies gasped. Rebeka jumped, and Katria turned in her seat. Over the years, Katria had seen him in formal attire, but this time he wasn't going to meet a contact or charm information out of someone.

This time, he was hers.

The slim-fitting black jacket he wore over a silvery gray shirt drew attention to the thick muscles in his arms and shoulders. Her heart skipped. A single onyx stone served as a substitute for traditional neck garb, making his sleek appearance all the more elegant. As was his usual style, he did nothing special with his hair, leaving it to fall as it would around his face and to his shoulders. She also couldn't help but notice he'd opted not to go with the tight pants that seemed to be in current fashion, instead wearing a more casual loose fit to his black slacks.

She wanted to return the compliment that he looked gorgeous as well, but all she could manage was a pitiful, "Thank you."

Rebeka cleared her throat, "If that'll be all?"

"Yes, thank you," Sean said in dismissal when Katria continued to stare at him.

"Thank you, Rebeka," she called out as the woman quietly exited the room.

Sean smiled and held his hand out as he drew near to her. "I didn't want to make you walk down the stairs alone in your first ball gown."

"Oh... I didn't think about that," Katria admitted. "Will you be helping me down all the stairs I encounter this evening?"

"Of course."

She took his hand and lifted herself and the heavy weight of her layered dark green satin skirt and golden velvet embroidered top. "I didn't allow her to put a dozen clips in my hair. I won that battle."

"I think the simplicity of your style is going to make some jealous tonight."

She chuckled in disbelief. "Or make sure we don't get any more invitations."

"If you can promise that, I'll make sure she doesn't do your hair at all next time."

Katria couldn't help herself, she laughed and jabbed her elbow into his side. "I don't think you'd win that one."

Sean released her hand and then looped his arm through hers as they approached the stairs, leaving both her hands free to tackle the skirt. Katria grabbed as much cloth as she could and lifted, attempting to free her foot enough to make sure she didn't trip. With slow, methodical steps, Sean led her carefully down the wide staircase. Davis waited at the front door for them, opening it as they neared. Cold night air rushed in, and Katria briefly wondered if she'd need more than her gown. Then again, she didn't think she could freeze to death with the layers of material she wore.

"Have a good evening, primary guardian and guardianess," he said with a bow as they exited.

"I don't know how I'll get used to all the attention everyone gives us," Katria stated as she was helped into the carriage waiting at the curb.

Once she was seated, Sean climbed in after, pushing on the section of her gown that had fallen out of the door. "You will, I promise."

She collected the ridiculous volume from him, rolling her eyes. "Are the other women going to be dressed in so many layers?"

"I'm not sure, I've been out of the social scene for quite a long time," he remarked distantly, his attention shifting to the window as he sat across from her.

An odd tension filled the cab, and Katria wished she could see more of Sean's face than the passing gaslights allowed. She glanced out the window too, focusing on the tall shadows of brick houses against moonlit clouds as they went by. Nerves began to take over, and she fidgeted with the opal dangling around her neck. She'd insisted on simple because she wasn't a showy person. Her life depended on her going unnoticed. Now she realized her minimalism would likely draw more attention than she intended.

Sean remained unusually quiet the rest of the journey. Which was just as well, Katria was too anxious to make idle chatter. The carriage pulled off into a long line. Katria noted the couples dressed in opulence as they walked by. One woman already fanned herself with a decorated silk fan despite the frost forming on the edges of the sidewalk. Sean pounded on the roof, signaling they'd also be exiting instead of waiting. The door opened. Sean stepped out first, then helped Katria.

He wrapped her hand around his forearm and walked with a sense of authority she'd only seen when he was at the First Intelligence Office. Katria drew her brows together. Was there something he wasn't telling her? She didn't have long to contemplate as they approached the sprawling white painted brick mansion. Oil lamps tucked behind wide pillars illuminated the front of the building. Paper-wrapped candles lined the long walkway, creating a beautiful path of color.

A crowd had gathered at the wide-open double doors. A soft murmur fell over the group as they slowly stepped away, allowing the couple of honor passage. Sean removed the invitation from his inner jacket pocket, not that they needed it, Katria noted. Everyone already seemed to know who they were.

Another line had formed at the doors to what she assumed was a ballroom. She resisted the urge to stand on her tiptoes to get a better look at the brightly lit room. Graceful music flowed from the open doors, mingling with the dull noise of conversation.

Katria leaned close to Sean and whispered, "This man is just a key guardian?"

"I told you my house was small when compared to others. This house is the average."

Katria took the time they waited to glance around. Landscape paintings hung from gilded frames on the two-story foyer walls. Black marble polished to a high sheen created an elegant floor. A curving staircase with a carved floral banister swept to the second floor. Sean's house was downright modest compared to the wealth this house displayed.

The little two-story, three-bedroom cliffside house she grew up in suddenly seemed special. Normal. She sighed. What she wouldn't give for *normal* again. But as Sean had pointed out late last night, they'd given up ordinary long ago.

Their turn in line finally came. Sean handed the man standing at the door their card. He accepted with a faint bow before loudly calling out their ranked name. Every person in the room seemed to turn their direction in an audible shift. Sean tensed.

"Here we go," he said under his breath, and then pasted on a grin that changed his whole face from attractive to devastating.

Why hadn't she thought to bring a fan? She suddenly found herself needing one. Katria's fingers dug into the soft fabric of his jacket sleeve as they swept into the room, every eye upon them. Sean patted her hand, and she relaxed a little.

He leaned close and said softly into her ear, "Smile. You look like you're walking in front of a firing squad."

"Am I not?" she whispered in return.

All he did was give her a wink.

Shoving her nerves deep down, she shifted near to him

as though he'd said something sweet and gave an appropriate smile. If she could play a taunting sister, annoying ward, and interfering cousin, she could be a wife for real this time.

Deep red liquid swirled in the fluted glass Katria stared into. Around her, the room buzzed with conversation. Somewhere in the crowd, her husband mingled, having left her standing with other socialites, none of whom seemed too eager to get to know the Primary Guardianess Wintersfall.

Katria was rather grateful, unsure what conversation she'd have with the wealthy ladies. One woman had so many trinkets clipped and woven into her hair that Katria wasn't sure how her hair remained on her scalp with so much weight. The others *oohed* and *aahed* over the vast array of bracelets, rings, and necklaces they wore. Each woman seemed determined to outweigh the other in precious metals.

She took a shallow sip of bitter wine, scanning the crowd for Sean. A small group of women heading her direction caught her attention. The confrontational glint in the lead woman's eyes and the way she flexed her jaw made Katria set her wine glass down on a small side table. Social skills were not her area. She didn't need the temptation of throwing the liquid if any of the women proved to be bothersome.

The lead woman, who was at least a decade older than Katria, stopped within arm's length. She patted her perfectly coifed dark red hair behind her ear, looking down her nose as she did so. Beaded baubles clinked lightly together, reminding Katria of a wind chime. "I see Sean didn't inform you about our fashion standards here in Sziveria."

Katria caught the woman's familiar use of Sean's name and smiled softly. "He didn't, no. My stylist elite tried, but I forbade her from making me look silly. I enjoy the freedom of being able to look around without hurting myself."

A blonde behind the woman gasped, covering her bright pink lips with her hand. She nudged the leader with her fan. The woman frowned and swatted behind her back. She rolled her shoulders and composed herself. Dark gray eyeshadow made the hateful gleam in her brown eyes all the more menacing. Katria remained calm and took a deep inward breath.

"We have standards here," she bit out.

"You mentioned them already," Katria replied with a smile and a polite nod. She decided to turn the tables. "Who are you?"

Deep crimson bloomed across the woman's face and along the exposed skin of her chest. "I'm Ms. Carlie Milbourne, my father is the Primary Guardian Keswickland."

Deciding she needed the wine after all, Katria grasped the flute. She took a slow sip. With her attention still on her glass, she stated, "I do believe *social standards* dictate you should have started with that, no?"

Carlie fisted her hands. The blush on her chest turned to an angry scarlet. If she breathed any harder, Katria feared her barely contained breasts would spill right over the top of her dark blue velvet bodice.

"Don't tell me what our society's standards are, you-you *Ruthenian*." Carlie spat the word like Katria was a diseased mongrel. "Everyone knows you people are barely civilized in that frigid nation. How could he have married *you*?"

Katria took another sip of her wine as she pretended

to contemplate the woman's question. "I do believe it was our mutual attraction, not to mention our unending passion for each other. Why else do people get married? Is it different here in Haven City?"

Carlie screeched and turned on her heel, the charms in her hair made little soft *tink-tinks* as she stalked off. Two popped free, and one of her entourage hastily caught them, running after her friend.

Sighing, Katria searched the crowd once again. Somewhere in the crush of bodies, her husband was probably enduring boring, incessant conversation. She shook her head with a little smile. *Her husband.* Eventually admitting the fact wouldn't make her belly do flips. Maybe.

An open door to the greenhouse gardens caught Katria's attention. She set her glass down after checking for her husband one last time and then retreated into the slightly cooler greenhouse. The noise of the gathering faded. She ventured down the wide cement stairs to a walkway, dimly lit, just as the front had been, with colorful paper bags and tea lights.

A couple dashed away behind a curtain of ivy draping from the exterior wall to the balcony. Their laughter of delight floated on the faint breeze coming from the few open glass panels. Beyond the protection of the conservatory, a film of silvery ice coated everything. Only the hardiest of plants survived the constant winter nights in their post-cataclysm world.

Katria sighed as she kicked at a stray pebble, knowing she couldn't miss the warm evenings she'd only read about. On nights like tonight, however, she longed for air that was fresher than the humid glasshouse offered. Perhaps one day they'd travel to an equatorial country like Italyssa, or even southern Westica, where a more temperate climate ruled.

The tea lights illuminating the route became sparse the deeper she ventured. She glanced over her shoulder and noted she could no longer see the balcony over the tall trees. Katria eased down on a cement bench in front of an expertly carved shrub. Her skirt fluffed around her, and with a sigh, she dropped her hands onto the mound of fabric with a *whoosh*. Closing her eyes, she leaned back against the cold seat, enjoying the silence.

A familiar deep voice called her name, and she sat forward, peering down the narrow path. Sean walked at an even pace towards her. She smiled, genuinely happy to see him. Before she could stand, a hand clasped over her mouth. Katria reached up, grabbing at her assailant's arm, but she wasn't quick enough as another arm snaked around her shoulders.

An unknown attacker pulled her over the back of the bench faster than she could struggle. Rough cement scraped across the exposed skin of her shoulders, leaving a burning trail. The bushes swathed her in darkness. Twigs snapped and snagged on the long lengths of her gown and into her hair as someone dragged her through them. The arm around her shoulders moved to her waist, pulling her up tight against a male form.

Oh heck no.

Katria licked the man's hand, drooling all the saliva she could manage. Shocked, her assailant quickly moved his hand away from her mouth. With her upper body now free, she arched her back and lifted her feet, putting her full weight onto one arm. Unable to maintain a hold, his arm caved beneath her, and she landed hard on the ground. The man didn't have time to react, as her husband crashed through the bush and sidelined him, knocking him to the ground. Katria snapped her foot out, connecting it with her assailant's temple as he landed in front of her, knocking him out cold.

Sean rose and then reached out to help her. Wincing at the pain in her shoulders and back, she slowly stood.

"Are you okay?" he asked, looking her over.

She brushed at the leaves sticking at odd angles from her dress. "I'll be fine."

"What were you thinking coming out here alone?"

"I thought these events were safe."

"For everyone but us, they are. Or have you forgotten who exactly we are and why we're here?"

Katria frowned and snapped at the bottom of her skirt to dislodge sticks and dead leaves. "I haven't forgotten. Why do you think I came out here in the first place? I don't belong here."

Sean fisted his hands at his sides to keep from dragging her into his arms. When she'd disappeared into the bushes, his heart had nearly stopped. All thoughts of why he'd come looking for her vanished. Now, as she revealed why she'd sought solitude to begin with, he remembered.

Across the room, he'd observed Carlie Milbourne's confrontation. Knowing the woman held some bitter emotions towards him now, he could only imagine what she'd said to his wife. When Kat disappeared out into the greenhouse, he'd assumed the worst. Turned out that hadn't been what he should have been concerned about.

He stared down at the unconscious man and pushed at him with the toe of his boot. The attacker didn't budge. Sighing, Sean knelt down and searched through the man's pockets. "Nothing. No identification or note." He glanced around, noting for at least the time being, they were still alone. "We need to do something with him."

"Will someone notice him here?" she asked, looking around, too.

Sean pointed to the second path that curved

around the trees. "Possibly. There's likely a tool shed down this path. If you get the door, I'll get him."

Kat waited until he'd hefted the man onto his shoulders before moving ahead. They walked deeper into the greenhouse, finally finding the shed. Kat held the door as he dumped the man inside. Shovels and rakes clanked and fell over him. Sean made sure the man's feet were securely inside before closing the door. When the guy woke up in a couple of hours, he'd stumble out and no longer be their problem. Unless he tried again.

They made their way back towards the house in silence. Moonlight filtered in through the glass above, shimmering between the high branches. Long, dense shadows covered the ground, and Sean kept close to Kat. While the man had acted alone, there was a slim chance he'd arrived unaccompanied. Glancing at her, he noted the dirt, leaves, and twigs still in her hair and stuck to her gown.

"We're going to have to give you a good reason to look like such a mess," he said with a sigh.

"Oh?" she asked, her stride slowing. "What do you mean?"

He stopped when he made out the high rear exterior of the mansion through the trees. "I mean, unless you want to explain why someone would wish to snatch you out of a greenhouse from a party, we have to come up with another explanation."

"I suppose miscreants can be at any gathering," she surmised, touching a finger to her chin. "But I really don't know why someone tried to snatch me. Do you?"

Sean knew better than anyone how dangerous a social function could become. He frowned as another dark memory threatened to surface. "Yes, bad guys can be, and no. I don't know why someone tried to take you.

Maybe we could have asked if you hadn't kicked him in the head."

She frowned. "Sorry, it was a reflex from Kevin's training. What do you suggest as cover for my appearance?"

He reached for her, wrapping his arm around her waist and drawing her close. "Seduced by your husband."

Katria's breath hitched on an excited flutter. She knew his plan was all for show, to keep them from being suspected of anything foul. Especially since a man lay unconscious in a tool shed. But she also knew it meant he might kiss her. After last night, even the idea of a kiss from her husband was enough to quicken her pulse.

Sean's body pressed into hers, all warm, hard muscle and male. Katria resisted the urge to touch him. He walked her backward until she came up against a tree. He braced an arm above her head. The bark rubbed against the scratches on her shoulders, and she winced, arching her back and pressing her palms onto the rough surface to force the distance.

"What's wrong?" he asked softly. His free hand unbuttoned his jacket, then his shirt.

Katria blinked a few times to focus her thoughts. "When he pulled me over the bench, he hurt my back."

He straightened away from her. "You said you were fine."

"I *am* fine," she reiterated. "The tree just made it hurt, is all."

"Let me see." His warm palms touched her shoulders and he eased her around. He tsked and brushed a finger between her bare shoulder blades. "Scrapes, but no blood. You sure it doesn't hurt too much?"

She blinked, her mind struggling to notice the pain with the distraction his touch caused. "No, not so much."

"Good." He stepped around her and shrugged off his jacket, laying it on the ground. He motioned to it.

Katria stared at the coat, her heart racing. "W-what am I supposed to do?"

Gently, his knuckles brushed across her jaw. "How can you be so deadly and yet so innocent?"

She stared up at him, at the way his amber irises caught the faint illumination of candle and moonlight. "Because I served with honest men who didn't see me as anything more than a valued team member."

His hand fell to his side. In the soft paper defused light, she made out the troubled expression on his handsome face. "Is that how you wish to remain?"

Katria's breath caught in her throat. He was giving her an out, an opportunity to stay a team member, nothing more. She knew he'd respect her decision and do everything in his power to ensure their relationship didn't become blurred further. Deep down, however, that wasn't what she wanted, not really. Yet, what she wanted, she couldn't have. Could she? She took in his now disheveled state, his jacket off, his shirt nearly completely open, revealing the defined muscles of his chest and stomach.

The unfamiliar sensation of vulnerability crept into her. Nerves fluttered in her stomach. She wrung her hands. The moment she realized she was behaving like some distraught weakling, she dropped her arms to her sides. Still, the fragile emotion remained.

Instead of asking the important question to herself, she asked it aloud. "What would happen if I said no?"

"I don't know," he answered truthfully.

A female voice called their ranked name from the balcony.

Katria glanced over her shoulder. "Perhaps we'll need to have this conversation later."

"Agreed." He sat on the ground.

Joining him, Katria followed his lead. She undid a few buttons along the side of her gown and pulled one sleeve completely off her shoulder while he took one of her shoes off and tossed it haphazardly away from them, yet still within reach. He wrapped his arm around her waist and carefully laid her down, half covering her with his torso.

When she went to wrap her arms around him, he whispered into her ear, "Under my shirt."

Oh, summer sun, under his shirt? She closed her eyes. A new type of nervousness mixed with anticipation made her pulse race. Gathering courage, she slid her trembling fingers along the skin of his back under his shirt. Hot, lean muscles rolled beneath her touch. With the physical contact, the line between playact and reality blurred.

His mouth found hers, and she parted her lips without hesitation. The edge of his tongue glided across hers. He tasted of the sweet, smoky liquor he favored. With his equally smoky and warm scent surrounding her, the mixture enticed. Desire coiled fierce and deep in her stomach. She pressed her hands into his back, holding tight as he deepened their kiss.

The cool yet humid night air of the greenhouse brushed across her leg as he eased the skirt of her gown up. Sean forced her knee to rise, pulling it against his side, his fingers trailing low to her hip. A delicious tingle formed at her center.

"Oh, my goodness!" a woman shrieked.

Sean slowly pulled away, but not before giving her another soft kiss. Katria sighed in disappointment, lowering her leg while he pulled her dress down.

"Oh my... oh dear... I'm so sorry, Primary Guardian Wintersfall," the woman stammered. "I guess three years wasn't quite long enough for the two of you, hmm?"

Katria glanced over Sean's shoulder. She took in the woman, wearing a bright fuchsia gown which fitted past her plump rear, where it flared at her thighs. The satin accented every voluptuous curve of her figure. Little charms glittered all over the gown, matching the ones adorning her hair.

"Key Guardianess Wystone, I'm sorry, we thought we'd ventured far enough off the trail not to be seen," Sean replied calmly, helping Katria rise into a sitting position. He then gathered her shoe for her.

The guardianess waved a hand, "No one saw you, silly. I feel terrible for interrupting your moment of solitude. I truly didn't mean to."

After putting her shoe on for her, Sean stood and then helped Katria up. "If you found us, anyone could have."

Key Guardianess Wystone's hand flew to her full chest as her eyes swept over Katria. "Oh, dear child, well, never mind why I came out here, you two best leave by the greenhouse door."

"Were you looking for us?" Sean asked, taking Katria's hand.

The woman's reaction to Katria's appearance had her thinking she must look worse than they thought. She edged behind Sean's back, leaving her husband to extricate them from the situation.

"It was time for your honorary toast, congratulating your marriage. My servers couldn't find you, so I decided to look myself. But, I'll of course let everyone know we kept you two love-birds long enough." She waved towards the right side of the conservatory. "Now go along, it's that way. I can't promise that you won't be seen, but at least you don't have to walk through the house."

"I'm sorry, I didn't consider congratulations."

Their hostess smiled. Wrinkles hidden by make-up

appeared at her genuine show of delight. "Vernon and I were young once, too, and I believe just as in love with each other. Now, go on and enjoy the rest of your evening. I had the honor of hosting Haven City's most talked-about couple, whose affection for each other leaves every other couple in shame. What more could I ask for?"

Sean bowed formally. "Thank you."

She turned to walk away and then stopped. "Oh, one more thing, Vernon did wish to speak to you about something, do you mind if he stops by your house?"

Sean tensed faintly, and Katria found herself holding her breath. The entire reason they'd shown up and her venturing off alone had caused him to miss it.

"No, of course not. The key guardian is welcome to arrive anytime."

The key guardianess's shoulders relaxed and she smiled. "He'll be pleased. Thank you."

They waited until she cleared the bend before heading to the greenhouse exit.

"I'm so sorry," Katria said as he held the door for her.

"It's not your fault."

They rushed across the lawn. Katria realized he hadn't buttoned his shirt, and her dress was still half undone. What a sight they'd make if spotted. Their coach was closer in line than it had been when they arrived, and Sean waved to the chauffeur bundled up on the driver's bench. Thankfully, everyone still seemed to be inside enjoying the festivities. With a huff, he landed in the seat across from her, the edges of his shirt falling across his lap. He didn't seem at all fazed by the cold air or his half-dressed state. "I don't know whether this night was a success or a complete failure."

Katria fumbled with the buttons along her side. Rebeka had secured the tiny fastenings, and Katria realized she'd not be successful on her own. Giving up, she dropped her hands in her lap. "We know for sure now someone is after us."

"After *you* at least. And they knew we'd be present."

Katria frowned. "Why after me? My involvement in the team is even more unknown than yours. Does that narrow anything down?"

"Maybe to get to me." He sighed, closed his eyes, and dropped his head back. "Who knows. As for narrowing down suspects, it leaves ranked society or those associated with them."

Katria glanced out the window to keep herself from staring at the tempting column of his exposed throat, and the strong curve of his jaw. "Half the city, then."

"I'm still not discounting Key Guardian Wystone."

"You invited him to the house," Katria reminded him, alarmed.

Sean remained relaxed. "Do you think he can do anything to either of us in that house?"

Understanding made Katria breathe a sigh of relief. "You won't be alone."

"When am I ever alone during an important or potentially risky meeting?" he asked, straightening to look at her, a sensual smile curving his lips.

Katria's heart raced, but not from the thought of having to be her husband's usual protection detail. The seductive smile and the exposed span of his torso had her quickly looking away from him. What would he do if she slid onto his lap, wrapped her arms around his shoulders, and demanded he kiss her? Probably oblige her. Katria closed her eyes.

"Are you okay?" he asked.

She took a sharp inhale, terrified he somehow read her naughty thoughts. Or felt her sudden desire in the air.

Choking on the air, she nodded. "I'm fine, yes... my shoulders are hurting a little." She hoped he bought the lie. Though with her coughing bout, the scrapes across her back did ache.

They arrived at the house, and Katria couldn't get out of the carriage fast enough. She didn't even wait for Sean or the coachman to get the door. She took the stairs as fast as her heavy gown would let her. Behind her, the steady scuff of Sean's booted feet followed. With longer legs, he didn't have to do much to match her stride.

"Why the rush?" he asked, not even winded.

She paused at the top of the steps to catch her breath and waited for Sean to open the door, assuming it was locked. "I don't exactly want to freeze to death *or* be caught looking like this."

Sean pulled a leaf still attached to a small twig from her hair. "Is that all?"

Heat flooded her cheeks, and she turned away from him. "Yes."

"After you." He opened the door with a sweep of his arm.

She stared at the revealed entryway in shock. "You have a fortune in my closet, and you leave the door unlocked?"

"It's not as if the house is empty," he whispered, and then walked by her when she didn't go inside.

"Yes, but no one is awake right now."

After she was inside, he closed the door. One by one, he fastened each lock, looking at her as he did so. She pressed her lips together in an annoyed frown.

Sean motioned to the now secured door. "Happy? Now they have to take the extra step of breaking the door down."

"At least it's a deterrent."

"If someone wants in, they'll find a way, locked door or not."

"For someone who knows the dangers out there, you sure take a careless approach to your home's safety."

His hands settled on her shoulders, and he met her stare. "I can't make this house any safer than it already is. The true dangers out there don't care about locks. We both know that. But, if it makes you feel better, I'll bolt every window and door in this house."

"My father always did," she found herself saying before she could stop herself.

"Then I will." His hands fell to his side. "After I look at your back. Come on, upstairs."

Katria wanted to argue that she didn't need any help; she was fine. He didn't give her the chance. Before she could find her voice, he headed up the stairs. Rebekah waited in Katria's room, reclining on the window seat that overlooked the greenhouse gardens. A bright lamp secured on the recessed wall burned above, illuminating the book she read. She quickly rose when she noticed Katria enter closely behind Sean.

"My guardians, good evening."

"Evening," Sean replied. "I'll be helping Primary Guardianess Wintersfall tonight."

Rebeka's eyes widened in a gasp when she finally seemed to notice the couple's disheveled state. Of course, Katria wasn't surprised. Her husband had still failed to button his shirt, and much to Katria's irritation, Rebeka's stare hadn't left his sculpted torso.

"What happened?" Rebeka asked, her hand flying to her mouth. "Are you okay?"

"I'm fine, I fell in the gardens and landed in a bush. Sean ripped his jacket and shirt coming to my aid," Katria explained easily. "I have a few scrapes he wants to make sure are okay, that's all."

"Of course." Rebeka collected her few personal items from the window seat. "I'll see you tomorrow."

They both moved out of the doorway so she could pass by. Sean closed the door and —simply to annoy her, she was sure— locked it.

Katria crossed the room and then laid a hand on the knob to his bedroom door. Raising a brow, she met his curious stare. "Are you sure you locked the right door?" she asked mischievously.

He closed the distance between them. Each step he took made her heart beat that much faster, until she was sure even he could hear it racing.

"Would you feel safer?" He braced his forearm on the doorframe.

Her fingers fell from the knob and she slowly shook her head. "No," she whispered.

"I didn't think so," he replied softly, leaning in close. "Now let me look at your back before I lose what little willpower I'm hanging onto."

Katria turned around. She wanted to be brazen. To be one of those seductive women she'd once witnessed teasing men. To tell Sean that he didn't need to self-control when it came to her.

Then again, as his hands made expert work at getting her dress off her shoulders, maybe it was for the best. In Haven City, she was learning her husband didn't trust his heart to his women. And she suddenly realized she didn't want anything less.

"Who is Carlie Milbourne to you?" she asked.

He paused and then pulled her away from the wall and into the light. "Are you sure you want the answer to that question?"

"I think I should know the answer. The woman seems to hate me, I'd like to know why."

She lifted her arm for him as he carefully undid all the tiny buttons running along her side. He fell to a knee, his attention on his task as he answered, "We carried on a relationship for several years, until I left."

"Were you going to contract with her?" Katria tried to tamp down the sharp rise of jealousy. What did she have to be jealous of?

Sean snorted out a laugh and shook his head. "No. Ms. Milbourne was between husbands when she and I were together. She likes them wealthier than I am. I was simply... a safe distraction while she looked for something better."

"Wealthier than you?" Katria asked in shock. "Does she know about your ridiculous fortune in jewelry?"

"She's very aware. Carlie made every effort to deprive me of a few pieces over our years."

Our years. Katria tried not to let the sentiment sting. "And the wealth you offered her to wear wasn't enough?"

"No."

"And men keep marrying her?"

"She's very good at seducing older, lonely, wealthy men. Her last husband was nearing seventy and owned half the Westican Trading Fleet."

Troubled, Katria turned to face him, holding her gown to her chest to keep it from falling. "She didn't make it sound like she was interested in anyone but you tonight."

Sean's smile was cold as he stood. "She doesn't like to lose."

"I don't understand."

He forced her back around and then gently pushed the sleeves of her gown completely off her shoulders until they fell to her bent arms. "She didn't end the relationship, I did, three years ago. When I returned, married to you, she was upset she didn't get to seduce me again, and then break things off first."

Katria drew her brows together. "Should I be concerned about this woman?"

"She will likely attempt to cause trouble, yes, but nothing more than rumors."

Agitated, Katria glanced over her shoulder. "Are there any other lovers I should be concerned about?"

"No."

"Good." She let the gown fall to the floor in a puddle of satin and velvet. In a low-backed silk slip that fell to her knees, she let Sean examine her aching shoulders. "How bad is it?"

"You're going to be sore tomorrow, but otherwise just scrapes and forming bruises, nothing is deep or bleeding anymore."

She stepped out of the ring of fabric and Sean didn't waste any time gathering a soft, thin cream cotton robe Rebeka had left on the bed. Katria slipped it on. Tying the sash around her waist, she watched him head to his door.

The unusual tension between them made her frown. "I'm sorry, I know I have no right to be upset about Ms. Milbourne, or Cora... or anyone else. I'll try to be better."

He rested his hand on the doorknob and stood between the two rooms. "Kat, you don't know me, not really. And no matter how real or pretend this marriage may be, you're still my wife. I didn't tell you about my previous relationships because I don't think about them much. They are very much in the past."

Katria wrapped her arms around herself. "You didn't... love any of them?"

Sean sighed and pushed his fingers through his hair. "No."

"Did they love you?" she asked, but didn't know if she wanted the answer.

Slowly, he shook his head. "No."

He didn't give her the chance to say anything else, slipping into his room. The door closed with a soft *click*. Katria stared at the barrier between them.

Before tonight, she'd never given much thought to love or romance, to forever between two people. Now, she realized if she were going to give over the body she almost lost to a bullet, she didn't want anything less. Rubbing her arms through the robe, she knew falling in love with Sean Blackbain wouldn't be difficult. If she were honest, she'd admit perhaps she already had, long before a document gave her permission.

❧ 11 ❧

T*he next day*
        Haven City Enforcement Services
East Street Division

Jᴏɴᴀᴛʜᴏɴ Hᴜɴᴛᴇʀ, Kᴇʏ Gᴜᴀʀᴅɪᴀɴ Aꜱʜᴇʀᴡɪᴄᴋ, scanned the pages of the open file he carried, avoiding other enforcemen negotiating the crowded halls. He came to his small office, packed with file cabinets, shelves, stacks of papers, and various colored files. Eventually, he'd go through everything and put things in order according to his system of organization, but every week seemed to add dozens more cases to his over-congested load. Perfectly styled glossy black hair, a slender neck, and squared shoulders in a teal blue gown with a peach silk overlay made him come to a dead stop.

The woman turned in her seat, a playful smile teasing her lips and sparkling in her pale gray eyes. "There you are, I thought I was going to have to search you down."

Jonathon snapped the folder shut and picked his way through the mess. "What are you doing here, Ms. Dandridge? I don't have any new information on the Daniels case."

She tsked and waved a hand. "Stop it with the *Ms.* nonsense. How many times do I have to ask you to call me Cora?"

Flexing his jaw in annoyance, he sat. Jonathon returned his attention to the contents of the folder in his hand. "At least one more time."

In the enticing manner in which she always seemed to move, she leaned forward, resting her forearms on the surface of his desk. The cut of her gown was low enough to give him a perfect glance down the front, revealing her full, firm breasts. Jonathon sighed and kept from rolling his eyes at the ploy she always attempted. Somehow, by logic that continued to defy him, he managed to resist.

"You're lucky I adore a challenge," she teased.

"We seem to have differing opinions on what lucky is."

A soft, sing-song laugh escaped from her smiling lips. "I so love being around you. No one dares speak to me the way you do. Everyone else is always so polite, formal... boring."

He set the folder on the desk and met her gaze. "Is that what it takes to be ignored by you? Be dull?"

The tip of her tongue touched her upper lip, and a predatory glint he recognized all too well entered her stare. "Jonathon Hunter, you couldn't be boring even if you tried your hardest."

Mirroring her posture, he braced his arms on the desk and leaned forward. "Maybe I'd surprise you this one time."

"You always surprise me," she admitted with a soft

smile. Then she finally sat back, resting her arms on the chair. "And I'm hoping you'll continue to."

"I already told you I don't have any new evidence, I wasn't lying."

"As disappointed as I am to learn about that, I am trying to put the public at ease. The victim is the sixth woman to go missing in two months. I'm not here for the Daniels case, or any of the others. Well," she tapped her fingers on the edge of the seat, "that's not entirely true, I am here about one, but we'll get to that in a moment."

Intrigued, Jonathon clasped his hands together. "Very well, I'm listening."

For what he believed was the first time, he watched Cora Dandridge fidget. She sighed and smoothed an imaginary strand of hair behind her ear. "My brother needs your help."

Jonathon raised a brow. "Primary Guardian Kynhaven needs my help? Doesn't he have the near-unlimited resources of the FIO at his disposal?"

"Not for this particular situation." All traces of humor left her beautiful face. "I don't know what's going on specifically, he's being rather cryptic—"

"Likely for your own good."

"So he keeps insisting. However, neither he nor the others are home enough to make any contacts or even know the condition of the local or national government."

"And you think I can help them somehow learn, or introduce them to someone who can?" he asked in confusion.

"Well, as *the* top investigator for the Haven City Enforcement Services, you know better than anyone where they should possibly start looking, or not, or... I don't know. I'm not entirely sure how these things work."

"What things?"

She waved a hand around. "You know, these secretive someone-wants-you-dead things."

Jonathon stared at her. "*You* don't know about all that? Really?"

An alluring flush bloomed across her cheeks. "Well, okay sure, a few intimidations might have come across my desk over the years, but nothing ever came of them. That's not the case for..." Her words died, and she cleared her throat and glanced at the cabinet closest to her.

"For who?" he asked when she failed to continue.

"Primary Guardian Wintersfall," she said under her breath.

Seething anger filled Jonathon, and he jumped out of his seat, pointing at the door. "Out of my office. Now!"

She didn't budge or even bat an eye. Instead, she sat further back in her chair and regarded him with a nonchalant stare. "Sean is not responsible for what happened, and you know it."

"Do I look like I care how responsible the man was? I'm not going anywhere near him, and I can't believe you would ask me to."

"Sit down, Jonathon. You're going to draw attention. I'm not going anywhere, and we're going to continue to have this conversation like the two adults we are."

Slowly, Jonathon returned to his seat. He tried to steady his breathing and regain some semblance of composure. "No, I'm done with this discussion. If you want to stay sitting there while I work, that's up to you."

She sighed heavily again. "I figured you'd be stubborn. I mean, you're stubborn enough to keep turning me down, I didn't really think I'd win this fight."

"Then why bother?"

"I might have come across something you will find most useful." She stood and then carefully made her way around to him. Propping a hip against the edge of his desk, half sitting, she forced him to turn and face her. "Valuable enough for me to come to your office." She leaned forward, close enough to touch a finger to his chin. "I waited almost an hour for you, and made a proposition I knew you wouldn't go for. And I kept the thread of information to myself. I didn't tell my editor. I need you to do this for me. For my brother, Sean, and his... wife, and Kevin. They're my family and they're in trouble."

"Who's the one drawing attention now?" he couldn't help but ask.

A teasing smile sparkled in her pale eyes. She slid closer to him along the desk. Papers shifted under her, crinkling and fluttering to the floor. "You know how much I enjoy attention."

"Especially the mischievous kind."

"All the better," she admitted. She wrapped an arm around his neck and, before he could stop her, she slipped onto his lap.

"You're going to get me dismissed."

"Doubtful."

Knowing she wasn't going anywhere until she had her way, Jonathon kept his hands safely at his side. Somehow, the witchy woman always managed to land in his lap. "What is this information that I won't be able to do my job without?"

She leaned close enough for him to take in the soft, clean fragrance she wore and whispered into his ear, "I may have discovered who stole the reported magic lily dust shipment three months ago, arriving from Alexandria."

"The one that didn't even make it into port and made Import and Immigration Regulation Agency look foolish? The one rumored to have sunk in the Ceylon Channel in a windstorm?" he asked skeptically, ignoring the tightening in his gut. He did not need more of the pink powdery mind-altering, immorality-inducing drug out on his streets. More drugs meant more crime meant more missing kids. At least, that'd been the norm for the past two years.

"What if it didn't sink?" She trailed her fingers down the buttons of his shirt, tapping on each one before moving to the next. "What if the ship was deprived of its cargo in the middle of the night, voluntarily? And the ship itself was, oh, I don't know, renamed, changed ownership, and the old name simply went to the bottom of a channel no one can investigate?"

"You're not just talking about possible stolen drugs, but insurance fraud as well. That ship had a massive payout; it was worth close to half a million raimarks. Because the IIRA failed to confirm the illegal contents, the insurance company paid the claim."

"I know," she exhaled, her lips brushing against his ear. Jonathon closed his eyes and took a slow breath to regain his self-control. "Now you see why I'm so confident? You need this information." She rested a hand on his cheek and forced his face to turn until her mouth hovered over his. "And I need you."

He opened his eyes. "You are wicked."

"So everyone keeps telling me. So? Do we have a deal?"

"If I say yes, will you get off my lap?"

She ran her thumb down his lips, her eyes focused entirely on his mouth, and Jonathon found it hard to breathe. "I rather like being here. You know that."

"Cora..."

"Finally, my name." Her lips touched gently to his before she stood. "Is this a yes?"

Jonathon held up his index finger. "I will meet with him one time. Once."

"Excellent. See? I did say you'd surprise me again."

Not just her, Jonathon had amazed himself. Somehow, he'd managed to agree to meet a man he'd rather see dead.

S ean paced before his desk in the upstairs loft of the library. He'd asked Davis to bring Kat. He glanced back at the letter from Cora informing him of Key Guardian Asherwick's agreeing to meet with them. The man would not arrive in a good mood. The tension wouldn't be something his wife could ignore or leave unquestioned. At least part of his family's dark past was going to have to be exposed. Running a nervous hand down his face, Sean stopped, trying to ignore all the what-ifs swirling in his mind. The library door opened and then closed behind her. Kat called for him.

"Up here," he answered.

She took the stairs along the left wall up, her hand trailing along the thin rail. "Why are you not downstairs?"

"It feels quieter up here. And it's usually a little warmer."

Once on the landing, she ventured to the wall of windows overlooking the conservatory, which rose an additional story above the house. "The view is better as well."

"Won't be too much longer, and they'll have the

pathway uncovered at least. I didn't know plants could take over so quickly without the proper care."

"Oh yes, my mother worked daily on ours."

He joined her at the window, clasping his hands behind his back. "Do you know much about plants?"

Resting a hand against one of the crossbeams, she shrugged. "A little, I guess. My mother tried to teach me, but my sister was more interested."

"You have a sister?"

"Are you doing anything particular with the greenhouse? Does it grow food or is it just for show?"

Sean drew his brows together at her evasion. Apparently, her sibling wasn't a topic she wanted to discuss. Not that he blamed her. He didn't want to venture there himself.

"Mainly show. I try to grow some food to have some fresh produce for winter, and for the staff to take home if they wish." A thought occurred to him, and he turned to face her. "Would you like to take over the design?"

Shocked, she met his stare. "Why?"

"There's not much I can give you to make your own here, the house is what it is. However, the conservatory grounds are currently unplanned. If you'd like, you can do with it whatever you wish. Turn it into food, or a flower garden, or an orchard. Maybe some of everything. Its footprint is larger than the house, almost a half a block."

She pressed in closer to the glass, her other hand resting on the surface. "My mother restored an entire species of plants believed lost after the Cataclysm. Lovely flowers that smelled unlike anything else in the world. Herbs that healed sickness. I wish I had her passion. I don't know if I could give you something as pleasing as a garden architect could."

Sean smiled in encouragement. "It doesn't have to be

perfect, just yours, something you'll enjoy spending time in."

"I'll think about it," she said, returning his smile. "Is that why you called me in here?"

How I wish it were. He shook his head. "No, afraid not."

Turning away from the window, he made his way to the desk and then sat on the edge. He clasped his hands between his knees and took a deep breath. If she thought having a ranked husband was a burden, how would she feel after learning what he was about to share? He hoped she wouldn't hate him or her new name.

She came to stand in front of him, a troubled frown on her beautiful face. "What's wrong? Did you learn some new information?"

"No, not yet. But Cora managed to convince an investigator with the HCES to help us. With his experience in solving the unsolvable and his knowledge of the city's inner workings, he'll likely be able to provide insight we're not seeing."

"All right, that sounds great."

"It is, I'm very thankful she was able to get him to agree." He took a deep breath. "There's just one thing I need you to know about him."

She crossed her arms over her chest, shifting her weight onto her back foot as she contemplated him. "What's that?"

"He hates me."

"Oh," she said softly, clasping her hands together. "What did you do?"

"I didn't do anything," he said with a sigh. "My brother, however, assaulted a good number of women, and Asherwick's sister, Ramsey Hunter, helped see him convicted."

Kat gasped, her eyes wide in astonishment. "As in..."

Frowning heavily, Sean said, "As in he's in prison for

rape, with no chance of seeing freedom again. It turned out that Miss Hunter witnessed him with a victim. When she came forward with the woman, the authorities couldn't ignore it. Miss Hunter's testimony and the victim's medical exam, proved accusations were true and forced them to acknowledge the other victims."

"I don't understand why they ever would have ignored other victims to begin with," she stated, her voice uneven with anger.

Sean steepled his fingers and brought them to his chin in thought. "How can I explain this... There are certain things the authorities will look past when it comes to the ranked and the wealthy and the lower class, provided it stays contained."

"What do you mean contained?"

"Not an entire city or town is affected, rather what's considered a minor injustice here or there. The burden of proof always falls to the accuser. Those in powerful positions often use their money and influence to prevent proof from reaching the accusation hearings, so authorities drop the cases before fully investigating them."

Her face pinched in a deep frown. "And your brother made sure that happened?"

"Yes, until he accosted a woman at the wrong house, and they couldn't."

"I didn't even know you had a brother," she said softly, glancing away from him.

"Not exactly something I care to discuss."

"And this investigator holds your brother's crimes against you? His sister wasn't hurt, was she?"

"Depends on your definition of hurt. Ramsey Hunter was ostracized afterward. Her promised broke their engagement, and everyone canceled her invitations to their events. Society doesn't like being turned against, regardless of the crime. I don't think it's so much *me*, but rather my family, my name."

Kat's focus remained on something only she could see outside. "That's terrible. What's your brother's name?"

Sean flexed his shoulders and braced his hands on the ledge of the desk, feeling as if speaking his brother's name would somehow return the unseen curse he'd escaped from so many years ago. "Joel."

"And he's younger than you?"

"No," Sean said with a shake of his head. "He's five years older."

That brought her attention back to him. "Was he a Gen-Heir?"

"Yes."

"He was the heir to the rank?"

"Yes," he said with a heavy sigh.

"Did you want it?"

Sorrow settled over him. "No, and I never expected it. I was just going to join the military, get away from all the phony facades people in this city keep up, the shallow pretenses. The responsibility that no one ever cared to teach me anything about, because I was never supposed to have it. And then," he ran a hand down his face, "and then Endowment and Revocation approved the change from Joel to me, and I was Primary Guardian Wintersfall. Either I did what the elected crown's leadership asked of me, or I lost everything."

"How long did you have the rank before they sent you away?"

"A month."

"And when I was assigned to you?"

He thought back, counting the years that had passed. "I think two years at that point, but I'd only been back in the country for one week, and no one knew I was home."

Kat raised a brow and gave a sarcastic tilt to her head. "Except Ms. Milbourne, perhaps?"

He grimaced. "She *might* have known, yes."

"Still between husbands?"

"You will hate my answer, so I think I'll keep it to myself," he said.

She raised her dark brows. "Isn't that an answer in and of itself?"

"No," he drew out.

"Fine, I suppose it doesn't matter anyway."

Sean took in her rigid stance, the way her foot tapped against the hardwood, and the flush of pink gracing her cheeks. He wondered what he'd sense if he took a step closer and invaded her space. "Are you... jealous of her?"

"No," she snapped, her hands fisted at her sides. "Why would I be jealous of a woman who has no respect for much except money?"

"Kat," he began softly, waiting until she met his gaze to continue. "You can't be jealous of her or any other woman. If you're serious about keeping this marriage a professional front that we have to endure until we figure out what's going on, you have to see me as no one special."

A faint glimmer of hurt entered her cerulean blue eyes. "Is that how you see me? No one special?"

"I should," he admitted, sliding a foot forward until his weight shifted further onto the desk. "But, no. You've been special since the moment I took responsibility for you, and I don't want my name to be your ruin. You never asked for taint of my family, and you don't deserve it."

She stepped closer until they stood mere inches apart. A soft, almost sad frown settled on her face, and deepened in her gaze. "Sean, they married you to the one woman in all of Sziveria whose reputation you had zero chance of ever being able to ruin. I'm a marksman, naturally gifted with the ability to take out a target over seven hundred feet away." She turned her attention to the floor, her shoulders falling as her brows pinched together. "What man would ever marry me knowing what I've done... what I'm capable of, and can still do, if asked?"

The tremble in her voice gave away how hard it was for her to say those words. An unfamiliar need to comfort crept into his heart, a desire he found himself unable to force away. Reaching out, he grasped her wrist and pulled until she stood between his legs, her chest nearly touching his. She kept her face downcast, her hands clutched tightly together.

"A future husband wouldn't know if you didn't tell him," Sean stated quietly, ignoring the pinch in his gut. He didn't want Kat to have another husband in the future, but it wasn't a choice.

She finally met his gaze, the vivid blue of her eyes filled with a pain only time could lessen. A pain he recognized in himself. "This isn't a life you leave behind. You may have a black mark next to your name, but we both know mine would be worse."

If only there were just one. After tucking a strand of her silky hair behind her ear, he brushed his fingers along her jaw. "You are making a very compelling case for this marriage."

"Everything is turning quite gray," she admitted barely above a whisper.

"And what about my brother? Does knowing his actions still make things gray for you?"

She touched a hand to his jaw, her focus centering on his mouth. "You are not your brother. I don't even know the man, so why should his crimes affect how I view you? I *know* who you are." She lifted her eyes to his. "You're Sean Blackbain, and my life has been safely in your hands for three years. And I'm still alive and *no one* has been able to touch me."

A fierce surge of protectiveness flowed into him at her words. And no one would *ever* touch her but him. What the possessive emotion meant for him, he wasn't sure yet, but he'd worry about the repercussions later.

Everyone had told him for years that he and Joel were nothing alike. His brother's corruptions were not his and didn't reflect on him as a man or an individual. But not until his wife spoke the words did he truly choose to trust that. If this incredible, strong, smart woman saw him as something other than the second choice of the Sziverian government, and a societal reject, maybe he was...

Closing the distance between them, his lips captured hers. Without hesitation, she accepted his advance, her mouth opening. Her arms wrapped around his neck and her chest pressed against his, leaving no space between them. The loose lengths of her hair tangled in his fingers as his hands slid up her back. He wanted to explore every inch of her.

Sean slanted his mouth over hers, deepening the kiss. He broke their embrace long enough to switch their positions and lift her onto the desk. Returning his lips to hers, he didn't give her the chance to get situated. He leaned over until she lay beneath him, her legs moving apart to accommodate him. Cool air brushed across his skin, her hands sliding under his shirt and along his back.

Sean pushed the skirt of her dress up until he could slip a hand beneath. His fingers found the warm, soft skin of her thigh, and she lifted her leg, her foot bracing on the edge of the desk. His tongue explored her mouth, seeking out all the soft crevices. She tasted of sweetened tea and citrus. The heady combination of her strong emotional desire and physical need coiled under his touch, feathering into his person, heightening his own need. Many, many times he'd been here before, his Sympath abilities informing him of his lover's state of arousal, but nothing prepared him for the turbulent onslaught of Kat's controlled passion. Under him, she lay soft, pliant, but still.

The feelings flowing into him like a turbulent wave from her told a different story. She wanted with a ferocity he'd never experienced before. Stars above, what had he done? And how was he supposed to stop?

Her hips pressed into his with a quiet whimper. Instinctively, he returned the gesture. A shiver of pleasure raced through him at the intimate contact. With their emotional state coiled and fused together through his touch to her bare skin, he continued sliding his hand along her silken thigh. At her hip, he encountered the line of her panties. He slipped the tips of his fingers beneath the edge and instead of shying away, Kat's leg fell open, her low body seeking his caress. And oh, how he wanted to *touch*. Would she be at the start of her arousal, or fully immersed and wet for him? Suddenly, he found his control going from strained to near non-existent.

Every nerve in him wanted to keep going, to push the measly scrap of fabric aside, to feel the heart of her inches from his fingers. To bring the pounding emotions seething beneath her surface into manifestation, until she writhed and cried out beneath him. But she wasn't a lover to part ways with when the time arrived. Nor was she a quick reprieve from a stressful mission. She was a stunning woman who had never known love. Sean knew the man who'd have her would deserve her heart as well as her body. And he wasn't that man. He was a bad risk; one he wasn't willing to allow her to take.

Breathing heavily, he broke their kiss and rested his

forehead against hers. "I seem to lack some serious restraint around you. I'm sorry."

"I do as well." She exhaled, her hands slipping from under his shirt. Her blue eyes seemed somehow brighter when filled with passion, and now a hint of annoyance. "And I'd appreciate it if you stopped apologizing. If I didn't want you to kiss me, I'd stop you."

He trailed a thumb down her kiss-swollen lips. "Not a good thing to say to me right now."

"Then either stand..." An intensity in her stare that had his pulse quickening again. "Or finish what you were going to do."

"As much as I'd love to act on where my very impure thoughts are taking us, I don't think it's wise." He straightened and helped her stand. In long flowing folds, her gown returned around her legs.

"Probably not," she agreed, but her disappointment was evident in the firm set of her lips and jaw. She shook out her dress and then smoothed her hand down her stomach. "You'll let me know when the investigator arrives?"

"Of course."

She nodded and then, as if nothing abnormal had occurred between them, headed down the stairs. Sean went to the banister, his brows drawn in thought as he watched her leave. As the door closed silently behind her, he couldn't help but feel as if a small part of his heart had walked out with her.

❈   13   ❈

Body still humming with an intense yearning she didn't even know she could feel, Katria shut her bedroom door and then sagged against it, closing her eyes. Two more seconds, and she was certain his hand would have been giving her an experience she had only ever imagined.

Frustrated with her apparent lack of self-control and the situation she found herself in – desiring a husband she couldn't seem to touch – Katria stalked to the cabinet where she'd hidden her rifle. Old habits died hard, and she needed an outlet. She grabbed the gun and a box of ammunition and then headed for the basement training room. No one would bother her there, or ask questions, or entice her with sensual promises they couldn't fulfill.

On her way to the indoor range, she lit the wall lamps. Once inside, she set her rifle and the case on an empty table with two chairs and a stack of paper targets. At the end of the long, narrow room, she lit enough lamps to illuminate the target area completely. Back at the worktable, she removed a set of rubber earplugs from her ammo box. When they were in, she clapped her hands to ensure they were indeed dampening the sound. She didn't need to be deaf before thirty.

The familiar routine centered her. Her nerves calmed, and a sense of grounding flowed through her. Focusing on a long inhale, she ran her hand along the cool wooden stock of her rifle. Sitting, she leaned into the weapon and closed her eyes. She exhaled slowly and then drew air in measured breaths, allowing her senses to shift and become merged with the steel and wood of the weapon.

After a few steadying exercises, she opened her eyes, her attention on the paper bullseye over a hundred feet from her. She armed her rifle and kept her concentration fixed on the tiny red center. Katria placed the correct level of pressure on the trigger. The bullet exited the barrel on a hard kick with a puff of sulfurous gray smoke. The red dot disappeared. Katria smiled.

An hour later, a pile of spent targets had formed on the table beside her. Bullet casings littered the floor. She sighed and sat up, not quite happy with the last shot. Soreness radiated from her shoulder, and she gently rotated the joint to ease the pain. A bruise would cover the entire area by tonight. At least she'd have a different ache to focus on.

Since inflicting more abuse on her sore body wouldn't change anything, she stopped, laying the rifle down and then removing the earplugs. A faint movement outside the range caught her attention, and she glanced over her shoulder. Kevin made his way towards her, and she sighed. She wasn't in the mood for conversation.

When he opened the door, she began gathering the bronze casings off the floor. "I take it the investigator is here?"

"Yes, and no one could find you. Sean was about to tear the house down."

Katria paused and glanced up at him. "Really?"

He squatted down and helped her, dropping the reusable shells into the nearly empty box. "Really. I told him I was pretty sure I could find you. He didn't know I'd brought you down here."

"Does he know now?"

"Yes, he does, thankfully. Next time, he won't panic so much."

She drew her brows together. "I forgot I asked him to find me when the investigator arrived. I should have told him where I would be."

They stood after collecting all the casings. Kevin kept hold of the box while she picked up her rifle.

"Are you okay?" he asked, his dark gray eyes searching hers.

"I'm fine, why?"

"You took over a hundred shots, that's why."

Katria rushed from the range, embarrassed. What was she supposed to say? *I can't have my husband, so I decided to shoot my gun instead?* She didn't think so.

"It's not because you learned about Joel, is it?"

"Who?" she asked and then remembered Sean's brother's name. "Oh. No. I don't care about him. He's in prison where he belongs."

"I knew you wouldn't care." Kevin matched her stride. "Sean wasn't so convinced."

"Yes, he seemed very concerned, I'd think he'd ruined me or something." She snorted as she headed up the stairs. "As if I have to concern myself with reputations."

"Well, in the world we come from, reputations are everything. They're as important as the ranks or family names they represent," he explained, holding the door open for her at the top of the stairs. "You're lucky you never had to worry about that."

No, her family name was *not* reputable. A niggle of

guilt danced in her stomach and she frowned. Sean was attached to that name, even if he didn't know yet. Maybe *she* was the one who should be worried about ruining *him*.

"Sean shouldn't worry about it either." She took her box of spent bullets from him. "He's probably one of the more honorable men in the city when he's home."

"Ranked society will see it eventually."

At the door to the hall, Katria found herself hesitating. Kevin was the only person she knew who could understand the frustrations she faced. Her hand on the doorknob, she looked up at him. "Can I ask you a very personal question?"

His gaze narrowed on her. "I suppose that depends on how personal."

Taking a chance, she questioned, "Do you love your wife?"

Eyes wide, he huffed out a heavy breath. "Wow, uh, that wasn't what I thought it'd be. My marriage is similar to yours. We didn't have the choice."

"So, you don't?"

He glanced away from her with a frown. "We've been apart more than we've been together. We don't know each other very well. That's not easy on a marriage."

Katria decided to risk one more. "How do you think she feels about you?"

A scowl darkened his face, and he reached for the door. "I'd rather not think about that, to be honest. I'm not the best person to be asking about relationships."

Dejected, her shoulders slumped. "I don't have anyone else to ask."

"I'm sorry. I wish I had a more positive outlook on things. Honestly, I've seen more of you in three years than I have of her. You probably know me better, too."

"The life of an intel guardian seems to mess everything up."

"Risks we all took when we agreed to put country before self."

"Still..." Unhappiness filled her. "I don't feel like it's fair."

"It's not." He squeezed her shoulder. "Don't worry, Kat. Sean knows what he has with you, and if he doesn't, it won't take him long to figure out."

"I hope it's soon," she said under her breath.

Kevin chuckled. "Funny you two were able to go three years cohabitating without any tension, and then one piece of paper suddenly shifted everything."

"I didn't think it would matter," she admitted. "I mean, I'd been so many things to all of you over the years. I could be a wife, nothing had to change."

"But you really are a wife, not just being told you're one."

"I know. That's been the hardest part. Everything is real." Vulnerability settled over her. "I can't disappoint him."

Kevin wrapped his arms around her and pulled her into a brotherly hug. "You won't."

She accepted his embrace, comforted by his assurance. "How do you know?"

"Because you care about him."

She huffed skeptically. "Caring isn't enough."

Kevin put her at arm's length, his stormy gray eyes fixing hers with a serious gaze. "Kat, it's always enough."

"Import and Immigration is currently investigating Key Guardian Wystone for smuggling charges," Jonathon Hunter stated.

He tapped a pencil on a notebook spread open on his lap. The enforceman wore exactly what Katria imagined. No-nonsense dark gray slacks. A plain button-up light gray shirt. An unbuttoned black coat with the HCES emblem on the left breast, with his enforcement and guardian ranks underneath in bright yellow thread. He wore his medium brown hair cut short. At the start of the day, perhaps, he'd likely brushed it to one side, but weather and life had left the top a bit disheveled.

Sitting in a loose circle of chairs and settees in the center of the library, everyone regarded each other over the information. Katria glanced at her husband sitting beside her, the small divan they occupied leaving little room between them. Mason sat in a chair across from them, beside Kevin, though Mason kept glaring in Cora's direction. She'd entered the room last and insisted her brother keep his place, taking the space on the small loveseat beside Jonathon. Every few minutes, she seemed to inch closer to the enforceman.

Mason couldn't seem to tolerate his sister's obvious effort, and he stood, pointing at the chair. "Cora, sit here."

"I'm good," she insisted.

"It wasn't a request," Mason bit out, closing the distance between them.

Rolling her silvery gray eyes and growling out a sigh, she stood. "Fine."

"For the love of stars!" Sean barked. "It's like minor academia in here." He stood and crossed the distance to his desk. When he returned, he dragged two chairs with him. "There, now all the adults can have a chair. Happy?"

Cora inspected her fingernails. "I was perfectly fine."

"Thank you," Mason helped Jonathon replace the small couch with the seats.

Deciding to get the meeting back on track, Katria stated, "The charges wouldn't affect us."

"Not unless they're fake, like the assignment someone gave us in Gaula," Kevin pointed out.

"I can't attest to the charges," Jonathon said. "But I know the Sziverian National Investigative Division is examining it."

Cora folded her legs up onto the chair and relaxed to one side, her lavender silk gown cascading to the floor. "I wrote an article about it a month ago. They believe he was using his position at the FIO to manipulate dock workers into forging cargo manifests."

"To what end?" Sean asked.

"I don't know," Cora replied. "No one ever came forward with any information when I asked."

"Well, he wants to speak to me about something, and considering the attack on Kat at his house, I have to assume his departure from the FIO is relevant, whatever the cause," Sean stated.

Cora's eyes widened, and she looked at Katria. "Are you okay?"

Puzzled, Katria raised a brow. "I'm fine. Why wouldn't I be?"

Mason snorted softly. Kevin cleared his throat. Cora glanced between the two of them and then, with a suspicious glimmer, focused her attention back on Katria. "You weren't fazed at all, were you?"

"Cora," Sean began, "she's an FIO operative. She helped me hide the body."

Jonathon straightened, his dark blue eyes wide. "Body?"

"Unconscious," Katria clarified. She didn't need her husband getting hauled off to jail by a man likely looking for a reason to. Though so far, the tension Sean had worried about didn't seem to be an issue. "Not dead."

Jonathon pinched the bridge of his nose. "I never should have agreed to this. I'm not involved with whatever it is you all do. I could get dismissed if I'm caught."

"Will you stop it with the *they're going to dismiss me* nonsense? You're the best investigator in the entire city. You'd have to hide the corpse yourself before they'd release you," Cora stated, exasperated.

"He has a point, though." Mason settled back in his chair. "With this group, you never know when we'll need to hide a body."

"Or seven," Katria said with a sigh, remembering a mission that had gone sideways two years ago.

Kevin laughed. "Oh, that's right, we did have seven we had to figure out what to do with, didn't we? That was a bad night."

Jonathon stared slack-jawed across the distance at

Cora. She glared at her brother. Mason shrugged carelessly and picked at imaginary lint on the arm of the chair. "What?"

Leaning forward, Cora fixed Mason with a glare. "You better stop. You need Jonathon's skills, and alienating him isn't going to help you."

The two of them stared each other down. Katria couldn't help but note the identical, powerful silvery gray coloring of their eyes and glossy, straight black hair that fell almost midback on both of them. Even their glowering expressions were remarkably similar, which she knew shouldn't have shocked her, since they were twins.

"Can we *please* find another time to talk out this family squabble?" Sean said, and then turned his attention to Jonathon. "Don't worry about what we do, it doesn't concern you. And if it does, a certificate of custody will land on your desk for us, I promise. What I need to know is if anything is going on in this city that would require one of the top special teams to be home all at once?"

"Don't you think you would have been told if there was?" Jonathon inquired.

Kevin shook his head. "Not necessarily. The FIO often puts us in situations with limited information. We each possess a unique skill set that allows us to complete tasks effectively. Only in this particular case are we missing the key link – the *what*. Without it, we can't move forward."

"There may not even be a *what*," Mason argued. "We could just be waiting for reprimands."

Sean drummed his fingers on the armrest. "No, there's something, I know so."

"Look," Jonathon began, scrubbing his hands over his face. "This city is eating itself alive with crime. I have a serial murderer that I can't find and the killer is one more victim away from the SNID picking up the case. I have heard about magic lily dust being smuggled into the city, despite strict enforcement of cargo from countries known to process the substance. Somehow, they're still managing to smuggle that crap in, and keep half the population in a state of fake euphoria or the morgue. The addiction has reached such pandemic heights that people are selling their *children* to fund their habit, or stealing children to sell. Not to mention the violent crimes that come with addiction as a whole. Take your pick."

Katria met Sean's glance. He brushed his fingers along his bearded jaw. "Things weren't that bad when I left three years ago. I haven't heard of magic lily dust."

Jonathon shrugged. "Well, they're that bad now."

Katria turned towards Jonathon. "So, how long has this been going on, if you had to narrow it down?"

"Well, drugs have always been a minor problem, though magic lily dust itself showed up around five years ago, and has taken off in the past two years. And the trafficking too, just more towards adults than kids. The child situation seemed to explode," he glanced at Cora, "two years ago as well?"

"Around then, yes," Cora answered with a nod. "And it's been impossible to narrow down how exactly they're disappearing. They just are."

"No one is talking about it. I've seen nothing in the papers," Kevin stated, frowning.

Cora worked her bottom lip between her teeth. "I know. We've been told at the paper that the subject is too depressing to cover. Even the addiction situation seems to be off limits."

"Things are staying very contained, it's true," Jonathon confirmed.

"Why? People have a right to know their families are in danger if kidnappers are randomly taking children." Mason looked between Cora and Jonathon. "Is that what's happening?"

Cora fidgeted and glanced at Jonathon, who tapped a pencil on his thigh. Katria frowned as dread rose in her belly. What was happening to Sziveria?

Jonathon looked around at them all. "If the kidnappings aren't considered a violent crime, I'm not assigned them. Here lately, most of them seem to be disturbingly *non*-violent. Parents making the exchange for a month's supply of dust, or orphans disappearing from orphan houses without any signs of struggle."

Sean leaned forward. "Like the caretakers are in on it?"

"I've discreetly tried to investigate that," Cora confessed with a long exhale. "And I haven't found any evidence of it. The caretakers seem genuinely distressed when a child or two goes missing. Most of the suspicion seems to be falling on people who expressed interest in adoption."

Sean sat back, his fingers tapping along the back edge of the couch. "Drugs, human trafficking, and an investigation into an FIO agent forging cargo manifests. Sziveria seems to need her guardians about now."

Mason nodded. "Yes, but why not say something? If they mean for us to help either the SNID or even local enforcement, we need to know what to look for."

Steepling his fingers against his mouth, Sean mused, "Unless they don't know where to begin themselves." He glanced at Jonathon. "Besides your violent crime investigations, what sort of resources are being thrown at the problems?"

"I'm not sure." Jonathon raked a hand through his already messy dark hair. "The thing is, I'm not even sure something *is* being done."

"Why do you think that?" Mason asked, leaning forward and bracing his elbow on his knee.

"Because most of the kids who go missing aren't from Gen-Heir families. They're from the gen-common population."

Sean scratched at his beard in thought. "It's not affecting the guardians, so they aren't putting their attention on it."

An ominous sensation grew in Katria's stomach. She took a steadying breath. "Isn't that the whole purpose of guardians, though? If not to protect everyone, then why have the positions at all?"

All the men looked at each other, expressions grim. Katria gritted her teeth. "No one else matters on our soil? We've worked for three years to keep the monsters at bay in other countries, only for them to have free rein here?"

Jonathon's troubled, dark blue gaze met hers. "I didn't notice the lack of attention until now. It's just been a problem that has become almost..."

"Normal," Cora stated on a soft breath, wide-eyed. "Oh, my goodness. How? How has this happened?"

Mason flexed his jaw. "To have become normal, it had to happen in phases. People became numb to the problem. They felt unaffected, so they could easily look the other way. If what you're saying is true, someone is strategically coordinating the abductions and the drug sales. Is anyone combating any aspect of the issue at all?"

Cora's forehead pinched in frustration. "I'm not sure. I haven't heard of anything, but I haven't looked beyond the orphan house abductions. Do you want me to make some inquiries?"

"Discreet might be best," Mason advised with a pointed look at his twin.

"You'll have to use trusted resources," Sean added.

"Yes, whom to trust is going to be the biggest hurdle," Mason concurred.

"I know where we can start on our inquiries," Kevin began, but Jonathon rose.

"I think I've completed my part in helping. I'm not so sure I want to know where your investigations may lead, or the method." He bowed his head toward Cora. "I'll expect to see you tomorrow. You have some information I need."

"A promise is a promise," she said with a little smile.

"I'll see you out," Katria said, rising. Walking him to the door was her chance to speak to an investigator, and she wasn't going to let it go by.

Jonathon gave another gentlemanly nod to everyone in the room before following behind Katria. Once she was sure they were clear of anyone hearing, she paused and touched a hand to the back of his arm.

"Key Guardian Asherwick, I was wondering if I could ask you a favor," she ventured.

He stopped near the door, his face twisted in discomfort. "Primary Guardianess Wintersfall, I'm pretty much out of favors when it comes to this house."

Katria let out a held breath, her hand falling to her side. "I understand, however, my husband isn't to blame for the sins of his brother. And I think we can both agree, he's worked very hard to make amends to our country for a crime he didn't commit. I *do* need help, and I don't know who else to ask. If you won't, can you at least give me the name of someone you trust who might at least listen?"

Sighing heavily, he looked at the ceiling and muttered, "Fine." Then, turning his attention back to her, he asked, "What do you need?"

Relief mixed with anticipation, so she kept a careful check on her reaction, simply giving what she hoped was an appreciative smile. "Thank you. Almost four years ago, someone murdered my mother and sister. I was told that the Sziverian National Investigative Division would be taking over the incident, but I have not received any updates since then. I was hoping when we arrived in Haven City, I'd hear something, but I haven't."

"And you need me to check on it for you," he guessed with brows drawn.

"Yes, if you can."

He opened the notebook he'd been holding and flipped to a clean page. "What are their names? And you said four years ago, can you give a more exact date?"

She could give him an exact hour if he wanted it. Tamping down the sorrow that threatened as the date forever carved into their headstones appeared in her mind, she replied, "Margaret and Anyka Nachemir, March third, eight-thirty-two."

Confusion registered across his face. "I thought..." He sighed and flipped the notebook closed. "Never mind."

Katria's heart skipped a beat. Had he made the connection that her name in the paper wasn't the same as the name she'd given? She'd known the risk was huge, but finding the murderer was more important than a fake name. Deciding not to question his line of thought, she smiled. "Thank you. If you ever need anything, I'll owe you a favor."

"I seem to be collecting those." His attention shifted to the partially open library door. "I don't know what I'd need from... actually, I don't know what you do."

"Are you sure you want to?"

He pressed the pad to his mouth, his stare meeting hers. For a moment, she wasn't sure if he was going to answer. Then he tucked his notebook into his inner jacket pocket and said, "I'm curious, so yes."

Taking a deep breath, she said, "I'm a sharpshooter."

"I'd be in some trouble if I needed a favor from you."

"Well, I'm the person who takes care of trouble."

An unfamiliar and altogether uncomfortable feeling of jealousy rose within Sean when his wife walked out the door with another man. He hadn't taken his eyes off the empty frame while a conversation he was positive he needed to listen to happened around him. The sudden, intense clap of hands together forced his attention to Kevin, who waved when Sean looked at him.

"Hello, there, welcome back," Kevin teased.

Cora grinned with bemusement. "I don't think Jonathon's going to run off with her."

Kevin chuckled. "It's the other way around. *She* isn't going anywhere."

"Fine, I get it, I'm listening," Sean growled, annoyed at how transparent he must have been.

Mason leaned forward and rested his elbows on his knees. "As I'd been saying, I think the first place we need to look is in our files. Someone who knows us knows we'll be watching them for any changes to our status. They may leave us a clue inside."

"How?" Sean asked. "They're locked in a cabinet in Voklane's office."

"Which I've gotten into once already," Kevin reminded him. "It's not like that floor is secure, it's just offices."

"Floors that contain personal information," Sean felt the need to point out.

"Plus, we work for them," Mason stated in defense of his plan. "It's not as if they can arrest us for being in our workspace."

"We don't work *in* that building," Sean argued.

"And you watch me have the biggest fit in grown man history if they say a word," Mason retorted. "We should be able to come and go as we please with what we do for this country."

"While I agree," Kevin began calmly, "I also believe caution is warranted. If security catches us prying around, we can arouse suspicion we don't need. Voklane's office is fairly simple to get to, however. I can check the files tonight."

Cora rubbed her hands together, an all too eager smile on her face. "What fun this is. Sounds like you men have a plan. I've never been able to sit in on a covert meeting before."

Mason fixed her with a concerned frown. "And you won't again. Asherwick was right; neither of you needs to be involved in this."

She waved his apprehension away. "I'll be fine. Besides, who knows when one of my contacts may come in handy with all the subversive stuff going on? I already said I'd make some inquiries about who may be helping drug and abduction victims. I can help."

Mason shot a desperate glance Sean's way. Sean shrugged. "You allowed her to come to the meeting, my friend."

"Because of Asherwick." Exasperated, Mason pointed at his sister. "She all but said either she came or neither of them did."

Cora smirked. "I'm stubborn that way."

Kat still had yet to reappear. Due to his distraction, Sean's usual involvement with organizing their next step was suffering. Irritated, he rose, knowing he'd be useless until she returned. "I'll be right back."

The collective snickers at his departure didn't improve his dark mood. Out in the foyer, he searched the open space and found her closing the front door. "What has taken so long?"

She flinched and spun around. Her rich black hair cascaded around her arms. A tense line replaced the rosy fullness of her lips. "Was I gone long?"

"We've already planned out the next step without you."

In a show of indifference, she shrugged and walked past without looking at him. "Then you didn't need me, did you?"

Annoyed and confused, he took wide strides and caught her, grasping her upper arm to force her to stop. The immediate sensation of anxiety coursed along his nerves from the contact. "Is something wrong?"

Kat twisted and yanked her arm free, her eyes an unnatural blue with the worry he'd detected. "No, of course not. It's nothing."

"It doesn't seem like nothing," he said carefully.

A small amount of tension left her frame as her gaze dropped to her hands. "I just thought you trusted me more than this."

Sean looked at her, contemplating her unusual reaction and the way she averted his stare, and knew without a doubt, there was more she wasn't saying. However, he didn't have the right to ask anymore of her. "I do trust you," he admitted.

He took her chin in his hand and made her meet his stare. The anxiety and worry from earlier tingled along his senses from her again. Yes, there was something she didn't want him to know. So, he added, "And maybe someday soon, you can trust me, too."

Katria's heart raced as Sean headed back to the library, hands fisted at his side.

How had he known?

Because that was his Gen-Heir ability. He could read people. That included her omission. He hadn't said another word to her, likely perceiving she'd remain silent. Guilt nagged at her. She pressed a hand to her stomach to ease the discomfort.

She could have told him then and there, should have laid it all out. Who cared about their team waiting for them? If she wanted a marriage, she had to trust her husband. But fear had taken over, and then frustration had set in at her weakness. She'd shut down when she should have been honest.

Overwhelmed by the emotional day, she retreated to her bedroom. No one would miss her now anyway. Sean had already walked in alone and likely hadn't expected her to follow.

In her room, she sat on the edge of her bed, staring at her hands. She should tell Sean about her name. About her father. About her past. How hard could it be to say *I'm Katria Nachemir. Katerina Nachesa doesn't exist. She never did.*

If she found speaking the words too difficult, all she'd have to do is find their marriage contract and place it somewhere easily visible in his room. He'd see her name this time. She wouldn't even have to say anything. But then he'd know, and suddenly his knowing the truth of her identity had her chest constricting and her breath faltering.

From the beginning, her identity had been false. Why? Who needed her name to be kept a secret? And was it for her protection, or his?

In the world we come from, reputations are everything.

Kevin's words echoed in her mind, and the pressure in her chest increased until a sharp pain splintered through her ribs. Gasping, she leaned forward and tried to catch her breath, bracing her hands on the bed beside her. She closed her eyes and focused on her heartbeat, centering her thoughts. She did not panic. Ever.

Hopefully, they'd soon return to regular assignments, and this marriage business would be behind them. But the memory of his lips on hers, of his skin beneath her hands swept into her mind and Katria knew there was no going back to how things used to be. And if she were honest, she didn't want them to. Of course, that would require her to be *truthful*.

Maybe once away from Haven City, she could be when the concern for his reputation and family name wasn't so important anymore. Perhaps by then she'd also know more about what happened to her mother and sister. She wouldn't have to worry about whether it was from her father's identity or what he'd done in the past. Or if it turned out to be precisely that, how could she avoid the same fate?

Settled by the thought process, she took a deep breath. The tightness of anxiety finally subsided. Now to figure out how she was supposed to be a wife... for real. Or if that was even what her husband desired.

❧ 15 ❧

"Y ou're sure we have to attend this?" Katria asked, yanking the royal blue satin of her gown away from the door before the carriageman closed them in. She brushed her fingers along the heavy sapphire and diamond necklace draped over her collarbone. The elegant piece featured three layers of rich blue stones, surrounded by smaller diamonds. Sean had insisted on something more adorning for the gathering than a simple drop pendant. Knowing she wore a fortune around her throat didn't help the edgy sensation grating her nerves.

"Yes, we have to go," Sean stated firmly, his attention out the window. "Our host is an arch guardian. One does not simply ignore the request of an arch guardian."

She flexed her jaw. "I don't care what an arch guardian thinks."

That brought his attention to her, something which had been lacking since their little fight a week ago. Katria hated to admit the weakness, but she'd found she missed him.

"I'd keep that to yourself."

Frowning, she had a sudden urge to kick his shin. She should keep that to herself as well. His out-of-character detachment had her more on edge than the impending social engagement did. When the silence continued to stretch as the carriage bounced down one brick road after another, Katria couldn't help but glare in the darkness.

"You can't stay mad at me forever," she said. A week since her conversation with Jonathon hadn't improved either of their moods. Not that they'd had a chance to talk about it, since Sean had been busy and mostly absent.

"I'm not mad at you." The curtness of his tone implied otherwise. She wished she could see his face. He heaved a heavy sigh. "I *am* frustrated. But not with you. It's been almost two weeks now and not a damn word from the FIO. Nor have we gotten any closer to learning why we've been called home in the first place."

"Well, we haven't been released. Someone has to say or do something at some point."

"I don't think we want them to *do* anything."

She grimaced. "That's true, likely wouldn't end well for us."

A sudden brightness outside the windows drew Katria's attention. She leaned forward. Short lamps lit a winding drive beyond a looming wrought iron fence. Katria gasped at the imposing three-story granite house at the end. Two round towers rose against a dark sky. Steep slants created an imposing roofline. The mansion was masculine in design, characterized by hard angles and a bleak gray and black palette. The architect designed the building to show-case its owner's power.

A line of carriages moved along with quick ease, making it apparent someone directed the flow to keep things organized. When their turn arrived, a footman in green livery opened the door, his black gloved hand propped up to accept hers. He didn't even look at her as she stepped out, his frame straight and professional. Once Sean was clear of the door, the employee closed it and then motioned for the following vehicle, a sleek black ariot, to pull forward, directing their carriage to drive away.

"Efficient." Katria continued to watch the quick succession of guests vacate their rides.

Sean leaned close. "Would you expect anything less from the guardian of special teams?"

Surprised, Katria's attention snapped to him. "Our top superior? This is *his* house?"

"Yes." He angled his body and motioned towards the dark street. "And the other five arch guardians live on this street as well. Welcome to the Arch District."

Butterflies danced in her stomach. "Have you ever been invited here before?"

"I haven't been home enough to be invited to much of anything since I was endowed with my guardian rank."

A sudden thought occurred to Katria, and she touched his arm. She moved off to the side, away from prying ears, and Sean followed. "We could ask him, surely he'd know the reason we're in Haven City."

Sean shook his head, frowning. "No, we can't ask him anything."

"Why not?"

"Chain of command, we have to go through Voklane, who then has to go through his superior." He rubbed the back of his neck. "Kevin could ask, but he won't."

Confused, Katria drew her brows together. "Why could Kevin ask?"

"He's married to Arch Guardian Synintel's daughter."

"I see." Kevin's words about his obligatory marriage

came back to her. Was the relationship with his father-in-law a tense one?

"If there's a reason he invited us, other than as a professional courtesy, we'll find out soon enough."

Wishing they'd stayed home now, Katria looped her hand through Sean's offered arm and pasted on a smile as he escorted her inside. The entrance hall teemed with overflow from the sprawling ballroom, separated from the hall by broad, two-story arches. Intense laughter radiated from a large game room to the right. Katria leaned forward and peered through the wide doorway. A group had gathered around a card table. Two men slammed their hands on the surface in amusement, while another tossed his cards to the side.

The atmosphere was amiable, inviting. Not what she'd expect from a man in such a powerful position. Attendants weaved through the crowd, carrying silver platters with flutes of various colored liquids. Guests simply reached out and took what they wanted without a word spoken. Gentle, lively music radiated from the ballroom. Glittering chandeliers immersed the crowd below in warm light. The host had arranged a buffet of cold meat, cheese, fruit, cakes, pies, and bread beside the game room. There was no dancing. Everyone mingled, spoke in groups, played games, or partook of the food.

"This is very nice," she commented, taking it all in.

"Yes, no announcers, no attention on anyone specific."

Katria glanced up at him, noting a hint of frustration on his handsome face. "Does that worry you?"

His expression relaxed. "No, I don't mind not being the center of attention one bit."

With their arms still linked together, Sean led her around, politely nodding and commenting to others as they passed by. Katria disliked the superficial kindness everyone seemed inclined to show, including herself. The gathering seemed like one large acting game. Smile this way, comment that way, be pleasing to the eyes, and the ears. While it was only her second event, Katria didn't know how much longer she could pretend to be *civilized* for these people.

Sean took them to a more secluded corner near the terrace, which led to the greenhouse gardens. He leaned down and whispered in her ear, "Don't wander outside this time."

When she turned to meet his stare, he didn't back away, leaving them close enough together that if she stood on her tiptoes, her mouth would meet his. The temptation made her lick her lips. "Are you leaving me alone again?"

"No, I don't plan to. But if for some reason I do..."

"I promise, I'll stay inside."

For a brief moment, his forehead touched hers. "Thank you."

Katria ignored the sudden thump of her heart and nodded. They made a few more rounds of niceties and watched a game of dominoes after she admitted she had no idea how to play the ancient game. Sean had been surprised, but not disappointed. Once again, Katria felt entirely out of her league. Who didn't know how to play games? Especially ones that had been around for over a thousand years?

After what seemed like hours, but had probably been closer to one, Katria asked, "When can we leave?"

Sean looked around the room. "I don't think anyone will miss us."

"I don't think they would have missed us if we hadn't shown up," she grumbled under her breath.

He cast her a sideways glance. She blushed, but he remained silent. They'd passed the ballroom arches into the entry hall when a footman dressed in a rich green uniform with large silver buttons down the front stepped into their path.

"Primary Guardian Wintersfall, Arch Guardian Synintel needs a word before you leave."

"Of course he does," Sean growled out. "Show me the way." He turned and grasped her hands. "I'll be right back. Do not leave the inside of this house."

"You already told me that."

He fixed her with a playful stare. "You're stubborn."

"I promised."

He released her hands and followed behind the attendant. Katria melted into a nearby shadow and watched the door close on the other side of a sweeping curved staircase. Maybe now they'd finally get some much-needed answers.

Arch Guardian Synintel stood with his hands clasped behind his back before a window overlooking the drive, which still teemed with activity. The weak light in the room illuminated the faint gray streaks in his otherwise dark brown hair. The pale silvery gray of his formal attire did little to soften the man's rigid stance. Even though Sean couldn't see his face, he figured the man's expression was as severe.

"Where is my son-in-law?" Synintel inquired without turning.

Sean stopped halfway into the room. The tricky question caught him unprepared. "I'm not sure what you mean."

With a less than warm smile, Synintel turned, his hands still clasped. His light brown eyes fixed Sean with a sharp stare. "I understand we've bred into you men to be fiercely loyal to each other, but as your superior and as an outranking guardian, I'm asking you again, where is Raiventon?"

While Sean didn't mind taking orders from the man on a slip of paper, being intimidated was another matter entirely. And since Kevin had made no effort to see his father-in-law, boss or not, Sean wasn't going to betray his friend's wishes. Easing into a relaxed posture, he shrugged his shoulders. "I really don't know. The last time I saw him was in Voklane's office. Maybe you should ask your lackey. Voklane seems to enjoy keeping secrets."

Synintel strode up to him and snapped, "Do not make the mistake of making an enemy of me."

Knowing he had to tread lightly, Sean remained composed. "I wouldn't dare make you an enemy. I can't give you an answer; I don't have one. Master Guardianess Raiventon is more likely to know his whereabouts than I am."

"He has made no effort to contact my daughter since the team's arrival."

"Really? I'm not sure what to say to that." Sean made a show of thinking, scratching his chin and jaw. "Is he in some sort of trouble?"

"If he doesn't report to either my office or Voklane's, he will be."

"But he isn't now?"

Synintel took a long breath and pressed steepled fingers to his mouth in a rare show of patience. "Look. I've already said I'm willing to overlook your loyalty to a team member over your superior. I need to know where Kevin Merrick is, and I need to know now. It's not a matter of his being in trouble, it's..." He took another deep breath. "Personal."

Sean raised a brow. Well, now, wasn't this interesting? And here Sean had always figured Synintel did everything in his power to keep his daughter and son-in-law apart. Sean wasn't even sure Kevin could tell him what Lorraina's eye color was if he asked. "Personal, sir?" He then cleared his throat. "Perhaps if I *do* see him, I can deliver a message for you."

A sigh of exasperation escaped Synintel. He rubbed his thumb between his pinched brows. "Besides arriving at my door? I think I've made my need for his physical appearance pretty clear."

"Yes, sir. Anything else?"

For a second, Sean didn't think the man was going to answer. Then on another long-suffering sigh, he said, "When I married Raiventon to my daughter, I expected him to be a husband when he's home. His place is at her side."

Sean raised both brows now. While Sean had no way of knowing how often Kevin had been allowed to venture home in the five years he'd been married, he guessed not often, since where Sean was, so was Kevin. His skill set was vital to most successful missions. Synintel's outrage was a joke. Like the rest of them, Kevin didn't even get vacation time to come home to visit.

Sean wanted to ask why the desperation to have Kevin, who had been married to the arch guardian's daughter, was needed *now*. Then again, maybe this was simply a case of fatherly outrage. Perhaps Lorraina had complained to Daddy Dearest about her husband's neglect. Either way, something that hadn't mattered for the past five years suddenly did.

"I see," Sean somehow managed with a neutral expression. "If we somehow manage to cross paths, I'll be sure to convey your... messages."

The older gentleman narrowed his intense, raptor-like stare on Sean and stepped back, looking him over. Sean didn't flinch. "I knew I chose a good leader in you, I just didn't realize how damn good. *When* you see him next, not *if*."

Synintel didn't give Sean the chance to reply, stalking past him and slamming the door in his wake.

Sean let out a pent-up breath. "You owe me big time, Kevin."

When the door opened again, he prepared for round two. But when he turned, he couldn't keep the shock from registering on his face. "Ms. Milbourne."

Carlie pressed her body against the door to close it, her dark eyes taking him in. "I have waited all night to get you alone. I never thought that clingy wife of yours would leave your side long enough." She sauntered across the room, dropping her satiny pink gloves, cream knit shawl, and pulling the sleeves of her puffy fuchsia gown down her shoulders. The small charms in her hair twinkled and flashed in the low light.

Before he could protest, she was on him, her fingers pressed to his cheeks, her lips capturing his. The force of her lust slammed through him in a torrent of demand, making his mind reel. The fullness of her breasts crushed against his chest as her hips fit against his. He grabbed her shoulders and tore his mouth free, pushing her away, breaking the physical contact she had with him.

"What are you doing?" he asked, keeping hold of her upper arms to maintain distance between them.

Desire clouded her dark brown eyes, her gaze focused on his lips. "I've missed you, and I know you've missed me too. You never went a night home without sending me word. I figured—"

"I'm married."

A coy smile turned her lips. "Oh, come now, since when has that stopped anyone?" He let his hold weaken a second too long as she slipped back against his body, her mouth taking his earlobe between her teeth before she whispered, "You're the only man who's ever been able to satisfy me."

Sean closed his eyes at her warm breath and the memory of their long nights together. Weeks of sleeping near a woman he couldn't touch, mere feet away, had his nerves on edge. Carlie would be a welcome reprieve. But, as he pulled back and looked at her face again, she wasn't the one he wanted to see under him. Her eyes weren't the ones he wanted to see full of hunger for him.

Taking her hands, he steeled himself against the strong force of her yearning seeping through his skin and stepped back. "I'm sorry. I'm not that man anymore."

Sean realized he meant the words the moment he'd spoken them. Kat had changed something in him, making him want to be the man she saw, not the one everyone else perceived him to be.

Anger flashed across her face, splotching her neck and chest in ugly red. "Not that man anymore? Were you only *that man* when *you* needed something from me? If that's the case, then I'm calling in my favors."

She launched herself at him, and out of reflex, Sean twisted. Carlie sailed to the floor, landing hard at his feet with a heavy thud. A cry of distress escaped from her. For a second, Sean almost decided to leave her lying there. But that would be cruel, and cruel he was not.

Lowering to his hunches, he helped her rise to her knees. "Are you okay?"

She sniffled. "I'd be better if we were down here together."

Sean sighed and stood without helping her further. He made his way toward the door. "Goodbye, Ms. Milbourne."

The fabric of her dress rustled as she hurried to rise. "Wait, please!"

Against his better judgment, he paused, hands clenched at his side. "What?"

"I'm sorry, I am. I just... I'm not very good on my own, you know? I had so much hope in your return. I'm still really confused about your marriage." She grabbed his hand and pulled it to her chest. Gone was the lust, desperation, and anxiety curled into him from the contact. "You'd sworn never to marry, and I believed you."

"People change."

Tears welled in her eyes, and she nodded, stepping close enough to hug his forearm. "Yes, I know, I always hoped that, well—"

The study door opened. The bright light of the entry hall flooded in a perfect line straight to them. A slender, tense womanly form shadowed the door. An unspoken curse formed in Sean's throat, and he eased his arm free of its female captor. Kat's hand slid down the door as she strode into the room. As she neared, the intense cerulean of her eyes focused on Carlie.

"Kat," Sean said in a low warning.

She held up her hand near his face, stopping before the woman. "Ms. Milbourne, I see you think my husband still belongs to you."

Carlie's shoulders straightened. "He was mine long before he was yours."

Sean wondered when exactly he'd become property.

"I see." A weak, shallow smile graced Kat's full lips. She lowered her hand and slid a low, dangerous glance to him. "Sean, why don't you explain to this woman that I am not the one to cross."

"I'll do better." He pulled his wife into his arms. His mouth found hers in a possessive kiss, and she didn't hesitate to let his tongue slide past her lips, her eyes closing. Everything about this woman drove him crazy. Deepening the embrace, he molded her frame to his, his mouth slanting over hers as his tongue toyed inside her mouth. When he broke the kiss, her gaze fluttered to his. Keeping her stare, he stated with complete honesty, "My wife is the only woman I want."

On a whiny huff, Carlie stalked past them, leaving her discarded trail of items on the floor. Charms tinkered and clashed in her dramatic wake.

Breathing ragged, Kat's hands pressed to his chest. "Why did you say that?"

Sean clenched his jaw, a desire he'd never felt for Carlie or anyone else raging inside for the woman in his arms. But he couldn't let her know. At some point, reality would dawn on her of the hard life she'd be in for as his wife. Slowly, he put distance between them. "She wouldn't listen to anything else."

A flicker of hurt crossed over her beautiful face, her hands falling to her side. "Oh."

Sean hated the lie, hated the pain he knew he caused. Even when he wasn't trying, his family's nature seemed to seep through. "Kat, I'm..."

She shook her head and turned from him. "It's okay, I understand. We can talk about what Synintel said on the way home. I just want to leave."

Katria stared out the carriage window, fighting the sting of tears, hating the emotional turmoil raging within her. They hadn't said one word to each other since leaving, and unlike on the way to the event, she didn't want to speak to her husband. Everything was a show for him, a means of keeping their cover intact. At what point would she realize that she'd never have his?

From her vantage point near the stairs, she'd observed Arch Guardian Synintel leave. The scowl on his strong face and clenched fists at his side told Katria her husband had not been compliant. She'd been about to cross the distance to the study when Ms. Milbourne beat her to it, entering the room so fast she'd been nothing more than a blur of fuchsia and cream fabric.

Then the conversation war within her mind had started.

Katria had no claim to Sean. At no point had either of them agreed to, or stated a desire, to have their marriage be anything more than a façade.

Yet a strange churning sensation developed in her

stomach as she imagined the woman's hands on Sean. Imagined him kissing Carlie the way he'd kissed her. Touching Ms. Milbourne the way he wouldn't touch her. A cloud of jealous rage settled over her, and before she could stop herself, she was at the door, pushing it open. And in her far too active imagination, the shot if she'd had a pistol would have been too easy.

Sean, however, seemed to know just how to diffuse her, taking her in his arms and kissing the reason back into her. Right now, she almost hated him for it. Almost. Because Katria knew if he'd said anything other than, "*She wouldn't listen to anything else,*" she'd love him.

Groaning at the memory, she sank low in her seat. Her head dropped against the wooden wall behind her. Who was she kidding? Even after his cutting words, she couldn't deny her heart was a lost cause. The best hope she had now was that he'd continue to leave her alone as he'd done the past week.

The carriage came to a sudden, lurching stop. Katria gasped, bracing one hand on the ceiling and the other on the seat beside her. Her hair rushed over her shoulders and around her face. Sean's booted foot slammed into the edge of the seat, next to her thigh, keeping him from hurtling across the distance and into her lap.

He turned his head towards the small panel in the back used to speak with the driver. "What th—"

Cold air rushed in, and before she could even turn to see who had opened the door. A firm hand grabbed her right upper arm while another seized her right ankle. With a swift yank, an unknown assailant pulled her from the carriage by her limbs before she could even scream in protest. Her unrestricted foot caught on the short stair. Her balance already uneven, she tumbled to the ground. Hard brick connected with her hip, and she cried out. Her captors didn't seem to care, dragging her toward a dark alley.

Kicking, she freed her captive leg, but they seemed ready for that, grabbing her left arm and moving faster. The moment she was clear of the carriage and past the threshold of the alley, three men jumped inside the vehicle. Katria's breath lurched in her throat. She struggled, trying to gain a foothold on the icy brick beneath her feet.

"We have to be quick," a deep voice growled to her left.

"I know," the other man to her right bit out.

Terror was not an emotion Katria was prone to. *Panicking only dulls your senses, making you miss things*, Kevin's voice stated in her mind, echoing from years of training sessions. She had to observe. Look for an opportunity. Trying to calm her racing heart, she repeated his words over and over. The duo dragged her past a stack of crates, deep into the shadows that no one walking or driving past would be able to see beyond.

One man finally released her, and Katria grabbed the smaller crate, crashing it into his face. He grasped at his eyes on a cry of surprise as splinters and small staples flew everywhere. A piece of jagged wood remained in her hand, and she slashed at her other captor. He was quicker than his friend, however, and he dodged her swipe. Grabbing her neck, he slammed her up against the wall. Pain burst in her back and ached in her throat. Heightened adrenaline levels made her lungs demand air. Katria tried to remain calm, but her assailant squeezed until instinct won out and she dropped the wood. Her hands flew to his wrist in a feeble attempt to make him lessen his hold.

"You're a pretty one. I don't usually get pretty ones." He leered. "Too bad it's so dark."

Except, she wasn't just a pretty face. Time for a different strategy.

Lifting her knee, she sent it into his groin. He howled and stumbled away from her. A deep cough racked her sore throat as her lungs filled with precious air, but she didn't allow herself to linger in the relief, shoving off the wall. The door to the carriage banged against the side and a man flew out, landing on the ground, unconscious. If she made it back to Sean, then what would happen? Opponents outnumbered them, and she carried no weapon. However, they would be stronger together. She did a quick survey of the man on the ground as she bolted for the carriage, and noted they weren't carrying guns either, likely having decided they were too loud.

A heavy object slammed into her back, and she went sprawling on the ground, her palms sliding along the uneven brick. Tiny bits of debris and rock fragments bit into her skin. Weight landed on her torso, pinning her down. Fingers tangled in her hair and yanked her back and up. She cried out as pain radiated from her scalp.

"Not so fast, pretty. We aren't finished yet." His hot breath coursed across her cheek, and she shuddered.

A set of arms wrapped around her, locking hers in place, making her kicking legs useless for much else than trying to slow their progress back into the alley. The other man kept a firm hold on her hair, meaning his buddy had come back, too. Finally, the pressure on her scalp released. Katria's head snapped forward, her hair flowing around her face, blocking her view.

The man holding her spun them around to face his partner, his arms still banding around her chest. "Take care of it now!"

"But..."

Her captor shoved her forward. "No buts, we aren't being paid for nothing else!"

On a stumble, she reached forward to brace herself. A sharp, slicing pain spread across her left side. She struggled to take in a breath as she sank to her knees.

"Get the goods and let's go!"

Fingers clawed at her chest. A hard yank forced her forward. The catch on the sapphire necklace snapped. Booted feet retreated down the alley. When she realized she *couldn't* take in a deep breath without seeing stars, she dropped her weight on her left hand, her right rising to the fire in her side. Wet-hot warmth covered her fingers and flowed over her palm. The only thing she could think before the panic took over was, *I can't go through this again!*

Sean landed a solid punch in one man's gut, while the other attempted to block his exit by any means necessary. That's all they'd done, just stood in the doorways, keeping him from leaving. He'd managed to get a solid kick to one in the head, but someone new had been right there to take his place. Punching the second man blocking the door in rapid succession in the ribs, depriving him of air, Sean sent his palm sailing into the center of the man's chest, who flew back, joining his friend on the ground, coughing and gagging. With a swift back kick, Sean sent the third one crashing through the street-side door.

At once, he had a clear view of the alley, and he leapt from the carriage. In the deep shadows, he barely made out Kat's hunched form making no effort to rise.

"Kat!"

She stirred, but only enough to sit back. Her palm lay face up. The glistening, black shadow covering her pale skin made his stride slow. *No... oh no.*

He fell to his knees beside her, grasping her hand. "Where?"

Her eyes fluttered closed. She wavered. Her breathing was harsh, too erratic.

Sean gathered her against his chest and stood, careful to shift her weight evenly. He took long, purposeful strides, giving the man who still struggled to rise from the beating a swift kick to the head as he strode past. The other man who'd landed on the road was gone.

Gradually, he laid her on the floor of the carriage. On her back with the gas light feet from them, he could see the dark red bloom covering the entire left side of her gown. Grasping the torn fabric, he ripped it further, exposing the deep, angry gash in her side. Touching her hot skin, he probed. She writhed under his touch, and he clenched his teeth.

"I'm sorry, my love, I am." He continued to examine the wound. "Take a deep breath for me."

"I-I can't," she gasped, her bloody hand sliding down his wrist when she tried to grasp it to get him to stop. Fear, anxiety, and panic slithered through his muscles and made his teeth clench.

If he weren't careful, her emotions would drag him under in a tide of his own panic, and he'd be useless. "You can, you have to."

In shallow pants, her chest rose and fell. Blood poured from the wound. He shook his head. "No, you have to do better than that. Just one deep breath for me, come on, Kat."

Her hand tightened around his wrist. He blocked the increased push of her emotional chaos. With an effort that he knew cost her greatly, she filled her lungs with air. A fresh wave of crimson trickled from the gash. A sigh of relief almost had him collapsing next to her. The blood was free of froth or bubbles. They hadn't punctured her lung. After pushing her feet the rest of the way into the carriage, he lifted the top of the seat and pulled out a blanket. He draped the soft covering over her trembling body.

Taking her hand, he pressed it firmly against her wound. "Hold this here, I know it hurts, but it'll slow the bleeding. We aren't far from the house."

Sean closed the doors and then jumped into the driver's seat. His carriageman lay slumped, unconscious, a small knot forming at his temple. After checking and finding a strong pulse in the man's neck, Sean pushed him out of the way. That he was alive was enough; he'd have to deal with the rest later. He had to get Kat home and stop the bleeding.

Sean's educational focus had been in medical science. As a Sympath, he was uniquely qualified to deliver compassionate medical care, and before his primary rank endowment, had planned to work for Health Services, earning his medical science officer certification. But then he'd been made a team leader, and his medical instruction had come in handy. They couldn't risk taking wounds to hospitals, and providing Sean had all the necessary equipment, he could fix any injury.

Urging the horses into a gallop, he took the ride home a little more recklessly than he meant to. Being unable to check on Kat, hear her voice, and know she was okay left him anxious. When he arrived at the house, he parked the carriage in the carriage house himself. He unhooked the horses and met the stable boy halfway to the stables. After handing them off and telling the boy to make sure the driver was okay, he ran to his wife.

She lay trembling under the blanket, but conscious.

Sean lifted her into his arms, wincing at her cry of pain. The door opened for him, and he was about to have some fly-by excuse for Davis, but it was Kevin on the other side. Grateful, he didn't bother to ask why his friend was waiting at his house after midnight.

"She's been stabbed. Dining room."

Kevin bolted into action. "How did it happen?"

"We were ambushed on the way home. Her necklace is missing. Might have just been a robbery."

A dark frown crossed Kevin's face. "Or made to look like one. Does your staff live in the house?"

Sean had the same sentiment, but there wasn't time to consider the details at the moment. "No, except for Davis, but he's on the third floor."

Kat's slender frame trembled in a heavy shake. Kevin collected the plates and silverware into neat stacks. Sean huffed in annoyance. "Just shove it all to the side!"

Dishes and silverware clanked as Sean laid Kat on the wide surface. Her fingers gripped the edge of the table, her eyes shut tight in pain. The heavy shadows in the room prevented him from getting a decent look at the wound.

"I need more light."

He and Kevin went to work lighting all the candles. Kevin climbed onto the table, one foot braced on each side of Kat's bent legs, and lit the chandelier.

"Better?" Kevin asked, hopping down.

"Better."

Sean tore the gown further to examine how far the cut went. "They hit her rib. Had they not, it would have gone clean in."

Kevin leaned over with a low curse. "She wouldn't have survived that."

Sean shook his head, grasping her shoulder as she went to twist away from him. "Going for the heart." He met

Kevin's stare and straightened. "I'll be right back, I have to get my kit. Will you get some water, clear shine, and towels from the kitchen? It's just through there."

Kevin nodded, and Sean headed to his room. Upstairs, he found his medical kit and removed the necessary items. Tools in hand, he returned to the dining room to find Kevin neatly arranging everything near Kat's right side. Sean grabbed a chair and sat.

Knowing the routine, Kevin began to hand him the things he called for. Within moments, he had the dried blood cleaned away. Blood pooled on the table and dripped in heavy splats to the hardwood below. Sean frowned. Hers wasn't the first puddle of blood to grace his floors.

After threading the curved suture needle, he set it on a towel and stood, leaning over her. He smoothed her hair back from her forehead and waited until she opened her eyes. "I have to close the cut now, it's going to hurt, but it'll be over as quickly as I can, okay?"

Something dark flickered in her brilliant blue eyes. With a force he didn't know she possessed, she flew upward. She shoved at his chest and made to stand. Sean grabbed her wrists and pinned them to her chest. Twisting side to side, she fought to get free of his hold. The color had begun to seep from her skin, and he knew if he didn't close the wound, her blood loss would be too significant.

"You will *not* use anything on me!" she screamed at the top of her lungs. "I won't go through it again. I can't! Let me go!"

A low growl escaped her throat. Sean pushed the full strength of his upper body into hers, laying her out on the table. Warm, wet heat soaked his shirt, and his heart skipped a beat. She arched against him with a snarling cry, her feet kicking the table's surface.

"Kevin!" Sean roared.

Kevin moved with a swift, barely discernible motion, his hand at Kat's neck. A second later, she lay limp under him. Breathing heavily, Sean straightened and took in her now peaceful form.

"How long will she be out?"

Kevin shrugged. "It's different for everyone."

Sitting back down, Sean took hold of a pair of scissors and cut a larger section of her gown across her belly and under her as far as he could go, careful to keep her breasts hidden as the fabric fell away. "What in the arctic was that reaction for?"

Kevin didn't have a response to Sean's rhetorical question. Pulling the material away and down to her hip, Sean took in a sharp intake of air at what they saw.

"She's been shot before," Kevin whispered.

Sean touched a finger to the pale, round scar just above her left hip. Lifting her slightly, he eased her over enough to see where it exited. Only a thin scar near her spine was visible.

A hissed curse escaped Kevin. "She must have been awake when they removed the bullet."

"And stitched her up," Sean guessed with a grim frown. He gently returned her to her position. "Let's not repeat the event for her. Hand me the shine."

Quickly and methodically, Sean set to work, compartmentalizing away that he was working on his wife. Focusing only on the wound and the need to close in the lifeblood seeping out. Minutes later, a neat, long row of stitches curved along her side. He smoothed a thick cream on. Kevin helped wrap a tight bandage around her midsection.

Sean lifted her off the table. He had to work to get her limp frame in a comfortable enough position to carry. He laid her on her bed. In his room, he grabbed a comfortable cotton shirt for her. Bits of dirt, mud, and likely stuff he didn't want to contemplate stained the bottom and front of her now ruined ball gown.

Shifting her slack form gently more onto her stomach than her back, he removed the cut top half of the gown and eased the shirt onto her, completely covering her before rolling her over and removing the skirt portion. He situated her under the blankets.

For a second, he stared at her beautiful face, pale from her ordeal. A knot formed in his chest. Tenderly, he grazed his knuckles across her forehead and down her cheek, pushing wayward strands of her midnight hair to the side. He leaned over and touched his lips to hers in a tender kiss.

Before he stood, to ease his frazzled mind, he touched two fingers to her throat. Relief flowed through him at the steady pulse under his touch. Leaving her door open, he headed back downstairs. Kevin was cleaning up, a bowl with bloody towels in the center of the table. He stopped when Sean entered the room.

"What brought you here tonight?" Sean asked, stretching his neck to one side to ease the tension that had been building up.

Kevin wiped smudges of blood off his hands with a clean, damp towel. "I found something. But it can wait until tomorrow."

Sean shook his head. "She'll be asleep for hours, if not all night."

Kevin raised a skeptical brow.

Sean chuckled. They'd both been through a knife wound, or eight, in their time of service. The first couple of nights were always the hardest. "Okay, maybe not all night, but likely at least a few hours."

Kevin went to the library, and Sean followed. He

retrieved a file from a small table beside the door. "I went to Voklane's office like we talked about, searched through our files and discovered a notation on Kat's information page. A small file number scribbled in the corner. Mason was able to get me a layout of the warehouse location in the records district."

Sean raised his brows. "That couldn't have been an easy task."

"It took me a solid week to search that warehouse for the correct section and row," Kevin stated with an annoyed frown. "Anyway, I did find the file."

"And?"

Frown still in place, Kevin flipped it around to him. "And I have no idea what to make of it."

Sean accepted the file and then wandered back to the dining room for better light. He flipped it open, scanning a well-organized table of information. "Christopher Survaine, Anabel Hollins, Edwin Wisnik, Aleksandrov Nachemir, Henry Castien, Mark Plewright... these are all top assassins in the last fifty years."

"There are twenty-five of them on the list."

Sean continued to review the data. "And their known children?"

"With birthdates and last known locations. Someone compiled the list in eight-twenty-seven."

And all the names were crossed out except for three. Christopher Survaine, Alexandrov Nachemir, and Henry Castien. "Survaine has a son listed, Caidon, and Nachemir has two daughters, Katria and Anyka. Anyka's has been crossed out. Henry Castien has two children on the list, a daughter and son, Lucianna, and Joshua. Both have question marks next to their names." Kevin crossed his arms over his chest, his frown deepening. "Has Kat said anything about her family?"

Sean's attention focused on Katria Nachemir. "No, just that she grew up outside of Old Helston."

Kevin accepted the file back from Sean. "Nachemir, Old Helston. Maybe it's time to find out about her family."

❧ 17 ❧

Searing pain tore Katria from unconsciousness. With a hiss, she pulled herself up against the headboard, the action leaving her breathless and fighting nausea. She tried to remember what happened, and how she had managed to get into her bed, but the night was a blur after the carriage ride home.

"Here," Sean's deep, tender voice began, "take a sip."

Too exhausted to do much more than turn her head, she glanced in his direction. He held a glass of water. Carefully, he helped her take a drink. The cold liquid glided down her throat, and she collapsed against the soft mound of pillows.

"Thank you," she managed to croak out. "What happened?"

He made her take another slow, but long drink before he answered. "You panicked. We had to make a quick decision about what to do, so Kevin rendered you unconscious."

Katria winced as another deep throb pounded in her skull. "Is that why my head hurts so badly?"

"No." He kept the glass at her mouth until she sipped again. "That would be from blood loss."

He set the glass down on the nightstand and settled back into a chair beside her bed. She drew her brows together.

"Have you been there all night?"

"It's only been two hours."

Katria glanced around the dark room. Only the soft glow of the fire provided any light. Her eyes fluttered closed as exhaustion once again threatened to claim her. "Oh. For that long then?"

"Yes."

"Why?"

"Because I was worried about you. And because I thought I could wait, but I can't. I have to ask you something."

Curious, Katria rolled her head to the side and met his shadowed stare. "What?"

He scooted to the edge of the chair, his hands clasping between his knees. "Kat..." He sighed. His head dropped, his pale brown hair falling over his forehead. "Please don't lie to me."

Katria's heart began to race. Why would he ask that? "W-why would I lie to you?"

"I don't know," he whispered. His gaze lifted again to meet hers. "But I'm asking you now not to."

"Okay." Suddenly, sleep was the last thing on her mind.

"Kevin found a notation in your file, and when he retrieved the information, it was a list of the top known assassins in the world."

On top of her now rapid pulse, her breathing became heavier. She wasn't ready for this. Her hands fisted in the sheets.

Sean continued. "There were only three names left

uncrossed, along with four known children. Caidon Survaine, Katria Nachemir, and Lucianna and Joshua Castien."

The sting of tears burned behind her eyes. For three years, she'd waited to hear her name from his lips. She closed her eyes and took a deep breath, regaining her composure.

"Is your father Alexandrov?"

"Yes," she confessed on a mere whisper, her eyes still closed.

"Was he the reason for the old bullet wound you have?"

In the two hours she'd been unconscious, Sean had discovered every secret she'd ever kept from him. Some nap.

"I don't know. Voklane recruited me by saying he'd have the murder of my mother and sister, and my attempted murder, investigated."

"That's what you were talking to Asherwick about last week?"

Another splitting pain tore through her head, and she winced, bringing her arm up to her forehead. "Yes."

Sean helped her rise and take another drink. "You need to finish the water before you fall asleep again."

She didn't know how she'd possibly fall asleep now. He propped pillows up behind her and eased her back. That's when she noticed she was wearing a soft, cotton, short-sleeved shirt.

"Did you... change me?"

"I didn't think you wanted to sleep in a blood and garbage-covered gown, so yes, I did. Don't worry, I didn't peek. Much." He gave her one of his winks, and she flushed. "It's the most comfortable thing you could wear right now."

She didn't argue. "Thank you. For everything."

He nodded. And then he did something unexpected. He laced his fingers through hers. "Why didn't you tell me about your family? Your father?"

"I don't know. I guess I was scared about how you'd react, knowing who my father is. I know him as a good man, but most do not. Plus, I didn't know why they provided you with a false name for me. There has to be a reason, right?"

Sean brought her hand to his mouth. Her pulse quickened, but for another reason entirely. How was it possible that she sat in mortal pain, and he managed to bring fire to her veins still?

"I'm sure there is, yes. And we'll look into it. Also, when you're better, I have some things I have to tell you as well, but they can wait. You need to get some rest."

His hand pulled free of hers. Katria kept the groan of displeasure to herself. The chair scraped across the hardwood as he stood. She grabbed the edge of the sheets and pulled them into her lap, wishing he wouldn't leave her. Katria knew all she had to do was ask, and he'd likely stay by her side. But glancing at the chair he'd vacated, that wasn't the most comfortable place for him to spend the night. Her bed, however... her breath hitched in her throat. Before she could say anything, he disappeared behind his door.

Left alone in the dark silence, Katria stared at the flickering light under his door until it too faded. The dull throb in her side brought back the memory of the knife slicing into her flesh. The darkness seemed to rush in, enveloping her until she felt a scream rising in her throat.

To her terrible shame, panic, once a rare experience for her, seemed to be becoming normal. Disgusted, Katria forced the fear away. Pushing her hands into the mattress, she rose and took several, slow, deep breaths. The pain reminded her she was alive. Not dying and not bleeding to death.

Throwing her feet over the edge of the bed, she took a moment to steady herself as the room swayed around her. Sean's door was only a few steps away. Convinced she could make it, she stood. Again, she waited until her sense of balance returned. Breathing evenly, she shuffled the distance to his room and opened the door. Her heart hammered in her chest. He lay half covered, his bare back to her, deep shadows playing across the muscled plains from the low burning fire.

If fiery pain weren't radiating from her side with each pitiful step, she'd have contemplated whether his nude state continued past the sheet. Katria decided, however, that she didn't care one way or another. Since she didn't want to allow him to say no, she pulled the blankets back and eased onto the mattress beside him without a word.

"What are you doing?" he asked softly, rolling over.

"I can't be alone," she admitted, hating the crack in her voice.

To her relief, his arms encircled her shoulders, pulling her close. The warmth of his bare skin and the smoky, wickedly tempting scent of him surrounded her. His cheek dropped onto the top of her head. Katria grasped his forearms and closed her eyes, savoring the safety of his embrace. How long had she wanted to be here? Held so near every inch of him brushed against her. Years. Only now she was hurt, a slicing ache distracting her from the moment. Figured she'd get her way *after* a catastrophic event.

Sean's hold on her tightened. "I almost lost you tonight. I can't... I can't lose you."

His words were pained, desperate. Katria's heart thumped against her ribs. She shifted in his hold until she could lift her head, their forehead and noses touching.

"I'm not going anywhere," she whispered, her hand stroking down his cheek to the stubble on his jaw.

His lips touched hers in a slow, gentle kiss. Katria's stomach fluttered. She tried to roll closer to him, but he wouldn't let her, his hold softening until he splayed a hand along her uninjured hip over the blankets, holding her still. In a seductive lick, the tip of his tongue teased along the seam of her lips until she opened. His mouth moved leisurely, exploring in unhurried, tender sweeps. The composed assault built an intense need at her center, and she grabbed his wrist.

Sean pulled the sheet down her thighs. Cool air brushed across her skin. She shivered as a mixture of anticipation and nerves built deep in her belly. His arm came out from under her shoulders, and she settled onto the pillow. He pulled his mouth free, and she opened her eyes. Braced on his forearm, he looked down at her. His gaze searched hers. In the shadowed light, his irises were pools of amber. His fingers toyed with the ends of her long hair.

"What?" she asked nervously when he remained silent, simply looking her over.

"You're so beautiful."

"It's going to take two hours to get the knots out of my hair, and I have…" She felt the thick bandage wrapped around her. "Yes, I have three inches of dressing around my ribs. Beautiful is not how I feel."

He kissed her again, open-mouthed, slow, and seductive, until her toes curled into the mattress and her body tightened. "What about now?"

Little by little, her muscles relaxed when he raised his head, smoothing a tangled lock of hair from her temple, and as they did, a sharp pain stabbed at her side. She hissed and went to grab the wound, but Sean caught her wrist before she could.

"Don't, that'll just make it worse. Relax. Breathe," he instructed, easing her arm across her stomach.

Katria obeyed, squeezing her eyes shut and trying to ignore the focused heartbeat throbbing in her wound. "I hate this," she whispered.

"Me too." He tenderly pushed strands of hair from her cheek and temple. "I have you in my bed and there's not a thing I can do about it."

She opened her eyes and found him smiling through frustration. "You only allowed me here because I'm hurt and don't want to be alone."

His gaze roved over her face and lower. "No, I'm afraid you're making me too selfless. If you'd crawled into my bed on any night, I wouldn't have let you leave."

Shocked, she shifted her head on the pillow to see his face clearer in the low light. "What?"

Slowly, his fingers traced to her collarbone, where he brushed the tips of his fingers along the curves and hollows, sending curious sensations through her body that somehow lessened the pain. "You are a temptation I'm finding myself increasingly unable to resist."

Annoyance and anger flared through her and she found herself tensing all over again. The pain only added fuel to her frustration. "Stupid thieves," she hissed.

He kissed above her brow. "Indeed."

She gritted her teeth. "I would have climbed into bed with you a week ago had I known."

He chuckled faintly and then whispered, "Go to sleep, Kat."

"How am I supposed to sleep after that confession? That's not very fair."

"None of this evening has been fair," he said, caressing

her arm draped over her belly. "And you need rest, so hush, and go to sleep."

The memory of all his pulling back, of refusing to allow anything but unfulfilled passion to linger between them, had her asking in a small voice, "Do you really want me?"

His fingers pressed into her forearm and he dropped his forehead to her temple. "More than you can imagine and I want to admit."

Katria turned her head until her lips brushed his. "I can imagine a lot."

"And it's more."

"When?" she asked, suddenly desperate, wishing she knew how to ignore the hurt enough to make him show her all he had been holding back.

"When you're ready."

"Do I get to decide that, or do you?"

He cupped her jaw and forced her to meet his shadowy gaze. "Now is not the time for a discussion on important decisions. You're hurt and exhausted."

Katria disagreed, but sighed through her need to sulk. "Fine. But *I* get to decide when I'm ready."

He said nothing, just kissed her forehead again and pulled her close into the warmth of his body. Even though he acknowledged his desire to change the direction of their relationship, Katria knew the battle was far from over.

❧ 18 ❧

Bright light seared across Katria's closed eyes and she groaned. Attempting to turn away from the blinding sun, she regretted the movement as a wave of queasiness swept through her stomach, followed by a stabbing pain in her side and head. She resettled onto her back and threw her arm over her eyes.

"Oh, primary guardianess, I'm so sorry," Rebeka said, closing the door and immersing the room back into the dark. "I thought you'd be awake. Primary Guardian Wintersfall said to help you bathe and dress. I thought you were in your room, but... well... you aren't."

Feeling too terrible to care about the girl's embarrassment, or any that she should or shouldn't be having, Katria waved her comment away. "It's fine. I just need a minute."

Katria remembered the agonizing throb the morning after her gunshot wound, and the stabbing wasn't even the same caliber. If she could get through a bullet, a knife shouldn't be an issue. Controlling her breathing, she tried again, this time with Rebeka's help. Together, they managed to get her to her bathroom, cleaned up, and re-bandaged.

Rebeka didn't ask any questions, leaving Katria to believe Sean must have given some sort of explanation for her condition. On the bed, wrapped in a towel, Katria struggled with the pain and pounding in her head, feeling like a MagnaRail train had run over her.

Rebeka opened and closed every drawer in the chest with a frustrated sigh. "I don't know what to get you to wear."

The comfy cotton shirt she'd worn and the pajama pants she remembered Sean wearing came to mind. "My husband's room, his sleeping pants with a drawstring and a cotton shirt."

Rebeka's nose crinkled. "You'll be seen in that?"

Exasperated and drained of any patience before the woman even woke her up, Katria asked, "Where am I going?"

The glass of water Sean had instructed her to drink before falling asleep still sat full on the nightstand where she'd left it. Regretting not listening, she reached for it now. Rebeka returned with a pair of soft, dark blue bamboo pants and a cotton shirt three times too big for her. They both looked like a warm summer afternoon. Setting the empty glass down, Katria took the clothes from Rebeka. She slowly eased into the comfortable materials with her stylist's help. Rebeka left with a quick flourish of her skirts to tidy up the bathroom and bedrooms.

After convincing herself for a solid five minutes she wouldn't die walking down the stairs, Katria ventured to the library. Sean worked behind his desk, several ledger books open in front of him, a scattering of papers surrounding them. A platter, half full of pastries, sliced fruit, and cuts of what appeared to be ham, rested on the left corner, next to a tall porcelain cup of coffee.

The moment Sean noticed her, he sat back in his chair. A pencil flipped in his hand as his gaze followed her slow progress across the room. In a white button-up shirt and brown pants, he looked comfortable and relaxed. The morning light streamed in through the wall of windows beside his desk, making his hair appear almost golden. She had to be married to the sexiest man in all of Sziveria.

"My clothes never looked so good on someone else," he said with a sincere smile.

Katria mustered a half-smile as she rounded the desk, thankful when he tossed the pencil to the side. She climbed onto his lap and curled against his chest. She wasn't one for whining or for weakness, but he offered what she needed. Safety. "I feel like I'm dying."

He wrapped her in a warm hug and kissed the top of her head. "You aren't."

"I know." Taking easy, deep breaths, she fought the sharp, slicing fire at her side. "I didn't think I'd ever have to go through this type of pain again."

Sean's hold on her tightened. "I know, and I'm sorry."

Comfortable in his embrace, Katria relaxed into his frame, her calves and feet settling onto the chair at his thighs, her back supported by his arm and chest. She rested her head on his shoulder and took a deep breath. All night, his warm, smoky scent surrounded her.

"What did you tell Rebeka? She didn't seem at all shocked by my injury."

His fingers toyed with the end of her braid. "The truth. Thieves robbed us and you were hurt."

The memory of the violent yank of jewels tearing from her neck had her hand flying to her throat. "Your necklace! Oh no, I'd forgotten they'd taken it."

"Your health and safety were more important. It's just jewelry."

With a sigh, she dropped her hand. "Do you think that's what it was? A robbery?"

"I'm not sure, could be. We left the party early, and anyone watching for an opportunity could have considered us a good target. That doesn't answer the question, though, why attempt to kill you?"

Shocked, Katria met his somber amber gaze. "Kill me?"

His fingers caressed up and down her arm, and Katria's focus began to slip. "Had the blade not ricocheted off your ribcage, it would have gone through the bones and into your heart. It's a hard strike to make correctly. You're fortunate they didn't know how to do it the right way."

A shudder wracked through her. Sadly, it wasn't from the growing desire her husband was building inside with a simple touch. "I remember them saying they weren't getting paid to do anything else."

"And then they took the necklace?"

She nodded. "Yes, after they stabbed me, one man told the other to *get the goods*."

Sean's hand had gone from absently rubbing her arm to caressing down her back, careful to keep clear of her injured side. Katria closed her eyes, wondering if this moment was what it felt like to be loved. If so, count her finished and in for the long haul.

"I have to admit, that sounds like a robbery. But the men didn't do anything to me."

"Maybe they didn't get the chance."

His fingers slipped under her shirt, stroking her back, up to the bandage, and down to the waist of her pants. Katria took a long, slow breath. In less than a day, her husband had gone from teasing at a distance to downright tempting all at once. An insatiable, and slightly annoying throb began at her center.

"Maybe," he said, his tone distracted, thoughtful.

All thoughts of the robbery and necklace fled in the face of baser desires. The worst part was that she didn't know what to do about it. Ask him to stop? Tell him to keep going, but somewhere else? No, that wasn't very lady-like, and he'd probably say she wasn't ready again, anyway. Plus, she didn't know the boundaries between a married couple Did they even have any *if* they'd decided to make their marriage genuine? Katria drew her brows together. The authenticity of their marriage needed to be addressed.

Straightening on his lap, she looked at him. "Are we married?"

His hand stopped at her hip, and he gave her an incredulous stare. "I thought we had established that weeks ago."

She shook her head. Nervous, she stood, albeit slowly and with this help, but she managed to put distance between them. That's what mattered most right now. She had to think clearly, and his constant touches put her in an unfamiliar haze.

"No, not what we were before. Are we..." She swallowed and steadied her back against the desk, hating her angst and the weakened state of her body. "Are we *really* married?"

He raised a brow. "As in neither of us is going anywhere?"

Katria waved in agreement, her heart pounding. "Yes, as in exactly that."

Slowly, he rose to tower over her. Katria pressed her hands onto the desk surface. The edge pushed into her hips. Papers slipped under her palms, but before she could fall back and cause herself additional pain, Sean's arm was under her back, supporting her weight. His other hand braced on the surface, closing the distance between them. The strength of his presence and his body quickened her pulse.

Sean leaned in, his mouth barely a whisper from hers. "I would not have admitted what I did last night if I didn't want you to be my *wife completely*." His lips grazed across hers, and when she rose for more, he pulled away. "The question now is, do you want me to be your husband?"

Elation swept into her heart, and had she been feeling better, she would have launched herself at him. But fatigue still gripped her, and the odd angle she stood at increased the already throbbing ache in her side. All she could do was nod and manage a weak, "Yes."

He kissed her softly before straightening and taking her with him. Settling once again onto the chair, he pulled her back onto his lap, but didn't let her lie against him. His hands smoothed along her cheeks to her neck. "This isn't going to be easy."

"Because it's been so easy up to this point," she bit out sarcastically.

Humor mixed with a bit of annoyance flashed in his eyes. "It'll be different."

"No." She shook her head. Finding his hands, she interlaced their fingers. "Just more personal." Then a new thought occurred to her. "Why weren't you upset about my father?"

He let loose a heavy sigh, bringing their hands onto her lap. "Well, the chaos of last night *might* have taken the edge off the information. There isn't much I can do now. I'm married to the daughter of one of the most dangerous men in the world. At least I have her on my side."

Katria couldn't help but tease, "You're likely married to

the most dangerous woman in the world, and she's *definitely* on your side."

Sean straightened until the distance between them was close. His hands slid from hers and up her back. He whispered against her mouth, "And I'm very thankful for that."

His lips closed over hers in an intense kiss that had her hands fisting in his shirt. The gentle, enticing caress of his fingers smoothed under her shirt to her shoulders, where he pressed her gently against his chest, forcing her arms to his back unless she wanted them pinned. A bulge strained against her thighs through Sean's pants, and she had the urge to straddle his lap. She'd just worked up the courage to be bold when a heavy knock sounded on the library door.

With a growl, Sean pulled his mouth away and snapped over her shoulder, "What?"

The door opened a crack, and Davis's voice drifted in. "I'm sorry, but Key Guardian Asherwick is here to see Primary Guardianess Wintersfall. He wasn't willing to wait."

Sean sighed. "And he shouldn't have to. Show the man in."

His hands slipped from her shirt, and she asked, "Should I move?"

"Do you want to?"

Glancing at the chair across from his desk, away from him and the safety he enveloped her in, seemed too far. "He's here because of my mother and sister."

He brushed a stray lock of hair away from her cheek. "You didn't answer me."

Katria shook her head. "No."

"Then you don't have to go anywhere."

Sean arranged himself on the chair so she could sit back against him comfortably. He wrapped his arms around her and grasped his hands at her hip. The action was both possessive and protective. Katria tried to fight the dread in the pit of her stomach, thankful Sean had allowed her to stay where she was.

When Jonathon finally entered, his handsome face was stern. He paused when he took them in, and then with a shake of his head, continued. "I guess a woman crawling onto men's laps is the new thing now."

Katria glanced over her shoulder at Sean, who raised a brow.

Jonathon waved the file he held dismissively and cleared his throat. "Never mind."

"Did you find something?" Katria couldn't wait for formalities, not that Jonathon seemed to care for them.

Sitting in the chair to the left, he gave a curt head shake. "Not really, which is interesting."

"How so?" Sean asked.

Jonathon sat back, laying the folder on his lap. "Well, I had a contact at the SNID look into the case, and there was no record. I didn't have him dig too deep because technically, he wasn't supposed to be looking. But on the surface at least, no investigation was ever started."

Anger and betrayal filled Katria. She'd been lied to. Used. Sean rubbed a hand softly along the top of her thigh while his other kept a firm hold around her waist. Katria tried to relax. "You found nothing at all?"

"Not at the SNID. I radioed the enforcement office in Old Helston, and the investigator in charge told me the case files had gone missing." He picked up the files. "But he had some notes at his house that he kept around for cross-referencing when he took cases home. He sent me those."

Confused, Katria stared at him. Another wave of disappointment flowed through her. "I don't understand.

With all the evidence missing and only a few notes sent to you, how does that help?"

"Well, here's the thing: he has notes on statements from your father, from your physician, and from the housekeeper present that day. But there's nothing from you." Jonathon set the file on the desk in front of him and perched on the end of the chair. "I'm hoping that you can give me enough information that I can figure out the crime scene. The sketches are missing, as are the complete statements from all the witnesses, but I've worked with less."

Katria took a deep breath, ignoring the sharp pain it caused. She'd given up her life to have the murder case of her mother and sister solved... No, that wasn't true anymore. Her choice had led her to Sean, and the chance at a future she had only once dreamed about.

Maybe she should let the investigation go. A heavy sorrow she hadn't experienced since their funeral threatened to break her. She couldn't relive that afternoon. Biting her lip, she looked away from Jonathon.

But then she'd never know why.

She'd never know who'd robbed her mother of her next great botanical discovery, or her sister of growing into a woman and experiencing falling in love like Katria was.

For them, she had no choice but to go through their deaths again. Everything to this point in the last three years had been for them, and she wasn't going to stop now. "Okay, what do you need to know?"

A shadow of regret crossed over his face. "I'm sorry, I have to know everything. Every detail you can remember."

Sean's hand took hers, his thumb caressing over the back. "You don't have to do this."

She took a deep breath, suppressing the anguish. She'd

learned how to control the consuming emotion years ago. "I do. It's okay."

Jonathon opened the file and then reached across the desk to pick up a pencil Sean had lying near a ledger. "Start at the beginning, before their murder."

Katria fought against the churning of her stomach. "We were eating lunch on a blanket on a small slope overlooking the Sovereign Channel, not too far from the house."

"You could still see the house?" Jonathon asked.

"Yes, but it was small. We probably walked five minutes before we found a place Anyka liked."

Jonathon flipped a sheet up and made a note. "And everyone was on the blanket facing towards the water?"

"We were more to the side, facing the cliff line."

The pencil scratched. "And how was everyone arranged?"

Katria closed her eyes and searched her memory. The warmth of the sun seemed to glow across her skin from that afternoon. Her sister's laughter to her left floated on the ocean breeze. "My father was lying behind me, talking to my mother, who was putting things back in the basket behind my sister, to the left. Anyka was struggling to put a lid on a jar, the threads kept..." She squeezed her eyes shut, her sisters laughing, having given way to her temper. "Getting stuck. The lid rolled away from her, and I leaned forward to get it for her."

Jonathon sat silent and then asked, "So your father was behind you, and your mother was behind Anyka, both your mother and sister were to your left?"

Katria nodded and opened her eyes. "Yes, Anyka was sitting more forward than I was, and my mother was more on the corner edge, behind her."

"What happened next?"

Pain. Excruciating confusion. Katria locked every ounce of emotion away as she spoke. "Everything just went to chaos. Fire exploded in my hip; my sister fell to her side, and my mother fell backward. Neither moved again. My father used my hip to steady his gun and managed to get a few shots off before he realized exactly what had happened."

The pencil stopped moving in Jonathon's hand, and his dark blue gaze met hers. Sean's hold tightened around her waist and hand. Then Jonathon went back to his paper. The silence became unbearable. If pacing wouldn't hurt, she'd be out of the chair.

Jonathon tapped the pencil, his lips drawn in a stern line. "The autopsy results were missing as well. Do you know if the shots were accurate?"

Katria flexed her jaw. "Very."

"Where?"

Sean shifted under her. "Asherwick..."

Jonathon cast her a sorrowful look. "I'm sorry, I have to know."

For three years, Katria had blocked out the sight of her sister's limp hand still holding a silver lid, of her blue eyes staring at nothing as blood trickled between them. All of Sziveria must have heard Katria scream that afternoon. "Head."

"And your father had been lying down directly behind you?"

"Yes."

Jonathon glanced up, and the trouble clouding his eyes made Katria's heart race. "I don't think the assassin intended that bullet for you."

Gripping Sean's hand so tightly in her anxiety, she was sure she drew blood, she stared at Jonathon. "What do you mean?"

Jonathon straightened, slowly laying the pencil down. "The shots were true for your mother and sister. Your father was lying behind you. You'd moved when the bullet hit, blocking your father. I think he was the first target."

"He was the biggest threat," Sean voiced, tense.

"The killer knew he'd protect his family, so yes, I'd say your father was a threat that had to be eliminated first. Then your sister and mother."

"But why?" Katria asked, trying to push back bitter emotion.

"That I can't answer."

Katria's mind reeled. Her father, her sister, her mother, but not her. She'd been an accident. A second shot hadn't been fired at her to finish the job. "It was me," she whispered. "An assassin killed them because of me."

"Kat, you don't—"

Her stomach rolled, and a burning sensation rose in her throat. "I'm going to be sick."

Struggling off Sean's lap, she reached for the edge of the desk, stars dancing in her vision. Her abdomen heaved, and she gagged, falling to her knees. A trashcan appeared under her the second the glass of water from earlier that morning spilled from her mouth.

Agonizing pain tore through her side at each convulsion of her torso. She couldn't breathe, each attempt triggering another wave of nausea until she choked and dry heaved. When nothing remained in her stomach to come up anymore, she rolled to the floor on her back and covered her face with her hands. And for the first time in over three years, Katria relented to tears.

✾ 19 ✾

A deep red bloom spread across the side of Katria's gray shirt. Her body trembled with each sob. Guilt, sorrow, and confusion flowed from her in strong waves. All Sean wanted to do was gather her against his chest. But in the violence of getting sick, she could have torn a stitch, or all of them. After lifting her shirt enough to expose the bandage, he eased the edges of the gauze back and inspected the seeping wound. Everything looked intact.

"What happened?" Jonathon asked, crouching behind her.

Sean couldn't help but glare at the man. "Besides you?"

"Oh, don't give me that crap, Wintersfall. When it comes to who's worse in whose book, I'm still winning."

Sean conceded. That much was true. "We were robbed last night."

"Did you report it?"

Exasperated, Sean's glower returned. His incredibly strong and emotionally reserved wife had fallen to pieces, and all Jonathon could talk about was a robbery gone wrong. Granted, it was the enforcer's job, but Sean's mind wasn't on the events from the night before. "Can we discuss this later?"

Asherwick rubbed the back of his neck and looked away. "Yeah, sorry, of course. Old habits."

Sean gathered Katria to his chest. Her hand fisted in the front of his shirt as she buried her face against his shoulder. Hot tears soaked through the fabric. He lifted and then carried her towards the fireplace. Arranging her on the thick cushions, he pulled back, but she didn't relinquish her hold.

He brushed wet strands of hair off her cheeks and took her hand in his. "I'm going to see Asherwick out, I'll be right back."

Her grip tightened, and she pulled on his shirt. "Y-you can't l-leave me."

A sharp ache pierced through his chest. He peeled her fingers from his shirt. He kissed each palm before laying them across her stomach. "I'll only be a second, I promise."

The moment he stood, she curled into herself, her face disappearing under her hands. A silent sob wracked her shoulders and shook her body. Fisting his hands at his side, he forced himself to step away.

Jonathon tucked the folder under his arm and headed for the door. Sean followed.

"Did you want to tell me about that robbery now?" Jonathon asked, pausing before he reached the front door.

Sean stopped and crossed his arms over his chest. "Why? So, you can have another unsolved case on your desk?"

"No, so I can compare it to others and see if there's been more. Who knows, maybe I'll find something interesting you can utilize or even help me with. I can have the street crime force monitor common barterers for what was stolen."

Sean shook his head. "I doubt they'd be foolish enough to trade it within the city."

Jonathon shrugged. "You'd be surprised. They may be clever when it comes to choosing their targets, but then greed sets in, and they want their money."

Sean relayed the pertinent information to Jonathon about the robbery. He took notes on the outside of the file folder.

"I'm surprised the medical scientist didn't report it, to be honest. Did you pay him not to?"

Sean flashed a smile. "No, I didn't call one. I'm a medical science officer."

"Well, isn't that convenient," Jonathon stated.

"Yes, that was the point of it, I believe."

"Can't have people dying on you when you're interrogating them, I suppose."

Sean laughed. "It does come in handy for that when necessary. Usually, however, I use the skill for my team."

Jonathon frowned. "I was joking."

"I wasn't. Although I typically prefer subtler methods of collecting information. It's easier when they don't even realize they've given anything away."

Jonathon's gaze narrowed, then widened. "You're a Sympath." Jonathon shook his head, disbelief still on his face. "I know another Sympath, but she uses her abilities in trade brokering."

"Peace is usually our end game, too." Then Sean took a chance and held out his hand. "Thank you for helping my wife."

Jonathon hesitated and then gave him a firm shake. "Well, I couldn't say no, she said she'd owe me one. I figured having a sharpshooter on my side couldn't hurt. I'm just sorry about the result."

Sean was, too. "You have a favor of an interrogator, too, if you ever need one."

Jonathon chuckled. "I'm more likely to need the medical training."

Sean made a quick trip to his room to get new bandages and salve for Katria before heading back to the library, while Davis saw Jonathon the rest of the way out. Sean took a deep breath, hoping he hadn't been gone too long. The second he walked in, he knew he had been.

Sitting stiffly before the fire, she stared into the dancing flames, her hands folded neatly on her lap. The loose t-shirt gathered on her thighs, the bloody stain deepening in color as it dried. Sean approached her with caution. Her gaze shifted to him and then back to the fire. She remained motionless. The broken anger in her vivid blue eyes tore at his heart.

"There's no way he didn't know what Jonathon discovered by my witness testimony alone," she stated calmly.

Sean crouched down before her, forcing her gaze from the flames to him. He set the bandages on the couch next to her. "Who?"

"My father. He knew the assassin intended the bullet I took for him."

"You don't know—"

"I don't know that?" Her eyes flashed, and a delicate pink tinged her ashen cheeks. She pointed at her chest. "*I* don't know? I know! I think I would be *the one person* who would know! And he was ten times better than I could ever hope to be! He'd have figured out the intended targets within seconds of their death."

Sean didn't dare tell her to cool down. The last thing his beautifully angry bride needed to be was calm.

However, she was injured, and any additional stress she put on herself, she'd be paying for later. Crossing his legs, he sat, quiet and collected, the heat of the fireplace at his back. Time for a little subtle intervention.

"You're right, his skill is unmatched, but you're still early in your career. As for him knowing or not knowing, he was in as much grief and shock as you were. Intense emotions can cloud our perception of things. If the investigators didn't see the crime the way Jonathon did, they wouldn't have relayed that to your father." When she opened her mouth, he held up a hand. "*If* he made the connection, it could have been after you left."

A tear slid down her cheek as she looked past him to the fire. "He didn't speak a word after their death. Not one. He sat in a chair looking out toward the cliffs from morning to night." She shook her head and whispered, "He knew. And he didn't have the courage to tell me."

Grasping her calves, he squeezed gently until she met his eyes. "Would you have wanted him to?"

She tilted her head to the side, and her chin quivered as fresh tears spilled over her lashes. She tore her gaze away. Her legs trembled under his touch.

"Kat?" he inquired softly. "Would you have?"

She choked on a cry. "No."

Sean caught her as she sank to the floor. He pulled her onto his lap and held her close. Her forehead fell to his shoulder, heavy sobs wracking her slender frame. The tears she denied herself while he'd left her alone burst forth. Tenderly, he ran his fingers along her back and rested his cheek on her head.

By the time she stopped crying, his feet had gone numb. Sean tried to wiggle his toes, but they'd forgotten they were part of his body. Sniffling, Katria straightened from his shoulder, completely soaked from her tears.

"Sorry." She brushed her hand down his clothing as if she could dry his shirt with a touch.

Sean glanced down at the tear-stained patch. "Don't be, tears wash out." He pulled at the front of her shirt. "Blood does not."

She gasped, taking the fabric from him. "Am I okay?"

"I wouldn't have left you alone for a second if I didn't think you were okay. You didn't pull any stitches. You've just released some pent-up fluid. You're fine." He motioned to the small pile of first aid supplies on the couch. "I brought what I need to fix you up."

Her hands collapsed to her lap. A sad, yet determined expression settled on her face.

"What?" Sean asked when she didn't speak.

"I have to go home." She looked at him. "I have to speak to my father."

"Okay, we'll go."

She shook her head as if he didn't understand. "No, today... tomorrow. I have to go."

Sean sighed. "You can't travel in your current condition. Old Helston sits on the other side of the country, to the south, not the east. It's a long, uncomfortable trip."

Katria slipped from his lap back to the couch, her finger tapping on her bottom lip. "We could take the MagnaRail. The last stop on the line is at Port Anchor. It's less than a day from there."

Hesitation filled him, and he rubbed the back of his neck. "I don't know."

Her hands fisted on her thighs. "You say I'm in no condition for the *more* you refuse to give me, and now I'm in no condition to travel. I'm just hurt, not dying!"

Had any other woman other than the strong-willed, fierce beauty sitting before him spoken such brazen words, his jaw would have dropped. And at her words, he couldn't help but rise to his knees, despite the protest of his stiff joints. He cupped the back of her neck and whispered into her ear, "Don't tempt me."

Her heavy breath rushed across his hair, and he smiled, rising to his feet. Tiny needles tingled in his toes up to his ankle.

"Davis!"

The man appeared in the doorway. "Yes?"

"I need today's paper, if you please."

Davis bowed and disappeared.

Katria stared at Sean. "You couldn't go get the paper yourself?"

Sitting next to her, he lifted a foot and began to massage the life back into it. "I pay the man to do things for me. Currently, all he does is answer the door, bring me the mail, and perform his normal household duties. Let him be useful."

Her frown indicated she didn't believe him. "It's the paper."

Davis arrived with a neatly folded paper and handed it to Sean sharply.

Before he could leave, Sean asked, "Davis, will you please tell my wife you didn't mind getting the paper for me?"

The butler clasped his hands behind his back and regarded Sean with furrowed brows. "What is that?"

A smile danced on Sean's lips. "She seems unsure of your duties and feels I was being lazy."

Giving a short bow, he turned to face Katria. "I assure you, Primary Guardianess Wintersfall, he was quite in the right to ask me to fetch him the paper."

Cheeks pink, Katria gave a curt nod. "Thank you, Davis."

Sean snapped the paper open. "Yes, thank you, Davis."

"Is there anything else you," he turned towards Katria, "or the guardianess needs?"

Sean met Katria's stare over the top of the paper, and he raised a brow.

"Um," she began, "how about something to drink?"

Davis's expression became neutral. "Do you care to be more specific? Something warm, cold, sweet?"

Katria fidgeted with her hands. "Sweet."

With a bow, he departed. Sean laughed, turning pages until he found what he needed.

"Very good, however, next time do be more specific. Whatever Davis brings you, you're to drink."

"Oh." The enticing flush continued to tint her skin. "I didn't think about that. I've never had anyone just bring me what I wanted before."

"I know. You'll grow accustomed to it." He folded the paper open to the page with the MagnaRail schedule and laid it on the couch between them. "Looks like there's a departure tomorrow at eight a.m. We missed today's. It connects twice. We'll arrive in Port Anchor if there aren't any delays by four a.m. the next morning."

"And add another thirteen hours to that, so almost two days."

"By carriage or ariot alone, it'd be close to five days. Two is better."

Davis arrived with a wooden tray. He set it on the side table beside Katria. "Enjoy."

A softly steaming cup of hot chocolate and a plate of cheese with crackers rested on the tray. "Thank you, Davis. This is wonderful."

"You're very welcome. If there is nothing else?"

"Nothing else," Sean said with a smile.

"Very good."

Katria picked at the snack and sipped at the chocolate

drink. Sean simply observed her. At the soft curve of her neck whenever she glanced at the plate before choosing her next morsel, at the way she slowly eased the food into her mouth. She tucked her feet under the baggy clothes, hiding the perfect body he'd been desperate for last night. Still ached for now. She was stunning, and she was his.

A heavy sensation settled in his stomach. He couldn't mess this up. The selfish curse his family existed under couldn't destroy what was building between them. He couldn't let that happen.

And yet... he still found himself unable to tell her about his past.

Her gaze met his, and she frowned. "What is it? What's wrong?"

Shaking the dark thoughts away, Sean gave her a shallow smile. "Nothing. I was just wondering if you're sure about this trip. We could go in a week?"

"No, I can't sit here for a week dwelling. I have to go now."

"All right, I'll have the tickets purchased. Have Rebeka help you pack."

"Should I bring my rifle?"

"Probably not a bad idea." Then, as an afterthought, he added, "Just don't let your stylist see it."

❦ 20 ❦

The Helmstreet MagnaRail station buzzed with activity. Barterers called out their wares to passersby as messengers darted through the station, delivering whatever anyone asked for. An ocean of people moved in assigned lanes based on destinations: enter, exit, tickets, baggage, and boarding. Katria marveled at the chaos. She'd ridden the MagnaRail twice. Once to Haven City, and once to the port that took her on the journey to her new life. She'd met the team that would soon become a part of her life in a passenger car. She smiled at the memory.

A deep chill still hung in the morning air, and Katria wrapped her arms around herself. The crowd of bodies did little to warm the vast space, which was open to the outside, with nothing more than a high canopy providing cover from the elements. There were two distinct lines. Ones for priority passengers and one for everyone else. They waited in the shorter, priority que.

Sean rapped their enveloped tickets against his leg, his attention constantly shifting over the multitude. He stood stiff beside her, keeping almost a full body-length between them and the next couple in line.

Katria looped her arm through his and shifted until their hips touched. "You're nervous."

"I'm just looking."

The rumble and gentle hiss of a train arriving penetrated the noise of hundreds of conversations. Their line moved forward a few feet as a boarding gate swung open. Within minutes, they were onboard, walking through narrow corridors to find their passenger room. Sean had made sure they rode in comfort and privacy, securing them a suite.

Dark hardwood floors and walls, paired with brass accents, made the tight space between the wall and the row of rooms feel even smaller. Not even the large windows with rounded corners seemed to penetrate the dimly lit corridor. Katria kept close to Sean's back as everyone filed to their destination. They walked three cars before locating their room.

Sean slid the narrow door open, but not fast enough for the person waiting behind them. In a huff, he shoved past Katria, knocking her against the wall. The sudden jolt sent a flash of pain through her side, and she struggled to take in a breath.

Jaw clenched tight, Sean grasped her elbow and helped her into their suite, his eyes flashing an *I told you so*. "Are you okay?"

She could do little more than nod, feeling a little foolish for thinking she was ready for a trip so soon after a near-fatal injury. But safely in their room, what more could happen?

Inside, the suite was decorated just as darkly as the hall with rich mahogany wood floors and walls, soft, deep red upholstery, and dark golden curtains over the window.

Katria slid her hand over the indulgent fabric on the bench and then sat.

"This is really nice."

He closed them in and secured the privacy lock. "Yes, the company has taken excellent care of the cars."

After hanging his coat in the tiny space provided, he took hers. Katria stared out the window as another train, five tracks away, glided past, the multi-colored freight cars little more than a blur. Another passenger train slowed to a stop beside them, blocking her view, and she sighed. That train would have to wait until theirs departed to offload and reload, which meant it wouldn't be long.

"It's so busy here," she marveled.

"Have you forgotten how busy the Port Scarborough station was?" He took a seat across from her. "That station has twenty-three tracks. This one only has fifteen."

"I don't remember much from that, no. I had other things on my mind."

He lifted his ankle onto his thigh and rested his hands over his calf. "Such as?"

Katria cast him a facetious stare. "Oh, I don't know, being alone with three male strangers in a passenger car barely big enough to house all of us?"

Sean nodded, humor dancing in his whiskey colored eyes. "I can see how that would be distracting."

She raised her brows. "Maybe a little bit."

His expression sobered. "Were you really afraid?"

"Stunned, I think, would be a better word. They assured me I was working with honorable men, and since nothing untoward happened to me during training, I believed them."

"My only thought was, I had a young woman on the team who'd never even left the country before, let alone served it. Pretty pitiful for someone who's supposed to pick up on emotion, hmm?" He smiled sheepishly.

"I'm sure you perceived I was a bit nervous."

His attention shifted to the window. "Perhaps." Then he sighed. "Are you *sure* you want to do this? We can still get off the train."

Katria joined his gaze out the window. "I'm positive. I can't help but feel the answer to their death may give us some answers, not just me. I don't know to what, but why else make the note in my file about my identity? And why hide my identity at all? No one said I wasn't to be *me* at any point in my training."

"Maybe to keep you safe."

That brought her focus back to him. "Keep me safe? From whom?"

"From anyone looking to take down a Nachemir, and all the notoriety that would come with such a feat. It'd be a career high for those building a name."

Katria frowned. She'd never considered her name a threat. Her father had never seemed concerned, so she hadn't either. "Someone did already, though, didn't they?"

His intense gaze grew dark. "Not a Nachemir active in their profession."

A tremble of apprehension twisted in her stomach. "Then changing my name, maybe makes sense. But why keep it from you?"

He gave a nonchalant shrug. "Who knows. You kept it from me, too."

A niggle of guilt made her sigh. "Not on purpose. I saw my fake name in the newspaper and assumed there was a reason." She waved a hand. "Then, you know, secrets and all that."

"Speaking of those—"

"Yes, speaking of those, we never did get to discuss why Arch Guardian Synintel needed to talk with you."

Something flickered across his handsome features she couldn't place, and then it was gone, replaced with a gentle smile. "You were stabbed afterward. When were we supposed to talk?"

"So, what did he say?"

"Nothing."

Katria narrowed her gaze. "What do you mean nothing?"

"He wanted to know where Kevin was."

"Oh. And?"

Sean shrugged. "I didn't tell him. If Kevin wants to be found, he'll tell his father-in-law where to find him."

"Did you at least tell Kevin?"

His shameless grin made her stomach flip. The man was too good-looking. "I forgot."

"You are going to tell him, aren't you?"

A hiss sounded a second before the train suddenly lurched. Caught off guard, Katria's body shifted, and she gripped the seat, her abdomen tightening. A sharp ache tore through her left side, and she winced. Katria braced for the faint sense of weightlessness that accompanied the MagnaRail's transition into smooth motion.

Sean shook his head, exasperation clear on his face.

She took several slow breaths before relaxing against the seat again. "I'll be fine."

Concern entered his gaze. "The entire journey is going to be that way for you."

And he hadn't been joking. By the time they arrived at Port Anchor, he had to practically carry her from the train. Sean hired a driver to take them the additional thirteen hours to her home locality, though she paid dearly for it. Twice, the pain overtook her, and they had to stop to let her out, so she didn't get sick in the carriage. Not even the salve Sean had brought to numb the pain took the edge away by the time they reached Old Helston.

Night blanketed the landscape when the horse-drawn vehicle came to a slow stop before a plain two-story, pale brick house with a wide porch. Katria lay across the seat, her head on Sean's lap while he stroked his fingers through her hair. She was thankful for the darkness. An angry scowl hadn't left his handsome face since he helped her off the train. His frustration she could deal with, but the pain was rapidly becoming something intolerable. Sweat covered her body, chilling her until she trembled.

Sean's hand fell from her hair as he sat forward. "I think we're here."

"Okay." She tried to rise but failed.

He helped her sit in slow increments. Once she was fully upright, he paused until she let him know when she was ready for more. She waited for an intense wave of nausea to clear before nodding. The cabin bounced as he jumped out of the door. Katria scooted the distance to the door and then held her right hand out. Instead of grasping her hand, he took hold of her forearm, while the other reached for her left upper arm. Thankful for the help, she gripped his strong shoulders and eased out of the carriage. Cool salty air whipped around them, and Katria closed her eyes. How she'd missed the way the constant ocean breeze brushed against her skin and teased her hair.

"Can you walk, or do I need to carry you?"

No way was she going to show up at her father's front door with her husband carrying her like some weakling. Gritting her teeth, she opened her eyes and pulled herself as straight as she could manage. "I can walk."

Sean kept a steady hold on her upper arm as they shuffled their way through the overgrown yard. Light shone from a single window, and Katria's stomach tightened. She wasn't ready for this. What had she been thinking? Her step faltered. Sean reached around, his arm steadying her.

She grabbed his arm, her fingers digging into the fabric of his coat. "I don't know if I can do this."

"Too late now, we're here. I guarantee your father saw the carriage stop, and he's watching us now." And under his breath, she caught, "Probably through a scope."

If she hadn't felt like a carriage had dragged rather than carried her, she would have elbowed him in the side. Therefore, she simply agreed. "I would be."

Sean muttered a rare curse. "We should have at least sent a message ahead of our arrival."

Yes, that would have been the logical thing to do, but it seemed Katria hadn't been thinking too rationally the past couple of days. Hence, the excruciating situation she found herself in, suffering through pain and anxiety.

Breathing heavily through her clamped jaw, she succeeded in making the three steps to the porch with his help despite her shaky limbs. "Next time, make me listen to you, at all costs."

"And tame the ferocity out of you? Never. I'll just stick around to make sure you don't kill yourself when you're too stubborn to listen to me."

He hadn't looked at her as he said the sincere words, too focused on where her feet seemed to land. And she realized, then, without a doubt, that she loved him. She even found her lips parting to tell him as much when the front door opened.

Katria's gaze locked with crystalline blue eyes, which, like her Gen-Heir ability, she'd inherited. Already barely able to take in a breath, her lungs stopped working altogether. And when her vision faded and blackness enveloped her, she welcomed the darkness.

Sean barely caught Katria as she slumped forward, unconscious. He hauled her weight against his body before lifting her into his arms.

"What is wrong with my daughter?" Alexandrov barked, his Ruthenian accent clear in the harsh pronunciation of his words.

Sean took in the tall, broad-shouldered man. The only thing that betrayed his age was the gray in the short black hair at his temples and the wrinkles around his eyes. With a stern face and a flashing blue stare, Sean recognized immediately that Aleksandrov Nachemir was every bit as intimidating as Sean assumed he would be.

"She was hurt a couple of days ago, but that didn't stop her from insisting she come see her father. Do you have somewhere I can lay her, or are we going to have a conversation on the porch while I hold her?"

Alexandrov's gaze narrowed, but he conceded and stepped away from the threshold. "Her bedroom is upstairs, on the left."

Sean entered the house, noting the living area to the right and the dining room to the left, and a hall that led to a few doors at the back. The staircase was only a few feet inside, and he headed up. On the small landing, he noted only two doors: one on the left and the other on the right. With some finagling, he opened Katria's bedroom door.

In the silvery moonlight, he could make out muted greens and ivory tones. A medium-sized, cream-painted wood framed bed took up most of the quaint room. Sean gently laid Katria down, smoothing the long strands of damp midnight hair from her face. He looked her over before rising, making sure her even breathing was as strong as the pulse in her neck.

Briefly, he considered staying with his wife. But then

he figured, he'd be something of a coward not facing the assassin, and a coward he was not. After laying his coat over the top of a chest-style dresser, he silently exited her room and headed downstairs. Alexandrov sat in a chair facing the window, his back to the rest of the room. Sean frowned and wondered if the chair was the same one Katria had mentioned he had never left.

"She is okay?" Alexandrov asked without turning.

Sean cautiously entered the sparsely furnished living room. "She's fine. She's barely slept for three days. I tried to persuade her to wait until she healed, but as you know, your daughter can be very stubborn."

Finally, the man turned in his seat. "And you are?"

Leaning against the wall near the recessed windows, Sean crossed his arms over his chest. "I'm her husband."

Confusion and a bit of her hurt crossed over Alexandrov's face and stiffened his shoulders. "Do you have a name, husband?"

"Sean Blackbain."

Alexandrov looked him over, from his booted feet to his finely spun black wool slacks and teal button-up cotton shirt, and shook his head. "There is more to your name, yes?"

Sean couldn't help but smile. "Yes, I'm Primary Guardian Wintersfall."

The aging assassin leaned back, folding his hands over his stomach. "My daughter, a ranked guardian. I believe the position would suit her."

"She doesn't agree."

He gave a short chuckle. "Then why marry you?"

At that question, Sean couldn't help but frown. "She didn't have a choice." And then he added quickly when the man became rigid. "Neither of us did."

"How is that possible?"

Sean raked a hand through his hair. "The FIO assigned her to my team, but apparently, we couldn't travel together or sleep in the same room unless we were married. We just found out a couple of weeks ago."

Alexandrov sat forward slightly. "And you bring her here when she demanded it?"

"Yes."

"I see." When he relaxed, so did Sean. "And why now?"

"Because she wouldn't leave her mother and sister's deaths alone. She discovered that someone meant the bullet she took for you."

❧ 21 ❧

A terrible dryness in her throat was what finally stirred Katria from a death grip on sleep. Everything ached when she moved. She decided rolling over was a better start than sitting up. Shifting onto her right side, she buried her face in the warmth of the pillow and tried to convince herself to at least open her eyes.

Subdued light streamed in from the windows on either side of her bed, and Katria blinked grit away. A seagull cawed its song not far from the house. The familiar rattle of the glass panes from a heavy ocean gust made her glance around. Cream bead board walls with soft green trim came into focus. The narrow chest style dresser that had held her childhood treasures and clothes had Sean's jacket flung over the top of it. Two travel chests sat against the wall near the door, beside the low-burning woodstove. She was in her room. How did she get here? And where was Sean?

The soft scraping of wood against the floor made her aware she wasn't alone. Despite the discomfort, she rolled onto her back and looked to the other side of the bed. Her father leaned forward, his forearms bracing against the mattress. Katria gasped and flinched, scooting close to the edge of the bed. Her sudden shift in position caused the cashmere underdress she'd been sleeping in to pull tight across her side and shoulder.

Sadness entered his sharp blue gaze, and he shook his head. "Oh, my *Katya*, what have you done to yourself?"

The question seemed to inquire about more than her physical condition. She tried to speak, but her parched throat wouldn't let any words out. He stood and went to the bathroom off the corner of the room. He returned with a half-full glass of water and presented it to her as if he were holding a peace offering.

Katria raised a trembling hand and accepted the water. Rising enough to bring the glass to her lips, she sipped the cool liquid, savoring the relief.

When the water was gone and the ache in her throat had dissipated, she attempted to speak again. "Where is my husband?"

"Ah, yes. I like him. I think he is good man for you."

Irritated, she handed the glass back to him. "I didn't come here for your approval. Where is he?"

"Downstairs. He said we should have time alone, and I agreed."

She did not. She wanted answers, not a family reunion. "Why didn't you tell me?"

Alexandrov didn't pretend not to understand. "You have to know, I made enemies, *Katya*, a lot of people wanted me to suffer. Leaving me without my family would have done that. I thought you were the third shot, not the first, which would have accounted for the inaccuracy."

"I wasn't the third."

"I know, your husband told me what the investigator thought. No one ever spoke to me about their deaths after that day. No one ever returned. And you and I never spoke of it for me to have your perspective."

"You never spoke to me at all," she said quietly, though she wanted to scream the words. Tears burned her eyes and she breathed them away.

He shook his head, sadness pinching his face, aging him. "I know."

Katria forced herself to focus on what else had said. "So, you didn't know you were the intended target, not me?"

Alexandrov shook his head. "No, but after I heard, it made sense."

"Why?" she asked, hating the shakiness of her voice.

"Because, then you would have nothing to leave behind and no one to convince you not to go into that life. And removing me from your life *would* have been the smartest thing to do. I am the only one who could hurt them if they hurt you."

Despite the remorse that she'd misjudged her father, she couldn't help but scoff. "Did you even notice when I left?"

Shame flickered across his face, and he looked away. "After a couple days, I realized."

"A couple of days." Shaking her head, she chanced on rising into a more seated position, thankful when searing pain didn't assail her.

"How did they do it?" His gaze met hers once more. "How did they convince you?"

"An investigation into Mom and Anyka's deaths on a national level."

Surprise entered his vivid blue stare. "The government?"

"Yes." She glanced down at her hands. "And I didn't

have you to ask if I was making the right choice, so I simply agreed."

He leaned across the bed, his fingers touching hers. "My thoughts would not have mattered to you."

Tears stung behind her eyes, and she shrugged. "We won't ever know, will we?"

"*Katya*, you were never the emotional one of my daughters, but you are fiercely loyal. If someone promised to find who took my Maggie and Nyka from us, how do you think you would have said no despite my opinion?" His thumb lovingly caressed the back of her hand. "And you did find out."

She sniffled and shook her head. "Not like you think. I had to promise a favor and have someone outside look into it. There was nothing to be found, *Ahtyshka*, everything had gone missing."

This time, he sniffed, and she stared at him. Tears glistened in his eyes. "I have missed being called father by my loves."

Raw emotion tore through Katria. She took a calming breath. She'd cried enough tears over her loss. There wasn't anything left. She didn't have the emotional strength to dwell on her father's pain. Of course, he had lost, greater in many ways than hers. A wife, a daughter, and in the end, almost two daughters gone. No, that was a rabbit hole she dared not get stuck falling down.

Glancing around her sparsely furnished room, she noted the long shadows crossing the floor. "How long did I sleep?"

His hand slipped from hers as he straightened in his seat. "Almost a full day. Your husband said your journey was not a good one for you."

"That's true."

"Why not wait?"

"I had to know."

He tsked. "So stubborn. Nyka was not as stubborn as she had her mother in her. You..." Alexandrov shook his head and stood. He pointed at his chest. "Too much of me."

"I think my superiors are rather happy with that," Katria stated dryly.

"Sean shared a few stories with me this morning. I am not happy you chose this life, but I am thankful for who you are living it out with."

Her heart softened at his words, and she couldn't help but smile. "Me too."

Aleksandrov nodded. At the door, he paused with his hand on the knob. "Clarice should have dinner ready soon, if you are hungry and can make it downstairs. If not, I will have her bring it to you."

Katria raised a brow. "You have a cook?"

He shrugged. "Cook, housekeeper, gardener. I was no good at taking care of everything. The house was a wreck."

"I'm feeling better, a full day of rest seemed to be what I needed. I'll be down in a few."

Cautiously, she slipped her feet to the floor after the door closed. She waited a moment, and when neither extreme pain nor nausea assailed her, she rose. At the chest, she found one of her simple black gowns. She let out a sigh. Her normal. And yet, frowning, she couldn't shake the trouble settling deep in her gut.

The implications of the conversation she had with her father came rushing back. Someone had wanted to leave her with nothing. To give her zero reasons to say no to them. Any appetite she had vanished.

"Finally awake?" Sean asked, laying the paper down he'd been reading as Katria shuffled into the dining room.

Still ashen and moving at a pace half her normal speed, she seemed to force her smile. She'd showered, her damp hair hung down her back, and she had brushed it from her face. The fitted torso and flowing length of her simple black gown accentuated her figure. From the soft swell of her breasts, flat plane of her stomach, to the gentle curves of her hips, she was perfection. He wanted to explore every alluring inch of her. Funny how he'd kept himself from noticing before and now, dressed in what seemed to give her security, he couldn't help but stare.

"You shouldn't have let me sleep so long."

"You needed it."

She eyed the paper as she slowly lowered herself into the chair adjacent to him. "Anything interesting?"

He snapped the paper and nodded. "Oh, yes, it's very exciting in your home locality. Let's see... there's a young couple who just moved to town, and he's a banker. They're very excited to have a competent man of numbers around. Oh! A new fishing venture has arrived, they will have five seats open on their vessel, young men need apply. And, the very tragedy is that Mrs. Gordillo's sweet cat has been missing for two entire weeks. Anyone with information on where the kitty could be will be handsomely rewarded."

She perched her elbow on the table and dropped her chin on her hand. "Is that so?"

Folding the paper in half, he laid it on the table. "Says so right here. I seriously considered going into town today to help with the search party."

Doubt crinkled her face. "Search party? For a cat?"

"Did I mention the reward is for the grand sum of ten raimarks?"

She smiled at him. "You don't say."

Sean leaned forward and whispered, "Apparently, this is

the most exciting thing to happen in a month. There's a betting pool on who finds the cat first, and where."

Sweet, sing-song laughter escaped past her lips, her face relaxing. "And what stopped you from joining in the hunt?"

His heart clenched as color seeped into her cheeks and merriment danced in her eyes. She was beautiful. "I didn't think my wife would appreciate my leaving her to look for a cat."

"How perceptive of you."

He leaned forward and rested his chin on his palm, his face close to hers. "I've been known to be insightful a time or two."

She shook her head, her attention shifting from him to her father as he strode into the room. Sean straightened and kept a sigh internal as their playful banter came to an end. Alexandrov had been curious about the last three years of his daughter's life, and while Sean didn't blame him, he didn't know how much Katria wanted her father to know. He kept things mainly within the team, focusing on what they did and how they functioned together. The retired assassin had turned out to be more level-headed than Sean had anticipated. Although, in hindsight, he wasn't sure why he had expected anything less. His wife was equally as composed.

"You are in for a luxury." Alexandrov rubbed his hands together as he took a seat at the head of the table. "Clarice has made her squash casserole."

They ate and kept the conversation light and safe. Sean noted Katria barely touched her food, her fork pushing the yellow lumps of creamy squash around on her plate. She excused herself before the men had finished eating. Alexandrov watched her leave, concerned. When she didn't return, Sean excused himself and searched the house for his wife. Every room came up empty, but he remained calm, remembering this wasn't the first time she'd gone missing on him. A door at the back of the house led outside, and he pushed it open.

A narrow brick path led to the greenhouse. Between the house and the conservatory, Katria sat on a bench swing facing the cliff. The ocean's waves crashed in a gentle lull below. With the wide expanse before her, she seemed somehow small, lost. The climate was more temperate in the far southern end of the country, and only a faint chill drifted on the spring breeze. They had until the sun fully set before the air would become uncomfortably cool.

Easing down on the swing beside her, he laced his fingers through hers. "You've had a rough couple of days."

"That would be an understatement." She looked at him. The setting sun cast her in the warm, peach glow. The wind toyed with the long locks of her midnight hair. "Did my father tell you his theory?"

His attention settled on her full mouth. Her soft pink lips ignited a desire in him to kiss them. Two days without the feel of her mouth on his was two too many. Discussing her father was the last thing he wanted to do. Shifting his focus to the rolling waves below, he centered his thoughts.

"Yes, he did."

"And?"

"And I think it's very possible, and likely accurate."

Her fingers tightened around his. "They'd been buried three months when Voklane came to see me."

That information made him frown. "I don't think we can jump to conclusions."

"What else is left?"

Sean decided to be a little more rational. "While I'm

your leader, Voklane is mine. I have to trust him until he proves otherwise."

Her fingers slid from his. "I don't."

Sean angled his torso on the swing, his arm resting along the back edge. Wisps of her hair fluttered across his arm, and he resisted the urge to play with the long strands. "That's true. But do you trust me?"

Her gaze snapped to him. "What kind of question is that? Of course I do."

"Then *do*." He curled his fingers into her silky tresses. "We'll formulate a plan on how to question him when we return that won't raise any suspicion from someone watching."

Her jaw set in a hard line, and she returned her gaze to the ocean. "I'll be watching."

❦ 22 ❦

A stair creaked beneath Katria's foot on the way up to her room. Behind her, Sean leisurely followed. She'd known by the condition of her bed that he'd slept beside her last night, but she hadn't been conscious. She was now. And she recalled he slept in nothing but a pair of thin pants.

Her heart hammered. She tried to focus on the plan Sean had promised they'd formulate for their return to Haven City. But the memory of her husband's solid, muscled body and the confession of desire he'd given her tore through her thoughts.

If she weren't careful, he'd see right through her, literally.

Squaring her shoulders, she pushed the door open and entered her childhood room. An oil lamp burned on the bedside table, and a faint glow from the woodstove cast everything in long, soft shadows. Sadness overtook her desire. The bedroom had once been a happy space. Her sister had run back and forth, taking toys or a ribbon from her dresser, anything that would rile Katria and make her chase after. At twelve years of age, her young life had been cut far too short. And for what? So Katria would be the one behind a trigger.

She clenched her fists. "They made a mistake taking my family from me."

"One I'm sure they've realized," his deep voice said behind her as the door clicked shut.

"What chance do I have that they're oblivious to my digging?"

He went to the seat her father had occupied earlier. Lifting a foot, he pulled his boot off. "I'm not sure, since I don't know who *they* are."

"If it's our government?"

His gaze simply locked with hers before going back to focusing on his boots. That's what she thought. A sense of trepidation set over her, along with hopelessness. She sat heavily on the bed, her fingers intertwining on her lap. The springs squeaked in protest.

Lost in the impossible thoughts of unraveling her family murder mystery, she jumped when Sean's hand slipped between hers. She lifted her head. He crouched before her, elbows on his bent knees. The small flame burning beside the table gave the amber of his irises an ethereal quality. Shadows defined the strong angles of his face. Katria's breath faltered.

"I need you to prepare for the eventuality that you may never learn the truth."

"I can't give up," she whispered more to herself than to him.

His hand tightened over hers. "I know, and I'm not asking you to."

The warmth of his hand and nearness of his strength had her mind going fuzzy in a way only he could seem to make happen. All she had to do was slip forward, right off the bed, and she'd be in his lap. His arms would wrap around her, and he'd pull her close. Katria found her gaze dropping to his unbuttoned shirt. He must have been in the process of removing it when he decided to detour to her. If she held her hands out while she moved, they'd slide right along his muscled chest. She bit her lip. The thought was oh so tempting.

"Stop." The word came out as a growled command from her husband, and she tore her attention from his torso to his face. His jaw clenched, and his eyes closed, as he turned from her. "You have to stop."

"I'm not doing anything."

"Kat," he began through gritted teeth, "you forget my Gen-Heir ability."

Confused, she shifted to the edge of the bed. "You're a Sympath, I haven't forgotten."

His labored breathing caused his chest to swell. "Then you don't know what that truly means."

Katria pulled her hands free and ran them up his tense forearms. His palms braced on her thighs, and still he didn't look at her. "You perceive emotion."

"At sight, yes, sympathetic." He took a deep, shuddering breath. "Empathic at touch."

He could feel her desire. Katria's hands lifted from him as if her touch were venomous. "Why didn't you take your hand away?"

Finally, his face turned, and Katria gasped at the fire burning in his gaze. "I should have."

And then his mouth captured hers in a possessive kiss. Her back arched into his chest. He moved over her, his hands sliding from her thighs to the bed. Katria grabbed his shoulders, but a layer of fabric denied her the smooth expanse of his skin. Frustrated, Katria used ab muscles that weren't ready to be used yet to suspend herself above the bed. She ignored the fire in her side, a more profound need urging her forward as she yanked the shirt down off his shoulders. His lips devoured hers, his tongue teasing and tasting every part of her mouth.

The heat of his skin met her palms. Her hands slid over his shoulders to his back. He pulled her tight against his chest and, using his knee on the bed, eased her backward, further onto the mattress. A sharp pain tore at her ribs, and she gasped, pulling her mouth free to catch her breath.

Sean rested his forehead against hers. "You're not ready for this."

Lying on the mattress, she grabbed his face, forcing him to meet her stare. "I'm more than ready, and you *know* I'm not lying. Let me handle my pain. You can't feel that, can you?"

"No."

He rose long enough to throw his shirt off to the side. But instead of returning to her like she expected, he rolled onto his back and pulled her with him. She tumbled across his chest. His lips caught hers for another bone-melting kiss.

Katria moved along the hard length of his body, her hands exploring every inch of his chest. She slid her leg over his thighs and straddled him. Fierce desire stole through her as the bulge in his pants pressed against her through her dress. They had far too many clothes between them.

Sean seemed to feel the same, for within seconds, he expertly had her dress join his shirt on the floor. His mouth hardly left hers during the process. His hands played havoc with her senses, caressing every inch he could reach. With a groan, he gently switched their positions again. Naked beneath him, Katria wrapped her thighs around his hips. Her fingers delved into the lengths of his hair.

Braced above her, he kept his weight from settling. He reached between their bodies, and her heart raced in anticipation. But instead of touching her, he rose further, almost breaking their kiss. Fabric rustled, and his legs moved beyond hers. The shift of his hips against her lower body brought a yearning so deep within her she thought she might cry.

His mouth tore from hers, and she opened her eyes, confused. The weight of his knee beside her hip shifted the mattress. His touch slid along her center, and had she not been so desperate for the contact, she would have been embarrassed at the slick heat he discovered. He groaned, dropping his head to her shoulder, a heavy breath rushing across her dampening skin. Katria arched beneath him, unable to stop from spreading her legs wider, the unfamiliar need to feel his stroking deep within her making her hips rise.

Gently, he massaged her clit in slow circles, causing her to gasp and then he went lower, pressing the tip of his finger just inside. She moaned, her fingers sinking into his shoulder and tried to say without words she wanted *more*. But still he played, teasing her with butterfly strokes and whispering caresses until she almost sobbed with need.

Then, when she thought she'd go mad from his tempting, the hard length of him pressed into her inner thigh, hot and heavy. His hand slid from between their bodies to run along her forearm to her wrist, leaving a damp trail. Her pulse quickened as he took her wrist and guided her to his erection. In wonder and a little trepidation, she explored his aroused state. A smooth bead of fluid leaked from the head and her body seemed to respond in kind, something she would have thought impossible. His hips pressed forward, and carefully she guided him into her, gasping at the pressure.

Katria pulled her hand free as he pushed inside her. She wrapped her arms around his back, closing her eyes and focusing on a building sensation of pleasure. Slowly, he worked his way deeper into her. With each thrust, he inched further until a sharp, tearing pain tensed her muscles. He didn't stop, continuing to move in a slow, measured pace. The discomfort subsided, and as she relaxed, his movements quickened. He moved over her, his hips brushing hers with each powerful thrust.

Her nails dug into the flexing muscles of his back, and she clenched her teeth, desperation rising for something she knew only he had the control to give. Soon she was crying out for release, his heavy breath in her ear, and his moist skin beneath her hands, adding to her frenzied state. A piercing wave of pleasure tore through her, and she arched off the bed, her chest pushing to his, taking him deep inside. His growl of release joined her moaning cry.

Breathing fast, she collapsed onto the bed, and he fell on top of her. The weight of his torso pushed against her wound, and she could do little more than squeak at the burst of pain. Cursing, he quickly rolled off her, pulling free. She gasped at the sudden, sharp emptiness within her.

Sean let out a heavy sigh, his arm falling across his face. "Are you okay?"

Steadying her breathing, she tried to distinguish between the heated gratification still thrumming through her core and the aching throb in her ribs. "I'm fine."

He shifted onto his side and gently caressed her cheek. "Are you sure?"

"Yes, I'm sure."

"I told you we should have waited." He sat and then stood from the bed.

"Waited? I'm pretty sure three years was long enough," she argued.

He cast her a glare that teased more than threatened. Katria lifted onto her elbows and couldn't help but lick her lips at his completely naked form. Every part of him was strong. From his thick, muscular thighs to the roll of his shoulders as he walked. And she'd had him.

Her heart fluttered.

Now they were joined as husband and wife, completely.

He retrieved a white jar from his chest. Returning to the bed, he fell onto his stomach next to her. The bed bounced and the frame creaked from his sudden weight, and she laughed at the little smile he directed at her. On his elbows, he opened the jar. "Lie back."

Katria obeyed. Tenderly, he soothed ointment over her stitches, his attention wholly focused on his task. Katria's heart swelled to the point that she thought it would surely burst from her chest. The words tumbled out on a breath before she could contain them. "I love you."

The only indication that he'd heard her words was a faint pause to his tender touch across her injury. When he finished, he replaced the lid. He gave her a long, gentle kiss before speaking. "I have something for you."

Thankfully, her words hadn't caused a barrier to go up. She smiled softly. "What?"

"Hold tight." He left her again.

Back at the chest, he returned the cream, pulled on a pair of sleep pants, grabbed a cotton shirt, and something she couldn't see. He handed her the comfortable loose-fitting shirt and waited until she had it on before sitting next to her. Then he gave her a small black box.

Crossing her legs, Katria tucked tangled locks of hair behind her ears. She accepted the box. "What is it?"

"Open it."

Nervous, she looked over the small box. The shiny lacquer exterior gleamed in the warm, dim light. She slowly opened the hinged lid. Neatly nestled inside were two golden rings made of intertwined bands. Sean reached in and pulled out the smaller ring. He took her left hand, and her heart pounded. Meeting her eyes, he slid the ring onto her finger.

"You didn't get a normal engagement or a celebration. You didn't even get to hear your husband promise he'd be a good man to you." His hold on her hand tightened, his fingers sliding over the ring. "We chose a life that takes away any chance at normal we could ever hope for. I know this will never be enough—"

Her lips over his stopped his words. The box tumbled from her hand as she grasped his cheeks and kissed him hard. "Learn this now, husband," she whispered, her eyes closed, heart open. "*You* will always be enough."

"And you," he said huskily against her lips, "will always be my wife."

Katria's steady breathing brushed against Sean's chest. Her cheek rested in the hollow of his shoulder, and the length of her body ran against his. The soft skin of her thigh pressed to his, her hips cradled along his side, played havoc on his restraint. In slow, measured breaths, he rode out the wave of desire. Sean knew he'd never get enough of her.

He combed his fingers through the long length of her hair, entranced by the way the warm glow from the woodstove made the midnight strands shimmer. The dim light caught on his ring as he let the silky tresses fall. His other arm draped across her back to her hip.

She loved him.

The knowledge made his heart both swell and ache. When she'd said the words, the truth of them had flowed through him like a tidal wave. She'd meant every syllable. And the part that scared him the most was, he'd almost returned them. Only the uncertainty of the emotion made him hold back. What did he know of love? No one, not even his parents, had loved him to the depths he'd experienced tonight from Katria. The sensation was new, exhilarating, and downright terrifying.

The meaning of the word, or what actions accompanied the sentiment, was foreign. Yes, he wanted to protect her, know she was content in their relationship, and please her at every turn. Was that love? Sean sighed. He didn't know, and he certainly didn't want to mess up where her heart was concerned. At some point, though, she'd expect him to say the same.

Then, of course, he couldn't ignore the dire future in store for them.

He wasn't sure when in their lives his family seemed to lose their ever-loving minds, but the hard fact of his ancestry was that they did. They always did. A deep, insatiable need to fulfill a selfish desire sprang forth, and like a curse, a Blackbain couldn't resist the compulsion. So far, he'd kept a careful check on any impulses. Nothing was allowed to rule him. And so far, he'd won. But what if one day he didn't? What happened when the day came, and the yet unknown addiction lurking in his veins sprang forth?

His hold around her waist tightened. He couldn't hurt her the way everyone else in his family had hurt someone. Soon, he'd tell her the truth. Because as he rested his jaw against the top of her head, closing his eyes, he knew she was the only one who could save him.

❧ 23 ❧

gentle fog blanketed the early morning landscape. Rising from the ocean, tendrils of fine mist swirled along the ground and in the delicate light of dawn. Katria disappeared around the back of the house, following the narrow brick path to the greenhouse, leaving Sean alone with her father. Again. The hired carriage was packed and ready to depart when they were, but at the last moment, after her quiet goodbyes to her father, she'd slipped away.

"Her mother's work is in there." Aleksandrov motioned with his chin to the greenhouse, crossing his arms over his broad chest.

"She told me her mother was a botanist."

"Yes, brilliant woman. I *almost* felt guilty for taking her away from her work in Ruthenia on pharmaceutical plants. But she adapted and changed her passions and focus. She enjoyed bringing long-dead plants back into the world." He shook his head on a sigh and a frown. "I think she felt her work somehow made up for mine, in the end."

Sean took a slow, steady breath. A knot formed in his stomach. "Her mother was Ruthenian as well?"

Aleksandrov nodded, his attention still on the empty pathway. "Yes."

Sean bit his tongue to keep from cursing. He hadn't known, though he'd suspected... *of course* he hadn't known, how could he have? All those years ago, he received information about Katria's training, not her family. Not that the knowledge would have mattered, he hadn't known she'd be his wife. He didn't even know for sure her father was Ruthenian until a few days ago. Being of full-blooded Ruthenian heritage presented them with significant hurdles to overcome. Hurdles Katria might not have been willing to endure had she known of them. He wanted to bellow a curse.

The old assassin slid his gaze away from the path to Sean, who met his stare with a clenched jaw. Understanding slowly lit Alexandro's brilliant blue eyes. "Ah, yes, well, there is a positive, I suppose. If things don't work out, you likely won't have to worry about children."

"And if she wanted children?" Sean asked softly.

Aleksandrov took a slow, deep breath. "I don't know. Ruthenian women aren't permitted to marry outside of our heritage. *Katya* is lucky. She won't ever know what we rescued her from."

"She was still married off."

"Ah, yes, but not like you think. I am assuming the contract is limited, and without having to worry about children, you both will be free."

Sean's stomach clenched. He didn't want to be *free*. When he'd told her last night she was his, he meant the words. But he couldn't deny her a family in the end if she wanted one. Something from his understanding, only a man of Ruthenian blood could give her.

"Explain to me about the genetics."

Aleksandrov shifted his weight and cleared his throat.

"Ah, are you sure you wish to have this conversation with *me*?"

"Since you're the only Ruthenian I know, yes. Plus, she's your daughter. You should want her to be happy. Kids may be what makes her happy. I have to help her understand." Sean sighed and shook his head in disbelief. Only his luck. "If it comes to that."

Silent seconds passed, Alexandro's stare intense on him. Finally, his father-in-law nodded and directed his attention to the ocean beyond the house. "You know of the history?"

"The legend of genetic engineering in humans and what eventually became the Ruthenian nation? Yes, we learned of it in academia."

"Not legend, fact. Ruthenia was the first to record genetic inheritance. Not just eye color, or hair, or height, but actual talents that grow when nurtured with correct pairings. For generations, Ruthenia carefully cultivated her genetics to produce the strongest talents that would make her a formidable nation. During the process, our scientists found our women select the genes their offspring inherit. Rejection is high. As a result, our men adapted. We know when our women are..." A pained expression crossed his face, and he shifted on his feet again. "I knew when my Maggie was, oh, how to say... ready? Able to conceive? We call it in her phase."

Sean raised a brow. "When she was ovulating?"

Aleksandrov snapped his fingers and grinned. "Yes, that. We know, Ruthenian men, we can, I don't know, smell it, I guess? We bond, as mates, and as a result, we know when our women are ovulating. When Maggie and I were ready for children, we ah..." The aging man turned red, and Sean bit the inside of his lip to keep from laughing. "We didn't leave the bed for days. It's that way in

Ruthenia; it's known as conception phase, and when we enter that stage, no one is allowed to bother us. Here in Sziveria, the practice is unknown."

The corner of Sean's mouth lifted. No, sex was not such an open topic in their nation. Their more modest culture had rubbed off some. The elder Ruthenian was bashful discussing the subject. "So Ruthenian women have never married outside of the country?"

"Some. About thirty years ago, a prestigious beast master married a Sziverian woman. Their children became somewhat famous in our land. If someone proves their lineage back to Ruthenia with strong Gen-Heir traits, officials may grant permission for such a pairing."

Sean rubbed the stubble on his jaw in thought. "I will have to research the bond. I'm sure there's something in my medical journals."

Aleksandrov glanced at him. "You *must* know when she's in her phase. It's the only way even to try, when you both are ready."

Katria's father left out even then, they'd be lucky. Yet another reason he should have kept his hands to himself. Or rather, his entire body if he were honest. One more topic to add to the already difficult conversation Sean would have with his wife.

Sean wasn't sure if he wanted to have children. His Sympathic ability wasn't the only inherited gene passed along. Did he want to curse another generation of Blackbains? He raked a frustrated hand through his hair. The sun glinted on the band Katria had slipped onto his finger. Now it seemed fate had chosen for him. For them. How would he tell her she'd unknowingly become stuck in a marriage that might prove to be fruitless? Sean clenched his jaw. The bigger question, perhaps, was whether he'd be willing to let her walk away if she decided children weren't something she could do without.

Four nights later, Katria found herself clothed in yet another uncomfortable formal gown. She'd refused to wear anything poufy and was thankful Rebeka put her in a navy dress with only one sheer top layer of silk. A couple walked past their group for the third time. They stood under a walkway near the wall with Jonathon Hunter. Katria controlled the urge to stick her tongue out at the couple's obvious attempt to eavesdrop. They weren't the only ones making an overt effort, either. What was with these people?

"Seems the two of you sharing the same breathing space is a hot topic tonight," she bit out. "I don't know how we're supposed to get anything accomplished."

"Don't worry." Sean brought a small glass tumbler of liquid the same color as his eyes to his lips. "The buzz will die down shortly, and we'll find somewhere quiet to set things in motion."

Sighing, she twisted the ring on her finger. The object proved to be an unexpected stress reliever. "I don't see why we couldn't have met at the house as we have been."

"Because someone is going to notice our little gatherings and know something is up, that's why."

"But Kevin can't be here," she argued.

Sean frowned. "He doesn't need to be, not for this."

Jonathon raised his glass to his lips, taking a sip. "I don't really, either."

Sean gave him an annoyed sideways glance. "No, but you invited yourself anyway."

Jonathon shrugged. "What can I say, noticing three-fourths of a covert group all in one place, my curiosity is piqued. Since this is *my* city, I like to know what's going on in it."

"Your city?" came a woman's husky voice. "And here I thought it was mine."

Katria turned as Cora sauntered up to them, a wine glass perched delicately in her slender fingers. A stunning pale gray gown with shimmery accents brought attention to her distinctive silvery eyes. Like Katria, she'd shirked the ridiculous hair fashion and wore hers in unbound black curls around her shoulders. Three strands of pearls draped across her neck, the last strand settling above her breasts.

"Since the safety of the city beats the excitement of gossip, I'm afraid I win this one," Jonathon stated with a raised glass.

Cora edged past Katria until she stood beside Jonathon. "We could share."

Jonathon's expression took a serious turn. "I don't share."

"Well, isn't this just a fun night?" Katria grumbled. She almost reached for her husband's drink, realizing now why he'd grabbed one.

Mason joined them, pushing his large frame between Cora and Jonathon. "This is convenient. With enforcement-boy here and miss-writes-when-she-shouldn't, no one will think our conversation is anything but casual."

Jonathon angled his body, which wasn't as tall or large as Mason's, but equally fit, and glared. "Enforcement-boy?"

"Enforcement-man? Enforcer-man?" Mason tapped his finger on his chin. "What is it they call you again?"

"Mason," his sister warned.

"What?" he snapped, his pale eyes flashing.

"You're being ridiculous." Cora placed a hand on her brother's jacketed arm. "Act your age, for once."

"If you'd stop flirting, I wouldn't have to resort to immaturity," Mason said between clenched teeth.

Cora bristled. "Stop flirting? There's nothing wrong with my flirting with whomever I want. You aren't in charge of me. In fact, I'm a solid hour older than you."

Sean stepped forward, creating a half-circle of the group, and pointed at the bickering siblings. "Do not make me banish the two of you from this little discussion. And *you*," he gave Mason a hard frown, "I actually need. So behave."

Like two chided children, they pouted. Katria bit the inside of her bottom lip to keep from laughing.

Jonathon lifted his left arm and his jacket fell away to reveal a simple, thick silver band around his wrist. A band that marked him promised to another woman for marriage. He fixed Mason with a glare. "And the promises made with this band don't belong to your sister, so back off."

Sean dropped his hand at his side on an exasperated sigh. "And here I thought Asherwick and I standing in the same vicinity would cause a stir."

Cora laughed. "Oh, come now, Sean darling, you know wherever I am, voices follow."

"Yeah, well." Sean ran his hand down his face. "As your brother so kindly pointed out, the two of you are providing great concealment. Let's act like the grown-ups we are, and get this conversation done so we can socialize like normal people."

Cora snorted and then motioned to Sean, Mason, and Katria. "Normal people? You three?"

Another couple walked past. Katria looped her arm through Sean's and delivered a small, ladylike laugh, keeping up appearances that their little social circle was mundane in conversation.

Cora quirked a brow. "Well, aren't we catching on quick. All right, talk, before people start purposefully slowing down."

Sean didn't waste any time. He briefed everyone in the circle about the visit with Katria's father and what they had learned. When Jonathon's part in the recollection came around, he glanced down at his boots, scuffing them along the floor. Katria tried to remain relaxed, but as Sean laid out her broken past, heartache made her tense. Sean's hand rested on top of hers, and he gently stroked his thumb along her wrist in a soothing action, not missing a word. She glanced up at him. Her husband, so attuned to her needs, no matter how small.

Jonathon furrowed his brows. "Who exactly is Aleksandrov Nachemir besides Katria's father?"

"Only one of *the* most infamous assassins of our century," Cora stated, excitement bubbling in her words. "This is amazing, I mean, I would win every journalism award in the inhabited world if I ran with this story."

Katria's heart leapt into her throat. All four shouted in unison, "No!"

Cora held up her arms in defeat. "All right, calm down. I was joking, of course I'd never do that."

Several people nearby turned and stared. Cora gave them a little wave, and they returned to their conversations.

Sean cast Cora a stern frown, and then continued. "We have to talk to Voklane, but we can't do it in his office or one of the houses. If he's blameless, we don't want to bring any negative attention on him."

A contemplative look crossed Mason's handsome face. "Didn't you and he used to play chess before he commissioned you? At Atherton Square?"

Sean nodded. "Yes."

"Then that's perfect, invite him to a game of chess. I'll research the area and find a position for Kat and me. You can let him know you're not alone."

"I think the HCES needs to sit in on one of these little meetings," Jonathon stated. "They're rather efficient."

Cora glanced at him with a raised brow. "What else do you exp—"

A shriek tore through the crowd, followed by a series of screams. Katria's grip on Sean's arm tightened. And then a single shouted word, *rabies*, rang out in the room, and all chaos broke out.

Human Rabies Syndrome.

Katria didn't waste a second. She leaned back. Pressing against Mason, she reached past him to Jonathon. She'd noted the swell of the pistol at his back, which he'd attempted to conceal earlier in the evening. There was no hiding a gun from a marksman. Before he even realized her intent, she lifted his jacket and pulled the weapon from its holster.

"Hey!" Jonathon argued, coming around, but Mason's arm stopped him.

"Shut it," he barked and then fixed his stare on Katria. "Stairs just outside the room, to the left. They will take you to the walkway above. You'll have a clear view."

She nodded quickly and kept to the wall, away from the pushing, shoving, and clawing happening all around. As she slipped past, she tried to get a glimpse of the victims, but too many panicked guests blocked the savagery she knew was happening. At the door crammed with people desperate to get out, she went to the floor and crawled through the space between struggling legs. The bulky pistol clanked on the floor and bit into her palm.

As Mason had told her, a narrow stairwell, directly to the left of the door, led upstairs. She took the stairs as fast as her gown would allow. On the walkway, she rushed around the edge. She gripped the railing and leaned over to locate the infected individual. A sobbing, frantic woman, gushing blood from her arm, reached out to a terrified man who had fallen and was kicking out to get past her.

Katria continued to run the edge, her focus shifting along the scattered, bleeding injured who now only had weeks to live and would suffer the same fate as their attacker. With every second she failed to locate the diseased assailant, more people suffered bites. She arrived at the location where their group had gathered below, and had an unobstructed view of the room from the back. A man stood hunched over a woman who convulsed in his arms. Katria's gaze narrowed.

When the man stood, the woman fell to the ground, limp. He turned. Blood dribbled from his mouth and soaked the front of his yellow shirt and pants. His eyes didn't search as they looked forward. His head tilted, and his fingers twitched. In less than a second, he was on another person, his movements inhumanly fast.

Katria dropped her knee to the ground. Using the railing, she braced her forearm, locked her grip, and targeted the center of the man's head. The gun whispered to her senses. Confident in her aim, she pulled the trigger, controlling the recoil to keep the bullet true. The crack of the shot rang out as the infected's head snapped back, and he fell to the ground.

Mission accomplished, Katria slipped the gun through the railing and dropped it into Sean's waiting hand below. She moved to the back wall, staying out of sight from anyone below, and watched as Sean shoved Jonathon forward, the gun in his hand. Her lips twitched, and she tried not to laugh at the confusion and shock on his face.

A small crowd began to gather around Jonathon, clapping him on the back, shaking his hand in gratitude. Sean's pace kept with hers along the opposite wall below. Mason stayed with Cora behind Jonathon. In the aftermath, the survivors wailed in terror and sorrow, knowing full well their outcome. Within minutes, Health Services would arrive with a containment unit and the bitten would be taken to a quarantine facility on the outskirts of Haven City. Katria closed her eyes against the pain in their cries, knowing she could do nothing. She couldn't dwell on their injustice.

Sean waited for her at the bottom of the stairs, his hand reaching for her. She wound her fingers through his and kept close.

His lips were in a tense line. "I think this party is over."

"What makes you say that? I bet his lover, or lovers, will make things quite interesting when they find out who was shot."

"I'm sure it'll all be very dramatic. Cora says thank you for a story where she might get to paint Jonathon a hero."

Katria snickered. "I bet she does."

§ 24 §

Jonathon threw his pistol and badge into his desk drawer a little more forcefully than necessary. The objects slid and clanked against the wooden interior before coming to a rest at the back. He used his knee to shut the drawer and then fell back into his desk chair. Heaving a sigh, he pinched the bridge of his nose.

No matter how hard he tried, he couldn't sway Cora away from the article she was determined to write about the night. Events he didn't even bring about. The woman hadn't been fooling him about her abilities. While Jonathon could hold his own with a gun, it usually took him a shot or two to make his mark. She'd hit the bullseye with a pistol and no scope. How? The feat seemed impossible to him.

"I thought I heard you enter," a sweet female voice said from the doorway.

Jonathon glanced up to see his sister, Ramsey, walk through the study door. She tied a fluffy pink night coat tightly around her small waist. Her black curls fell in disheveled chaos around her round face. She brushed her fingers under her violet eyes and yawned.

"You look exhausted. Why are you still up?"

She plopped down in a seat across from his desk. "Because I live such an exciting life."

Jonathon snorted. "Yes, the bird nest outside your window is the epitome of thrilling."

She stared at him with an air of boredom. "Fine, I live an exciting life through you. Now, out with it, I want to know how the social went."

"You could go with me, you know. You're always included on the invitations."

A frown darkened her pretty face. "As a courtesy. No one wants me there, and you know it."

"Ramsey..."

She held up her hand. "How many times do we have to have this conversation? I can't stand their whispers or their distrustful looks. Like I'll know all their secrets if they so much as meet my gaze. I'm fine."

Jonathon sighed, knowing full well the near five-year fight with her would continue. Only now he had a bigger problem than a social recluse of a sister. She still didn't know he was working with Sean Blackbain. Or that he'd been at a party where a rabies outbreak happened. And while one he could still keep from her, the other he couldn't. He opened his mouth to tell her about the evening when a sharp knock sounded on the front door.

Frowning, he stood. Ramsey followed him into the entryway. He knew it wasn't anyone from Haven City Enforcement Services to collect him. They'd use his radio to call him whenever an emergency or a case requiring his attention arose. So then, who could be at his door so late? He swung the door open quickly. Dancing silver eyes greeted him.

"Well, hello there, hero," Cora said with a seductive smile.

Jonathon glanced past and noticed she was alone. He frowned. "Miss Dandridge, to what do I owe the pleasure?"

She pushed past him, removing her cloak with one elegant sweep. "I have to interview the hero of the night, don't I? Can't go to my editor tomorrow without words from the man who saved hundreds of people from a terrible demise."

"What is she talking about, Jonathon?" Ramsey asked, her arms crossed.

Jonathon opened his mouth to tell his sister the truth, but Cora began speaking. "Your brother killed a rabies-infected tonight."

Ramsey's jaw dropped. "An outbreak happened at the social?"

"Yes, but—"

"Yes, and he was stellar!" Cora proclaimed, clasping her hands together in a loud clap of excitement.

Against his better judgment, Jonathon wrapped his arm around Cora's waist and his other hand over her mouth and gave his sister a shallow smile. "It wasn't me. The shooter can't be named. No, I was never in any danger. Yes, Miss Dandridge is going to run with it in the paper tomorrow. No, I can't convince her otherwise." Then he forced Cora into his office and released her. Once she passed the threshold, Jonathon turned to the doorway and said to his sister before closing them in, "I'll be right back."

"I always wondered how it'd feel in your arms. Now I know," Cora stated breathlessly.

Annoyed, Jonathon leaned against the door and

crossed his arms. "As Primary Guardian Kynhaven said so eloquently earlier tonight, shut it."

She braced an arm over her waist and touched a finger to her mouth playfully. "My, a little testy, aren't we?"

"Why are you going to write the story?"

"Because a hundred and fifty people witnessed the attack, and everyone there knew you were the only one who had a gun to stop it."

"A footman could have a gun."

"Hardly. Sean made the only decision he could when the other attendees gave you credit." She surveyed him. "Why are you so opposed to playing hero? You'll probably get a promotion."

"Because I didn't do anything to earn praise."

Cora sighed. "Valiant to the end." Then she nodded her chin towards him. "Who's the girl?"

Jonathon turned his attention to the silver band on his left wrist. "Woman."

"Ah, of course." Cora smiled. "So?"

"I don't see how it's any of your business."

She closed the distance between them and took his wrist in her hand. Her finger traced the curving metal. "I can't believe I never noticed you were promised before."

"That's because you didn't want to."

A pout turned her provocative lips downward. "That's true."

Jonathon pulled his wrist free. "How can you..." He sighed and dragged his hand through his hair. "How can you risk your life in any meaningless relationship? You saw the risks first-hand tonight."

She took a wide step away from him. "Contrary to what people think of me, my relationships are rarely meaningless. Just because a promise or contract doesn't come of them, doesn't mean I don't appreciate the time. I had my chance at love, and now it's gone."

Jonathon wanted to ask what love had to do with protection. Without a minimum year, honored by over ninety percent of those who entered into a contract, the risk of becoming infected with human rabies syndrome was very real. The marriage ensured they kept the promise to remain faithful for the duration of their relationship, regardless of how short it may be. If Cora couldn't accept a single year, what must have happened? The hurt etched on her beautiful face pulled at his compassion. Jonathon wanted to reach for her, but Cora was a dangerous woman to hold.

From experience, he knew how limited his self-control was when it came to her. So, he kept his arms crossed. "I'm sorry to hear that."

"But not sorry enough," she said with a sad smile. Then she stepped forward again, her fingers tracing over his forearm. "I am careful, you know. You don't share me while you have me."

"You've mentioned that before."

"Yes, and you've considered it." She rose on her tiptoes, her mouth rising towards his. "I know so."

Before she could kiss him, Jonathon slipped away from the door. "I take my promise seriously, Miss Dandridge."

A predatory gleam entered her gaze, but she didn't follow. "At least let me know the name of the woman who is earning such loyalty from you."

"Why do you care?"

She shrugged. "Consider me curious about my competition."

"Competition?" Jonathon laughed. "Woman, you'd be bored with me before she stepped foot back in this country."

"Bored?" Her eyes narrowed. "You aren't one of those who douses the lights and jumps under the covers kind, are you?" Her gaze roved from the top of his head to his booted feet. "Because that would be a real shame."

Jonathon fisted his hands to keep from growling. "You will never know, so stop attempting."

She sighed and waved a hand. "We both know I enjoy torturing you too much for that. But very well, I'll stop for tonight."

"Will you change your mind on the article as well?"

"No." She opened the study door. "But I'll try to tone down your role."

"I appreciate that," he said, following her into the foyer.

At the front door, she swept her cloak back over her shoulders. Once outside on the steps, she turned to face him, her beautiful face set in determination. "I must know, please tell me who she is."

Jonathon braced his forearm above himself on the open door and met her curious stare. "Sylphine Seartavos."

Cora's eyes widened, and she made a choking sound. "The Italyssian trade heiress, Sylphine Seartavos?"

"Yes, the very same."

Bright pink flushed across her cheeks. "Well, I do have competition."

Jonathon simply smiled and closed the door. He made sure to bolt all the locks before heading back to his study. Tomorrow, some made-up story about the rabies-infected would end up in the paper. Cora never needed him for anything other than her entertainment.

"What about Sylphine?" Ramsey asked, rising from the stairs.

He hadn't even noticed she'd been waiting. "Miss

Dandridge wanted to know who I wore the promise band for."

"Oh. Why?"

Jonathon cast her a Do I really have to say why stare before returning to his study.

Ramsey followed him. "You weren't in any danger, were you?"

Considering the company he'd been with, he'd likely never been safer. But the genuine concern and fear in his sister's voice had him turning to face her. "No, I wasn't, I swear."

"Who shot the infected then?"

A pang of remorse burst through his chest. Ramsey was going to hate him, and she had every right to. "Primary Guardianess Wintersfall."

The color drained from her already pale face. Disbelief widened her eyes. "What? When did... how did he...?"

Jonathon immediately realized his sister had the wrong man on her mind. He reached out and steadied her swaying form. "No, Ramsey, Sean Blackbain's wife. Her name is Katria. Remember, Endowment and Revocation gave the title over to him after his brother's guilt and incarceration."

"A-and you were with them?"

He knew he had to tread carefully. She was giving him a chance to explain, and he couldn't lose it. "I investigated the murder of Katria's family members." She didn't need to know at the woman's request.

"No one else could handle the case?" she asked, a tinge of color returning to her cheeks.

"Ramsey..."

His sister looked away from him and shook her head as if clearing away thoughts. "You're right. You're the best at solving crimes, and Primary Guardianess Wintersfall didn't do anything to deserve my anger." She took a deep breath. "If the woman fired the gun, why isn't she in the article?"

"Because she's FIO commissioned, she can't be in the paper. No one can know she can shoot a gun." Especially of her caliber. He'd never met anyone capable of what he'd seen tonight.

"I see. Thank you for telling me, I know you probably shouldn't have."

Jonathon chuckled. "Who are you going to tell? You don't even leave the house."

She shrugged, and he dropped his hands from her. "I do when Sylphine visits."

"You should even when she doesn't."

"I'll think about it." She turned to leave and then paused. "I'm happy you're acknowledging your promise, even if it is just to keep the two of you from being pestered by pursuers. A sister can hope."

"Ha, ha," Jonathon joked. "Keep hoping, little sister. Sylphine can do better than me and we both know it."

"Actually," Ramsey said with a mischievous gleam in her eyes, "I think she knows she can't."

And with that, she flounced off, and Jonathon was left wanting to drop his head to the desk.

Sean glanced at his wristwatch for the third time and frowned. Voklane was late. Not very professional for a First Intelligence Office guardian. Sean sat at a chess table in the center of Atherton Square, facing a five-story, light-brown brick building. When Voklane arrived, his back would be to Katria and Mason. There only task was to watch the meeting and ensure no one made any attempts on either Sean or Voklane.

"Blackbain!"

Sean turned in his seat. Ryan waved as he moved through pedestrians, taking a stroll on the comfortable summer afternoon. Sean stood from his seat. When Voklane arrived at the table, Sean shook the man's hand.

"Sorry, I'm late, two ariots and a bicycle crashed into each other on Highlands Street, causing a carriage to over-turn." Voklane had a smile pasted on his face, though the emotion didn't show in his light blue eyes. "I was pleased to get your invitation. I was hoping one of you would make a move soon."

Sean motioned to the seat across from him. "Shall we begin our game?"

Before sitting, Ryan glanced over his shoulder. "Where's your wife?"

Opening a simple, polished wooden box, Sean answered, "Across the street, in a vacant room, watching."

Some of the color drained from Voklane's already too pale face. He accepted the white stone chess pieces Sean handed across the table. "Alone?"

"No, Kynhaven is with her."

The information seemed to appease Ryan, for he relaxed in his seat. "And he's keeping her calm?"

Sean raised a brow. "My wife isn't overly emotional, Mr. Voklane."

Voklane met his stare. "Unless she's upset, and then it's not so easy to help her see reason. Her psych evaluation from training said as much. I take it since you wanted this meeting, one of you found my little message in her file."

Sean began to set up his black stone game pieces. "Yes, we found the list and a very talented investigator concluded that someone killed Kat's family specifically to force her into becoming an assassin. Why did you lie to her about examining the murders of her family?"

"I didn't." Ryan's face remained impassive as he set up his white chess pieces. "A week after you completed your first team assignment, I filled out the report."

Sean frowned. "There's no record of any investigation at the SNID. Even the records are missing from her home locality."

Voklane glanced up from positioning his queen. "That is not of my doing."

"But you did know she was the only one who was supposed to be left alive?"

"I know the arch guardian told me to make sure she

said yes to my offer before anyone else could make her one."

Sean paused halfway to setting a pawn before his left bishop. "What do you mean, anyone else?"

Voklane braced his forearms on the table and sat forward, his voice lowering. "A little over four years ago, Arch Guardian Synintel gave me a list. He told me to look into all the names, record where they lived, and how old the children listed were, and not to share this information with anyone. So, I did. Only one child was of legal age, and one close."

"Survaine and Nachemir." Sean slowly continued to add pawns to the front row.

Voklane nodded. "Yes. Survaine said someone had already approached him with a proposition who'd discovered his talent. He didn't provide me with any further information, and I didn't ask. It wasn't my job. I did make him an offer, one he accepted."

"And Nachemir?"

"She was a little trickier. She wasn't yet of legal age, so we had to wait. Alexandrov would never have agreed to his daughter following in his footsteps. Synintel hoped her father would shield her from whoever was looking for their assassin. Then word came of the murders of her mother and sister. Synintel wasted no time. I didn't know she'd been shot too, but in hindsight, that likely let me get to her first because they were waiting for her to heal."

"Is that why her name was changed on the documents filed?" Sean asked. "And how did our marriage contract have the correct name, but the one Cora Dandridge looked at from Records Department had Kat's false name?"

Ryan studied the board and then made the first move with his knight. "Yes. Synintel wanted a buffer, and giving

Kat a name no one would know seemed to have worked. As for the marriage contract, we just made sure the fake one was what a records keeper could pull."

"I think someone knows. There's been an attempted kidnapping at a party we attended, and someone stabbed her and made it look like a robbery gone bad," Sean told him, also leading with his knight.

Ryan's attention shot up. "Someone attempted to murder her?"

"I think so."

"She all right?"

Sean met his gaze. "I made sure she was all right." Sean moved a pawn to be open his rook. "And placing her on my team?"

Voklane took a deep breath and pushed a pawn forward one square. "You mean making her your wife?"

"Team first." Sean moved out a pawn two squares.

Voklane moved another pawn forward one square. "Synintel wanted her on a country loyal team. If she were on a trustworthy team, no one would be able to approach and sway her allegiance. We don't have a team more loyal than yours."

"Was there a concern she'd be approached once on a team?" Sean moved his bishop out across the board.

Voklane countered with a pawn. "I don't know how much you've heard since being home, but things are a bit of a mess here. We believe that at least some of the drug smuggling and human trafficking operations were planned in advance. To what end, I can't answer. However, if someone has an agenda and is slowly weakening the spine of this country, we had to have Katria on a team we were sure was a hundred percent vetted. We couldn't risk someone compromising her from the inside. Since the entire purpose was to keep Katria Nachemir not only on our side, but sane in the process, we had to be strategic and place her with the right team on the first try."

Sean retreated the bishop to his pawn row. "What do you mean, keep her *sane*?"

"The reason the FIO contracted you two together. Your Sympathic abilities are crucial to Katria, along with your composed leadership style."

Confused, Sean looked up from the board, folding his arms on the table. "I don't understand."

Voklane met his stare. "How much do you know about her father?"

"Just that he was renowned for his skill."

Ryan shook his head. "No, he was renowned for his ruthlessness. Until he met Margaret Havrenko, who became his wife. We had to make sure Katria never reached that stage to begin with."

Sean drew his brows together. "You placed her with me to keep her level?"

His lips drawn in a serious line, Voklane leaned forward. "She would be a lit fuse without you. Do you really think she would have allowed us to meet and talk this out if you hadn't initiated it? She'd have shown up at the FIO with a rifle and demanded answers regardless of the consequences. And there wouldn't have been anyone with the skill to stop her."

The truth of Ryan's words hit Sean like a punch to the gut. He glanced up at the window, from which he knew Katria watched.

"You're helping her win a war she doesn't even realize she's fighting," Voklane said softly. "Imagine the damage someone else could have done if they'd simply let her loose on the inhabited world."

Sean pushed aside thoughts of the alternate reality his

wife might have faced and refocused on their game. "What happened after she and Survaine were commissioned?"

"There was no discernible consequence if that's what you're asking. It's been quiet. There wasn't anyone shouting in my office or demanding answers. No one even asked how I knew to find two Gen-Heir sharpshooters with extraordinary ability even within their field."

"But Synintel knew."

Voklane nodded. "Yes. My only consolation in all of this is he still trusts me implicitly, and I know I'm his first choice when it comes to making sure those within the FIO are loyal."

Sean asked the next question quietly. "Have you discovered any who are not?"

"I have my suspicions, but I can't act or share on any of them. Yet."

"You can't tell me anything." Sean frowned, disappointed.

"Nothing except to keep moving in the direction you already are."

"Is this why we were called home?"

Voklane shook his head. "I don't honestly know why you were sent those orders. But since nothing has come down, it very well may be."

Sean suddenly wanted to swipe the pieces off the table in frustration. "Are we to get nothing that can help us?"

"I'm afraid I can't divulge anything Synintel doesn't clear."

Sean's gaze narrowed. "He cleared this conversation?"

"Yes."

With a growl of annoyance, his focus followed a little gray bird hopping about under the table beside them. "I'm going to have to convince Kevin to meet with the arch guardian."

"That would be wise, I agree."

"I'm going to need more. Kevin won't go see the man with what little I have, especially since nothing is tied to much more than my wife. I don't think you understand how deep Kevin's hostility lies."

Voklane shrugged indifferently. "Then you're going to have to be the one to get it."

"Let me see if I understand this correctly," Katria began, pinching the bridge of her nose as she paced before the fire in Sean's room. "Someone killed my family to get access to me, and now that they can't have me, they're going to make sure I don't live long enough to figure out who they are."

Sean opened his mouth to reply, closed it, then tried again. "Well, I didn't say that, exactly."

Katria glared at her husband. "You didn't have to say it, *exactly*. These individuals, whoever they may be, have worked very hard to remain hidden. My little quest to solve their crime has them on edge. And your meeting with Voklane today likely made things worse."

She collapsed on the small couch next to him and tried not to let the despair welling up inside take over. "I can't help but feel I've made a mistake and made them too aware of me."

"I will concede, knowing what we know now about Voklane's involvement in commissioning you, that yes, they will know you have another piece in your puzzle. However, they have no idea *what* you know. They can suspect." He turned to face her, and his knee shifted onto the cushion. "But there was never a chance of you forgetting their crime."

"How could they have kept themselves so secret for so many years?"

A dark frown crossed his handsome face as he fixed her with a serious stare. "That's not the biggest problem."

Katria regarded him warily. "What do you mean?"

"Whoever they are, someone high in the ranks informed them that we were being sent home before we even knew."

An uncomfortable, heavy sensation built in her stomach. She pressed her hand to her abdomen. "Why do you think that?"

"The human rabies syndrome infected was somehow released on the floor in Gaula to attempt to kill you. There's no other rational explanation. And in light of all the information we've learned since returning to Sziveria, it makes sense. If they killed you before you could even make it home, no one would have given those murders another thought."

"That means the attack..."

Sean nodded and finished for her, "In the greenhouse was for you. I'm thinking the robbery, like you conjectured, was another attempt against you."

A dull ache blossomed from her injury, and she rubbed beneath it. "And now that I know more, they'll be trying again."

"Now that *we* know more."

Katria stifled a gasp and turned to face him. She grabbed his calf and squeezed. "Do you think they'll hurt Mason and Cora? I know they're going to try for us again, they'd be foolish not to at this point, but Mason was with me today."

"No, I don't think so. Neither Mason nor Cora pose a threat to them. Kevin *might*, if they suspected he were involved in also helping investigate. You, however? You can make sure they don't even know they're in danger before they're gone from the inhabited world. You are a very real threat to them if you figure out who was behind the gun, and who was behind the orders." His hand slid over the top of hers.

Katria let out a long breath. "And now you're in danger, too."

Sean leaned forward, closing the distance between them. His hand caressed under her jaw to the length of her hair hanging over her shoulder. "I was never safe, because I can't allow anything to happen to you."

Fierce protective love stole through her, and Katria grabbed his hand, holding tight. "And they aren't allowed to take another person from me."

❦ 26 ❧

The intensity of her devotion coursed up his arm like fire, searing to his heart until he almost yanked his hand free. Almost. Sean realized what he had to do, and he needed the strength of her love to do it. Knowing that he never said anything about his past would make her feel less for him. He couldn't put off the inevitable any longer. If she loved him *that* much, she needed to know *who* she loved. Bringing her fingers to his lips, he kissed her hand gently and squeezed before rising.

Taking a deep breath, he helped her stand. "I have to show you something."

As they left his room and ventured down the hall, he pointed at the doors. "My parents' suites used to be across from us. Our rooms used to be a single guest suite. I had it converted when I became the owner of the house."

She paused, forcing him to as well, looking at the closed doors across the hall from them. "Why?"

"I wanted no part of the unhappiness that played out in those two chambers." Continuing down the hall, he pointed at two doors. "That was my room, and that one was Joel's."

He stopped at the last door on the right and slowly pushed it open. Inky darkness greeted him. Katria pulled a burning candle from a stand across the hall. The flickering glow barely penetrated the chamber's depth. Sean released her hand and eased into the room. He'd always rushed through here when he headed downstairs, always kept his focus on the hidden door in the wall. Tonight, he allowed himself to stare at the rug, forcing the memory of fear away.

"This used to be my mother's study. Her sanctuary, she'd called it. A space we were expressly forbidden to enter." Katria remained in the entryway, holding the candle like a beacon for him to return to. Shaking his head at the silly thought, he pushed at the rug with his toe. "Mother was late to dinner, and my father sent me upstairs to retrieve her. I checked her room, and it was empty, so I checked here."

The memory pulled at him, forcing his feet to move to the window. "She stood here, looking out, too still. For some stupid reason that I still can't figure out, I wanted to touch her. I called her name, and she did that weird tick thing they do when they hear a victim approach, but at my age, I didn't recognize the action for what it was. Before I even guess what had happened to her, she had me pinned against the desk. I grabbed what I could for a weapon and managed to find her envelope knife. I kicked away from her, slid across the desk, and landed on the floor, here."

Sean returned to the rug and, with his foot, sent it sliding along the hardwood floor. A dark stain caught in the dim light. "I had no idea how fast they were until that night. I barely had time to get the knife up before she landed on me. The blade stabbed deep into her neck, and still she attacked, trying to find any way to sink her teeth into me. It took me a second to realize I had to pull the blade free if I were going to survive. So, I did. But she didn't die right away, and I had to fight her, while her blood poured over us both."

He shoved his hands in his pockets and sighed. "The expiry official told my father he could either list that I'd been the one to kill her, or that the human rabies did. Thankfully, my father made the only decent choice in his life and agreed to the HRS. Over a week, there were seven other cases in the circles she associated with, confirming what everyone had always spoken about her, that she slept around voraciously."

Katria's hand gripped her chest, and her face was a mixture of horror and sadness. "I-I'm so sorry, Sean."

If only he were finished. "Ten years later, my brother was caught assaulting a stylist by Asherwick's sister. A couple of days after authorities hauled Joel off to prison, my father overdosed on opium. In less than a week, I was left without a brother or a father, a name completely in ruins, a rank I had no idea what to do with or even cared for, and a responsibility I was never supposed to have any part in. And that, my dear wife, is what you married into."

Finally, she ventured into the room, her frame stiff. "And their behavior is not yours. You've worked hard in your position and served your country faithfully. You've made yourself someone to respect."

Sean fisted his hands in his pockets, hoping to make her understand. "My father was addicted to opium. My mother to sex. My brother to sexual violence. My uncle died of alcohol poisoning before I was even born. My grandfather was dependent on gambling. My grandmother had to hide the family jewels to keep him from squandering them. My great-grandfather had a vice for rare vintage watches, so much so that my grandmother told me he had three stolen and a man killed for one."

The candlelight danced off the soft curves of her face as she studied him. "Are you saying your family struggles with obsessions?"

Jaw clenched, he nodded. "That's what lineage history has revealed."

"I see," she said softly. She grasped his wrist. An emotional calm slipped from her. No disgust, or fear. Only the placid depths he'd come to expect from his wife. Slowly, she backed out of the room, making him follow. "And what is your obsession, then?"

Out in the hall, she released him. Sean kept from reaching out to claim her sense of peace for himself again. She returned the candle to its holder and regarded him curiously. When he still didn't answer, she tapped her foot. "I'm waiting."

He pulled his hands free from his pockets and shrugged. "I don't have any that I know of. Yet. I've been cautious with alcohol, no drugs, I don't gamble, I don't have a compulsive desire to collect something."

She stepped closer, her finger trailed up his forearm to his elbow, her focus on her drawn path. "And women?"

Sean grasped her chin and forced her gaze to meet his. "Just you."

Her arms wrapped around his shoulders. "You are in complete command of your destiny. Not your ancestry, not what your father, mother, or brother did. You have truly impressive self-control. I'm just trying to help you see that."

"I can't seem to say no to you," he admitted with a soft chuckle. His lips touched hers in a quick, teasing kiss.

She rose on her toes. "The problem is mutual, I assure you."

Sean returned his mouth to hers, more than pleased when she opened for him, her tongue sliding along his. He took two steps forward, forcing her against the wall. She arched her back, pressing her soft yet firm curves against his torso. Desire shot through him straight to his groin. No woman in the history of women made his control waver like his wife. And now he knew the unbridled passion with which her body could love his, making him near weak in his need for her. Katria tore her mouth from his and, with a wicked giggle, shoved him away and then took off down the hall.

"We may be able to have each other anywhere, but the hall is not my idea of fun," she called out as she disappeared into his room.

"That's because you haven't tried it yet," he countered, taking his time following.

With each step, he took slow, deliberate breaths, his restraint returning. When he arrived in his room, he kicked the door closed and found her in a fight with her dress. He swiftly closed the distance and caught her arms above her head, the dark fabric covering her face. She stilled, and he walked her backward until her legs stopped at the mattress. Pushing her, he grabbed the dress. As she fell, the gown slipped free. Long strands of hair flowed around her, settling over her shoulders, covering her breasts.

Sean made quick work of his clothes before climbing onto the bed with her. She scooted back until her feet were on the mattress. When she went to kiss him, he dropped his mouth to her jaw and licked a path down her throat. He made a brief stop at her breasts, taking first one nipple, and then the other into his mouth, sucking until she cried out, her fingers tangling into his hair. After licking the hardened tips, he gently bit the underside of the fullness of her breasts and then moved to her stomach.

Her breathing turned ragged. In lazy circles, he traced his tongue between the hollow of her hips. His hands weren't idle, cupping her breasts, plucking at her nipples, and then caressing down her stomach, and lower to her thighs. Deliberately, he eased them open to accept his torso between them. Desire from her flowed in shocking currents along the pads of his fingers, nearly overwhelming him.

Continuing lower, desperate to know how responsive she was, he used his thumb and forefinger to part her folds and licked around her clit. Her knees pulled in, and her legs fell open at the same time her hips rose off the sheets, opening her completely to his questing mouth. On a deep cry, she bucked beneath him. Sean speared his tongue deep into her, licked and sucked at her clit, and teased until she ground against his face. The rising tide of her sexual hunger became his gauge for what she wanted more of, and what didn't excite her. Her body's response coated his lips and made his finger slide easily into her. Soon her emotional demand for release was a torrent threatening to overtake him. Rampant need left him shaking, had him imagining taking her harder than he had... harder than he ever should. And then, in the throes of her pleasure, as she screamed his name, an image twisted into his mind.

He might not be able to say no to her, but would he listen if she said no to him?

Sean's heart fluttered in his chest, and he shoved away from her, panic gripping him. Where had that notion come from? In the haze of anxiety, Katria's voice broke through. Her hand slid up his bicep, concern snaking its way into thoughts.

"Don't," he managed to growl out, pushing her hand away.

She didn't listen. Instead, she climbed onto his lap before he could stop her, and he gritted his teeth. Her wet core slid along the sensitive flesh of his erection, and he dropped his head back, swallowing against the need to thrust up into her welcoming heat.

"What is wrong with you?" she whispered, touching the exposed column of his throat.

"I don't want to hurt you." He braced his hands on the bed to keep from touching her.

"You were *not* hurting me." She shifted, gliding her slickness along his shaft again until he shuddered. "Does this feel like you were hurting me?"

"I think it's you," he confessed, closing his eyes.

Tenderly, she cupped his face, lifting his head. "What is?"

"I can't say no to you."

"So, you said." She caressed her thumbs across his pinched forehead. And still, she continued the slow, maddening rock of her hips, as if she didn't even realize what she was doing to him.

He shook his head, his breathing rough, from his fear and from the control he needed to keep from locking himself into her body. "No, I can't... what if I can't let you say no to me?"

Much to his relief, she stilled, and he knew she understood his distress. "I have a BACR-18 and I'm pretty good with it."

"Kat," he groaned, opening his eyes to find her staring at him in complete seriousness.

"I'm not playing. But you won't ever hurt me."

Unconvinced by her trust in him, he shook his head again. "You don't know that."

"Yes." Her fingers smoothed into his hair. She leaned forward until her nipples brushed his chest. "I do. How long have you allowed yourself to live with this worry? That no matter what you do, something is going to consume you?"

Since I killed my mother to save my own life. Since guardians dragged my brother off, screaming the things he wanted to do to Ramsey Hunter, no human should ever utter. Since I found my father dead in a pool of vomit on his bedroom floor.

Defeated as the memories took over, he closed his eyes. His head fell forward to rest against hers. "From the day I knew something would."

Katria's fingers pressed into his scalp. "Look at me, Sean Blackbain."

Obeying, Sean lifted his gaze.

Her thumb traced over his lips before she gave him a soft, delicate kiss. Her lips plucked in adoring, undemanding grazes. Her tongue traced his mouth until he opened. Then she slowly touched her tongue to his, easing into exploring his mouth as though it were his first kiss and *she* were the experienced lover. Love so pure ebbed from her mouth, driving away the pain and fear. He wrapped his arms around her, lost in the sensation. When she pulled back, a faint smile graced her lips.

"Could you ever hurt me?" she whispered.

"No." And he knew then, he never could. She was light to his darkness, just as he was to hers.

He held her tightly, a shuddering gasp escaping when her hand encircled his aching shaft and she slowly lowered herself onto him. Slick heat encircled him, and they both moaned. Once he was far enough inside, her hands gripped his shoulders. In slow, deliberate movements, she rolled her hips and rose just enough to drive him crazy. With every descent of her body, she kissed him, but never moved her mouth away, her heavy breaths fanning across his lips and mingling with his equally uneven exhales.

Soon, her reserved movements were too much to bear, and Sean rolled until he had her beneath him. At her urging, her hips rising to meet his, he increased their pace. He slammed into her, his fingers digging into her thigh to hold her in place. Beneath him, she thrashed and sought pleasure with the same wild abandon as he. The bite of her nails radiated through his shoulders and scored down his back as he brought them both over the edge, the hoarse cries of their climax mingling.

Breathless, she relaxed beneath him. "See, not hurt."

Exasperated, he rested his head next to hers. "What am I going to do with you?"

She shrugged and wiggled under him. "I like what you've been doing."

Sean lifted on his forearms and stared down at her, amazed. "You didn't even care about my family's past, did you?"

A pucker formed between her brows with her frown. "Of course, I care. I care because they hurt you. Every one of them hurt you. Your mother's irresponsibility has left scars deeper than mine could ever go. Your brother's cruelty has ruined lives. Your father's addiction left you without a father. Yes, I care. Do I care what everyone outside this house thinks? No. They can rot in their opinions. They make no difference to me. If they knew what lineage I came from, they'd run away screaming. But I told you that."

Then Sean realized she'd had to accept every horrific deed her father had committed. Had to choose to see the man he was, not the man he'd been. She'd grown up seeing the present, not the past. And she'd done the same for him. How had he missed that?

Because his fears had blinded him.

"How did I get you?" he whispered more to himself than to her.

"You can thank the government for that," she quipped and then hugged him tightly with her arms and legs.

"Any other woman would have been convinced she'd married a monster," he said into her hair, returning her hug with a fierce one of his own.

"That's because every other woman doesn't know the true definition of a monster."

❧ 27 ❧

A strange, muffled thump caused Katria to roll away from the warmth of Sean's still body. The unmistakable creak of a board sounded beyond the bedroom door. Katria gasped, bolting upright. Sean's hand grasped her wrist. In the barely visible light of the dying fire, she caught his quick motion to his lips for silence. She nodded, and he signaled toward her room as he slid from the bed.

Katria retrieved his pants and shirt from the floor. She tossed him his pants and then slipped into his shirt. She was almost to her room when he held up his fist, and she froze. Slowly, he lowered himself to the floor in front of his door. Katria kept her breathing calm in the waiting and worked on the shirt buttons. He held up three fingers, then two, and she crept into her room.

Three intruders. She had two minutes.

Once she was certain the room was clear, she rushed across to the armoire to retrieve her BACR-18. Dropping to her knee, rifle in hand, she removed the scope. The subjects would be too close for one. She loaded four rounds and placed an additional two in the breast pocket of Sean's shirt. Rising, she chambered the first round. Silently, she crossed the distance to her door and pressed her back against the wall, her hand on the knob. Seconds to go.

Resting the barrel against her forehead, she controlled her breathing, slowed her heart, and focused her attention on the task soon to be at hand. The rifle was a comfort in her hands, whispering its secrets, waiting, like her, for their task.

"Now." Sean's voice was her cue.

Opening the door, she swung around, rifle raised. In a split second, she identified the silhouette of two targets in the hall. She fired, the sharp sound muffled the interior design of the rifle. She braced against the recoil, chambered a second shot, adjusted aim, and fired again. All before either intruder could react to Sean's single word. Their heads snapped back, and they slumped to the ground. Katria remained patient, slowly sliding the bolt forward to chamber a third round. The remaining man's head appeared from behind a doorframe. Modifying her aim by a fraction, she took the shot. He disappeared from view, a telltale *thump* letting her know the bullet was accurate.

Katria raised her rifle after clearing the chamber. Sean stepped into the hall, edged to the stairs, and carefully looked down. He returned, relaxed. She lowered her gun and joined him at the bodies.

"They picked the wrong house," she said, toeing the limp body. "Why did they go into that room?"

Sean stuck his head in and then straightened. "That was my mother's room." His gaze met hers in the deep shadows. "It would have been yours if I hadn't changed things."

He knelt beside one of the bodies, grabbing the man's face, slack in death. "Do you recognize him?"

Katria leaned forward and glanced down. "I couldn't see them in the alley, if that's why you're asking."

With a sigh of disgust, Sean released him and stood. "I don't like this."

Katria leaned against the wall, propping up her foot with a bent knee, and rested her elbow on her hip so her gun sat against her shoulder. "What's there not to like? They broke into our home and knew right where to go. At least they thought they did. How long ago did you have the house rearranged?"

"Five years."

"Who knew the layout of the house before?"

Sean ran his hand through his hair. "This house? Who doesn't know? I think that would be a better question. Between my mother's wild affairs downstairs and my father's opium nights, this house had more foot traffic than a MagnaRail station."

Katria dropped her head to the wall. "Another robbery gone wrong?"

"No, no, they are desperate now. Whoever *they* are."

His gaze swept over her, and Katria found herself straightening, her cheeks flushing. "What?"

"You put my shirt on."

She glanced down at the haphazardly buttoned shirt, the edges framing her lifted thigh. "It was the quickest thing I could think to put on."

Sean stepped across and reached for her hip. He closed the space between them, his frame pressing into her. Before she could ask what he was doing, his mouth covered hers in a searing kiss.

As quickly as he started the kiss, he ended it. "You look incredibly sexy."

Breathless and amazed that he could see anything more than the assassin she was seconds ago, she nodded towards the bodies. "I just killed three men in your house. You should be thinking about what to do with them."

A boyish grin crossed his face. "I was distracted."

"Clearly."

"Go put on something else." When she moved past him and towards her room, he amended, "That doesn't belong to me."

She couldn't help but grin. After changing into one of her simple dresses and tying her hair back, she replaced the scope on her rifle and added a shoulder strap. Carefully, she set the BACR-18 in the front corner, ready to go if they needed to leave the house. Somehow, she was going to figure out how to make sure her rifle went wherever she did. When she returned to the hall, Sean had already begun cleaning up.

"Where did they go?"

He glanced up from where he knelt, wiping spattered blood from the door. "Downstairs. I already radioed Mason and Kevin, they should be here within the hour."

"Did they have any identification on them?" she asked.

He shook his head, ringing the sponge free of pink tinted water. "No, nothing, just like the one in the greenhouse. They did have knives, and one of them had a diagram of the house."

"Where will you take them?"

"Old City Ruins. No one will find them there, except maybe the criminals who call it home, and they won't say anything."

Katria sighed and knelt beside him, pulling a sponge from the soapy bucket. "We aren't supposed to deal with this when we're home."

"No, but home seems to be unsafe at the moment, so

we are. Thankfully, it's nothing new and we'll take care of the consequences with little effort." Sean did another sweep of the soapy water across the door panel.

Katria frowned, staring at the deep red stain on the rug. "But unlike everywhere else, we won't be leaving in a couple of hours, where any chance for the authorities to solve the crime is erased."

He stopped scrubbing the wall near the door and met her gaze as she lifted it. "Trust me, no one will find the bodies where we're going to go. Enforcement services doesn't even send anyone into the Ruins."

Katria's stomach did an uncomfortable flip. "What if they were sent here just to be killed? Just to have a reason..." She couldn't bring herself to finish the thought.

The sponge plopped into the bucket, and Sean's wet hands covered hers. "Hey, they are not better or smarter than us. I'm positive whoever our unknown enemy is, they sent these people to make another attempt on your life. They're getting scared."

"Why three and not one?"

His hands fell away from hers. Still frowning, he went back to his task. "In case they had to hold you down."

Silently, they cleaned up the mess, finishing as the first glow of dawn broke the horizon. Energy spent, Katria sat against the wall, taking in the soft gray sky outside the window. Pale blue light filtered in, reminding her how little sleep they'd managed to get. Sean sat on the floor beside her, propping his forearm on a lifted knee.

"Do you think Kevin will take mercy on us and let us go back to bed after you deal with the bodies?" Katria asked, rolling her head along the wall until she looked at him.

"You're still on medical orders, so no training for you yet."

Exhausted, Katria closed her eyes, but nodded. "All right."

Within seconds, her consciousness fled.

Sean caught Katria as she slumped into him. Gently, he shifted her weight and rose, holding her tight to his chest. She nuzzled his neck, her warm breath caressing across the sensitive skin where his pulse began to race. He debated where to lay her, his room or her own. Since the night of her injury, she hadn't left his bed, and he decided he wanted to keep it that way.

He took the short distance to his room swiftly. The morning light had yet to penetrate the edges of the curtains. Sean laid her on the mattress. She rolled from his arms into the comfortable mound of pillows with a moan. Her knee rose, the edges of her dress sliding off her leg to her thigh. He fisted his hands, knowing if he traced his fingers up her soft skin, he wouldn't stop until she was very much awake and telling him exactly what she wanted.

"Knock, knock," the familiar male voice said a second before a faint tapping sounded on Sean's open bedroom door.

Sean slid a sheet over Katria's resting form before acknowledging Kevin. "Right on time."

Kevin raised a brow as Sean crossed the room. "Am I ever late?"

"Fortunately, no." Sean eased the door closed.

Kevin glanced around, his attention stopping at a large drying water stain on the hall rug. "The bodies are where?"

"Downstairs."

Kevin clasped his hands behind his back and headed down the hall. Sean fell in step beside him. "How much longer until Kat is healed?"

"Another week on the stitches, and I'd prefer another week after that to give the muscles more time to recover."

"The longer she goes without training, the slower her reflexes will be. Not the best time to be slow."

Sean kept calm, knowing his friend only wished the best for another friend. But Sean's concern for his wife went deeper than mere friendship. "And what good will she be torn open and bleeding again if you push her too hard, as you often do?"

Kevin grunted. "Fine. Two weeks."

Mason was waiting for them downstairs. He was hopping on one foot and inspecting the bottom edge of his boot.

Mason muttered a curse. "These are new boots, too, seriously?" He dropped onto the bench near the opening that led to a secret tunnel beneath Sean's house, which connected to the city's aqueduct system. "Why did I wear new boots?"

"That does appear to be the important question of the day: why did Mason wear new boots?" Kevin plopped down on the bench beside him and struck a contemplative pose. "Hmm, let's consider the reasons..."

"Oh, shove off it," Mason growled and heaved his shoulder into Kevin. Since Mason had a solid fifty pounds on Kevin's leaner frame, the man went tumbling off the bench, laughing.

Of course, had Kevin wanted to stand his ground, he could have. Mason would have been the one on the floor then. Sean shook his head and went to close the entrance.

Still fussing with his mucked-up boots, Mason motioned towards the door. "Those the dead guys?"

"Yes. We'll take them to Old City Ruins."

Mason grunted. "Best place for that nasty business, I agree."

Sean briefed them on the details from the meeting with Voklane yesterday afternoon, and the early morning attack.

During the accounts, Mason's frown had turned into a scowl, and by the end, he was up and pacing. "You do realize we could be dealing with anyone across a range of any of the services."

"It has occurred to me," Sean conceded.

"We need to get Kat out of the city until we can figure a few more things out," Kevin said.

Sean frowned. "She won't like that."

Kevin pulled his knee up and rested his elbow on it, fixing Sean with a serious stare. "She doesn't have to like it. I'm pretty sure you won't like a dead wife, especially since it wasn't *her* bed she was sleeping in."

Mason's eyes widened. "Well, that didn't take long."

Kevin snorted. "What are you talking about? They've only lived together for three years. Didn't take long, my foot."

"But they didn't know they were married then," Mason countered.

"And now they do. When you're in the company of your wife for a month, I'd like to see *your* self-control."

Mason's face contorted. "I'm not married."

"All things happen in good time," Kevin said with a cynical grin.

"Says the man who hasn't stepped foot into the house his *wife* lives in."

Before Sean could diffuse the ludicrous situation, Kevin had Mason pinned to the floor, a knee at his friend's throat. While Mason could hold his own, neither of them were a match for Kevin's speed or agility. They'd all be bleeding and angry before long. A pointless effort that Sean didn't have patience for.

"Enough! The enemy is out there, guardians, not in here!"

Kevin stood and then held his hand out for Mason. To Sean's relief, Mason accepted the peace offering and allowed Kevin to help him to his feet.

Sean held his hands out in a calming manner. "I know everyone is on edge and dealing with their own problems since arriving back in Haven City, but Kat is in trouble. Someone left her as a loose end, and now they want to take care of it."

Mason glanced at the closed entrance in the wall. "How did they think she'd be so easy to kill in her own home?"

"I asked the same question," Sean admitted. "They shouldn't have, unless whoever hired them to do the task didn't know the truth about Kat themselves."

"Or didn't believe it," Kevin corrected.

Mason's arms crossed over his chest. "How could they not believe it, given who her father is?"

Kevin shrugged. "Not everyone sees a woman as capable, especially those in positions of authority."

"We have an elected queen," Mason said.

"Yes, we have a queen, who some would say keeps having babies so she can stay in power longer," Sean said.

Kevin shook his head. "I think the pregnancy five years ago was an accident. I believe the words she spoke were, quote, a happy accident for our family, unquote, but that doesn't mean someone who didn't vote for her isn't angry. Yes, now we have her until the young prince reaches the age of legal adulthood at nineteen and can be elected if he's the choice of the Sziverian people. While the direction may be correct, I don't think our queen had any designs on staying in power through her children."

"Anyone been loud about being upset about the unexpected birth four years ago, then?" Sean inquired, mostly to Mason, who was home more than any of them.

With a disgruntled sigh, Mason sat heavily on the bench, resting his elbows on his knees and steepling his fingers. "No, not that I know of. She's been a competent leader. We have to narrow down the players. We're blind until we can at least attempt to know who we're up against."

Sean tapped his thumb against his thigh. "We'll figure out who's in a position of power to not only orchestrate, but also has access to necessary manpower, and if we can recall anyone showing discontent with our current leader. We need a *Directory of Guardians*. Mine is three years outdated."

Mason gave an apologetic look. "Mine is at Kyn Manor."

They both focused on Kevin, who took a step back. "Oh no…"

Sean exhaled, feeling a bit sorry for his friend. "We need that book."

"Do you know where your wife keeps it?" Mason asked.

Kevin dropped his head back with a groan. "Yes, she keeps it on a pedestal in the foyer. It's the first thing you see when you walk in the door."

Mason flexed his jaw. "I guess as an arch guardian's daughter, position and power *are* everything."

"That, or she wants to make sure everyone who walks through her door remembers she has power on *her* side," Sean remarked softly.

Kevin met his stare. "Fine, I'll get the stupid book." He pointed an angry finger at Sean. "But if she catches me, I'm blaming you."

"Sounds fair. But how about you just don't get caught? Now, let's go get rid of some trash before my basement starts to stink."

$\maltese$ 28 $\maltese$

Groggy, Katria rolled onto her back and spread her arms across the wide bed, finding the other side cold. What time was it? She rose, noting that she wore her dress and her hair was in a loose ponytail. Had she fallen asleep? Last she remembered she sat in the hall with Sean, who wasn't with her. Frowning, she tossed the blankets back and stood.

Shaking out the wrinkles in her dress and then fixing her hair, she headed downstairs. She was still tying the long lengths back when Davis appeared at the bottom of the steps. He held a simple white envelope in his hand.

"Good morning. Have you seen his guardianship this morning?" Davis asked.

"Earlier," Katria ventured, leaning forward on the railing and trying to see into the library. "He's not down here?"

"No, he is not."

Unsure of what to do, Katria tapped her fingers on the banister. "Did he leave?"

Davis's dark eyes regarded her. "I do not believe so, guardianess."

Katria considered what that meant, and then remembered what time it had been when she'd drifted off to sleep. She snapped her fingers and smiled. "Ah, I know where he is."

"Very good. Would you care to take some breakfast to him?"

Placing her hand on her hip, she nodded slowly. "Yes... Yes, I would. Thank you."

"Will any extra servings be required?"

Katria narrowed her gaze on the man's blank face. "That would be nice of you, yes."

"Will you please deliver this as well?"

Davis held out the envelope. Katria went down the stairs and accepted the note and then waited for him to return. A few moments later, he did, carrying a covered basket. He handed it off to her and departed. Katria raised a curious brow and then rushed up the stairs. She checked to ensure no additional staff were present before entering the empty room at the end of the hall.

Someone had already slid the rug Sean shoved away last night back into place. Katria's hold tightened on the basket, and out of strange compulsion, she found herself drawn to the secret the rug revealed. Using her foot, she eased the mat away until the dark reddish-brown stain on the light-colored wood floor came into the sunlight streaming in the window. Beside the long-ago dried puddle was a small handprint, likely where Sean had pushed himself off the floor and away from his mother.

Amid his recollection, his age hadn't registered, not really. Now, staring at the reality the child's handprint exposed, Katria's heart tightened. Instead of loving her sons, their mother had been living a selfish, indulgent life that almost killed one. How had Sean become such a good man? Full of compassion and patience? Neither of which she was sure his childhood included. Filled with anger over a past neither of them could control, Katria replaced the cover.

The muffled sounds of the men doing their morning workout reached her before she came to the last step. Sean was still in the pants she'd thrown him in the pre-dawn hours. Mason had discarded his shirt on the bench near the stairs, leaving him in pants and boots. Kevin had thrown off his button-up shirt, but he still wore a black, cotton, short-sleeve shirt and his pants. His boots lay toppled over near the stairs.

Sweat drenched all the men, their skin red from exertion. Strapped into a pull-up bar, Mason's muscles rolled with each strained movement as he forced himself to touch his toes, his long black hair flying with each sit-up. Kevin fought with a swinging bag, his actions swift and graceful, predatory.

The sight was familiar, but as she set the basket down, her eyes became transfixed on her husband. Running at a rapid pace up the set of training stairs in the center of the room, to the landing and down the other side and around again, he kept a controlled speed, as if he counted each second and made sure he never slowed. His hair fell in wet lengths, framing his handsome face. Sweat ran down his chest and back, darkening the waist of his pants.

The man was dangerously sexy and then some. This was far from the first time she'd seen him give his all during training. However, it was the first time she had an idea of what his body was capable of doing to hers, as she watched every muscle in motion. Exactly how he moved, how he felt, how he sounded with her. Her heart pounded, and she found herself fidgeting as the memory of his mouth on her skin swept into her mind and made her tingle in secret places.

Would she always feel a complete lack of focus around him? In twenty years, when she was sure to have put on a few pounds after having a few babies... She drew her brows together. Did Sean even want babies? Did she? Yes, she decided she did eventually want babies. They hadn't even discussed a family or their future, except that it would be a challenge with their mutual careers. Gripping the basket and the envelope tighter than she had been, Katria tried to stay calm.

So absorbed in her thoughts, she didn't notice Sean make his way across the room to her. His hand grasped her wrist, and she jumped, the basket falling to her feet. An apple rolled out and under the bench near Kevin's boots.

"Are you okay?" he asked, his hand smoothing up her arm to her elbow.

She stared at his hand, darker on her pale skin. Then she glanced up at him. "Do you want to have babies?"

Never before had she seen her husband speechless. Sean stared at her, his mouth open, his amber eyes wide. A strange choking sound came from him, but no words. Then she found her feet playing catch-up as he whisked her into the privacy of the stairwell.

She stumbled up the five steps he took to isolate them. Alarm raced up her spine when he twisted, pinning her to the wall. The scent of him swam in her mind. In that instant, she forgot why she was sequestered with him.

Then he reminded her. "Why are you asking me about babies in the middle of the training room?"

She kept her hands at her side, afraid that if she moved, she'd be running them up his damp skin. Probably not the greatest idea. She licked her lips. "Well, I just realized we hadn't talked about them. We haven't talked much about what to do with our future."

"And you decided *now* was the best time?"

"You asked," she reminded him.

A shaky breath rushed from him, and his eyes closed. "I asked if you were okay."

"Well, I was thinking about babies."

His fist touched the wall above her head. "Yes... we have established that."

Tense heartbeats passed, and still he said nothing. "So?"

"You want an answer now?"

"Is it such a hard question? It feels like a yes or no to me."

His warm gaze met hers, and Katria's breath hitched. "You do realize my answer may not even matter. You're Ruthenian and I'm not."

A slight tremor danced in her stomach. "What does that have to do with anything?"

Sean rested his forehead to hers. "You don't know?"

"What am I supposed to know?"

Sighing, his fingers brushed her cheek to her jaw. "We..." He heaved another long sigh.

Worry gnawed in Katria's stomach. "What do I need to be aware of?"

"When it comes to reproduction, our genetics are very, *very* different."

"How different? What do you mean?"

He glanced back down the stairs. "Are you sure you want to be having this conversation now?"

If he'd been wearing a shirt, she would have grabbed it and yanked. "Yes, yes, I'm sure. Now tell me."

"You go through what's called an ovulation phase in Ruthenia. If you were married to a Ruthenian man, he'd know, and his body would respond because you form some type of bond. You, in turn, accept or reject his genetic material. Usually it's rejected, which is why..." A pained expression came over his face.

Katria tried to remain patient. "Which is why what? Out with it, husband."

"Most Ruthenian couples don't leave bed during that time."

Katria flexed her jaw at the news. All day in bed being loved by her amazing husband? Where was the downside? "That doesn't sound so bad."

He choked on a cough. "Kat, I can't... I'm not Ruthenian." He leaned back a bit and waved a hand in front of his pants. "I don't function that way. I can maybe manage, I don't know, three, maybe four times in a day."

"And that's not enough?" Katria asked, not sure she was understanding the direction of the conversation.

"I don't know. From my understanding, it may not be. I have to research a little more."

He had to research their ability to have children. Katria let the information sink in for a minute. If he knew he had to research, then that meant he'd been thinking about a family. With her. The thought made her heart soar. "You *do* want to have babies. Some day. Even if it's difficult for us?"

His amber eyes searched hers. "You're okay with that? With us having to probably work really hard when we're ready to start a family?"

"Well, I can think of worse things to do than, you know..." She smiled. "I'm just glad we're on the same page."

His hands cupped her neck, his thumbs caressing along her jaw. Slowly, his mouth pulled across hers in a soft, tender kiss. "Wife, you can have as many babies as you want me to make with you."

Elated, Katria wrapped her arms around his neck and pressed her lips to his forcefully. He deepened the kiss, his body pressing to hers. She lifted her foot onto the step above, allowing him to fit perfectly into her curves. His hands left her neck to rest on her hips, pulling her against him. Katria barely had time to register his desire pressing into her when Mason's disgusted voice broke through her haze.

"No! No way! Stop you two, this is *not* the time!" Mason griped.

Katria knew she should be embarrassed, probably sheepish even, but she was responsible for the three dead bodies they'd had to dispose of earlier. The team strategist fussing at her didn't faze her in the slightest.

She pulled from Sean enough to cast Mason a glare. "He's *my* husband, so if I feel like kissing him, I will."

Mason growled and stalked off, a towel swinging angrily from his hand.

Sean chuckled, pulling on the tail of her bound hair behind her back. "He's grumpy this morning."

"I can see that."

Sean gave her a quick kiss before stepping away. The envelope crinkled in her hand as her arms fell away from his shoulders.

"Oh, I almost forgot." Katria handed him the now wrinkled paper.

He opened it, the bemused look on his face giving way to a somber frown.

"What is it?" she asked.

He called over his shoulder on the way back to the training room, "Wystone finally wants to meet."

Katria hurried after him. Kevin sat on the floor eating

an apple. Mason dug through the basket, a small collection of bread, cheese, and muffins on the bench beside him.

"Does he say what for?" Kevin asked after his bite.

"No, just that he has something he needs to discuss."

"Does he want to meet here, or at his place?" Mason asked, not taking his attention from the basket.

Sean looked the note over. "Here."

Kevin took another bite of his apple and nodded. "Good."

Katria sat on the bench beside Mason and took the basket from him. "What are you doing?"

"I haven't had anything decent to eat in a week." Mason took the food back with a yank Katria hadn't been anticipating.

"Why?"

"Cora fired our cook because the woman wouldn't add extra salt."

Katria raised a brow. "Can't your sister add her own salt?"

"Yes, but she said she pays the woman to make her food the way she wants, and if she can't listen, she can leave. So, she left." Mason sighed. "I liked her food."

Katria glanced at Kevin when he snapped into an apple, and he regarded Mason unsympathetically. "Then learn to cook."

Mason rolled his eyes. "I think my attempts would be worse than the housekeeper's."

Kevin sighed and looked up at Sean. "When does Wystone want to meet?"

"He doesn't specify, I guess I'm to return a letter with a time."

With a mouth full of biscuit, Mason managed, "Make it soon, if someone reads the notes between you two, and he is involved in whatever is going on, they won't want him talking."

Sean crossed his arms. The paper crinkled. "I'll tell him he can arrive today, at any time."

Crumbs fell to Mason's lap as he finished the last of the biscuit. "And don't be the one to answer the door, just in case it's a setup."

"I can't be two places," Katria felt the need to point out. "I can be upstairs when the front door opens, or I can be in the loft while the meeting is happening."

"The loft," Sean and Mason said in unison.

Kevin's dark gray eyes danced, and he chuckled. "I guess you're in the loft."

Above Sean in the loft, Katria lay out of sight. He tried to focus on the bank and investment statements he'd neglected over the years and still had to go over. While he decided to use the task to pass the time as he waited for Wystone to arrive, nerves and uncertainty made his attention waver. Checking his watch, he noted he had almost fifteen minutes before the man was due to arrive.

After pushing away from his desk, he headed upstairs, taking them two at a time. Katria sat on the floor against the smaller upstairs desk, one arm braced on a lifted knee. The silky fabric of her black dress pooled around her. Tendrils of hair had come free of her braid, framing her beautiful face. Her rifle lay before her, the muzzle flush with the edge of the second floor. He knew she wouldn't rise. They couldn't risk her being seen when their guest arrived.

She tilted her head and regarded him quizzically. "What's wrong?"

Sean braced himself against the banister in front of her,

crossing his arms over his chest. "Nothing really. I was just thinking we can't exactly hide the body of a key guardian if he does something stupid."

"I don't know. Your plan was very good for the three this morning. Wouldn't it work for anyone?"

"It's unlikely anyone but the one who hired those three will miss them. Society will notice if a key guardian is missing."

Her nose crinkled. "I suppose that's true, except he's on the verge of *not* being a key guardian any longer, isn't he? But, I haven't shot anyone at a meeting yet that didn't pose an immediate threat. If I can see his hands, he's fine."

Sean shook his head. "No, he needs to live regardless. *If* you feel I'm in danger, wound shot only, and make sure he has a weapon. We can explain that one away at least."

"And risk you?" She stared at him, eyes wide.

Sighing, Sean took the few steps to her and crouched down. While her possessive words warmed his heart, her skill made them unnecessary. "Do you really think he could beat you the moment you saw a weapon?"

Katria cast him a glare before looking away. "Why give him the chance?"

"You didn't answer my question." Gently, he grasped her chin and forced her to meet his gaze again. "Could he beat you?"

Her shoulders squared, and her jaw flexed in his hand. A hint of anger and annoyance flowed from her into him. He almost smiled, but instead found himself fighting against the sudden urge to kiss her. How did she do this to him?

A tremor of pride crept into her exasperation. "Of course not."

With little effort, Sean shifted to his knees and closed the short distance between them, settling his mouth over hers. The irritation rapidly changed to surprise. Her soft lips opened, and desire curled in his stomach a second before hers coursed through his veins.

Quickly, he broke the kiss, his thumb trailing over her lips, still parted. "I shouldn't have done that."

"Then why did you?"

"I can't seem to spend more than two minutes with you before I can't think of anything *except* you."

Like a graceful cat, she rose onto her knees until their height matched. Her arms wrapped around his neck, and she pressed her torso to his. She pulled a kiss from his lips, meeting his eyes. "Considering we work together, that could make things difficult."

Sean slid his hands to her hips, wishing she were even closer so he could feel all of her, his need for her straining against the seam of his pants. "I did tell you things would be challenging for us."

She seemed to have the same urge, for she pushed into him until he collapsed back onto the floor, and straddled him. Her eyes closed, and a shuddering gasp escaped her lips before she kissed him, her hips moved slowly over him.

Sean struggled to breathe. Of course, he was married to a woman whose blood seemed to run as hot as his and wanted him with the same desperation he wanted her. He pushed into her shoulders until her mouth pulled free and shook his head. "Kat, I'm going to have to explain what in the inhabited world I'm reading up here if you keep this up."

"I didn't start it," she retorted, her eyes the color of blue fire.

"True, and I promise we *will* finish later. But," he glanced at his watch, "sadly, we do not have time now."

She huffed, but climbed off.

Sean chuckled, grabbed her chin again, and gave her a swift kiss. "And a kiss can just be a kiss," he said against her mouth.

Mischief danced in her gaze. "Maybe if you weren't so good at all the other stuff, I could be satisfied with just a kiss."

He cupped her jaw in his hands and closed his eyes. "Primary Guardianess Wintersfall, you're going to be the death of me."

Katria's fingers trailed through his hair before she pulled away from him. "Go, before we get caught. You should have stayed downstairs."

He kissed her fingers before rising. "I'll remember that next time."

Heart in her throat, Katria's gaze trailed Sean down the stairs and to his desk. She devoted every ounce of her inner control to not following him. She knew she needed to learn to block out the way he made her feel, or rather, the way he could take away all other emotions except the ones she had for him. The man made it infuriatingly difficult, however.

Exhaling, she lay on her stomach beside her BACR-18 and rested her chin on her folded hands. She couldn't see Sean from her vantage point, but she could see the two chairs positioned in front of the desk. That was all she needed to see anyway. Still, she found herself pushing her toes into the floor so she could lean further forward until Sean came into view. He had a pencil in his hand, his arms braced on the desk while he shuffled between file folders and loose papers.

With his white shirt untucked and the sleeves rolled halfway up his muscular forearms, he looked relaxed, in control. Something she assumed he did on purpose. Katria simply watched him, admiring how his shoulders rolled with each slight movement, the way he'd absently tuck a stray lock of hair behind his ear that had no hope of staying. Her stomach did a little flip. Sean was hers and would always be hers. Curiously, she wondered if she could pull a Kevin and land like a cheetah on her husband's desk...

A sharp knock preceded the opening of the library door. Katria quickly slipped away from the edge and behind her rifle. Davis said something that didn't quite make it up to her. Sean's muffled voice carried through the room. Seconds later, a short, portly man dressed in entirely too many layers of cloth strutted into the room. A gold chain hung from his pocket, another draped around his neck, and another still adorned his wrist. Rings graced every pudgy finger. Katria figured the only thing missing was a golden cane. He slicked his graying hair to the side, and little untamed tufts feathered away from the style. *This* was the man married to the beautiful woman who had found her and Sean locked in an embrace in her greenhouse? Perhaps the ranked guardianship had changed Wystone over the years, or the woman married up, Katria speculated.

As the key guardian took his seat, Katria raised the rifle. She braced the barrel on her hand and fitted the stock into her shoulder. Leaning her head down, she peered through the scope until Wystone's round, already perspiring face came into view. He lifted a fluttering white handkerchief to his forehead and dabbed at the sweat. His attempt to use wealth to create a sense of courage seemed to be failing him.

Their voices didn't carry in the cavernous space that was the library, but Katria had learned over the years to read facial expressions. While she wasn't as skilled as Sean, she could read nervousness, anger, and any other strong emotion that would cue danger for her husband. So far, Wystone just displayed uneasiness to her. And provided he stayed that way, he'd be safe.

She kept a sigh internal, recalling Sean's request. The key guardian would remain safe regardless, if only to ensure her husband did. She didn't need him to join his brother in a prison cell because of her.

$$\maltese \quad 30 \quad \maltese$$

Sean regarded Vernon Payce, Key Guardian Wystone. Under the expensive clothes and fortune in gold, the nervous, not-so-little short man fidgeted and dabbed at beads of moisture along his brow.

He waved the white handkerchief about with a huff. "Scorcher today, real hot one."

Sean raised a brow, taking in the expensive wool pants, button-up shirt, vest, undershirt, and overcoat the man wore. In Sean's lifetime, Sziveria had never experienced a *scorcher*, and if they had, it wouldn't have been at the start of spring. "Indeed. Would you like to remove your jacket? I will make sure my staff keeps it safe."

Wystone waved the hankie again and pulled the breast edge of his jacket with his other hand. "No, no need for that, I can't stay long anyhow."

Sean inclined his head and folded his hands on his desk. "Very well, then I'm listening."

A fresh row of sweat appeared above Vernon's brows. He dabbed again. "Well now, I'm not quite sure how to start."

Sean kept his tone even, calm, and assuring. "How about why you chose to speak with me?"

"I know about your team and what you're often asked to do for intelligence. A fellow bureaucrat guardian likes to tell tales out of work."

Despite the hint of deceit in Wystone's voice, Sean kept his expression neutral. "Continue."

"Two years ago, I was approached, in my office at the FIO, to begin swapping out shipping manifests that were coming into Port Scarborough. I was informed that I would receive after-hours compensation for my time, since the work involved official government business. Additionally, I was required to file the original shipping manifests in the same manner as I submit my risk-level briefs for incoming ships from foreign nations. I didn't ask questions."

Sean nodded. "Right, because we don't get paid to ask questions."

Wystone's mouth turned into a grim line. "Yes, correct. So I did as I was asked. It became routine for me."

Reaching for his pencil, Sean flipped over a random sheet of paper. "Do you remember anything about the manifests?"

"The original or the ones I replaced them with?"

"Both."

Wystone rubbed his chin, the white handkerchief swaying in his grasp. "Let's see, they were rarely in the care of the same company or person, but I always put them into the care of one of the top five shipping companies that imports or exports goods for our country."

"Such as?"

"Westican Trading, House of Aishabai Trade out of Cairo, Floralantic Ocean Exports from Perazil, Cyrano Expeditions and Trade out of Italyssa, you know, the major players in world trade." Wystone waved his hand around as if Sean should have known the answer.

Sean jotted the names down. "But on the original manifests, it was always someone smaller?"

"Usually a person or a small merchant company. I rarely paid attention. I figured they probably weren't real anyway. I was the only one who ever showed up to *inspect* the manifests from a Sziverian government branch."

Sean stopped writing. "No one from Immigration and Import Regulation was there?"

"Nope, I already had the new stamped and approved manifests to swap out when I arrived."

"Who was signing off on the new manifests in an official capacity?" Sean asked.

"A shield guardian whose name I didn't recognize and can't remember, maybe a master guardian or two. Never anyone lower than a primary guardian, though."

Sean glanced up and met the man's dark stare. "And you can't remember any names at all?"

He tapped his wide chin again. "Solway? Solax? Sol something, and let me think, Middle some sort or another, Middleton, Middlewich? I'm not sure, something to that effect as well. I figure they're probably as real as the shipping companies on the original manifests."

Sean frowned and wrote down the potential names. "What else?"

"An unsigned note would tell me the time of arrival and the dock. I was usually the one waiting until the ship was tied off. Let me tell you, dead of October, before the harbor was near frozen, almost wasn't worth the money. I thought I might freeze." Wystone mock blew on his hands, a faint shiver wracking his rotund frame.

"The names of the ships on the original manifest never matched what arrived in port?" Sean asked.

Wystone shrugged again, fidgeting with the buttons on his jacket. "Like I said, I didn't pay much attention to the original documentation, and it was usually after dark when the cargo arrived. If I did happen to see the name of the ship, none of them seemed familiar."

Sean tapped the pencil on the half-filled sheet of paper. "What about cargo?"

"That didn't always change, usually resources, such as wood, clay, or wool. One shipment contained iron ingots, and the manifest was altered to indicate wood. I remember that because I found it odd. Raw iron is rare."

"Raw iron is incredibly rare," Sean agreed.

"The rail industry pays a great deal for it to keep the lines running."

"Yes, but why lie?"

"Market prices?"

Sean grasped the pencil between both his hands, thinking. He wasn't a logistics analyst, but he knew one, not that Kevin was currently speaking to his wife. Everything seemed to be funneling into his interceptor's hands. Sean sighed. "Perhaps. Why were you let go for this if it was part of your job?"

Wystone's hands fell to his lap. The rings *tinked* against each other. "Oh, you heard about that, did you? How embarrassing. Turns out I only *thought* what I was being asked to do was official. The last shipment I handled made me ask questions. Someone must not have liked my inquiries. I was released the next day and told it was because I was abusing my position in the FIO to help smugglers bring illegal goods into the country. I argued, how could I have done that without inside help? They said I didn't need inside help. I just needed a stolen or forged inspection stamp. I already had access to the manifest information for my position."

The key guardian's shoulders hunched forward, and he brought the hankie to his nose and rubbed it. Sean waited a moment before speaking again, watching him closely.

"Did they find the seal?" Sean asked.

"You know they did, right in my top desk drawer." He snorted, his attention still on his hands. "As if I'd keep something so damning in such an easily found location."

"What were the contents of the shipment you questioned?"

Wystone took a deep breath, his gaze rising to meet Sean's. No lies crossed the baron's face as he spoke. "A magic lily dust shipment from a vessel that supposedly sank."

Sean sat back. "I have heard rumors about that ship. The entire shipment was all the drug?"

"I'm not sure exactly if the entire ship was full or just a portion. Of course, it was coming from Alexandria, where magic lily isn't illegal, so the original manifest would have had that information. However, no one gave me the original manifest to exchange, as is normal. I wasn't even informed to conduct an assessment on the incoming vessel, which is why, at the time, I had no idea what the cargo was. My instructions were only to give them the forgery."

"When did you suspect drugs and not something else valuable, like say coal, cotton, or silk?"

Wystone tugged at his collar. "Over the last two years, I've suspected large shipments of drugs. As for this particular shipment? Someone on the crew gave me the drug to examine, as if I knew what to look for in quality or something."

Sean raised a brow. "And you said nothing?"

"I should have, I know that now. I should have refused and gone straight to Immigration and Import and reported the ship and everything I knew." He shook his head, and Sean thought for a moment the man might cry. "But I didn't. I, um, I figured maybe, being the FIO, they were setting up dealers, you know? Trying to dismantle things from the inside is what we're, I mean they're, known for," he explained in a rush. "Then, when they left out the original manifest, I knew whoever had been asking me to swap out the paperwork must have been hiding something illegal, and I... I was scared. I was in too deep by that point."

"All right," Sean said in a smooth, easy tone. "And what about the ship?"

"This time, I did recognize the name of the ship when it arrived. I had read a newspaper article written on its demise the day before." He dabbed at his forehead again. "I mean, the ship had become famous; it was a little hard to ignore."

"No one else recognized it at the port?"

"By daylight, I'm assuming the crew had changed the name to the one that was on the manifest I handed over."

"Under what company was the forgery?"

"Westican Trading, according to the paper."

Sean went back to tapping the pen against his chin in thought. "And they were also listed as the owner, or just the company handling the cargo?"

Wystone blinked and looked away, his face scrunched in thought. "I believe the new owners were listed as from Mark Inland, actually."

The answer took Sean by surprise. "Mark Inland? Nothing organized comes from that nation."

"Yes, I know. And Westican Trading is two oceans away from Mark Inland, why would they handle the logistics?"

Sean's mind raced, and he searched over his scrawled notes. "Where did the shipment originate from, again?"

Wystone shifted uncomfortably. "Alexandria."

Sean underlined the country when he found it. He wrote Mark Inland, and Westica off to the side. "And you asked what question?"

"Why it was reported to have been sunk, about the new ownership documentation, and about the magic lily dust. I asked about all of it."

"And without the original manifest, there was no proof of what you saw."

Wystone shrugged. "My word against no one else's. They are in the process of making one of the biggest national scandals out of me. My rank will be up for revocation at the next Endowment and Revocation meeting if they're able to make the charges stick."

The dejection across the man's face made Sean frown. "Synintel is on that council. Have you spoken to him?"

"How am I supposed to approach an arch guardian when my hands are supposedly so dirty? He couldn't be seen with me or even hinted at that he's spoken with me, you know that."

Approaching Sean, of course, wasn't an issue; his family reputation was already beyond tattered, so no one would think much about it. Sean made a quick note of all the new information. "I'm assuming the ranked guardian over your division won't speak to you, either."

Wystone shook his head. "No one at the FIO will meet with me. You have been the only one to agree."

Ah, the real reason came forth for why he'd asked to talk with Sean. He was the only one who'd listen. Sean sighed and tossed his pencil onto the desk. "Your situation intrigued me. I haven't been home for a long time, and when I do come home, things aren't... normal."

A spark of hope lit in Wystone's eyes. "Does that mean you think you can help me?"

"Without any evidence pointing to your innocence?"

Sean shook his head. "You know, at your hearing, the accusers have to prove your guilt, and so far, they have all the evidence they'll need. When is the next E and R meeting?"

The optimism faded. "Two months. And I don't have any idea how to prove my innocence. I was hoping you'd have some advice about that."

"I wasn't the one being sent to prison when Endowment and Revocation stripped the Primary Wintersfall rank from my brother. I had nothing to prove, and we couldn't exactly fall any lower."

The truth of the words deflated the key guardian further. "Ah, yes, a family possibly more disgraced than myself. Only you're at no risk of losing everything your family built. But you've served faithfully now, maybe you could say something? Speak to my character?"

He wanted to bitterly say he'd gladly lose everything his black-hearted family built, but he kept the words to himself. "I'll do what I can, but my opinion carries no weight in Haven City."

Wystone's calm demeanor evaporated, and he slammed his fist onto the desk. His jowls jiggled with the force, his face beet red. "I trusted them! And this is how my country repays me, repays my family for generations of loyalty?"

The soft, nearly indiscernible *snick* of a bolt sliding forward to chamber a round filtered down to Sean, but only because he recognized the sound so well. Wystone seemed oblivious to the danger his little tantrum placed him in.

Taking a deep breath, Sean leaned forward. "I need you to calm down."

Wystone's pudgy fists trembled, his knuckles splotchy purple as the rings bit into his flesh, cutting off the blood supply. "Am I supposed to let them just take my rank?

Allow them to drag my name through the garbage for their lives and ruin my wife and kids? I didn't *do* anything wrong!"

Sean softened his features to reassure the angry man before him. "No. And I don't think it's the government that's betrayed you."

Wystone's eyes turned into distrustful slits. "What do you mean?"

"The social issues plaguing this country didn't happen overnight. Nor do they happen without help in some seriously high places. Corruption is everywhere. While someone at the FIO *could* be responsible, that doesn't mean it's someone loyal to this nation or her ideals. You were played by forces outside your control, plain and simple. It's unfortunate, but you wouldn't be the first unsuspecting pawn in someone else's long-term goals."

Slowly, Wystone's fists relaxed. "I hadn't considered that."

"My team has. That's our job."

"Yes, of course." Wystone patted the wilted handkerchief beneath his chin.

Sean tread carefully, wanting to keep Wystone composed enough to keep Katria pacified. "I think whoever is orchestrating the drug supply may be behind your scandal. You asked the right question at the wrong time to the wrong people."

"How was I supposed to ask it to the right people? Isn't this rather serious?"

"It is, and I don't have the answer. I'm still in the dark myself."

Wystone sank back into the chair with a heavy exhale. "So, you can't help me, not really."

"I know in the reports your colleague files, I seem to have all the power and backing of a nation at my disposal.

But on home ground, I'm just a man with a bad reputation and a ruined family name. The higher-ups won't open anything I recommend. I don't even know if I can learn the identity of the person who has leveled the accusations against you and recommended your ranked revocation."

"How convenient for them, make sure the one who could bring them all down is completely disgraced," Wystone snapped in loathing.

Sean gave a taciturn smile. "Whoever is running things had a plan."

Wystone nodded sadly. He stood. "I hope you can do something with the information at least."

Sean rose from his seat. "I can assure you it won't go to waste."

"You weren't thinking of shooting him, were you?"

Katria shrugged, recalling the rush of adrenaline at Wystone's outburst. "That depended on him and where his hands went."

She leisurely descended the stairs. Her BACR-18 rested against her right leg in a relaxed hold while her left hand trailed the banister. Sean sat on the arm of the couch, his ankles and arms crossed. He regarded her with a mixture of curiosity and the heat she'd come to recognize as desire. Her stomach flipped, and she almost stopped.

"I appreciate you not giving enforcement services another reason to show up at my house." Sean grasped her rifle once she was within reach, tossing it onto the couch.

"Hey!" Katria rushed to retrieve her gun, but Sean's hold on her shoulders stopped her.

"Your BACR has been through worse, it'll survive a two-foot fall onto a couch cushion."

Katria growled. "My scope isn't so hardy. It can take hours to sight it in correctly."

Sean's hands fell on her hips, and he pulled her close, his still crossed ankles pushing through her skirt until she had to practically straddle him to stay upright, or fall into him. "Aren't you curious about what he said?"

"I'm interested in what made the key guardian so angry," she admitted.

His hands locked together at the small of her back, placing just enough pressure to pin her to his torso. Katria splayed her hands along his chest, deciding she did want to know before she gave into the urge to make her husband keep his earlier promise.

"He's convinced he has been betrayed by whoever his handlers are."

"And what do you think?"

"I don't know if you want to know that."

Katria studied his face. She allowed her weight to fall into him and traced the stern line of his jaw. "Are we in more trouble than I've put us in with my murderer search?"

Sean's arms tightened around her. "Love, we're in more trouble than we're going to be able to get out of."

31

I n a hushed skim of metal, Kevin slid his key into the
lock at the servant's entrance off the conservatory. The
lights in the two employee quarter houses behind the
mansion had gone off well over two hours ago. He'd
watched his wife's window for another hour before her
light dimmed, too.

His wife.

The notion was as ludicrous as it was a reality. Kevin
could break the wretched contract he'd practically been
blackmailed into simply by waltzing into his father-in-law's
house and proclaiming an illicit affair. The whole farce of
his marriage would dissolve. And so would his reputation
and career.

Sighing away his depressive existence, Kevin pushed
open the squeaky door. Darkness greeted him. The house
lights having been doused hours ago, only the weak silvery
moonlight provided dense shadows to work around. He
crossed through the pantry, morning room, and into the
spacious vestibule.

A large, dark rug covered the hardwood floor. Potted

plants made the space a more welcoming atmosphere than sculptures would have. Three padded chairs stood near the door, ready for guests who arrived by appointment to confer with the lady of the house on business matters. One of the top logistics analysts in the city, the Master Guardianess Raiventon, had built a reputation for herself that made her highly sought after.

The book Kevin required was on the pedestal he'd known it would be on. Stopping before it, he raised a brow at the open page. *Phipps Marion Geier, Shield Guardian Enbrackon.* Like every completed page in the hefty tome, the entry included a detailed sketch of the shield guardian, his role in society, and a short biography. Even in the murky light, Kevin could make out the arrogant young man staring off the page. Kevin had a sudden, unexplainable urge to tear the page out and crumble it in his palm. Men like this one had made his academia years a living nightmare. He slammed the cover closed on his face, the sharp sound echoing in the small space. Kevin winced and waited to see if the sound had traveled upstairs.

When all remained quiet, he gathered the book in his arms and turned to exit the way he'd entered. A large shadow crept through the doorway off the dining room, quiet and slow. Annoyance flashed through Kevin. Seriously? Not one sentry had been posted at the locked entrance gate onto the property, or at any of the three doors that led into the house. Which meant this intruder was just that – someone who shouldn't be in Raina's home.

Two more men stepped into the vestibule from the main corridor. Kevin rolled his neck and flexed his shoulders, taking a deep, centering breath. The tingling flow of adrenaline raced across his senses, sparking his nerves and setting his talent into motion. The three men converged on him, keeping a safe distance, as though they were unsure who should make the first strike. That they came for him, and didn't creep around looking for something to steal, told Kevin he had been careless. A small group had followed him and he hadn't even noticed. Sloppy.

Kevin spared them the torment of trying to decide who should move first.

With all the force he could put into his arm, Kevin heaved the massive book at the man near the doorway of the morning room. The tome slammed into his face, sending the assailant careening backwards through the opening. Kevin caught the book before it landed on the floor at the same time his outstretched form arced in the air into a side-kick. He sent his foot into the center of the intruder's chest. The second man went sailing backwards through the wide arch leading into the main corridor.

The remaining attacker growled and rushed Kevin. Crouching, Kevin let the book fall to the floor. Before he could stand, the man was on him, but Kevin had anticipated the scenario. As Kevin rose, he sent rapid, force-filled punches into the man's groin, stomach, diaphragm, and throat. Knocked out of breath and overcome with pain, the power of the blows sending a shockwave through the assailant's balls, intestines, lungs, and airway, the man's mind couldn't process all the harm at once. Grasping at his throat and his groin, the intruder began to panic, his eyes bugging from his face. In a matter of seconds, the anxiety would overtake him and he'd pass out.

Kevin picked up the book and brushed the wrinkles from his shirt. Strolling through the arch, stepping on the second man struggling to rise, the toe of his boot caught under the assailant's chin. The telltale *thump* in the vestibule made Kevin smile. All three down.

Now, to make sure none were lurking upstairs. Kevin took the steps two at a time. At the landing, he walked around the corridor, searching each room, skipping past the one in the back left corner. The floor was empty, quiet. For a dark second, Kevin almost decided to leave Raina to her fate.

But that's not the reason he'd been married to her.

With a curse, he slammed his fist on the banister and then stalked to her room. Kevin wanted to crash her door open to ease the frustration tearing at him, but he didn't. Carefully, he turned the knob and eased inside. The dim, warm glow from the woodstove illuminated enough of the bedroom to make searching simple. A soft rise in the center of the bed shifted, and Kevin froze.

At first, the Master Guardianess Raiventon didn't seem to notice Kevin, barely rising from her deeply cushioned mattress, thick blankets enveloping her petite frame. Then, as she went to lie back down, his presence registered. Scrambling against the headboard, she let out an ear-piercing scream.

"Why are you screaming?" Kevin asked calmly, stepping closer to the light of the woodstove.

She licked her lips, her wide eyes darting from the door to him. "Who... what are you doing in my bedchamber?"

"Raina," he began patiently, remaining still. "I'm not going to hurt you."

She pushed bangs that were too long from her pale brown eyes into the messy layers around her face. In the daytime, when everyone would see her, the guardianess's brown hair was without a strand out of place. Now, she appeared rather bohemian.

Kevin had always figured if pixies existed, Raina Merrick was one, petite to the point of appearing fragile. Her heart-shaped mouth was damp and slightly parted, accentuating the fullness of her lower lip. A small, slightly upturned nose brought out her round cheeks. The soft curve of her chin completed a face that many had described as adorable. Kevin hadn't quite decided if *adorable* was the word he'd use, but she was remarkable.

And she didn't relax one bit as recognition set in her jaw and hardened her eyes.

"Master Guardian Raiventon." She eased the sheet up to her chin and somehow managed to squeeze herself further against the thick wood of her headboard. "Again I ask, what are you doing in my bedchamber?"

"I guess I can be thankful you at least remember what I look like."

The sheet lowered in her tight grip to her chest. Her jaw flexed. "You're a difficult man to forget."

Kevin raised a brow at the admission. "Do you know of the men who attacked me downstairs?"

She gasped. "You were attacked? In this house? Are you hurt?"

She looked him over from head to toe.

Kevin tried not to fidget. Or laugh. "I'm fine."

Suspicion lit her eyes as she furrowed her brows. "Yes, you certainly appear to be."

Kevin rubbed the back of his neck. "I was making sure no one was in your room."

The sheet rose to her chin again. "And?"

"Safe. Perfectly safe."

The white fabric fluttered to her lap, and she slumped against the headboard. Heavy shadows cast the soft curves of her satin-draped torso in harsh relief. Kevin found himself unable to look away from the flat plane of her stomach, to the gentle swell of her breasts, up to the entirely too appealing curve of her collarbone. Before he realized what he was doing, he took a step towards her bed.

She tensed again, and he halted. What had he been thinking? Shaking his head, he turned on his heel.

"Wait!"

"What?" he growled without turning to face her.

"Am I... am I safe?"

Kevin fisted his hand at his side, his other gripped the book tighter than necessary. The question was a valid one. Completely alone, had the men downstairs been there for Raina, no one would have heard his wife scream. Until he could figure out how they managed to get in, this wretched house was his new home sweet home.

"I'm not going anywhere."

The bed squeaked, betraying her movement. "You're staying to make sure no one else is in the house?"

"Yes." He glanced over his shoulder. Big mistake. She'd risen onto her knees, the long nightgown pooling in shimmering waves. The weak light from the woodstove illuminated her petite frame. "But they weren't here for you, princess, so you don't need to worry."

Her shoulders squared as she straightened her spine. "I'm not a princess."

Kevin turned. "No, you're right, you're above one."

To his surprise, she held her ground, her chin jutting out, her nose lifting at him in the regal manner she held herself. "I'm just a master guardian's wife now."

Just a master guardian's wife. The haughty words made anger burn in his stomach. Even his rank was inferior to her. If only she knew how low her father had sunk her... Tossing the book on the overstuffed bed, he climbed onto the mattress. She gasped and hastily tried to scramble away from him, falling backwards. The satin slid along her bare thighs, revealing far more than he knew she wanted him to see. Kevin crawled over her. She squeaked, her hands fisting over her chest. Face scrunched in nervousness, she turned away, opening her neck to him.

Closing his eyes, Kevin bent low, careful not to touch any part of her. He inhaled deeply, taking in her sweet, feminine scent of peaches and sugary flowers. "Many would say, *princess*, you aren't my wife. Not yet."

"What do you mean?" A subtle tremor wracked her body.

"You know exactly what I mean. Look at me."

Still tense, her light brown eyes met his stare. "Is that what this is? You've come to claim me?"

"No." Bracing his weight on his left side, he wound a thick strand of her hair around his fingers, watching the light play on the varying shades of brown. "Do you remember what I said to you the day we met and were married? When you invited me into your bed anytime I wanted to be here?"

Underneath her clenched arms, her chest rose and fell, hinting at the faintest swell of her breasts over the satin neckline. "You told me no."

Kevin let her hair flow through his fingers and traced the tight line of her jaw to her chin, where he applied gentle pressure. Her lips parted, and her nervous tongue darted out, tempting him to take what he'd never dared. "You weren't listening."

"Then remind me."

Kevin slid his knees back, lowering closer to her until the heat radiating through the thin fabric covering her threatened to consume him. He brushed his bearded jaw along her supple cheek until his mouth hovered over hers. Another tremor flowed through her body, and a soft gasp rushed from her mouth, different this time, expectant. Kevin smiled. "When I come to your bed, it'll be because you want me here."

Her back arched softly, and her mouth rose, but he lifted, denying her any chance to start what he knew neither of them could. Rising swifter than she had a chance to react, he picked up the book and stepped onto the floor.

Knowing better than to look at her now, he turned and called over his shoulder, "I'll be in my room after I take care of the intruders downstairs." At her door, he grasped the edge. "And don't worry, I'll be gone before you're up in the morning."

"I want you to leave Haven City."

Katria glanced up from the book she was hardly reading and stared at her husband across his desk. Perhaps she'd misheard his ludicrous order. "Excuse me?"

Heaving a sigh, he braced his arms on the desktop and regarded her. "I'm serious, and I don't want to argue with you."

"Yeah, because you won't win." She turned her attention back to the page, tamping down a rise of anger.

Silence had long ago settled in the house, the staff having retired shortly after dinner. Katria hadn't wanted to sit upstairs alone, so she'd opted to keep Sean company while he continued to sort through three years of personal business.

"You never would have disobeyed me two months ago."

She flashed a glare at his softly spoken statement. "You never would have asked me to leave two months ago."

The weight of both their statements hit them simultaneously. Sean cursed, his hands digging deep into his uneven lengths of hair. Katria sucked in a lungful of air that suddenly seemed too thick to breathe and grasped the arm of the chair. Professional and personal had just collided. The ramifications could cost them if they weren't careful. Of course, they'd both been right – Katria never would have dared to violate an order, let alone mouth off to him, and Sean never would have asked her to go where the team wasn't.

Sean made to rise, and Katria held up her hand. "No, stay over there. My thoughts get all fuzzy when you're near."

His jaw tensed, but he settled into the seat. "Not helping."

"Well, it's true. I need my focus to be in my brain and not—"

"Fine!" Sean snapped.

Katria snickered. "I was going to say not on you."

He leaned forward, the fiery amber of his eyes nearly glowing. "Then make sure I stay."

Fierce desire shot through Katria until her lack of being able to breathe had nothing to do with anxiety. Crawling across the desk seemed a solid plan, but then their little problem would continue to hang in the air. "Why do you want me to leave?"

"You aren't safe here."

"I never was. But I'm safer with you than I am without."

"There have been at least three attempts on your life since we've been home, and one came far too close."

She frowned. "And where will I go that will be any safer? We know my father's isn't safe."

"If I figure that out, will you go?"

"No." An uncomfortable flutter had her pressing a hand to her stomach. "If I weren't your wife, would you be asking me to go?"

His head angled, and the dangerous gleam in his eyes had her spine straightening. "But you are my wife."

"I was your sharpshooter first."

Slowly, he shook his head. "Technically, you were my wife first. And your safety is my only priority."

Katria flexed her jaw. "You know I'm safest with you. If I hadn't been able to take out the three intruders, they wouldn't have stood a chance against you."

"I'm not Kevin."

"You aren't exactly helpless."

A smile tugged at his lips. "What is it going to take for you to obey me?"

She crossed her arms over her chest. "I'm going to remain insubordinate."

Sean rose to his full height and stalked around the desk, his eyes never leaving her. Katria fidgeted in the oversized chair, suddenly feeling very much prey to his predator. His hands braced on either side of the chair, and he loomed over her, his brilliant eyes nearly the same color as coals deep in a fire. Oh, she'd made him mad.

But instead of heated words, his head dipped low, and his mouth found her neck, easily accessed since her long hair was still bound behind her back. Slowly, his tongue glided down the tender flesh to her collarbone, forcing her head to fall back, a cold trail forming where he'd been. He worked his way to the other side of her throat and up. She barely noticed him kneeling.

"There's a distinct advantage to my knowing a few things you don't," he whispered.

Katria pressed into the cushion, hoping to put enough distance between them so the heat from his body wouldn't numb her mind. "I'm a quick learner, make sure you don't teach me anything you don't want me to know."

Sean's mouth hovered over hers. "Love, if you ever get it in your beautiful mind to seduce me into submission, I swear I won't stop you."

Katria didn't have time to respond, his mouth

capturing hers in an aggressive, possessive kiss. Heat coiled deep in her belly and pooled at her center. His tongue teased inside her mouth, making her forget she needed air to survive.

"Tell me you'll go," he exhaled against her lips.

Gritting her teeth, Katria shook her head. "No."

"I want you somewhere safe." His tongue licked a trail down the side of her throat. His fingers inched the skirt of her gown upward.

Struggling to form a coherent thought, Katria slid her hands along his strong shoulders. "I am safe."

His chin rested on her shoulder, and he sighed, fluttering the loose tendrils of hair at her nape. "Not enough."

Katria glanced at him. She smoothed her fingers into his disheveled hair and forced him to meet her stare. "I thought I already told you, you'll always be enough."

His mouth covered hers in a searing kiss that had her toes curling into the carpet. She vaguely noticed the quick movements of his shoulders or the way he maneuvered her onto his lap. He wrapped his arms around her back, holding her tightly to his chest.

"I want you to be safe. Always."

Katria rolled her eyes and hugged him. "Going somewhere you aren't isn't going to make me safer, Sean, and you know it."

"Fine," he growled into her shoulder. "We'll shelve the conversation for now."

"Good," she leaned back and grasped his face between her hands, "because I'm done talking anyway."

✸ 32 ✸

"**H**unter!"

Jonathon glanced up from his desk as his boss strolled into his office. Tall, thin with razor-sharp blue eyes, not one wrinkle on his black city-issued enforcement suit, the man in charge commanded attention.

"Master Prefect Hartland, what can I do for you?"

He tossed a slip of paper onto the desk. "Homicide at Emerald Street East."

Jonathon stood. "Over by Harlan Row?"

"Yep. Your part of town, right?"

He frowned, shrugging into his issued jacket, the embroidered large yellow letters HCES stood out brightly against the stark black over his left shoulder. Just below was the crest of the enforcement services, along with Jonathon's rank and name, followed by his ranked guardianship title.

"I live about two streets away, yes."

"Good, get your butt over there before that journalist I saw in your office a couple weeks ago beats you to it. I don't want this one in the paper before the facts are straight."

Jonathon didn't like the sound of that. "Anything I should be aware of?"

Hartland shook his head. "Just get over there and handle it."

Collecting his gear, Jonathon slung the pack over his shoulder and headed downstairs to the vehicle house. He was surprised to find his two-seater ariot already waiting. The thin metal door was open, the gears in park, the seat pulled back to make entry easier. Slinging his pack onto the passenger seat, he climbed in.

Jonathon slid the seat into a more comfortable position while he flipped the switch to start the vehicle. He properly hooked up the siren, which was powered by the same magnetic energy source as the vehicle. Shifting the vehicle into gear, he set out onto the busy street in front of the Enforcement building.

The sleek little vehicle maneuvered easily through the crowds of other ariots, bicycles, and carriage traffic, helped by the wail of the siren blaring on the roof. Within a half hour, Jonathon was on Emerald Street East, the large gathering crowd telling him where the murder victim likely was. He found a parking spot down the street. Pack slung over his shoulder, Jonathon made his way to the opening of a narrow alley.

The crowd slowly parted, revealing a well-dressed, rotund man lying face down, unmoving, in the center of the brick side street. The visible digits of his fingers were blue in the mid-morning light. A faint trail of blood led from the sidewalk to the body.

An enforcer stood from where he'd been inspecting near the body, a deep frown on his face. "Master Tribunii Hunter, what are you doing here?"

Jonathon glanced at the younger man's jacket and raised a brow. First Guardsman Nikolas Parby. "MP Hartland sent me."

"Well, I have it under control."

Jonathon ignored him and walked around the corpse. He stopped cold when he saw the dead eyes staring at the wall, and recognition hit him. "Key Guardian Wystone."

"You know him?"

"I'll handle this one, Hartman ordered me to."

"But—"

Jonathon crouched down. "I said I have it, First Guardsman Parby. Thank you for securing the scene until I could get here."

Parby's hands fisted at his sides, but he gave an abrupt nod. "Of course, my apologies, MT Hunter. I didn't mean to step out of line."

As a Master Tribunii, Jonathon was two ranks ahead of Parby. The young man had thankfully remembered his place in the pecking order before Jonathon had to remind him. Though what a first guardsman thought he was doing, investigating, was beyond Jonathon. Parby was a street enforceman and had yet to earn his qualified stripe for anything else. An uneasy feeling settled in the pit of Jonathon's stomach.

Parby stalked off, clearly angry.

Tough.

Jonathon had a suspicious inclination that someone at the office was about to receive an unhappy report from the young enforcer. After interviewing the enforcer who made the discovery and some willing witnesses on the street, Jonathon waited for the medical science investigator to arrive. The MSI delivered a quick account of the body's condition and cause of death before loading it into a wagon for the morgue at Health Services. Jonathon swept the alley, but came up empty, not having expected to find much. Someone had stripped the wealthy key guardian of everything valuable except his clothing.

After making a few extra notes, bagging what little he felt may be evidence, Jonathon packed up his gear and vacated the scene. He'd need to talk to the key guardian's widow, something he always dreaded. Hopefully, he wouldn't be the one to break the news. And thankfully, he hadn't been. While a mess, and clinging to a handkerchief as though it were a lifeline, Key Guardianess Wystone had answered his questions with poise. The only interesting tidbit she'd given was that her husband had visited Primary Guardian Wintersfall and hadn't returned home.

On the ride back to the office, he compared Wintersfall's address to the location where they found Wystone's body. The route Wystone took would have been the quickest. If the murder did indeed happen in the alley, the man had almost made it home. Back at the precinct, Jonathon parked the ariot and then headed to his office.

Parby stood from a chair in front of Jonathon's desk when he walked in. Jonathon paused, casting the young enforcer a wary glance.

"What can I do for you?"

Parby held out a piece of paper for him. "I thought I'd keep you from wasting any more time on the Wystone situation. If you'd waited for me to finish, I'd have been able to tell you at the scene, it's a suicide, not a homicide. It's why I was so surprised to see you."

Despite the shock of Parby's words, Jonathon kept his expression neutral. He accepted the paper written from an MSI at the scene. Jonathon recalled the swift description at the scene: *gunshot wound, not close range, instant death, body was moved to the alley and left, likely close to one this morning.* How was any of that a suicide?

"The medical science investigator gave me a depiction I hadn't considered as suicide," Jonathon said carefully.

Parby shrugged, stuffing his hands in his pockets. "They had a better chance to examine him at the morgue. No one is surprised. He was facing a rank revocation after all."

"There was no gun at the scene."

Again, the young man shrugged. "Everything was stolen except his shoes and clothes. We'll likely never find the gun. I'm surprised, to be honest, he was still in his clothes. Those were nice shoes."

Jonathon raised a brow. "Indeed."

"Anyway, I have been charged with the filing of everything, so if you have any questions—"

"Thank you." Jonathon handed him back the report. "I'll be sure to get you my information to file by this evening."

Parby exited on a swift turn of heel. Jonathon waited an hour before heading to Hartland's office, a stack of files in his arms. His leader motioned for him to shut the door when he entered.

"What in the arctic?" Jonathon asked the second the door was closed.

Hartland sighed heavily. "I know, and I'm sorry, but I need you on this."

"There is no *this*, master prefect. When a murder is ruled a suicide, I'm out."

"I'm not asking you to investigate officially, I know better than that."

Jonathon shook his head. "No. I don't need whoever was crawling all over Wystone's butt to be on mine."

Hartland leaned forward, his piercing blue eyes intent. "They likely already are. Or did someone mistakenly report seeing you with Wintersfall and Kynhaven?"

"You don't think—"

Hartland held up his hands and waved them in a gesture of denial. "No, I do not think the two primary guardians had anything to do with this. But I do think something is going on at the First Intelligence Office, and Wystone, who they recently let go, took his information to one of them. They haven't been home long enough to know the depth of his scandal to refuse meeting with him."

And Jonathon knew which one the dead man had spoken to. "Why do you want me involved in this?"

"You're the best I have, and honestly, the only one I know I can trust. Just be careful, and hide any notes you take where even a thief wouldn't think to look."

Jonathon raked his hand through his hair. "That bad?"

"Getting there."

"How?"

"Very carefully. Which is what we need to be now."

Sean glanced across the small round breakfast table at Katria. Poised like the ranked guardianess she didn't consider herself to be, she slid a forkful of eggs gracefully into her mouth, her attention on an article in the paper before her. The long black length of her hair was swept into a messy crown on top of her head, spilling over her shoulders, giving her a sensual, unkempt quality. She was breathtaking and completely his. How many quiet mornings had he spent, never truly seeing her? Too many.

Her vibrant blue eyes lifted and regarded him curiously. "What?"

Smiling, he shook his head, raising his cup of coffee. "Nothing."

The fork perched in her hand, and she raised an arched brow. "Nothing?"

"I can't admire my wife?"

"You don't admire well from a distance."

His lips twitched. "Is that an invitation?"

The fork clattered to her plate. "Do you need one?"

Sean set his cup down and rose, but a heavy knock on the front door stopped him. Davis's shoes clipped evenly on the hardwood. Katria leaned forward to see out the doorway into the foyer. Sean found himself doing the same. They weren't expecting visitors. Davis swung the door open and admitted the guest with a regal sweep of his arm. Jonathon Hunter stepped into the foyer. He took a glance around, noticed them in the breakfast room, and gave Davis a quick thank you.

Sean rose and motioned towards a chair on the other side of the table. "Asherwick, please, sit."

Jonathon closed the door. Katria straightened, pushing her plate away. Sean took a step closer to her. When Jonathon turned around, he raised a brow.

"Do I look like an assassin?"

"You don't have to kill someone to take their life away," Katria said softly.

Jonathon flexed his jaw. "No, a certificate of custody hasn't been issued for you, if that's what you're worried about. Is there something I should know?"

Sean relaxed and went back to his seat. He smiled at Jonathon and returned to his coffee. "No, we're fine."

Katria retrieved her fork, pointing it at him. "Nice uniform, it looks good on you."

Jonathon hesitated and then shook his head. "I don't think I'm going to get used to you two."

"It's best that way." Katria returned to her eggs and the paper.

Rounding the table, Jonathon moved his chair closer to Sean. "We need to talk."

"Clearly." Sean sipped his sweetened coffee. "Would you like a cup?"

"No, I..." He glanced at the steaming cup in Sean's hand. "Sure, thank you."

Sean went to rise, but Katria did instead.

"I'll get it, or rather, I'll have Davis get it. I think he'll pitch a fit if I attempt to use the kitchen again. He was quite specific last time." Katria disappeared out the side door into the adjoining dining room, muttering, "It's not becoming of a ranked guardianess to see to her needs, the kitchen is not..."

"She's having trouble adjusting," Sean said with a grin.

Jonathon gave him a droll stare. "I could see how having someone attend to your every whim would be difficult to accept."

Sean set the cup down. "Considering she still has to remain mostly independent, it has been. Primary Guardianess Wintersfall is currently overlapping between two worlds, both equally vicious."

Jonathon frowned. "Yes, I suppose that's true. I would ask Ramsey to come assist, but she'd likely never speak to me again."

Sean held up his hand and shook his head. "No, I couldn't accept anyway, and Kat's rather unique in her understanding of social niceties."

"Meaning?"

"She doesn't care about their existence."

Jonathon laughed. "Might do Ramsey good."

Sean shrugged. "It'd be your head for you asking."

"Very literally."

"You didn't come here to help my wife adjust to society."

Jonathon's expression turned sober. "No. Wystone was found dead this morning."

Sean's cup returned to the table so fast that coffee splashed onto his hand. He shook the hot liquid from his skin, ignoring the pain. "Where?"

"An alley on Emerald Street East."

"When did it happen?"

"The MSI said around one this morning."

"He was alive when he left my house around dinnertime."

"His wife said he never returned from your meeting."

Sean tapped his fingers on the table. "So where was he for all that time?"

Jonathon laid his open hands on the table. "Question of the day."

"Probably being interrogated by a Sympath for what he revealed to me."

"Interrogated how?"

Before Jonathon could react, Sean had hold of his wrist. "Do you hate me?"

"What? No." Jonathon tried to retrieve his wrist, but Sean held tighter.

"Does your sister hate me?"

"No." Jonathon tensed under his grasp.

The lie trickled like pinpricks through Sean's fingertips. "Lie. Would you arrest me if the certificate came to you?"

Jonathan resumed his attempt to regain his wrist. "I don't know."

Sean released him with a slow smile. "Lie."

Scowling, Jonathon massaged his wrist. "I had no idea you were capable of that."

"Most don't, and if they do, they often forget the depth. You don't usually perceive what you can't understand."

"Nifty little thing the FIO has in you. Answers without a scratch."

"That's the idea."

"Okay, so interrogated, dumped on the street, and shot before he could take another step towards home. Dragged into the alley to be hidden in the dark, but not so much that no one would steal what they could reach."

Sean wrapped his hands around his still-warm coffee. "He was shot? Where?"

"Chest."

The side door opened. Katria walked in and held the steaming cup out for Jonathon. "Then it wasn't FIO."

Jonathon accepted with furrowed brows. "What do you mean?"

Sean didn't protest when she forced his hand away from his coffee. He knew what she intended and welcomed her onto his lap with an open arm. Quickly, he learned that his embrace comforted her anxiety. The knowledge made his stomach tight and his chest clench. The sensation was becoming all too familiar, and something he was going to have to deal with sooner or later.

"We train for headshots, but when those aren't feasible, we cause accidents. Chest shots are too risky, too wide a mark, a heart shot isn't guaranteed."

Jonathon sat back. "The human heart is in basically the same location."

She shook her head. "There are too many factors. The brain is a much surer target. Also, since the human rabies syndrome pandemic, head shots are the most important to learn."

A tight line formed at Jonathon's mouth. "I shouldn't be discussing this with you."

"I have a feeling this is not an official conversation," Sean said.

"You're right, it's not. At the morgue, Wystone's death was ruled a suicide."

Katria tensed, but it was the only indication of her shock, not having been present when Jonathon imparted the news.

Sean rubbed his thumb along her forearm until she relaxed. "And with his state of affairs, it will come as no surprise to anyone."

"That's what my master prefect said."

"You trust him?"

"My MP?"

Sean nodded.

"Probably as much as you trust your leader."

Sean tapped his fingers against his rapidly cooling cup. "My interceptor is positive the man leading us is the only one we *can* trust."

"Which is exactly where I found myself this morning, having to trust my superior. What did Wystone say that was worth him dying for?"

"He confirmed what he'd been fired for, forging cargo manifests. But he didn't question them until a ship that was supposed to have sunk showed up in the harbor."

Jonathon snapped to attention, his dark blue eyes wide. "The *Mircea*."

"He didn't give the name."

Leaning forward, Jonathon waved his hand impatiently. "What did he say?"

"It showed up in port, he handed them an approved inventory sheet from Import Regulation, was asked to inspect a powder he suspected to be magic lily dust, and left. By morning, the ship had a new name and *new* inventory according to the manifests he provided."

"Was he given the old ones?"

"No."

Jonathon dropped his fist on the table with a curse. "The only proof he'd have."

Sean gave him a contemplative stare. "You know of this ship outside the article?"

"Yes, it's the reason I agreed to meet with you." Jonathon's jaw tightened.

Sean tried to excuse away the uneasy sensation in his gut at Jonathon's sudden concern. "Who offered you more information?"

Jonathon's jaw clenched. "Who do you think?"

With a curse, Sean helped Katria rise, but kept hold of her hand. "Davis!"

Sean yanked the door open and almost collided with his butler.

"Yes?"

"I need my ariot brought around immediately." He ran into the library, Katria struggling to keep up behind him. Over his shoulder, he said to her, "You write one to Kevin, I'll write the other, just pen *Int. CD*, nothing more."

"Okay," she breathed out. "What's going on?"

Sean ignored her, handing her a piece of stationery. He glanced up to see Jonathon waiting at the door. "Do you know where Kynhaven lives?"

"Yes."

"Go."

Sean didn't have to tell Jonathon twice.

$$\text{❧} \quad 33 \quad \text{❧}$$

When they arrived at Mason's, Sean had barely helped her out from the ariot before he ran to the house. Wrapping the cloak Sean had insisted she wear tighter around herself as bitter wind whipped through the courtyard, she focused on the bright red brick beneath her shoes. The front door was still halfway open, and angry voices carried outside. Katria slipped inside and silently closed the door, leaning against it.

"She is *my* sister!" Mason pointed at his chest and then to the door. "I should be the one out there finding her!"

Sean quickly side-stepped to keep Mason from getting closer to the door. "I already sent Kevin to collect her, which by the way, you know he can do much more efficiently than you."

"How is he supposed to find her in all of Haven City?"

"We all know Cora is nothing if not a creature of habit," Sean stated drolly. "Even after all these years, I figured she is likely to be one of two places when the sun is out."

Mason didn't seem convinced. His hands fisted at his sides. "She is my responsibility."

Sean rolled his eyes. "She's your sister, not your child."

The front door bumped against her back and then opened with such force that Katria would have fallen on her face if Sean hadn't moved quickly. Sprawling in his arms, she grasped his biceps, her chest slamming into his. The force of her body weight sent him stumbling backward, and before anyone could help them, they crashed to the floor, his strong frame taking the brunt of the marble floor.

"Oh!" Cora gasped, cold air rushing into the house with her. "I had no idea someone was on the other side, I just thought the door was stuck!"

Sean brushed hair from Katria's face, his expression tender. "Are you okay?"

Katria nodded. "Are you?"

"I'm breathing."

She couldn't help but chuckle, her hands sliding to his shoulders.

"Come on, you two," Kevin sighed, his fingers wrapping around Katria's arm.

Funny, she'd forgotten it wasn't just the two of them. Sean had an odd way of making everything else disappear.

"You're okay," Mason stated, hopping over Katria, still attempting to rise with Sean and Kevin's help.

"I'm fine," Cora insisted. "I don't know what the craze is all."

Mason's twin disappeared into her brother's massive chest and arms. His black hair flowed over hers as he rested his cheek on top of her head. "I keep telling you, someday you're going to get hurt if you don't stop digging for dangerous information."

"What are you talking about?" Cora asked, exasperated.

Katria observed them, sadness rushing through her. What she wouldn't give to be able to hold her own sister, to know with a simple touch she was safe. Only a still-warm hand that was *not* okay had been the last parting contact she'd had with Anyka. Wrapping her arms around herself, Katria retreated several steps.

"Where did you find her?" Mason asked Kevin, still holding Cora, who fidgeted in her brother's bear-like embrace.

Kevin shrugged and closed the door. "Extilis Square, where else?"

"Alone?"

"No, someone had pulled her into an alley by her arm."

Cora pushed against Mason's chest and, with great effort, put enough distance between them to look up. "What was that about, anyway? He asked me, 'who I told' and 'who gave you the information.' I had no idea what he was talking about, so I told him as much. Then Mr. *Do not even twitch without my permission* dropped in."

Mason released his hold enough for Cora to step away. "Then what happened?"

Cora pushed her hair back from her face and shrugged. "The guy twitched."

Kevin laughed. Cora turned toward him, hands on her hips.

"Does your wife know what you can do?"

Kevin shook his head. "No, not even a little."

"Poor woman," Cora sighed. Then she turned, her eyes grew wide when she noticed Jonathon. "All right, so what *is* going on? Why are you," she pointed at her brother, "upset about my doing my job? Which I will remind you, as a journalist, gathering information is a requirement. And why did Kevin have to rescue me?" She changed the direction of her point to Jonathon. "And why are you here?"

Sean provided a quick recap, and Jonathon interjected to clarify when necessary. The soft pink in Cora's cheeks had faded by the time they finished.

Kevin raked his fingers through his hair. "There's an entire shipload of magic lily dust sitting somewhere in Haven City, confirmed now?"

Jonathon nodded. "Basically. And while the drugs themselves aren't uncommon anymore, an entire shipload without any clue as to where it might be and provided by a foreign nation that knows the cargo is illegal in our nation is a serious worry."

Mason leaned forward, bracing his hands on his thighs. "Yeah, like when the drugs will be distributed. We're basically duty bound to find the damn stuff."

"We won't know where to start looking until we've narrowed down some suspects, or if it's still sitting somewhere waiting for a drug broker. Did you get the book?" Sean asked, looking at Kevin.

"Yes. And I had company waiting, too."

Sean raised a brow. "Not the master guardianess, I'm presuming?"

Kevin shook his head. "No, definitely not."

"And she was unhurt?"

"She didn't even know they were there."

Sean frowned. "They were there only for you?"

"Yes," Kevin answered.

"What now?" Jonathon asked. "We can't exactly start poking around where someone is willing to kill to make sure their secret stays one."

Mason shook his head, straightening. "No, we can't. We have to be very careful and start working backwards, starting with the new ship."

"Wystone didn't give it," Sean said.

Jonathon nodded towards Cora and asked, "Did you get the name of the new ship?"

She shook her head. "No, the dock worker wouldn't tell me anything except what I told you, the ship was renamed and the shipment offloaded."

"Then we start with the day before Wystone was released and see what ships came into port those two days. I doubt he waited to ask questions. He gave the name of the country of origin, correct?" Mason asked.

Sean nodded. "Yes, Alexandria for the original ship that was supposed to have sunk, Mark Inland for the new ship's country, and Westican Trading Fleet as who chartered the cargo. But we need to wait a little bit, we can't start looking now while they're expecting us to. I know Wystone likely couldn't lie, they know he told me, and they'll be waiting to see what I do with the information."

"And you want to do nothing?" Mason asked, his gaze unsure.

"I want to let things simmer down a little. A hot kettle boils over, and things are lost. I'd like this particular mess to stay as contained as possible."

Mason nodded. "I agree."

"So, nothing?" Jonathon asked. "Does that go for me, too?"

"That's up to you," Sean answered. "These three are my responsibility, you are not. What you choose to do is your decision."

"I'll quietly meet with Guardianess Wystone again and see if the key guardian told her anything, and make sure she doesn't speak to anyone else. I don't want another Wystone in the morgue. My MP told me to keep anything I find to myself and hidden somewhere even a thief wouldn't look to find it."

Sean's frown deepened. "That's not reassuring."

Jonathon shrugged. "Not really, but at least he was honest."

Mason grabbed Cora's upper arms, forcing her to meet his gaze. "And no more work, not for a couple of weeks at least."

Katria cringed, knowing firsthand the position Cora suddenly found herself in.

Cora's mouth fell open. "That's not fair!"

"They're killing people, Cora, and you know about their lie. It's not worth the risk. You can write from home, and if you want to go to Extilis Square, I'll go with you."

"No, absolutely not. They aren't going to make me a prisoner in my own home."

Jonathon stepped forward. "You aren't a prisoner, and your brother is right. It's not safe. If they can turn the murder of a key guardian into a suicide in less than an hour, someone high up is making the calls."

"This is ridiculous!" she seethed and then stomped past them both and up the stairs. "I am a grown woman! Being told what to do by a bunch of men is ridiculous. Point a gun at me and see what happens, I'll shove that..." Her words died as she reached the landing and turned.

"You'll have plenty of time now to find a new cook!" Mason shouted. A petite hand wound around the corner with a gesture no lady should give. Mason laughed.

"Spirited," Jonathon mumbled.

"I can think of another word," Mason sighed. "Thank you."

Jonathon shrugged. "I have a sister too. She's just as stubborn."

"Somehow I doubt that," Mason said, shaking his head.

"I should probably go before someone notices I'm

here, if they haven't already," Jonathon said, rubbing the back of his neck.

"Take the alley for two blocks when you leave. It's off to the left of the conservatory," Kevin offered.

"I can draw you a map for a back way to Wystone's if you'd like," Mason offered.

"Thanks, but my ariot is a double. I doubt it'll fit down all the side alleys."

"Won't be all alleys, mine is a double as well. I only use Mason's directions," Kevin stated.

"Okay, sure, I appreciate it."

Mason and Jonathon disappeared down a hallway. Sean looked at Kevin.

"Do you have the book with you?" Sean asked.

"Yes."

"Get it. Let's see if we can figure out who the players are."

$\maltese$ 34 $\maltese$

After countless hours of research, they'd managed to come up with a list of names for who could strategize to not only distribute drugs, but have enough power to change investigations. And who had the most to gain, and the most to lose.

Mason sat behind his desk, idly playing with the pen he'd used to draw Jonathon's map. Kevin sat in a chair near the door. Sean and Katria sat in front of Mason's desk, their chairs facing each other and the desk. Katria kept glancing around the overstuffed room. Sean had to keep reminding himself that more was in the room than his beautiful wife.

Kevin sighed, folding the list of names and regarding Sean. "I guess I'll need to speak to Synintel finally. Raina likely went to see him first thing this morning to tell him herself. At least he won't be able to lecture me about staying in her house."

When Katria glanced at Sean in questioning, he answered, "Kevin's wife's name is Lorraina. Everyone who knows her personally calls her Raina, except her father."

"And why have you been avoiding your father-in-law? He asked to speak to you weeks ago." Katria asked Kevin.

"Because he's a scab and I can," Kevin said with a smile. "I didn't have anything to say to him before. Now I do."

Sean reached across the distance to her, grasping her hand and her attention. "Please reconsider leaving Haven City."

Anger brightened her blue eyes and slithered along his senses. She tried to pull her hand free, but he wouldn't allow it. "No. Besides, there's nowhere to go they wouldn't think to look anyway."

"I have a place," Kevin offered.

"And Kyn Manor is a veritable fortress if I want it to be. Plus, my mother lives there," Mason chimed in.

Sean laughed. "With one sentence, whoever breaks in will be scrambling for the door."

Mason shook his head with a pitiful smile. "It's true."

"And why would I want to be all alone in either?"

"Kat," Sean implored, his hand squeezing hers.

"Your persuasive tactics won't work here either. I'm not going anywhere."

The memory of Katria's fingers digging into the arms of the chair, sexy little moans escaping her mouth, while he'd done his best to *persuade,* made him shift uncomfortably, fierce hunger tearing through him. Her knowing smile made him realize that his innocent little wife was becoming less innocent, thanks to him. He returned the smile, and hers faded, her cheeks flushing.

He leaned forward and whispered in her ear, "Don't play games you aren't willing to follow through with."

Desire flowed from her hand into his, and with a hiss, Sean pulled free as though she'd burned him. "I believe that was called a move? I told you not to teach me things you didn't want me to know."

Sean laughed and stroked his knuckles tenderly down her cheek. "They're lessons I certainly don't mind giving."

Pulling himself away from Katria's alluring gaze, he placed his attention back on Kevin. "When do you plan on meeting with Synintel?"

"Probably today or tomorrow. I have enough information to bring to the table, he might be willing to part with some himself."

"If he wants us to help, he better part with something," Mason grumbled, a pen twisting between his fingers.

Kevin sighed, pinching the bridge of his nose. "The arch guardian isn't forthcoming with anything regardless of how much help he wants. It's his way or no way, even if he asks the impossible."

"Which he'll likely do," Sean said with a frown.

"Yes," Kevin agreed. "He'll likely tell me we've done remarkably well so far, why get his name involved when it isn't yet?"

Mason pointed the pen at Kevin. "Yet."

Kevin gave a defeated shrug. "You can talk to the man in my place. He might listen better."

"You really don't like him." Mason dropped his arm on the desk with a frown.

"No. If he were on fire, I'd gleefully watch him burn."

Katria's shocked gasp had Sean glancing at her. She stared at Kevin as if she'd never seen him before. "I'm glad Sean didn't hold that level of animosity for being married to me."

Kevin snapped her a harsh glare. "I don't hold animosity for being married. I hold animosity toward a man who treats every person in his life like a pawn on a chessboard. His daughter included."

"Remind me not to get on your bad side," Katria muttered.

Kevin shrugged. "I thought you already knew that."

"Does *he* know that?" Katria asked.

Mason exhaled heavily, tossing the pen onto the desk. "He knows. He just doesn't care. He holds more pieces."

Katria rubbed her arms. "I want to go back to where the government was nothing more than orders on paper."

"To be blissfully ignorant." Mason sighed again and shook his head. "No thanks. I'd rather know who the vipers are."

Kevin flicked the paper he held. "With any luck, we're on their trail."

Katria propped her chin on her hands, resting on Sean's naked stomach, and stared at the partially open door to her room. "I don't think I want my room."

He stroked lazy lines on her back, stopping when he met the sheet barely covering her hips and then back up her spine, brushing long strands of wayward hair off her skin. Katria shivered, but not from cold. Soft morning light filtered in along the edges of the curtains. They should have risen hours ago, but Sean had told Kevin no training this morning before they'd left Mason's. A morning without obligation had been something no one had argued against.

"It's bigger than mine," he said.

"Yours is warmer," she argued.

"Only because you're in it."

Katria's stomach flipped. She shifted until her chest lay across his, and she could see his still resting face. Quelling the urge to trace the angles of his jaw and mouth, she admired the handsome features softened by his relaxed state. "How do you do that?"

"Do what?"

"Say all the right things."

"My nature, I suppose."

Katria chuckled, bracing her arms across his chest, unable to resist fluttering her fingers along the stubble on his chin. "Aren't I the lucky one?"

"That would be me."

A solid knock sounded on the door.

Sean growled. "What?"

"Sorry to disturb, but there's an enforcer downstairs wishing to speak with you," Davis's muffled voice came through the closed door.

"I'll be down in a moment."

"Very good."

Sean kissed her nose and rose out from under her. "Think good thoughts, I'll be right back."

"What sort of good thoughts?" she asked with a playful smile, not bothering to cover herself when he rose and the sheets went with him.

His gaze swept over her, naked, her thighs slightly parted from lying across him, and he growled. "That enforcer better have something good to say to me right now."

He swept over her, bracing his hands on either side of her shoulders and kissed her passionately. Then, as swiftly as he'd moved in, he was gone. He slid into his pants before grabbing a shirt and leaving the room. Katria took a second to let her heart rate return to normal and then left the bed to go to her room for clothes. An enforcer didn't show up for nothing. She had a feeling Sean would be back to change, not returning to her side.

Minutes later, dressed and tying her hair into a ponytail, she heard his heavy footfalls in the other room. Still fussing with her hair, she stood between the rooms and frowned. Sean sat on the couch in front of the fireplace, pulling on his boots.

"Where are you going?" Katria asked.

"Hunter wants to speak with me." He tied his boots with short, jerky motions.

"Why didn't he show up himself?"

Sean shrugged. "I don't know, the enforceman didn't say. He just delivered the message that Hunter needed to see me this morning, something that couldn't wait."

Katria moved to return to her room. "I'll go too."

Sean shook his head and sighed. "No, there's no need, I'll be back soon."

She went to argue, but his impatient glance told her she wouldn't win. Not this one, and she didn't feel like fighting. Their interrupted morning had been too wonderful.

"Fine." She wrapped her arms around his waist when he stood. "But we have a morning to finish."

Sean returned her hug and kissed the top of her head. He pulled teasingly on her ponytail. "Yes, we do, and you know I won't forget."

The administrator at the front desk for the Haven City Enforcement Services regarded Sean with the bored expression of a woman who wanted to retire a decade ago. She took the form she'd made him fill out and, in return, handed him the visitor's neck badge with Jonathon's information written on it, along with Sean's name. Sean found the entire sign-in process ridiculous. He should have had credentials that ushered him in with nothing more than a wave of a card.

But no one knew precisely what Sean Blackbain did, and Sziveria wanted to keep it that way.

After receiving convoluted directions to Jonathon's

office, Sean made his way to the wide stairs zigzagging to all seven floors of the building. A pulley elevator he didn't trust filled in seconds. The stairs were a safer bet overall. Sean took the steps with the heavy flow of traffic to the third floor. Another administrator, younger and wide-eyed, took note of him the moment he made the landing.

Sean showed his pass. The girl waved him on with a flippant toss of her hand and returned to watching the movement on the stairs. A maze of chaos lay before him, and Sean stopped. Hundreds of voices thrummed as people rushed along the never-ending corridor, their footsteps, papers, and urgency echoing off the walls.

Steeling himself against the throng, Sean pushed his way through the tightly packed corridor and tried to remember the turns he was supposed to make to find Jonathon. Finally, he located the small, stuffed office with Jonathon's rank, position, and name in thick, bold letters above the doorframe. The workspace was empty. Sean sighed and raked his hand through his hair. Did he wait or attempt to look for the man? One step back into the corridor told him the effort would be futile. So he waited.

And waited.

When Jonathon finally arrived, he was so engrossed in an open file that he would have slammed right into Sean when he strode into the office. Sean quickly stepped aside. Jonathon froze, glanced over his shoulder, and frowned.

"Wintersfall, what are you doing here?" The folder he'd been holding snapped closed.

Sean crossed his arms over his chest, a sinking sensation churning in his stomach. "You asked me to come here."

"I..." Jonathon's attention shifted to the door. He

quickly closed it and discarded the file he'd been holding on a nearby cabinet. "When?"

"Almost an hour ago now."

Jonathon scowled. "By message or person?"

"Person."

"Who?"

Sean recalled the introduction the young man had made and the golden embroidery on the black jacket. "First Guardsman Nikolas Parby."

Color left Jonathon's face, his dark blue eyes turned cold. Unease rolled off the man in waves, making Sean shift on his feet.

"He told you I needed to speak with you?" Jonathon asked.

Annoyed, Sean flexed his jaw. "Yes, why else would I be here? Are you saying you didn't?"

"No, I didn't. What did you leave behind that someone would want access to?"

Sean cursed and reached the door before Jonathon could. "My wife."

Snatching the door open, Sean came up against a wall of people.

"Clear the hall!" Jonathon commanded.

Like magic, everyone stepped into whatever room they were nearest, creating an unimpeded path to the stairs. The order resonated down each corridor by others passing on the directive.

"Nice trick," Sean said, breaking into a run.

"Only way to get out in an emergency."

"Can you get to Raiventon?"

"Where is he?"

Sean provided what he hoped was the address where Kevin could be found.

"What about Kynhaven?" Jonathan asked, shouldering past a group who hadn't heeded the call.

"No time, I'd rather have the man who can get my wife out of a situation versus think of all the different ways it could be done," Sean answered.

"Don't you need a strategy for the man, though?"

Sean shook his head and smiled grimly. "No, Kevin is a Gen-Heir at all the aspects of intercepting. Mason just keeps the casualties, and sometimes the time limit, down."

"They built the best in your team, didn't they?" Jonathon asked, shoving open the door to the buildings side stairs.

Sean cast him a dangerous grin. "Yeah, they did, and Cora unknowingly made it stronger by adding you to our little group."

Jonathon *tsked* as they ran down the stairs. "Bad day, bad guys."

"Let's hope so."

Unease shifted through Katria, an emotion she wasn't comfortable or familiar with. For what felt like the hundredth time, she glanced at the clock on the mantle in the library. She hadn't turned the page in the book on her lap in twenty minutes. Where was Sean? Almost an hour had passed since he'd left, and he'd been sure the visit wouldn't take long. Maybe it was more than he expected.

Sighing, Katria tried to refocus on the book. A rapid knock on the front door had her laying her book down and rising. She was at the library door before Davis. He hesitated and then performed a quick bow.

"First Guardsman Parby is here again."

Katria straightened her back, the apprehension returning. "What for?"

"He wishes to speak with you."

Katria glanced into the empty library, to the desk where her husband would have been able to give directions. But he wasn't here; he was with Asherwick, and the enforceman who'd collected him had returned.

"Show him in," Katria said, despite her unease.

Davis bowed again. "Of course."

Parby entered the house, his uniform hat bunched in his hands. He was around her age and gave her a sheepish smile.

"Sorry to bother you, Primary Guardianess Wintersfall, but Master Tribunii Hunter and the primary guardian thought it might be best for you to come to the office as well."

Katria couldn't help but take a small step back towards the library door. "Why is that?"

"MT Hunter is investigating the necklace that thieves stole from you. Primary Guardian Wintersfall felt your firsthand account would be better than his."

Her hand subconsciously went to her throat. The sensation of the heavy diamond and sapphire necklace being torn free prickled her skin. "I didn't realize that's why Hunter had called on him."

"Yes, of course, why else?"

Katria snapped her mouth closed and just smiled.

Davis had her cloak draped over his arm and offered her his forearm. "If you will allow me to escort you?"

Katria nodded and wrapped her hands around his sleeved forearm. Parby walked ahead of them down the brick stairs to a waiting black carriage. Davis draped the cloak over her shoulders. He shooed Parby's hand away and helped Katria into the carriage. Parby hopped in and waited for Davis to close the door.

The carriage pulled away from the house and rocked along the brick road. Katria slowly let a breath out, trying to subdue nerves that wouldn't listen. A sudden, fiery sting snaked up her thigh, and she cried out, grabbing Parby's wrist.

He yanked a syringe from her leg. "Sorry, guardianess, I have my orders."

"What did you..." The question drifted away as blackness claimed her.

The front door opened so swiftly that it ricocheted off the wall. Sean slammed his hand up to keep it from swinging back into him. He shouted for his wife, and silence greeted him. Fear raced along Sean's spine. Rushing to the library, he looked in. Nothing. He called again, heading for the stairs. Three steps up, Davis appeared through the dining room.

"She's gone, guardian," the butler remarked.

Sean's chest constricted, and he had to take a moment to find his voice. "Gone how?"

"The young enforceman, Parby claimed you sent for her from the HCES offices."

Sean eased down the stairs. "For what purpose?"

Kevin bounded up the front steps to the still open door, followed closely by Jonathon. Sean held up his hand to silence either of them, his attention still on Davis.

Davis cleared his throat and straightened his spine. "He said you requested Primary Guardianess Wintersfall for the investigation into her stolen necklace."

Sean cut a glare at Jonathon, keeping a close check on the fury threatening to rise. "Asherwick?"

Jonathon hastily reached into his jacket and removed his notebook. He flipped through the pages and cursed. "The page with the notes on the necklace is missing."

"What exactly did you write down?" Kevin asked.

Jonathon raked a shaky hand through his hair. "The

assault, injury, and the stolen item. I was going to compare them to similar crimes, see if there was a pattern."

"And?"

"And I hadn't had a chance to yet," Jonathon admitted.

Sean took several deep, calming breaths. "So whoever is after her knew how to convince her easily, they used Parby, an actual enforcement both she and I would trust, and now her kidnappers know she has a healing injury."

"It's completely healed, Sean," Kevin assured.

Sean fixed a cold stare on his friend. "Enough that she won't feel pain from it?"

Kevin flexed his jaw.

Sean went back to Davis. "What can you tell me?"

Davis sobered. "Parby took her into the private carriage of the Shield Guardian Enbrackon."

"If it were private, how do you know?" Sean asked.

Jonathon cursed. Kevin swiped his hand down his face.

Davis squished his nose as if he were about to sneeze and then composed himself. "His seal was on the interior."

Sean looked at Kevin. "Was he on the list?"

"Yes," the interceptor answered.

"What does he do?" Sean asked.

Jonathon answered. "He's over the Haven City sector of the Enforcement Services."

Sean stared in disbelief. "*He's* the first prefect?"

Jonathon nodded.

Cursing, Sean ran both his hands through his hair. "Damn. He can cover any crime in the city. Every single one."

"He already has," Jonathon stated grimly.

Sean sank to the step he still stood on. His wife was in the hands of the one man who could make her disappear. Somehow, he had to see past that. He had to focus on her as a team member in trouble, not the woman he'd fallen very much in love with. The rescue had to be nothing more than a mission, or he'd make a fatal mistake.

Taking a deep, centering breath in the same way he'd seen Katria do before she fired every critical shot, he cleared his mind of her. He met Kevin's stormy stare. "Wait until you get a window where she's alone. He'll likely not want to be present after he's ordered the kill. Intercept her then. Do not leave a trace you were present and harm no one."

Kevin gave a curt nod and turned to leave.

Sean took another shaky breath. "And Kevin?"

His friend glanced over his shoulder.

"Do nothing concerning the shield guardian. Just bring Kat back alive."

$\ncong$ 35 $\ncong$

T he soft, delicate sensation of someone toying with her hair pulled Katria from a deep, foggy sleep. Groaning, she tried to roll over, but sharp pain shot through her temple, and she hissed.

"Don't move too fast, the effects of the sedative won't wear off for at least another hour," a deep masculine voice said.

Katria lay still, trying to get her bearings. She was on her side, on a plush, wide leather couch. Forcing her heavy eyelids open, she tried to get the face of the man sitting in front of her to focus. His features blurred into three, then four lines, and a wave of nausea rolled in her stomach. Moaning, she pressed her hand to her abdomen.

"You will not puke on my couch. I suggest you keep your eyes closed and your mind calm."

"You're the one who ordered me drugged. If I puke on your couch, the one who stabbed me with a needle can clean it up."

He let out a sharp laugh. "Seems fair enough. But this is Cairoen suede, it won't survive stomach acid."

"I'll aim for you then."

He chuckled again. The faint tug on Katria's hair made her realize her hair had been unbound, and he was playing with the long strands.

"What are you doing?" she asked, hating the shakiness in her words.

"You know, I've heard how beautiful you are. You've been quite the topic of discussion here in Haven City. Having only attended what, three events? You certainly made an impact. And now that I've seen you for myself, I must say, no one spoke a single lie. If only you'd been the daughter of an arch guardian, my life would be perfect." He inhaled deeply and released a sigh of longing. "I always appreciated the scent of lavender on a woman. Simple, calming. Yours is more complex, I can't quite place it."

Katria kept still. A second attempt at opening her eyes had led to the same queasiness.

"Not going to share?" He tugged on her hair again, and she resisted the urge to turn her head. It'd only cause her pain. "Are you even with me?"

"Yes, I'm still awake. Trying not to be sick on you."

Her hair fluttered around her. "Ah, well, I appreciate that."

The sound of a chair shifting and then the feet moving along a carpeted floor indicated that the man was no longer sitting in front of her. Katria tried again to open her eyes, but the room blurred around her. She said a very unladylike curse under her breath, a new wave of stomach churning assailing her.

A match striking and flaring, followed by deep puffing, and soon the rancid scent of smoke made her mouth water in sickness.

"You know," he began, the hiss of air flowing over his lips cutting off his words. "I was quite disappointed in the *three* failed attempts on your life. I mean, I was told those men were experienced. Efficient. So I paid them well. But they were no match for you or your husband. But now I realize it was for the best. Now I have you here and where you are, one is sure to follow."

Having no patience for riddles, Katria sighed. "What are you talking about? And for your information, the men you hired were weak and ill-prepared. Did you really think you could eliminate an FIO operative with local street talent?"

He chuckled through another rush of air. "Well, I learned something, that's for sure. As for what I'm talking about, I'm talking about the training your husband won't be able to ignore and the man who will most certainly arrive to attempt to rescue you."

"Attempt? If I felt better, I'd laugh."

"My house is a veritable fortress, little assassin. No one gets in or out without my permission."

Katria kept to herself that Kevin had penetrated five actual fortresses. However, she didn't think her captor needed to know. "Are you keeping me alive until he gets here?"

"Yes, I doubt he'll be too keen on taking a body home. What good is that after all?"

"And why kill me at all if I'm just bait?"

Another rush of air. "You were supposed to die before you even left Gaula. My leader couldn't risk you stirring the hornet's nest when you came home and began asking questions again about your mother's death. Questions lead to eventual answers, and they couldn't have that."

"And my sister," Katria said softly.

"I'm sorry, what?"

"They took my sister as well."

"Ah, yes, well, vengeance is a tricky thing, isn't it. Not

quite the path one expects. Too bad the FIO beat my leader to you in recruiting."

A shadow descended over her. Katria swallowed against a tickle of fear.

"Such a shame. You could have been the greatest under our direction. The world would have trembled at your name."

"Why would I want to be feared?"

"Your father was feared. You have much greatness in you." Once again, a thick section of her hair was lifted. "Such beauty, such lethality." He sighed and released the tresses. "Such waste. You were the perfect age, too, old enough to mold, to master into perfection. Ah, well, others are rising, and we will soon have the means to match the talent the FIO currently holds."

"You lost Survaine, too," Katria winced after blurting out.

"My, you have been busy. Yes, but Survaine was too old anyway. He follows orders, but not without question. Youth is essential for blind loyalty."

Katria took a shaky breath. "Youth doesn't mean stupidity."

"No, it means pliable. You can change the heart of the youth, make them see blue where there is purple, or green where there is gray. You just have to use the right words. We make them see the colors differently; they see a new world."

"Like Parby."

He laughed. "Yes, young Parby, he's eager to rise, ready to see a new future where he has more importance than a mere commoner barely living as a street enforceman. He's ready for excitement! For a future he helped create."

"A future built on treachery and lies."

A sad sigh sounded near her, followed by the putrid

scent of spent tobacco. "My leaders said we won't be able to convince you to change sides now."

"I never would have agreed to begin with. Your leaders, whoever *they* are, murdered my family."

He sucked his tongue to his teeth. "Yes, I told them you had likely figured out the why, but not the who. Doesn't matter. By this evening, their secret will be very safe."

"Who are they?"

He clicked his tongue to his teeth in admonishment. "No, no, none of that."

"Why? I'm going to die anyway, aren't I?"

"Yes, but some words do not leave even my lips."

Katria sighed.

A lock of her hair lifted again. What was it with this man and her hair? "You aren't even scared, are you?"

"No, I'm nauseous," she snapped. "Trying not to be sick is taking all my concentration. If you wanted fear, you shouldn't have drugged me."

"I will remember that with my next victim," he said easily.

"Glad to know I'm not alone in my torture."

He inhaled deeply, and she kept her shudder internal. "Yes, I'm still working on how to handle her, if it is necessary. I'm hoping not."

"Don't be too hopeful, you'll be all the more disappointed."

His deep laugh grated on her raw nerves. "You are delightful."

"I try not to be."

"Really, it is such a waste that you have to die." A note of sadness tinged his words. "I wonder if your husband will continue to work for the government that has done nothing to help him protect the wife he had no choice in taking. I am surprised they let anyone threaten such a remarkable asset so easily. Makes one wonder, doesn't it?"

Attempting to swallow against the sudden dryness coating her throat, Katria focused more on her breathing than his goading words. "We're good at taking care of ourselves. Unlike some, we don't need our hands held."

Like she'd never spoken, he continued. "I also wonder if they'll choose a new wife for Primary Guardian Wintersfall. He couldn't say no, of course, his remaining in his title rests solely on his service to the country."

A cold touch brushed across her cheek, and Katria tried to shrink away, but the effort to move sent her head spinning.

"I doubt she'd have your fire. I can tell these things about women." He leaned in close, the fetid stench of tobacco on his breath churned her already rolling stomach. "And I have no doubt you've been a pleasant surprise to the primary guardian, who's taken tamer women in bed. Ms. Milbourne is a simpering joke. Ah, but Cora Dandridge was fun, I will admit. When the time comes, make no mistake, you'll be the same memory to him as all those other lovers were."

Even though Katria knew he was purposefully planting distrust in her mind, she couldn't help the ache his words brought. Being reminded of Sean's very beautiful, and likely very skilled, lovers twisted like a knife in her heart. Sean had kept no secrets from her, though, and if the cruel man thought he'd get a rise from her, he was in for disappointment. "Know him so well, do you?"

The man laughed, his touch tracing the curve of her jaw. "Of course, we graduated from The Sziveria Royale Academia together. He wasn't ranked then, but he lived up to his family's black reputation. I guess he could do so more freely."

Katria doubted that, but she wasn't about to argue with a maniac. "That was a long time ago."

"People don't change," he whispered into her ear.

She managed a snort. "Does time move on?"

"Yes."

"Then people change," she said without emotion.

"So sure of him are you?"

Not one for patience even on a good day, Katria snapped, "Why do you care? You're just going to kill me. How I feel about my husband has no relevance."

This time, when he laughed, it was a dark, menacing sound. "Oh, but doesn't it?"

Cold snaked up her spine in slivery fingers, and she released a shuddering breath. The realization hit her like a blow to the stomach. The kidnapper was purposefully manipulating her to see what she'd say, so when she died, he could tell Sean how much his helpless wife had loved him. Well, he could rot. She wasn't going to say another word about her husband.

"Ah, quick mind. You'd need one, I suppose, to be the top sharpshooter on the payroll."

The flex of her jaw must have given her away, or, like Sean, the treacherous man was a Sympath. It would explain his constant touching of her.

Katria cursed long and hard in her mind.

"You know, I asked those two lovely ladies if Wintersfall had ever bothered to love them. Do you know what they said?"

Silence.

"No? He never said he did. Has he said it to you?"

Katria focused on her breathing, slow in, slow out.

"No? I didn't think so. Do you think he'll realize it after you're dead? You know what I think? I think, like his brother, he's rather heartless. Probably doesn't even know how to love. Shame. I think you *do* fancy yourself in love with the scab."

Katria wanted to scream, 'What did Sean ever do to earn such hatred?' but she knew better. It was the rise he wanted. If he were a Sympath, he was getting a full dose of her anger without any words. He was getting the emotional high he seemed to crave.

"Not speaking anymore? I've managed to render the dangerous Katria Blackbain speechless. I'm all a-tingle with accomplishment."

Still, she remained quiet. Eyes closed, form relaxed.

His cheek came to rest on hers. How she hated being dazed into submission, or he'd be getting the fight he wanted, flat on his back with her knee at his throat.

"What if I tell you how I'm going to kill you? And that everyone will think your black-hearted husband must have driven you to it."

An intense, anxious pain swelled in her chest. *I can't lose you.* Sean's words echoed in her mind. She didn't need any other words to know how Sean felt about her. Her death would be his, and that society would blame him for it would be the ultimate blow to a man who had already taken too many in life.

"You're not taking my little sedative concoction very well. Another dose within the hour, and your body will shut down. An overdose in a city swimming with them. And knowing who you're married to, everyone will whisper, but no one will be surprised. The perfect crime."

Katria swallowed against the first wave of genuine fear she'd had, bile burning in her throat. A sharp knock sounded on a door which seemed impossibly far away. How she wished the world wasn't on a rocking chair so she could see around. Of course, the strange, fuzzy echo of the knock could have everything to do with the sedative wreaking havoc on her. A drug that would be the end of her.

Cold replaced where his cheek had rested against hers. "What is it? I told you not to disturb me!"

"I'm sorry, shield guardian, but Master Guardianess Raiventon is here, and you said always to inform you if the woman arrived, regardless."

A long sigh escaped him. "Yes, I did. I'll be right there."

His cool fingers caressed down her cheek. "Don't you move, you won't get far, and I don't want to have to pick you up off the floor when I return. I won't stop at lifting you if you make me touch your body."

The door opened. "You, stand here and make sure she doesn't even move."

Katria took the threat seriously when she attempted to shift her arm and could barely twitch her fingers. She was helpless and defenseless, two things she'd only been once in her life, and the outcome had been horrific. Same as the one about to meet her. Death and despair. Hating the tear that slid down her cheek, she tried not to give in to the panic threatening.

"Hey, Kat," came a very welcome, very familiar deep voice. A gentle touch wiped the tear on her cheek away. "None of that."

A wave of relief swept through her. She almost sobbed. "Kevin?"

"Who else?"

"I thought there was a guard at the door."

He huffed. "There was. A guard."

Katria furrowed her brow. "Oh. But I didn't hear anything."

"I know."

She knew he was smiling. "They gave me something, but I can't move very well."

"I know."

"I'll throw up on you if you move me."

"Won't be the first time someone has." He gathered her in his arms. "Come on, let's get you out of here."

Tensing as he lifted her, anger welled in her chest. "He's in the foyer, you can take him. All of this will be over."

"You think it's just him? And I can't touch him, Kat."

"Why not? He's a traitor, he admitted as much."

"He's a shield guardian and the first prefect for Haven City."

Indignation filled her until her barely working hands fisted. The shield guardian would get away with everything. And worse, he was the law. "He kidnapped me."

Kevin sighed, and she felt a faint jostle, followed by cool air. The rocking sent shafts of pain through her skull, straight to her stomach. She barely turned her head in time before she let loose what she'd been keeping in since she awoke. Gagging and choking, she coughed and tried to breathe as another wave ran through her body.

As though she hadn't thrown up her shoes in his arms, Kevin continued. "He may have kidnapped you, but to the rest of the world, he brought you here for questioning, which he had every right to do. Who do you think will be believed?"

The burden of proof always falls to the accuser...

Through her ragged breaths, Katria recalled what Sean had said about his brother. "Just like that, he gets away with it all?"

"For now, yes." Kevin adjusted her in his arms, and a sense of weightlessness assailed her before she sat in a low seat. "This is going to be extremely unpleasant for you."

The ariot jostled when Kevin sat in the driver's seat. Katria snorted and clung to the door handle as he reached across and she assumed rolled down a window when a rush of fresh air kissed her face. The brilliant light of the day burned even her closed eyes. She dared not try to open them.

"Yes, because all of this has been so wonderful," she said sarcastically.

He gave another long sigh, this one laced with regret. "Just... remember to breathe."

❧ 36 ❧

Sean paced by his vehicle to the building. He'd sent Jonathon home to make sure his sister was safe. Sean suspected why Katria had been taken, but he couldn't be certain, and Ramsey faced danger by association if Sean were wrong. The sleek black ariot Kevin drove appeared from around the conservatory, and Sean rushed forward. Katria sat on the other side of a small, open window, tears streaking her face, and the front of her gown a damp mess. Her hair was stringy from sweat, and she visibly shivered. But she was safe.

Still in leader mode, Sean approached the vehicle. He couldn't afford the weakness relief would bring. He'd be on his knees if he did. Kevin unfolded from inside, meeting Sean's gaze over the top. "What happened?"

"The kidnapper drugged her, and the concoction is not agreeing with her, not even a little."

"It's because she's Ruthenian. She metabolized whatever he gave her too quickly. Any other problems?"

"None. Smooth intercept."

Words Sean liked to hear. "Excellent."

Sean opened the door and grasped Katria's wrist, finding her threaded pulse. Fear and fatigue shivered along his senses with each of her heartbeats. He leaned closer and forced one of her eyes open. The pupil barely contracted, and she hissed at him. Yes, she was unquestionably high and very sick from it. A gift from her parents' genetics. Sean gathered Katria's weight until she tumbled from the small vehicle and into Sean's arms. She heaved, and Sean adjusted her so she could twist away, but there was nothing left in her stomach to reject.

In the house, Sean called for Rebeka. The young woman swept into the dining room and then followed after him at a quick pace, her hazel eyes wide, dark curls bobbing atop her head.

"Please draw Katria a bath, shallow."

"Will that be all?"

"Also, a cup of ginger lemon tea, please."

"You don't need any help?" the stylist elite asked.

Sean shook his head. "No, I have her."

Rebeka rushed ahead of him up the stairs and to Katria's room. Sean took the stairs more slowly. With each step, Katria whimpered, the faint jostle causing her to contract on herself. In her room, he gently laid her on her bed, where she rolled onto her side and curled into a ball. Rebeka splashed water in the tub. Sean wetted a washcloth, rang out the excess, and returned to Katria. A fine sheen of sweat covered her pale skin. He folded the cloth and wiped her face before draping it across her eyes. Another soft moan accompanied a full-body shiver through her form.

Gently, he smoothed her hair back and caressed her exposed cheek. "Shh, you're okay. It'll pass in a couple of hours."

"I'm dying," she said, her teeth chattering.

"You aren't dying, I promise."

Rebeka's head popped around from the bathroom wall. "The bath is ready."

"Thank you," Sean said.

"Are you sure you don't need anything?"

Sean shook his head. "Just the tea. Leave it on the side table, please."

She nodded and then rushed from the room.

Sean made quick work of Katria's dirty dress. The angry bruise developing on her thigh revealed the injection site. Closing his eyes against anger, Sean waited for his calm to return. She groaned in protest when he gathered her in his arms and gently carried her to the bathroom. Slowly, he eased her shivering frame into the warm, lavender-scented bath. On his knees, he gently lapped the steaming water over her until the trembling subsided.

He washed the sweat and vomit from her hair and continued to keep her warm with the water. Within moments, she slept. Only the even rise and fall of her breasts let him know she breathed without struggle. Sean dried her long hair first, hanging in long clumped strands over the rounded porcelain edge. Using the towel, he lifted her, not caring about the waterfall that blanketed his clothes as he pulled her close.

He almost laid her on her bed, then he remembered what she had said mere hours ago and went to his. Or rather theirs. He put her on the still rumpled sheets. After quickly changing into dry clothes, he dressed her in a cotton button-up and crawled into bed with her. Wrapping her in the soft sheets and his embrace, Sean rested his cheek on her still-damp head. He never wanted to let her go.

Once again, they'd managed to best them. Once again, they'd almost taken his entire world from him.

They would fail.

The pieces were coming together. The puzzle was still gray; the entire center was missing, but it now had edges. More importantly, they a name. He was under no illusions that Parby would *disappear* by morning. The young man had likely outlived his usefulness. But a shield guardian wasn't so lucky. And while none of them could do anything now, the man was destined to make a mistake at some point. All of them did.

Sean held Katria through the worst of the drug leaving her system. He caressed her hair as she tossed and turned in fitful sleep. And when Kevin and Mason arrived to check on her, he didn't leave the bed. He motioned for them to find a place to sit and wait with him. The world would destroy itself again before he left her side.

Comfort, warmth, and the soft, familiar stroke of her husband's fingers through her hair eased Katria from a fitful rest. She rolled toward the smoky, warm scent of him, her arm wrapping around his waist. A heavy pounding still thrummed at her temples, but it was better than from earlier. Now she could open her eyes. Which she did, and found herself staring into deep amber pools.

His fingers gently cleared hair from her face. "Welcome back."

"You keep having to put me back together."

His gaze softened. "Well, you keep getting broken on me."

"Aren't you the lucky one?"

He kissed her forehead. "I did say I was, didn't I?"

Katria frowned. Had that been today? He smoothed the crease from between her brow with his thumbs. A soft shift of fabric pulled her attention from him. Mason looked up from a sketch book, and Kevin rose from where he'd fallen asleep on the couch in front of the fire. They both moved to the bed, Kevin sitting beside her, while Mason sat near her feet. He grabbed her toes and squeezed them.

Katria pulled herself up until she sat against the headboard. Sean joined her. His arms encircled her shoulders and pulled her tight to his side. She didn't protest, threading her fingers through his.

"I get stabbed and wake up alone, I get drugged and everyone is waiting to see if I die," she said with a shallow smile.

"To be fair," Mason began, "I'd only just learned of your stabbing. Since I wasn't around when it happened, no one bothered to tell me."

"And you were never out of anyone's sight," Kevin added and then cut Mason a glare of annoyance. "And the world doesn't revolve around you. A lot is going on. Sean apologized."

"I didn't say the world revolved around me, I said I wasn't informed. There's a difference. It's not my fault if you mistake concern for arrogance."

Katria's brows pinched together. "When did the two of you start fighting like this?"

They both stared at her.

"We aren't fighting," Kevin said.

Mason smiled. "Fighting involves blood, Kat. You know that."

If she had the energy, she'd have glared at them both. "Then bickering. You're worse than siblings."

To Katria's shock, Mason's cheeks tinged pink. "My sibling has made my homecoming a national embarrassment. I don't even want to leave my house because of the things I hear people say about her. Aggravating Kevin is much safer than locking her in her room with a little hatch to pass food to her through until I have to leave again. Which, at the rate things are going, may be never."

Kevin gave a droll stare. "And I can't repeatedly punch my father-in-law."

Sean laughed. "You can't even punch him singularly."

Kevin sighed, his shoulders sagging. "I know. Sucks to be me."

"So, you're baiting each other?" Katria asked slowly.

Mason gave a sheepish smile, and Kevin nodded in response.

"Pretty much. Safer that we fight each other than the people we want to," Kevin said.

The heavy rise and fall of Sean's chest turned her attention to him. He stared down at her, concern in his amber gaze. "I know you're probably not feeling up to it, but the longer we wait, the further the memory is going to get due to the drug he gave you. We need to know what he said, if anything."

I think, like his brother, he's rather heartless. Probably doesn't even know how to love.

The words came back to Katria like a punch to the gut, and she tensed. Suddenly, she wanted to claw up Sean's chest and demand he proclaim his love. Demand he make a liar out of her kidnapper. She licked her lips. But a forced declaration wasn't the truth. *If* he ever told her, she wanted the words to be genuine.

Sean hugged her close, his cheek dropping onto the top of her head. "Shh, it's okay, just breathe."

She did, slow in, slow out. The steady rhythm of Sean's heart under her ear helped ground and remind her she was safe. The calm silenced the words once used as weapons against her. If only they'd stop bouncing around her mind like scattered bullets. "They're recruiting young adults, under twenty-one. He said older people tended to question authority."

Sean's hold relaxed, his fingers went back to combing soothingly through her hair. "Why did he reveal that?"

"He said I was the perfect age when I was placed on your team, but now I was too old, and the man you'd mentioned to me, Survaine, was too old to begin with. He confirmed that whoever is behind everything was also behind my mother and sister's deaths, but did not say who. And he wanted Kevin."

Kevin's spine straightened. "He wanted me?"

Katria nodded. "That's why he had me brought to the house, so Sean would send you. I don't know why."

Sean's strokes paused. "To kill him?"

"Maybe. I know he wanted me dead."

Kevin's gaze narrowed. "Did he say my name?"

Katria closed her eyes and recalled the conversation. "No, just that Sean's training would force him to send *the one* who could rescue me."

Kevin's jaw flexed. "Mason can plan that out, too."

"But you're the interceptor," Katria argued.

"True, but I'm hardly the only one qualified to rescue you. Sean could have as well, I'm only faster."

"Yes, my point."

Kevin shook his head. "Without my name, there's no way to know for sure he was talking about me."

Katria sighed, knowing he was correct and she'd made an assumption. "There's someone else he's after too, another woman."

"Did he give you any clues about her?" Sean asked.

"No, not really, sorry."

Sean squeezed her shoulder. "No, saying sorry, you've remembered so much."

Then she recalled the interruption and frowned. "He

had a visitor, actually, one he wasn't pleased arrived, but couldn't ignore."

"That took him out of the room," Kevin stated.

Katria nodded. "Yes."

"Did you see the visitor?" Sean asked.

Katria closed her eyes again and shook her head. "No, I didn't see anything. I couldn't open my eyes without the room spinning. But he said a name... oh, what was it... Master Guardianess Raven... No, Raveton? Something like that."

"Master Guardianess Raiventon," Kevin said so softly that Katria almost didn't hear him.

She opened her eyes and focused on him. His gray eyes had darkened, and the taut, lethal edge he often took before a fight had her inching closer to Sean. She recalled the interruption, to the name that had come through a door opened enough to deliver a message. The name Kevin had stated.

"Is that what you heard?" Kevin asked. "Master Guardianess Raiventon?"

"Yes," Katria whispered. "Do you know her?"

Kevin leapt off the bed and stalked from the room without another word. The door slammed shut hard enough behind him to knock a framed picture from the wall. Mason cursed. Sean's head fell back against the headboard.

Katria struggled to sit up more. "Who is she?"

They answered in unison, "Kevin's wife."

❧ 37 ❧

Like poison, the shield guardian's words snaked and wove into Katria's subconscious. Even in sleep, she couldn't escape his taunting. Images of her husband with women who could please him more, who'd given as much as her and come away without his heart, flowed through her mind in wicked, dancing shadows. In a panicked sweat, she gasped for air and came awake.

Alone.

Rolling over, she slid her hand across the cold sheet on Sean's side of the bed. She attempted a swallow to ease the dryness coating her throat, but her rapid breathing made the action ineffective. Why she expected him to be there, she didn't know. She woke alone more often than not. They kept different hours. They always had. Aware of her vulnerability, being partly to blame, she rose, tossing the sheets aside with an angry huff.

Katria didn't know how to handle her weakness. She'd discovered the fact quickly the day Sean left her alone after finding out about the murder of her mother and sister. And despite trying to remember how he'd held her, how he'd forced her to confront her emotions, Katria found herself slipping into a defensive state of mind.

The self-imposed wall around the betraying sense of feeling powerless was a safe haven. Comfortable. A lack of control could cost her everything in her life. Now she realized, a bit too late, that it may have truly taken everything from her already.

Resolved in what she needed to do, she straightened her back and left Sean's bedroom. In her room, she cleaned up, changed into one of her gowns, pulled her hair into a braid, and then went in search of her husband. An initial glance of the library showed the room to be empty, but the faint flutter of paper made Katria look up. She barely caught a glimpse of Sean's back before he disappeared from her sight. She closed the door before going upstairs.

Sean strolled around the desk, covered in a long sheet of paper. He leaned down, wrote something, and then rose again, continuing. Each time he bent over, hair would fall around his face, and when he straightened, he'd give a quick flick of his head to clear it away again. The motion was involuntary, showcasing his strong jaw and neck, making her want to run her fingers through his strands. Even in concentration, or perhaps because of it, the slow, deliberate walk around whatever he worked on was predatory and calculated. Katria's heart constricted. She loved him with every part of herself, and yet she loved alone.

"Did you sleep well?" he asked.

Katria jumped at the unexpected sound of his voice. He'd made no indication he was aware of her presence. He hadn't even looked up when he spoke. Fisting her hands at her side, she nodded. "Yes, thank you."

He glanced up. His intense whiskey-colored eyes

looked her over, and she couldn't help but tense under his scrutiny. "What's wrong?"

"Nothing," she said quickly, and then added before she lost her resolve and gave in to the overwhelming need to know how he felt about her. "Where is the list?"

Sean braced his hands on the desk. "What list?"

"The assassin list."

The pen he held tapped softly on the surface in a patterned rhythm. "Why do you want it?"

"That shield guardian said others were coming of age. I want to know what others."

The tapping stopped. "Why?"

Anxiety threatened to break her nerves. She took a deep breath and continued. "Because I can't let what happened to me happen to someone else."

For what seemed like forever, Sean simply stared at her. Then his attention went back to the paper in front of him. "No."

"No?" Pain laced through her palms as her nails bit into the tender flesh. "I didn't have a choice, Sean. They took everything from me and forced me into a life I didn't ask for! I can save someone else from that fate. We can warn them."

Still, he continued to focus on the paper, shifting down the desk, his mouth in a tense line. "No."

"I need to do this!" she pleaded.

His gaze shot back to her, the intensity in his eyes startling her into taking a step back. "Do what exactly? Warn a family that may never even be a target to begin with? Place unneeded fear in their lives? Or worse, lead the enemy you're so desperate to protect them from straight to their door? Or what about the dangerous assassins themselves who've worked hard to keep their families safe and who now will make sure no one can tell the secret of their location."

"My father couldn't save his," she reminded him, tears burning her eyes.

"But I can save mine. The answer is still no." Sean made a notation on the paper and then took a step back toward the to the left.

Katria moved closer the desk. Her desperation to force him to her will barely overshadowed her need to scream the actual reason for her fear. Losing him. Or rather, never having had him fully in the first place. "Please let me help them."

"No."

"Sean, please!"

His hands slammed on the desk so hard she jumped. And when he met her stare, a tremble raced through his arms. "Katria, do not ask this of me! I love you too much to lose you over someone else's agenda. They've made enough attempts at your life. Do not give them more reasons, or more opportunity." His head fell forward, shielding his face from her view. "I told you once I can't lose you, and I meant it. I can't..."

Katria rushed around the desk, tears spilling down her cheeks. What a fool she'd been, allowing the lies of a stranger to corrupt her thoughts. To control her emotions. And what a fool *she'd* been to think she could govern her feelings with an equally forceful manipulation. She grasped Sean's strong bicep and held until he moved his arm. She slid before him, her back against the desk. Taking his face in her hands, she met his tortured stare.

She kissed his lips. "I'm so sorry. Please, please forgive me."

Faint tremors still wracked his frame. Katria wrapped

her arms around his shoulders, pressing her body to his, hating she'd been the cause.

"Forgive you for what?"

Burying her face in his shoulder, her tears soaked into the fabric of his shirt. "He told me you could never love me. That the women you'd been with left your bed with nothing, and I'd be the same. A memory you cared nothing for." Ashamed, she choked on a sob. "And I... I..."

"Shh." His arms wrapped tightly around her waist, hugging her tight. "Don't."

Another wave of tears wracked her. She clung to Sean like a lifeline. "How? How could I believe him?"

Sean unraveled her braid and stroked his fingers through the long length. His other hand slid soothingly up and down her back. "Because I was a fool. I told you all the bad things about me and none of the good."

Sniffling, she pulled back until she could see his face. "None of the good?"

He clasped her cheeks between his hands, his thumbs wiping away the tears. His fingers massaged her neck beneath her jaw. The brilliant amber of his eyes shone with emotion. "You are everything to me, Katria. Everything. I didn't tell you I loved you because I didn't even know what love felt like before you. I wasn't sure if I even could, the emotion was so completely foreign to me, and it took me a long time to recognize it. Too long. I should have told you the moment I knew. I should have taken your lead and just said the words, but I was scared."

She raised a skeptical brow even as her heart threatened to burst from his confession. "You? Scared?"

He gave her a soft, fluttering kiss and whispered against her lips, "You have no idea."

"Why?" she asked, confused.

"What if I was wrong? What if I said the words and

they hurt you more than anything because I mistook my desire for you as love?"

Katria considered his concern, biting her bottom lip. "Then, how did you know?"

"How did you know?" he asked, his fingers tracing up and down her spine.

She shrugged lightly. "It wasn't any one thing, but a collection of small things. You've never asked me to be anything but who I am. When I didn't even know I'd strayed from myself, you were right there to help me get back. You loved me without saying anything." Tears swam in her vision again. "And still I believed the lies."

Sean kissed her, his mouth lingering over hers in an intimate embrace that stole her breath. "The lies of a manipulator are carefully woven, like a spider's web. Each word is meant to strike with precision, chosen for maximum damage. Very few are immune to them."

"I should have been stronger."

"My love, you were. Under the influence of what was likely an opium cocktail and the stress of being at his mercy, you came away with the experience of fretting over words, nothing else. You are amazing, and so strong." His forehead dropped to hers, his fingers tightened along her jaw. "I would have burned the city to the ground if something happened to you. They would have regretted the moment they decided to tear my house apart."

"They?"

"All parties, or none. No loyalty. No allegiances. I would have watched the empire of Sziveria crumble to dust."

Silent tears rolled down her cheeks. "You're the only one who could."

"And the idiots who made the dumb decision to come very close to killing you, twice, have made a powerful enemy, and too many mistakes to stay anonymous for much longer."

Katria let out a shuddering breath. "I think the biggest mistake happened when Parby openly kidnapped me."

"Yes, they're either stupider than I'm thinking, or they're in control of enough authority to believe they're near invincible."

"I'm betting authority."

"Yes. We haven't watched kingdoms crumble around the world to be foolish enough to think it won't happen to ours. This is a long road."

Slowly, Katria nodded. "Do you think whoever they are, that they'll give up on me at least?"

"If they're smart," he muttered under his breath, and she smiled. Then he straightened, and she looked up at him. His hands moved to her upper arms. An expression of seriousness hardened his handsome features. "Are you done trying to discover who pulled the trigger on your family?"

Katria considered his words. "I don't see how I could ever discover that, at least not anytime soon. Knowing the shield guardian worked *under* someone who initiated the attempted murders on me and my kidnapping, the person who made the decision is likely higher than we currently have the means to investigate. Or, has the resources to make sure any further attempts are met with dead ends."

"A dead end being you in the ground. You realize that, don't you? If you keep searching, they'll keep trying to stop you."

"I wasn't even looking anymore, and they still tried again."

Sean sighed. His hands caressed her arms. "I know, but from what you said, they had an ulterior motive. So? Can you let their murders rest?"

In the months since their return, she had learned enough answers to have a reason, if not a name. And while the motive hurt, it was more than she had before. Could she let it be enough? Her gaze swept over Sean's face, drawn tight with worry. Katria slid her fingertips into his hair and traced her thumbs over his cheeks and down to his jaw. She'd told him he'd always be enough for her, and now she needed to believe those words.

"Yes. I can't keep living in the shadow of their deaths. I have too much here in the present to let whoever tried to steal my life win because I didn't know when to let it go." She touched her mouth to his for a soft kiss and asked, "What about you? Can you walk away from the past everyone is intent on seeing in you?"

"I've thought about it, and I've decided to use the lack of scruples everyone expects from me to our advantage in the coming months as we unravel this mess we've been secretly tasked with."

Katria raised a brow. "How so?"

"They're limited in how creative they can get to make me back off when we start to become a serious threat at exposing them. They can't threaten to ruin me. My parents and my brother took care of the little problem years ago. They've already threatened you, it didn't go well, and if they try again, well, your BACR-18 is a quick problem solver."

Another disturbing thought occurred to her. "If Kevin's wife has been dealing with that shield guardian... Sean, I was in his presence for minutes, and he was able to get me to believe his lies." She closed her eyes.

He leaned forward and narrowed the space between them, his fingers sinking deep into her hair. "I know. Unfortunately, that's a fight we can't win for him. Kevin is going to have to become her husband if he's to save her."

Katria sighed in both happiness and apprehension. The emotions warred with each other. "I'm so thankful I have you to save me."

Sean pulled back, his amber eyes bright with disbelief. "Save you? Woman, do you have any idea how—"

She cut his words off with a firm kiss, her hands sliding deeper into his silken hair. The tip of his tongue probed against her lips, and she opened for him with a welcome moan. Sean deepened the kiss, his strong body pressing her into the desk. Everything faded except for him. No more confusion, fear, or anxiety. His mouth worked magic across hers while his hands kneaded her hips.

With a ragged breath, Katria broke their kiss and met his passionate stare. "I love you," she whispered.

He lifted her onto the desk. She didn't protest when he pushed her knees apart with his hips and pulled her to his chest. His mouth captured hers again for a searing kiss that left her even more winded.

Raining kisses down her throat, to her collarbone, he whispered against her skin in hot breaths, "I love you so much I can't think straight most of the time."

Desire curled fast and hard through her. Breath struggled to fill her lungs. "Good, because thinking is the last thing I want to do right now."

HAVE YOU REVIEWED THIS TITLE?

First, thank you! For authors, reviews are the best way for others to discover us and know that you, our awesome readers, love our work.

Look for Kevin's book next!

RAIVENTON - CHAPTER ONE

Haven City, Sziveria
  May 17th, 835 P.C.E (Post-Cataclysmic Event)

Bitter anger tore through Kevin Merrick, the Master Guardian Raiventon. Not bothering to knock on his father-in-law's front door, he flung it open. He turned to the left, past the curved staircase leading to the second floor. A servant in green livery with large silver buttons rushed into the foyer, sputtering a protest. Kevin held up his hand and kept walking.

The dark wooden double doors to the arch guardian's study were closed against intruders. Kevin ignored the bid for privacy and practically kicked them open, then slammed them shut with equal force. Henry Edmond, the Arch Guardian Synintel, leapt from his seat behind his massive desk. Recognition flared in the older man's eyes as he braced his hands on the surface and glared.

"Where in the arctic have you been?"

Kevin ignored the superior bite in Synintel's

words. "What was your daughter doing alone at Shield Guardian Enbrackon's house?"

Synintel smoothed a hand down the front of his long-sleeved maroon silk shirt, the buttons covered by a subtle seam of fabric. Nearing fifty, the arch guardian was fit and solid, knowing that power came not only from presence but also from stature. Gray liberally streaked his dark brown hair, which he kept neatly styled in the military standard he expected of those who worked under him. Of course, not all obeyed that unspoken rule. Kevin watched the faint motion of his hand with interest. The arch guardian was composing himself. He hadn't liked what Kevin told him.

"Enbrackon has taken an unhealthy interest in Lorraina these past few months. It's why I called you home." Slowly, he returned to his seat. "How did you find out she was at his house? Are you following her?"

"No, I do not need to spy on my wife. She's an adult who can make her own decisions. I found out because the shield guardian kidnapped Primary Guardianess Wintersfall."

Synintel's mouth gaped open. Kevin would have laughed if anger weren't still raw in his gut. "Did he harm her?"

"Why do you care?"

"She's an incredibly valuable asset. To lose her would be to lose our top sharpshooter. My other isn't exactly a team player."

Kevin fisted his hands at his side. "An asset? She's Sean's wife and as close to me as a sister."

"You saved her, correct?"

"Yes," Kevin ground out between clenched teeth.

Synintel nodded in approval and picked up his pen. "Good."

"What of Enbrackon?"

The arch guardian sniffled dismissively. "What of him?"

"Why was Raina at his house? And why hasn't he been arrested for treason? I know, as one of the top-ranking guardians, and only fifth behind the queen-elect, you can't possibly be ignorant of the discord and illegal behavior brewing in this country."

Synintel's pale brown eyes glanced up at Kevin before returning to the paperwork in front of him. His daughter had inherited those same eyes. "No, I'm not ignorant. As for why Enbrackon wanders free, I have no evidence. He's cautious. *They* have been very careful."

"Another reason you brought us home?"

"No, I already told you why I called you home."

Kevin frowned and recalled their conversation. "Because of your daughter's involvement with the shield guardian?"

Synintel sighed in impatience. "Yes. Now go home, do your job, and keep her safe."

Kevin closed the distance to the desk and slammed his fists down on the surface. Ancient snarling bronze dragons on the front corners, from a world one could only read about, jumped and rattled from the force. They sat in the open, daring someone to have the guts to break into the house and steal them. A testament to how powerful the arch guardian considered himself to be. Kevin didn't really care. Let one fall to the floor and dent. "I *have* been! For four years, at your every beck and call. I've been to every city but this one. I've been where *you've* sent us, doing the assignments you've demanded of us. So, don't tell me to go and do my job."

A flush crept onto Synintel's well-shaven cheeks. "I married you to my daughter for one reason, one you agreed to. Keep her secure."

Kevin leaned forward. "No, you married me to her so you wouldn't have to deal with some sniveling fool of a son-in-law."

"A sniveling fool, I certainly did not get. I have an impertinent one."

"Let me out of the deal, and you don't have to have one at all."

The arch guardian's eyes flashed. He gripped the pen so tightly that Kevin was surprised the thing didn't burst in his hand. "You know she made the contract binding for life. Only death or infidelity. Are you ready to admit you whored around on my daughter?"

Kevin's jaw ticked, and he took several breaths before he answered. "You'd love for me to say yes, wouldn't you?"

Synintel's grip on the pen lessened. "Not particularly. You are the only one who can protect her."

"And how is your end of the bargain coming along? Will I be keeping my master guardian rank?"

The little annoying sniffle Synintel gave when he didn't feel a question deserved his attention sounded again in the spacious office. "The next Endowment and Revocation Council meeting is in less than two months." His eyes took on a hard edge. "I'd suggest my daughter be well away from the shield guardian by that time."

Kevin straightened and crossed his arms over his chest. "Or what? You'll make sure your daughter is married to a baseborn? How do you think she'll take it? She already believes being a master guardianess is beneath her. I don't think she'll survive that blow. You have nothing left to threaten me with. I know you won't do that to her."

"And what of Primary Guardian Wintersfall?"

Kevin narrowed his eyes. A sinking sensation rolled in his stomach. "What of him?"

"His title is completely dependent on his staying in

service for me. I'd hate for anything to change that situation."

"You'd blackmail me with that?"

Synintel raised a brow. "Would it work?"

How he loathed this man. "I never said I wouldn't keep her safe."

"Good. I never said I'd be forced to do anything to make sure of that."

Kevin flexed his hands, the tightness causing his fingers to ache. "Someday the puppet strings you hold us all by are going to break."

An arrogant huff escaped Synintel's lips. "That day is not today. Make your presence known to society and your wife. There's a soiree at Shield Guardian Gisburne's house. The gathering will be crowded, enough people to see you and talk about it. I'll make sure Kynhaven's sister is present too. She's the best gossip columnist in the city."

"I don't have an invitation."

Without looking, Synintel opened a drawer to his right. A second later, an envelope rushed at Kevin from across the desk. "Now you do."

Dazzling chandeliers glittered light over jewel-toned fabric and the mingling voices below. Lorraina Merrick, the master guardianess of Raiventon, took in the shuffling scene with little interest. If she weren't duty-bound to attend at least five social gatherings a month, she'd stay happily sequestered in her gated home. But as the daughter of an arch guardian, she was essentially raised to be royalty, and royalty must always maintain its standards. Her father ensured she understood her role from an early age: duty, grace, and loyalty. Always be the perfect example of all three, at all times.

A server carrying a champagne tray offered her a drink.

Champagne was rare, the grapes only grew in Italyssa with great care. The import showed the guests how wealthy and generous their host was. Raina waved the server away with a flip of her hand, a bow of her head, and a kind smile. He returned the bow and moved on.

"Why so dull, darling?"

Raina snapped her attention to the male voice she hated to admit she'd been dreading. She didn't have the energy to deal with Phipps Geier, the Shield Guardian Enbrackon, tonight. He'd made a point to inform her at their last meeting that she wasn't pleasing him. As the wife of another man, she'd no right to be anything to the shield guardian but a professional adviser, as he'd asked her to be.

But Enbrackon wanted more. He'd made his desires very clear. He also wanted more *for* her. Over the past couple of months, she'd begun to believe he could help free her from her father's shadow. The question was, how far would she go to make sure that happened?

Shoving the uncomfortable thoughts away, Raina turned to him with a smile. "Shield Guardian Enbrackon, what a pleasure to see you tonight."

Eyes so dark brown they were almost black sparkled in the crystalline light as he bowed over her extended hand. He slicked back his shiny black hair, revealing the smooth planes of a face he considered handsome. Raina considered him pretty. Dressed in the elaborate wealth he personified, nearly every finger glittered with a ring. Only the finest fabric adorned his body in slacks that were purposefully too tight. A silver jacket with attention-grabbing, red embroidery showcased his broad shoulders, yet concealed his rounding stomach, paired with a matching red silk shirt and calf-high, glossy leather boots. A gaudy diamond brooch at his throat completed the ensemble. The outfit, designed to make him stand out visibly in the crowd, achieved its goal.

Enbrackon placed a fleeting kiss on the back of her hand, his hold lingering longer than socially necessary. "It's always my pleasure to see you. Why did you pass on the champagne? Truly is the best I've had."

"I don't enjoy alcohol."

He tsked and motioned for a server. The man appeared before them gracefully, lowering the tray for Phipps. Removing two glasses, he handed one to her. "Come now, darling. If you want to socialize with the top echelon, you must make them feel comfortable. They drink. Champagne is harmless, I think you'll enjoy it. One sip won't hurt, now will it?"

"I don't think it'll hurt anything, I just don't—"

Phipps sighed and lifted her hand holding the flute nearer to her face. He leaned close so only she could hear his words. "Lorraina, really, you can be so boring. I thought I told you boring just won't do. While you and I both recognize that you're above everyone else here, they dislike being reminded of it. And if they sip on wine, or champagne, or whiskey, while you sit with your hands in your lap, they'll hate you for it. You don't want to be hated, do you?"

A strange discomfort built in her chest. She stared at the bubbles in the golden liquid rising to the surface and slowly shook her head. "No, of course I don't want to be boring or hated."

"I thought not. See? What would you do without me? Now, take a sip and smile."

The thought of the sharp bite of alcohol hitting her tongue and settling in her mouth made her stomach roll. She swallowed and took a calming breath. "I don't think I can. I don't drink, everyone knows, and no one has cared."

Phipps cast her a dull stare over the top of his glass. He took a heavy drink before lowering it to his lips. "They cared, they were simply too polite to say anything. Now, one sip. You'll see. It's more like bubbly, white grape juice. You like juice, don't you? No reservations about that?"

Why did he make it sound as though she were some purist no one could tolerate? She frowned at the glass. Was she? "Don't be silly, why would I have an aversion to juice?"

"Because you're holding its cousin like it's poison. Drink, Lorraina."

The dry, sharp scent of alcohol hit her nose before the bubbles did. She wanted to both gag and sneeze. She quickly lowered the flute. "Not tonight, perhaps next time."

Phipps frowned, disappointment clear in the staunch line of his mouth. Again. "You said as much last time, to beautifully crafted red wine no less. Another cousin to juice."

Raina took a deep breath, staring at the champagne again. "The cousins don't seem to agree with me."

"Nothing ever does."

She lifted her gaze to his and caught the anger in the dark depths of his eyes. "Excuse me?"

He leaned forward again. His hand snaked around Raina's upper arm, his fingers biting into the tender inner flesh. "I am tired of your excuses. I try to help you, but you won't listen. You won't even try. What do you expect me to do? Work miracles for you? You can't even take a tiny sip of champagne. Now, take a drink. You will save yourself the future embarrassment of falling flat on your face when you refuse champagne offered to you by a princess and insult the woman into slandering your name all over Sziveria. I know you don't want that. Someday, you'll be there. Get comfortable now with what you don't like."

Raina gasped at his painful hold and the image he painted. Of course, she could never refuse something offered to her by a princess. And if the shield guardian was correct, someday she'd be free of her father and could choose her clients, which included princes and princesses. If someone wanted her to handle logistics for them, they wouldn't have to go through her father first, as they did now. Phipps was right. She had to get past her discomforts if she wanted to move in the circles he promised.

She ignored the sting of tears in her eyes. With a shaky hand, she lifted the rim of the fragile glass to her mouth. And still she couldn't. Despite Enbrackon's words, despite his physical pressure, her mind refused to let the substance pass her lips.

His grip tightened until she bit back a cry. "Take a drink."

"I—"

"How thoughtful of you to get me a glass, my dear."

The deep, smooth voice raced up Raina's spine like silk. *Kevin.* Not sure she had heard correctly, she turned as Phipps released her so suddenly that she swayed. The flute seemed to magically disappear from her fingers just as a gentle hand steadied her.

"Are you feeling okay?" Kevin asked.

Raina took in the dangerously handsome man standing before her. His stormy gray eyes looked her over with concern. She had to look up, way up, to see.

"I thought you were a dream," she breathed out.

Kevin raised a dark blond brow. "If that's not the best a husband can hear when he sees his wife, I don't know what is."

She shook her head and blinked. Now was not the

time, or the place, to relive a dream she now believed was a memory. "No, I... never mind. You're home."

Once again, she looked him over. Dressed effortlessly in black leather shoes, finely spun black wool pants and coat, and a gray silk shirt matching his eyes, he looked far more casual than the rest of the men in the room. Yet far more alluring. The simple style accentuated his lean, well-built frame. He'd done nothing special to flaunt his wealth other than wear luxurious fabrics. Nearly a foot taller than her five feet five inches, and inches taller than all the men in the room, he commanded attention.

And he was her husband.

His hair was short and not styled. Raina couldn't help but smile at how finger-mussed the strands appeared. She had a sudden urge to tame his wayward mane. A close-cropped beard, darker than his hair, brought out the angles of his high cheekbones, strong jaw, and perfect nose. As for his mouth, she dared not look at his full lips for more than a glance. If what she feared were correct, she'd come much too close to begging for his kiss nights ago.

If the faint smile turning his mouth was any indication, her examination amused him. She flushed, turned, and faced the crowd. "How long have you been home?"

The sensation of his hand settling into the small of her back made her shiver. He leaned close, which had to be a feat, and murmured, "What? No Master Guardian Raiventon this time?"

She gasped and turned so quickly she found her mouth a mere whisper from his. Oh, mistake, big one. Breath hitching in her lungs, she grasped the supple fabric of her gown's skirt to keep from grabbing his jacket. "The other night, it wasn't a dream, was it?"

Kevin didn't move away. The hum of conversation

around them faded, and she wondered if perhaps she shouldn't take a step back. "No, it wasn't a dream."

Then she remembered Phipps. She touched a hand to her mouth and turned. He was gone. "Where did Shield Guardian Enbrackon go?"

Kevin straightened, handing the champagne off to a passing server who likely wanted to hear their conversation more than be of service. "He knew what was best for his safety."

Wide-eyed, she turned her attention back to him. He set his face in hard, deadly lines. The gray of his irises grew dark until they were slate. Raina blinked. "Excuse me?"

Then, like a storm, the sun returned, and he smiled, all traces of lethality gone. "Why was he so intent on you drinking the champagne?"

"Y-you were eavesdropping on our conversation?"

"No, I was watching you continue to refuse the drink as I walked across the room. The shield guardian wouldn't let you. Why?"

"Oh." She didn't know whether to be flattered or not that he'd only had eyes on her, and so intently he'd understood her turmoil. Then a sliver of panic set in. What was she supposed to say? Working as he did for her father, Kevin would never understand, or sympathize, with her need for freedom. "He was just sure that I'd, um, really like the champagne. I've never tried any before."

"Does he own the label?"

Confused, Raina tipped her head to study him. Once more, his handsome face caught her off guard. At least her father hadn't married her to some short, fat man. No, he'd found the best-looking one in all of Haven City, shackled them together, and then made sure the man never set foot in her house again. Blinking, she realized she was staring and she'd forgotten the question. *Darn it!* "Does he what?"

Kevin raised a perturbed brow and repeated himself. "Does he own the champagne label?"

"No."

"Then why would he care so much if you tried it?"

Aggravated, Raina huffed. "Why don't you ask him?"

"I would have, but he slinked off like a bad cat. Now I'm asking you."

Her mouth fell open. "Are you always this persistent?"

He leaned closer to her. "I don't know. Are you always this evasive?"

Heat climbed up her cheeks. If social graces didn't dictate that she be the complete picture of respect to her husband, she'd be defending her right to privacy. The realization made her blush further. Less than five minutes, and he'd managed to rile her to the point of causing the gossip tongues to begin whispering. "I need some air."

When Raina made a move for the open greenhouse doors, Kevin caught her elbow and gently steered her in the opposite direction. He slid her arm around his and leaned close. "Unless you want every guest in this room to think you greeted your husband in the garden, I suggest we leave as expected. Everyone is aware of how long it's been since I was home."

The flush of her cheeks turned to fire. She quickly glanced at the floor and would have put space between them if Kevin's hand hadn't slid over hers and tightened to keep her near. His fingers were warm, rough, and calloused. Nothing like Phipps' soft, carefully manicured hands. Raina glanced at his hand and noted the small collection of scars running along the back and frowned. What exactly did he do for her father?

Out in the vast, circular vestibule, guests wandered in from the front door, the salon, the game room, or the dining room. Raina took a deep breath and smiled as they walked past. Several women waved when she caught their eye.

They waited on the bottom step for the groom to bring the carriage around. Kevin allowed the carriageman to help her inside, though he refused help for himself. He leapt in so swiftly, and with so little movement to the vehicle itself, Raina couldn't help but gasp. Once the door closed, she glared in the darkness.

"We could have stayed longer."

Kevin settled into the shadows, his long legs stretching as far as they could to her side. "We could have, but no one would have believed it. Your father insisted we make an impression tonight that no one will forget. He even made sure Miss Dandridge was present for a firsthand experience to write for the gossip column in the morning."

Raina let out a low, very unladylike, growl. "So, when my father snaps his fingers, you bow too, do you?"

"And you don't?" The words were quiet. No condescension, no mockery. Almost defeated.

The steam left her, and she slumped back against the seat. "Of course I do."

Though if she had her way, she wouldn't be under her father's control much longer.

Tantalizing shafts of silvery light brushed across Raina's face whenever an alley opened enough to let the full moon shine into the carriage. Kevin studied her in the quiet. Raina's rich brown tresses were elegantly braided and held in place as a crown by an assortment of simple ruby pins. The gentle angles of her face were beautiful in the shadowy depths. Softly arched brows, a heart-shaped mouth, with a bottom lip just full enough from the top to make them entirely too kissable, and a small, rounded nose.

Her petite frame and delicate features made him wonder if pixies existed, and he happened to be married to one. In comparison, he was a giant, towering over her by a foot, at six feet five, and more than double her weight. But the crimson silk flowing effortlessly over her curves reminded him that while small, she wasn't lacking. Firm, subtle mounds rose beneath the elegant material, drawing attention to her flat, narrow waist and the gentle flair of her hips. Breaking with fashion, she didn't wear pounds of fabric beneath her skirt, only enough to keep her warm.

No, what troubled him about her appearance was that she'd matched the embroidery color of Enbrackon's jacket. Kevin wanted to ask if their clothes had matched on purpose. If he'd noticed, others had too. He wanted to snap and demand the answer. But he couldn't. They'd spent hours together in their four years of marriage, not weeks or even days. She didn't know him any better than he knew her. Asking questions of her wasn't his right. Not yet.

"How long this time?" she asked, so quietly he almost missed the inquiry.

Kevin knew exactly what she asked. "Not sure, he didn't give me a timetable." That wasn't entirely true, so he added, "Probably two months, maybe less."

Her sharp intake of air was audible. "Two months?"

"Is there a problem?"

"No, of course not. I'm just... shocked. Father has never let you remain home for longer than a single night before one of his men knocked on the door. Sometimes you didn't even stay that long." Fabric rustled, and heavier shadows fell across her face and torso as she angled to face him. "Do you know why?"

"Why is he letting me stay home?"

Even in the darkness, he caught her nod.

Because you're playing with a wolf, and I have to make sure you don't get eaten. Kevin shrugged. "Who knows? Maybe he's ready for grandkids."

The gasping choke she made had Kevin smiling wickedly. "I can't believe you just said that."

"Can you think of another reason he'd keep me home?" He was allowing her to come clean on her own, if she recognized it. The faint fidget of her shoulders and thighs told him she did.

"No, not really. Maybe Father is allowing you to have a break?"

And she didn't take the chance. Great. He heaved a heavy sigh. "Maybe."

She squirmed again, the motion amplified by the gentle rocking of the carriage. "Were you really in my room a couple of nights ago?"

Kevin's gaze swept over her, lingering on her mouth, to the gentle curve of her collarbone that invited his attention lower to the soft swell of her breasts. He'd come so close to feeling all of her against his body. Dangerously close. He had to breathe against the hot pierce of desire at the memory. "Yes."

"Men really broke in?"

"Yes."

She released a shuddered breath. "There was no evidence. Not even your bed was unmade. I didn't think it'd been real."

"I've been in the house every night since."

Even in the dark, he could tell every muscle in her body tensed. "Really?"

"Yes. You didn't think I'd leave you alone in danger, did you?"

"Well, I... I didn't think it was real. My father would have sent men to patrol the exterior if you'd asked."

"Why? I'm your husband, I can take care of my house."

She chuckled lightly. "But they're trained."

Kevin couldn't stop the bark of laughter, and when he ran her comment back through his mind, he laughed harder. "Yes, I'm sure they're very skilled."

"Why do you laugh? My father only hires the best. You know that. They wouldn't let any harm come to us."

Thankfully, the carriage arrived at the house, saving Kevin from an argument he couldn't win. To be fair, Raina wasn't at fault for not knowing exactly what her husband was capable of. Kevin was in no hurry to enlighten her. The Master Guardianess Raiventon took her position in society seriously. Knowing she was married to a violent man capable of defeating multiple combatants in seconds likely wouldn't go over well.

Kevin helped her out of the carriage and then followed behind, watching the edges of the house closely. Satisfied no threats lurked, he took the row of stairs two at a time. A bright trail of light across the wide brick porch preceded the opening of the front door for them.

Portly and shorter than Raina, Mrs. Taft held the door open with both hands, beaming at her guardianess. Her silver hair was piled high on her head in a severe bun; her dark green uniform, complete with an ivory apron, was immaculate. "You look as beautiful as when you left." Her dark blue eyes moved past Raina when she noticed her mistress wasn't alone. She gasped, her hand flying to her ample bosom. "Oh my! Master Guardian Raiventon! We were not expecting you. Oh my, I don't have your room ready, or your place setting at the breakfast table, or—"

Raina set her hand on Mrs. Taft's shoulder. "It's okay, he's been home a couple of days. No need to fret."

Her mouth opened and closed like a beached fish. Pink darkened her cheeks. "Well, my goodness, how could we be so remiss! I'll have those girls' heads for their negligence."

Kevin shook his head as they entered the house. "As Master Guardianess Raiventon said, no need. I leave before anyone is awake most mornings. If I'd wanted special attention, I would have called you for it." Kevin cast her a sideways smile. "I'm just grateful you remembered me at all."

She waved her hand and laughed. "Forget you? Silly man, that's unlikely. We'll be sure to have everything ready for you now, whether you're here in the mornings, afternoons, or evenings, it doesn't matter. You're home."

"Thank you," he said, giving her a respectful bow.

Mrs. Taft returned the gesture and then closed the front door. "Tabby is upstairs waiting for you, guardianess."

"Thank you, Mrs. Taft."

Kevin waited until the robust housekeeper disappeared into the breakfast room before following behind Raina. "Tabby?"

With her fingers trailing up the rail, Raina headed upstairs. "Tabitha, Mrs. Taft's daughter and my Stylist Elite." She paused, and he took a moment to take in her beauty. The diffused warm light from the few candles still lit washed over her delicate features. "Will you be needing a valet?"

Kevin grunted. "No, I can dress myself."

She stepped down until she was at his height and then playfully tossed a hand through his hair. Kevin's breath caught at the sensation of her spirited touch on his scalp. Her pale brown eyes danced playfully. "You could use one, though, do something with this hair."

Blinking, he reached up and touched his head. "What's wrong with my hair?"

"Other than it goes any direction it feels like? Nothing at all."

Frowning, Kevin looked her over once more. Nothing was out of place. Remembering the last time he'd seen her, the sleepy mess of her hair and the way her thin silk nightgown had pooled around her knees had him almost falling to his. "Do you want me to change it?"

Her lips parted slightly, and her hand fell to her side. The tip of her tongue darted out, wetting her bottom lip. Kevin took a small step back before he did something stupid, like kiss her.

"No, not unless you want to. I think the disheveled look will grow on me." She cast him a soft smile and then turned, continuing up.

Kevin watched the sway of her hips and the way the gown molded to her rear with each step up, before sliding into place again. The cut of his pants suddenly became too tight, and he sighed. Two months. He had to make it two months.

Available now in all formats

My Dearest Reader,

Perhaps as you read this book you identified with the fictional characters knowing how it felt to be told they're something they aren't. Someone has made you believe a lie. They've said you'll never be good enough. You'll never reach your full potential. You don't have any talents. You aren't worthy. You aren't worth anything. They've made you question who you are and what you are capable of. They've made you feel like a puddle being stomped through and splashed away.

Close your eyes. Take a deep breath.

That isn't you.

Don't believe them.

You are beautiful. You are worthy. You are worth *everything*. You will reach your full potential because you have a goal to achieve and nothing will hold you back. You have a beautiful talent. Some you already know about, and some are waiting to be discovered years from now. A passion you don't even know you have yet. You are a treasure.

Did you know no one else can do what you do? No one else can take a picture like you, they can't see through the lens the same way you do. No one else can draw or paint like you, they don't have your vision. No one else can sing like you, they weren't given your amazing voice. No one else can play an instrument the way you can, their passion isn't the same. Whatever you do, whatever motivates you, drives you, fuels your excitement, helps you show the world to those around you in such an amazing way, is yours alone. Your gift. Your beauty. No one can take that from you, or tell you it isn't good enough.

Strive to reach the level of those who inspire you, knowing you will never be them because their way already exists. The world needs *you* and what you have to offer. Spread your wings and embrace your journey.

Thank you for reading Sean and Katria's story.
All my best,
Sarah Westill

What is the price of two sparrows — one copper coin? But not a single sparrow can fall to the ground without your Father knowing it. And the very hairs on your head are numbered. So don't be afraid; you are more valuable to God than whole flock of sparrows.
Matthew 10:29-31 (NLT)

ABOUT THE AUTHOR

SARAH WESTILL lives in Alabama with her US Army-retired husband. They have two sons – one they've successfully raised to adulthood – the other is still a work-in-progress, navigating middle school. As a full-on creative, Sarah lives to write, paint, teach, and meet amazing people while doing portrait photography. A veteran in the publishing industry working as a cover artist under the name Elaina Lee, she has been blessed to help hundreds of authors to achieve their own publishing goals for over a decade. To learn more about Sarah as she blogs her adventures, and about her Guardians, please visit her at sarahwestill.com or follow her on Instagram @authorsarahwestill